DEAD STYLISH

About the author

Lisa Armstrong became a journalist after graduating from Bristol University. She has worked on newspapers and magazines, and was Fashion Features Director of *Vogue* before becoming the Style Editor of *The Times*. She lives in North London with her husband and two daughters.

Dead Stylish

Lisa Armstrong

CORONET BOOKS
Hodder & Stoughton

First published in Great Britain in 2001 by Hodder and Stoughton
A division of Hodder Headline
A Coronet Paperback

10 9 8 7 6 5 4 3 2 1

A CIP catalogue record for this title is available from
the British Library.

ISBN 0 340 67453 9

Printed and bound in Great Britain by
Mackays of Chatham PLC, Chatham, Kent

Hodder and Stoughton
A division of Hodder Headline
338 Euston Road
London NW1 3BH

To my sisters,
Katie, Alison and Rachel

Prologue

Prologue

Chloe Capshaw felt the old familiar tingle that reminded her from time to time why she was still a journalist. It started in the pit of her stomach and worked its way down – rather inconveniently, as it happened, since it always made her either want to pee or jump into bed with the nearest male. She looked over at Angus on the subs' desk, with his scrubby beard and permanently hunched back, and decided the loo was probably the best option.

And to think she nearly hadn't worked this shift. It wasn't called the graveyard stint for nothing. Talk about tedious. The paper had more or less been put to bed by now. If only she had been. And preferably with George Clooney. Instead, she was stuck here, painting her nails, uttering the occasional comforting platitude to the odd hysterical hack who called in from a war zone, and waiting for *The Big Breakfast* to start.

She was pretty miffed to be on the news desk at all. She was a features writer, and doing a stint on news was a bloody

1

comedown as far as she was concerned. But if that's what it took to be considered for promotion to a higher position on that slimy pole she laughingly called her career trajectory, then so be it. That didn't mean she had to like it.

And then it had happened. Out of the blue she had taken a call from some snotty-sounding little bell-boy from Cape Town. She'd thought it was a hoax at first. She'd put the call on hold until she'd found her tape recorder. She'd played it back repeatedly since then. There was no mistaking the cat's-got-the-cream tone in his voice. The little shit. No thought for the victim, just a pair of very greedy eyes focused firmly on the main chance.

'Someone very big's just killed themselves. Slashed themselves to shreds,' the voice gabbled on.

'Where are you calling from?' Chloe interrupted.

'The Mount Nelson Hotel. But never mind all that. Are you interested in the story or not?'

The Mount Nelson. Chloe began to turn over the Rolodex of names and addresses that passed for her mind. Cape Town. Who the hell famous enough to warrant a dawn raid on Fleet Street lived in Cape Town?

'Who is it?' she asked, staring at the George Clooney screen saver picture on her computer.

'Uh-oh. You go and ask your editor how much he's willing to pay for an exclusive and then we'll talk.'

She raised her eyes. He'd clearly been watching too many episodes of *Drop the Dead Donkey*. And then she remembered who it was who lived in Cape Town. And he was a very big star indeed. Oh, please God, what if it really were Nick Wilde – and she had the inside scoop? He'd just been nominated for an Oscar. Christ, it was perfect. She scribbled down a telephone number and raced over to the night editor. Her heart was pounding, thudding, bursting. This was a story she'd been waiting for all her life. Prodigiously talented, handsome young actor with Hollywood at his feet throws it all away.

He'd been throwing it all away for quite some time, if the truth be told – and she was about to tell it. Leaving his wife, the beautiful actress Phoebe Keane, just as she was about to give birth to their twins hadn't been the cleverest move, in PR terms. Especially to take up with Martha Crawford, who wasn't that special. Not really any better looking than Chloe, and she definitely had smaller boobs. And when all was said and done, Martha was only a bloody journalist just like she was.

If Chloe had known that Nick Wilde had a predilection for hacks, she would have flirted a bit more blatantly that time she interviewed him. And probably made sure she had got her Dolce and Gabbana suit out of the dry cleaner's. He had been pretty charming, come to think of it. Distracted, but definitely not uninterested. She grabbed her notebook and dialled the bell-boy's number. It would mean a trip to South Africa, of course, and it was her birthday on Sunday. Couldn't be helped. This was a biggie. Definitely front-page stuff – and pages two, three, four, five and the centre spread if it really was Nick Wilde. It almost made putting up with Angus's halitosis worthwhile.

She drummed her fingers impatiently, waiting for the other end to pick up while images of Nick Wilde in his last but one film – *The Explorer*, her favourite, a five-hankie job about some doomed explorer who lived in the 1940s – floated unbidden through her mind. Unaccountably she found herself weeping. He was so very gorgeous. And then the strangest thing of all happened and she found herself hoping against hope that the body wasn't that of Nick Wilde after all.

PART ONE

Chapter One

'Kate, are you really not there, darling? Kate, I promise that I won't take up too much of your time. I'm not hysterical. I just need—' At this point her mother dissolved into tears and at least two minutes of tape were muffled by loud sobs. Kate sighed. Not a good start to Friday morning. And there was more from her mother. Another nine messages. She pressed the fast forward.

'Listen, don't complain that *I'm* never around—' Oh, Christ, thought Kate, Martha was on the warpath. '—when you screen every frigging call. Anyway, I just rang to see if you could recommend a cheap mechanic to fix the Escort's door so I can open it from the inside. That way I can throw myself out of it the next time I'm on the M4 ...'

She fast-forwarded some more.

'Darling, lovely to hear your witty message the other day—' The Fortnum and Mason Christmas puddingy tones of her father floated out to her. 'Yes, I do remember who you are and I'd love to get together. Can't do anything before the end of the month but—'

She pressed the button contemptuously.

'——so I wouldn't give the job at *A la Mode* another thought. Apparently the only qualifications required are an ability to pass the editor copious amounts of Valium and look fabulous with a fag in your mouth. But if you do feel like commiserating, how about dinner, tonight, with me and Podge?'

Eliza. It was her sodding idea that Kate apply to *A la Mode* in the first place. Now it turned out the job had gone before she'd even had time to redesign her CV. And she'd rather slash her new Gaultier than have dinner with Podge.

With phone messages like that, she thought, grabbing her coat and casting a fond farewell glance round her flat, who needed hate mail?

Kate Crawford wasn't the vindictive type but she couldn't help wondering whether anyone would notice if she murdered Max Horrowitz. He was ancient and seemingly without family after all ... This uncharitable notion left her so guilt-ridden she'd had to dive off the number 12 straight into the nearest phone box to call her mother.

Sadie was in one of her Troughs, which always made her incoherent. Kate couldn't get any sense out of her – not that the traffic roaring along Holland Park helped. So then she'd had to call her father at his flat in Dolphin Square to try to discover the cause of the Trough. As if she didn't know. The only time David Crawford, QC, and MP for West Fordingshire, ever experienced unconditional love was when he looked in the mirror. The only sacrifice he'd ever made was when he'd put himself on a reduced cholesterol diet. The only ... She could have gone on but there wasn't a lot of point: he hadn't been home. Probably showing one of the nubile clerks in his office his briefs. She'd have to try him later at the House.

She glanced at the delicate Edwardian numerals on her wrist, adorning what was possibly the world's most unreliable watch. She should have been at work half an hour ago. Or possibly an hour ago. Still, it wasn't her fault that she'd had to call her bloody irresponsible parents, or that the phone box had turned out to be so close to the dilapidated dump Max Horrowitz laughingly called his shop. The shop that should be *her* shop.

Honestly, thought Kate, looking at the chipped paintwork, some of the stock was so old it should have been requisitioned by a fossil museum. Once or twice, rummaging through the ancient zips and knitting wools, she had come across a pair of 1940s Wolsey linen knickers and a bar of Zixt Hand Soap, priced 4d. She'd snapped them up, of course. The knickers made an amazing lampshade, which, she thought mournfully, was the closest any of her underwear was likely to come to an electrifying time.

She peered through the dusty window. Closed. Punctuality clearly wasn't Mr Horrowitz's strong suit, thought Kate crossly, forgetting that she had never been on time for anything. He didn't deserve the shop.

She hovered uncertainly for a few more minutes, brooding about the phone call with her mother. If only Sadie would actually complete one of her wretched evening courses, Kate was convinced her self-esteem would come flooding back. But Sadie kept choosing the wrong topics. She was fixated with keeping up with Dad, which couldn't be easy given that he was one of the most brilliant lawyers of his generation. The youngest barrister ever to take silk. The linchpin of a law firm that was so famous for winning its celebrity litigation cases that the *Sun* had even featured it in one of its quizzes. The butt of *Spitting Image* jokes. (He even had his own puppet.) And a man so undeniably attractive he looked better in his wig-and-gown drag than Zsa Zsa Gabor.

They were *all* fixated with keeping up with him. If she could only get that shop, make a success of it, he might pay them all a bit more attention.

And he could start by going home more, thought Kate, tearing herself away from Horrowitz's. Make more of a fuss of Sadie. But apparently that was asking too much. After all, being nice to his wife wasn't going to get him a profile in *The Spectator*. And now he'd forgotten their anniversary. Men were bastards. Kate sighed and pulled up her collar. To cap it all, Max Horrowitz clearly couldn't be bothered to get out of bed. Dragging herself back up the street towards the bus stop, she called in for an overpriced cappuccino.

'Love the beret.' Roberto Spiga winked wolfishly at Kate from behind the fresh anchovies. Kate smiled back weakly through the fronds of her hair, which seemed to expand and shrink according to the state of her mental health. Anyone would think it was 1959 instead of 1989 the way Roberto conducted his flirtations, she thought disapprovingly. She was late enough as it was without queuing behind the six biddies already waiting. And her bank manager had told her that if she didn't make at least token attempts to economize in the next two weeks he was going to confiscate her cash machine card. If she could sustain the smile throughout the transaction, maybe Roberto would give her a discount.

'Salami salad. Hold the salad.'

He looked at her disapprovingly. It wasn't good for her to eat so much meat. It made her aggressive.

She shrugged helplessly. 'PMT,' she said, to try to embarrass him.

'You mean that bloody poky shop again,' he said, shovelling in some olives when she wasn't looking. They were excellent for the skin.

'For all the good it does me.' She meant it. Retail premises in the neighbourhood never came on the market unless one of the owners died. 'Why does no one round here ever snuff it?'

The six biddies turned round simultaneously and scowled at her.

'Well,' said Roberto, wrapping the salamis, olives and some rocket with a flourish and willing his erection to subside, 'I have some very, very good news for you.'

As it always had done whenever great events were in the offing, the 1812 Overture began exploding on Kate's internal soundtrack 'You don't mean Mr Horrowitz—' she began, suddenly breathless, caught between a pang of guilt, euphoria and a clashing of cymbals.

'Yup. Heart attack. Wednesday. You're a lucky, lucky girl. One pound thirty-four, please.'

'I trust you didn't charge me for the rocket,' said Kate tartly, handing him £1.35. 'Keep the change.'

Roberto gazed lovingly at her receding bloomers as she waltzed out of the shop. A minute later she poked her head back round the door. 'Roberto?'

'Yes?'

'I'm not paying for the bloody olives.'

He beamed. No one could tell him that that didn't constitute some kind of pass.

*   *   *

'Martha?' Donna Ducatti began innocuously, looking up from the immaculately typed list of bullet points that Martha Crawford had recently placed in front of her and on which she was currently painting her nails. 'What kind of fucking balls-up is this?'

'If you look really closely,' said Martha, who had got almost halfway across the studio – a record – before Donna's onslaught had begun, 'I believe you'll discover it's the news.'

She was in no mood for a screechathon. Especially when Donna would conduct most of it in DJ's italics. In fact, after last night's phone call from Jack, which had culminated in a cryathon and that pathetic message she'd left on Kate's machine, she didn't think she could face any more conflict. As it was, discovering that the key to the drawer where she kept a stash of *Hello!*s had gone missing had reduced her to tears that morning.

'*That*,' said Donna evenly, blowing on her left talons now that the revarnishing was complete, 'depends on your *definition* of *news*.'

Donna's peroxided mop was framed by another gauzy helmet of hair – that of her heroine, Mrs Thatcher, who gazed down at them all from the poster next to Donna's console. It made Donna's hair look as though it had a spare tyre. Which was fine, thought Martha spitefully, since the rest of her looked like a truck. Talk about Attila the Blonde.

'"Vaclav Havel agrees to hold the first free elections in Czechoslovakia for *forty years*." Oh that's *really* going to work them into a *frenzy* at the Dog and Duck tonight, *isn't it*?' Donna ran her angelic-looking blue-rimmed eyes down the rest of the list, her pupils pressed avidly against drifting turquoise contact lenses. 'And how many times do I have to tell you that *interest rates*, *up* or *down*, are of *no interest whatsoever* unless you also talk about *exactly* what it means for *mortgage rates* ... Cherrrist, it gets *drearier*.'

Donna waved the list around, allegedly in disgust, though really it was to make her nails dry faster. She sought support from Jem Parsons, her producer, seated behind the glass in the control room. He busied himself with one of the mixers.

'TU *fucking* C conference? Martha, for *fuck's sake*, news has to grab listeners by the *goolies*. It doesn't matter if it makes them *laugh*, *cry* or throw *up*, as long as it gets a *reaction*. Otherwise it's just ...' She rolled her eyes, scanning the room for a metaphor and giving up. '... fucking *shite*.'

'I'm sorry if the fate of the planet doesn't grab you by the goolies today. But for the moment we're clean out of celebrity suicides,' said Martha neutrally.

'Oh, spare us the lectures from the *Newsroom South-East* book of *clichés*. Listen, you *snotty* apology for a *hack*, you're not at *Bollocks* College now.' She riffled through the pile of *National Enquirers* on the console and brandished a picture of Liz Taylor on a stretcher. '*This* is news, Martha. Don't they teach you anything in journalism kindergarten? Ooops, I *always forget*. You never made it to the end of the *lessons*, did you?'

Martha lobbed back a scornful look. Donna really ought to be able to do better than continuously dredging up the matter of her curtailed stint on the BBC's graduate journalism course. What Donna couldn't understand, ever, was how, having been hand-picked out of thousands of applicants, Martha had chucked it all in halfway through. But then Donna hadn't met Jack Dunforth. Darling, lovable

Jack, who had suggested that it might be healthier for their relationship if they weren't constantly together. Healthier for his career was what he meant, according to Eliza. But all Martha had been interested in — obsessed about would be more accurate — was the health of Jack's sex drive, which was in turbocharge mode.

Just having been selected will open doors, he assured her. No one will ever bother to ask if you actually completed. In fact, he argued, some in the industry might argue that the combination of an upper second from Balliol and honours in journalism was over-egging the pudding. Traumatized at the thought of losing him, Martha had complied and, some months later, when the only doors that had opened had swung into the grimy reception area of BSR — and that was because Jem had taken pity on her — Jack dumped her. Or rather he had 'popped their relationship into the cool box' while he went and sizzled in New Orleans for MBC.

Even with her debt-fest, she hadn't been bowled over by the BSR job. But Jem's earnest-looking spectacles had seduced her. So when he'd told her that together they'd be able to create a new, honest and intelligent form of populism on local radio, one that could educate the masses, she had believed him.

Now she glared at him accusingly. So did Donna. Avoiding both their gazes, he took a call from Typhoon Glazing, who wanted to know why their jingle hadn't been played all morning. By the time he came off the line, Donna's earrings were spinning like manic satellites and her voice had reached blast-off. He looked at the clocks. In a laughable attempt at international gravitas, they had one set to New York time, one to Sydney's, and a third variable. It was

2 p.m. in Delhi. 'Time for a weather check, Donna,' he said hopefully.

'Fuck off,' said Donna and Martha in unison.

Jem's spectacles winked like flashers circling a public toilet. He flinched as Donna lobbed another personal insult at Martha and launched straight into the weather, without so much as a syllable from the Typhoon Glazing backing singers. Donna by name, Prima Donna by nature.

It was tragic. In their own way Donna and Martha were gifted broadcasters. Donna's populist instincts were infallibly spot-on and Martha had all the makings of a cracking little journalist. He'd been amazed how quickly she'd established a rapport with various local police stations that had given BSR some excellent crime scoops. In the first flush of her early enthusiasm she had even befriended some unsavoury underworld characters who had given her one or two excellent tip-offs. Donna had rewarded her by making her rewrite the weather reports.

Bright – though with recurring periods of fogginess when it came to affairs of the heart – and brimful of integrity, Martha was a workaholic who also cared passionately about the station, though perhaps not this one. If Donna and Martha could only establish a *modus vivendi* – if Martha could clamber off her moral crusade and Donna could get her snout out of the gutter for five seconds – BSR's news coverage might be unrivalled among local stations.

'Now fuck off back to that *dank little hole* you call an *office* and get me some news I can read out without sending *fifty per cent* of the audience into a *coma*,' screeched Donna.

'Would that be the fifty per cent that isn't already in one?' asked Martha, concentrating on the post-traumatic remains of Donna's last perm which, by rights, ought to have been submitted for the Turner Prize.

Having dismissed Martha, Donna swivelled back to the console, suctioned her pink, frosted lips against the microphone and began crooning along to the dying strains of Terence Trent D'Arbay, before segueing neatly into the Fine Young Cannibals' 'She Drives Me Crazy'. Her timing, as usual, marvelled Jem, was impeccable. She must have been born with amplifier leads leading to her heart instead of veins.

Martha slunk back to her cubby-hole, tripping over the flex to her fax machine, and wiped a prickly mohair-clad arm across her eyes, smearing the remains of last night's mascara over her cheeks. She must be depressed if Donna was getting to her this much. It was all Jack Dunforth's bloody fault. She'd give him popular journalism.

Donna ran her tongue lasciviously over her frosted lips, then flicked it over her teeth to get rid of any traces of lipstick before approaching the mike again. Flicking two fingers up at Martha's receding back – an involuntary reflex – she laughed an inimitable throaty gurgle that was a beguiling mixture of sweetness and crude suggestiveness. 'Now, Jem, me *old cocker*, who've you got on the line for me?'

'Hello, Dad?' The line was appalling. What with the roar of traffic racing along the Marylebone High Road just outside Morton's, Kate couldn't hear a thing.

'It's Elaine Fletcher,' said a voice patiently. 'Can I help you, dear?'

Elaine, thought Kate. What happened to Deirdre? Dad was getting through his secretaries at a record rate this year.

Ever since he'd been introduced to Sharon Weiner at a Leicester Square première and she'd allegedly told him how fascinating she found politicians, he'd been impossible. Even so, she'd decided to give him one more try on her way to work, now that she knew Horrowitz's was finally about to come on the market.

'I just wondered whether David Crawford was around. It's his daughter.'

'He's in Brussels. I'm sorry, I didn't catch the rest of what you said.'

'His daughter,' shrieked Kate, competing with the rush hour.

She shouldn't be calling him really. Not twice in one morning. The one thing she had gathered from Sadie's tirade was that her father was definitely in the dog-house. But then he always was. He was also the only one of them in the money. And given her current entente discordiale with the bank, he was her only hope of getting a loan to buy old Max Horrowitz's (the late Max Horrowitz's) place.

There was a pause. 'Really, dear,' said Elaine, sounding sceptical. Gratuitously so, in Kate's view. To listen to Elaine, anyone would think her father was inundated with swooning groupies. 'What did you say your name was?'

Bloody typical, thought Kate. At this rate she'd have to call Eliza for a loan on the pretext of asking for some advice about men or mortages – which was how she approached asking Eliza for most of her favours these days. It had come to a pretty pass when your oldest girlfriends from school were more accessible – and way more sensible – than your parents.

Eliza had everything, thought Kate enviously. A fantastic job, great legs, membership of the Groucho, a diaphragm that didn't sit on her bedside table collecting dust, and a conceptual flat in Primrose Hill, the main concept of which seemed to be that everything in it looked like something else. She had a sofa that looked like a giant pair of lips, a chair that looked like a piano, and a polished concrete floor that looked like a lake. No wonder she never cooked anything, thought Kate. Probably couldn't identify the oven.

If only Sadie and David could stop their infernal bickering. She ought to take the pair of them to the European Human Rights Commission for child neglect. Brussels indeed. If only she could stop being so dependent on her father. If only they all could. The problem was, for all his elusiveness, he was good at dishing out the rebates.

'Would you mind,' she began as sweetly as she could given the noise factor, 'telling him that Sharon called to let him know she's got the clap.'

'That was for all you *horny* girls out there,' Donna husked fruitily, flicking her fag ash over a pile of discarded news bulletins. 'And now, gang, as you know, we *should* be bringing you the *news*, but guess what? There *isn't* any. So we're not *gonna bother*. In fact, the world is *seriously boring*. Either that or there's been *another Martha Mix-Up*. Next week we're gonna launch a *competition* to see who can spot the *biggest* cock-up. In the meantime, to ease us into the weekend, there's a *Mega Mix* coming up. Thirty *straight-up* minutes of *get-down* music. No *boring* ads and no boring me.'

George Michael began crooning into Donna's head-phones, which had been hurled on to the console while she scrambled to the loo.

Jem clutched what was left of his mousey hair. What

with the previous interlude, Donna's Mega Mix meant they would have gone forty minutes without a single ad. Typhoon Glazing would not be happy. He ambled down the corridor to Martha's cubicle and waved the missing key to the *Hello!* stash in front of her. Nose-deep in the media jobs section of the *Guardian*, she looked up at him guiltily. 'That's the Dunkirk spirit, Marth,' he said wryly. 'When the going gets tough, send yet another application into *Woman's Hour.*'

Nothing – not missing a job lot of number 12 buses, the abortive phone calls to her father, not even the hideous new posters in the entrance lobby to Morton's advertising the grotesque collection that Kate had toiled on for most of last spring – could dent her newly restored good humour. She even smiled at Tatty as she tried to slide casually behind her drawing board and her collection of rare and endangered inks.

'Love the bag,' said Tatty, peeping round a brown plastic partition board, her cheeks glowing like polished damsons. 'New?'

'Not exactly,' said Kate, spilling the last of the extra-large cappuccino Roberto had slipped her on to a loose grey carpet tile. 'The guy on the stall said it belonged to Jane Austen. I hope so because I may need to offload it on the V & A.'

'Well, it looks jolly nice,' said Tatty sweetly, with more plums in her mouth than the entire output of Del Monte. 'I never know what to wear to work. It really drives Mummy mad. Freddie, on the other hand, seems to know instinctively.'

Freddie was Tatty's ghastly seven-year-old brother, whose distended features gazed down at them from a photo that had pride of place on Tatty's inspiration board, next to one of the gorgeous South African actor Nick Wilde. Tatty thought she could see a resemblance between them. Where, Kate couldn't imagine – perhaps it was that they were both, arguably, *Homo sapiens*. Nick had a sheaf of wheat-coloured hair and knowing, indigo-coloured eyes. Freddie had ... pudge. Lots of it. In fact Freddie, who had occasionally been known to visit Tatty at work during his school holidays with the express intention of putting them all off having children, had struck Kate as singularly unprepossessing. In Tatty's eyes he could do no wrong, even when he swallowed one of Kate's rare inks, mistaking it for some Tango. He was a surprise late baby, she had said, by way of explanation. The only surprise, thought Kate crossly, was that someone hadn't suffocated him.

'It is a bit intimidating, isn't it,' Tatty pressed on valiantly in the face of Kate's monumental indifference, 'knowing what to wear when you work for a fashion house?'

'You don't look as though it worries you.' The words were out of Kate's mouth before she'd had time to consider them. She felt evil and then she felt recalcitrant. It wasn't her fault if Tatty had all the style of a shantytown that had been ninety per cent destroyed by a hurricane. And was she to blame because Tatty was always on a diet? Tatty's mother, who sent her weekly food parcels, insisted that it was just puppy fat. Seal pups maybe. 'What I mean,' Kate carried on awkwardly, 'is that you don't look as though you'd ever get into debt over a torn handbag.'

That just made things ten times worse. Tatty, who had

palpitations if she parked on a yellow line for a few seconds, gazed at Kate admiringly and wished that she could be as utterly irresponsible in the face of impending financial meltdown. Instead she was destined for a life of sensible investments.

'Mark was looking for you,' she whispered loudly. 'He said it was quite urgent.'

Kate affected a yawn and pulled a dog-eared copy of *The World of Interiors* out of her bag. 'What now?' she said wearily. 'Stripes summit? Crimplene curfew?'

'New project,' said Tatty. 'I'm not sure if stripes are involved.'

Stripes were a sensitive issue. When Kate had arrived at Morton's two and a half years earlier, she had sacrificed hours of spare lunch-times rescaling Morton's stripes on Mark Lacy's computer, convinced it would make their lamentable knitwear look classier.

But altering stripes, let alone introducing some florals, had proved way too radical for Morton's management. The idea was firmly laid to rest, along with any ambitions Kate ever had for a future for herself within the company, even if, as Tatty had helpfully pointed out, they did offer their staff the best health and life insurance schemes in retailing. She didn't rush to Mark Lacy's office.

World news for 1989:
Fall of Berlin Wall
Rumblings of unrest in Romania — first publicly acknowledged
    demos for thirty years
Signs of disintegrating fabric of Soviet Union
More evidence of Thatcher's hubris: see speech declaiming intention
    to go on and on.

Growing paranoia about food scares — see dissertation on national pathologies
Green momentum

World news for 1989 as absorbed by BSR listeners:
Pamella Bordes cuts crotch out of Andrew Neil's trousers
Stench hit number one three times in a row
Claudia Schiffer signs as Chanel's new face — NB Donna thinks she looks common
Scorcher Morehouse, lead singer with Stench, goes into rehab

These two concurrent lists, endlessly revised in times of direst stress when she would perhaps have been better employed getting on with other things, represented Martha's most masochistic pasttime. Measuring the gap between what she was employed to do and what she thought she should be employed to do was a form of exquisite torture. What she should have been doing, of course, was compiling a bulletin that would meet with Donna's approval. She knew Donna mocked her to the listeners, because Samantha on reception told her so, in between wiping the soot which regularly floated through the doors from the main road off the reception desk and retuning the reception speakers to Capital Radio.

'Are they ready yet?' Jem's moon face poked round her door. 'Oh, Martha, not that lot again. Why do you do it to yourself?'

Martha shrugged helplessly. She knew she was behaving childishly, which made her even crosser. She had the moral high ground, after all. She ought to be striding heroically to victory, not stamping her foot as she stared oblivion — or at any rate a P45 — squarely in the maw.

'There are ways of making a difference, you know,' he began gently. 'Subverting from within and all that.'

'If you can find a way of turning Phoebe Keane's vital statistics into a parable on apartheid, do please feel free to share it,' she snapped.

'Any chance of a *few crumbs* of news – please, please, *please*.' Donna's wheedling sarcasm ricocheted tinnily round Martha's headphones, which were lying on her desk.

'For God's sake, Martha, c'mon,' pleaded Jem.

Donna's voice crooned on, terrifyingly calm. 'It's just that if you can't find *anything* of *any interest* for our *esteemed* listeners, Martha, sweetheart – just a few *teensy nuggets* to toss to their *atrophied* brains in the hope that it might *spur* some of them on to take *PhDs* in current affairs – we might have to kill you – strictly in the interests of making some *news*, you understand.'

Jem looked at her beseechingly.

Martha smiled sweetly. 'Flattered as I am by your faith in my omnipotence in this matter, I suggest that if you don't like the news, perhaps you could take it up with God.'

Over in Studio B, Donna made to rise from her chair but her spike heel got caught on a fraying corner of carpet.

'Now,' she screamed.

'Martha, for God's sake. She's not joking.'

'In case you hadn't noticed, I'm not laughing.'

'She'll fire you.'

'Hoo-bloody-ray.'

'You know how Jack likes a successful woman.'

Martha narrowed her eyes at him malevolently. 'You bastard,' she hissed, reaching for the phone and dialling Eliza's office number.

Jem smirked to himself. The Jack taunts worked every time.

Kate waltzed into the urinal-sized cubicle and eyed the grey plastic filing trays with their mounds of fraying buff folders that threatened to slide on to Mark Lacy's desk, causing a dangerous avalanche of bureaucracy. Since being promoted to head of department two months ago, Mark Lacy had been inundated with administrative details. It was pathetic what some people put up with for the sake of a company Vauxhall, she thought.

She sat down and found herself level with Mark Lacy's freckled gaze. Defiantly, she allowed herself a few seconds' appraisal. It was his more-in-sorrow-than-anger look, she decided.

'Sorry I'm late. Concorde's routed over Shepherd's Bush again and all the clocks stalled.'

Mark Lacy tried to suppress a smile. 'Really, Kate, if you expended half as much energy in getting here on time as you did on your excuses you'd be first in the building every morning.'

'Possibly. But it wouldn't be half so much fun.'

There was a silence.

'Sorry.'

'I'll pretend I didn't hear.'

Kate slumped back into the beige – a particularly nasty shade – chair. Mark Lacy really wasn't bad. He was even quite kind. She knew she ought to make an effort but she didn't know if she had any reserves of enthusiasm left for Morton's. Best to preserve them for other things.

'Look, I didn't call you in to beef about your time-keeping, though a bit more of it would be appreciated. I wanted to talk to you because I sense you're not as happy as you might be here.'

Kate said nothing. Her eyes began to glisten. Nothing caused her more anguish than the tragic subject of her sabotaged career.

'Is it the stripes?' began Mark gently.

Kate wiped a pin-striped arm across her eyes.

'I can see you're demotivated,' he tried again.

'Who wouldn't be,' said Kate, quivering, 'when everything here so clearly revolves around a bottom line – and a size-eighteen one at that? And yes, since you ask, the stripes were traumatic. Size matters, you know, and a three-inch gap looks so much better than a two-inch one. But everyone's so scared that profits might not show a twenty per cent year-on-year increase that they're terrified of taking any risk whatsoever.'

Mark waited until he was sure she'd finished. 'It may not be quite as bad as you think,' he began shyly. 'The management has given the green light to a project I've been researching.'

There was a pause pregnant enough for quintuplets while Kate tried to stem the waves of apathy. 'We want to launch a new youth line. Code-name Xtra. It's aimed at sixteen- to twenty-four-year-olds, so not that much of a leap of imagination for you. The figures are all here.' He nodded at a bulging buff file on his desk. 'They're quite thrilling, actually. It's going to be much more trend-conscious than anything we've ever done before.' He paused again. 'I'd like you to work on it.'

Kate's heart sank. Mark's figures never failed to send

her into a decline. Tracking trends didn't appeal to her in the slightest either. Morton's was grim, but as long as everyone accepted that, it was bearable. If they started trying to be hip, she didn't know if she could be held responsible for her actions.

'Great,' she said through gritted teeth.

There was a silence. Kate smoothed the ruffles on her bloomers. All she could think about was Horrowitz's. If she managed to get hold of it and make it a success, she was convinced everything else in her life would fall into place. The man of her dreams would materialize, her parents would stop bloody rowing, and her father would finally respect her. She made her mind up: she would give herself twelve months to turn Horrowitz's around, after which, if no headway had been made, she would resign herself to a life of Mark Lacy.

'Any questions?' said Mark hopefully.

Kate's eyebrows arched in minimal enquiry. 'Yes.'

He looked at her even more hopefully.

'Can I go now? Only I left my lunch on my desk and with Tatty's appetite you can't be too careful.'

His face fell. She couldn't bear those wounded grey eyes of his. And why did they have to be the precise same shade as Morton's carpets?

She tried to sound interested. 'I'd love to read the research,' she said.

'Oh ... right. Marvellous,' he said. 'I'll pull out the salient bits and get them photocopied for you.'

Perhaps there was hope after all. If he could only engage her imagination, he thought, she might stop taking so many liberties. And the upper management would stop asking if he'd sacked her yet.

'Off anywhere nice?' asked Tatty later, trying not to sound inquisitive. It was only just after lunch, and Kate was already packing up her bags and Mark Lacy's beige files.

'Home. Got a stack of research and you know how bad the buses are,' said Kate vaguely. 'Tell Mark I'm in the buff, in preparation for our first meeting. He'll understand.'

At three seconds to ten, Martha skidded into Studio B with a perfectly wrought BSR version of the news. She had done what she always did *in extremis*: called Eliza. When she and Eliza put their minds to it, they were a dream news team, prioritizing gossip and steaming through Eliza's precious little red contacts book. She had quite a collection of names in it now which Martha frequently availed herself of in order to polish small, offbeat stories into glittering Donna-sized nuggets. She'd had a tip-off about a memo that had been circulated to TUC members ordering them to smarten up, which she'd spiced up with a typically controversial quote from Katharine Hamnett, whose home number Eliza had just acquired. Eliza had also revealed that Sleeky Head, the men's hair products which she had recently signed up, had just conducted a poll that showed that eighty per cent of their customers preferred sex in the morning.

'What the hell has that got to do with hair conditioners and dandruff treatments?' grumbled Martha, while she worked the story into something fit for a Prima Donna.

'Absolutely nothing,' crowed Eliza triumphantly. 'It's a completely gratuitous question I added at the last minute, purely to get us some column inches in the tabloids.'

Martha made some disapproving noises.

'Oh, come on, M. You've got to admit this system is

working beautifully. You get stories. I get coverage. Now, did I tell you about the actress who refused to wear the dress Sir Vincent Lambert designed gratis for her to go to the *International Gazette*'s theatre awards on Monday unless he threw in his boyfriend's jewellery? It was good stuff as well, all forked out for from the Duchess of Windsor's auction.'

'Sharon Weiner, don't tell me,' said Martha. 'How despicable. Still, it's not exactly *Panorama* material, is it?'

'Correct on both counts. And you're not exactly working on *Panorama*. Which is why you and the story are perfect for one another. I'm sure you can shape it into something.'

Despite her misgivings, Martha had to admit that the process of compiling news stories, of spotting teeny little loose ends in the press and following them up until they connected to something bigger, was hugely enjoyable. If only she could put her skills to worthier ends.

Donna ran a practised eye down the list. 'Since you so *obviously* can do it when you *deign* to put your mind to it, Miss Po, I'm going to have to *insist* that you apologize to the *lovely listeners.*'

Martha rolled her eyes and headed for the door.

'So, gang, Martha's got something to say to you.' Donna pressed her *2001: A Space Odyssey* fanfare jingle. 'Come back, Martha, *sweetheart*, and tell the *gang* how *sorry* you are about the *Martha Mix-Up.*'

Martha stopped in her tracks. Donna was serious. She was actually going to make her apologize on air.

'*Grovel*'s the word that springs to mind. *C'mon*, Martha.'

She looked at Jem behind the glass but couldn't catch his eye.

'Ooh, she's gone *all sulky*. Or is it just *time* of the *month*? Honestly, some people would slit their vocal *cords* for a chance to come on this mike. Tell you what. Phone in if you want Martha to *grovel*. Inventor of the most *grovelling apology* wins a night out with *Marth*.'

The console's red phone lines began blinking like strobes. The listeners were becoming addicted to Donna and Martha's Row-In. As yet no one had heard Martha's voice on air. The suspense was killing them. 'Going to line *nine*, Jem,' said Donna, eyes flashing in time with the console. 'Line nine? Oh, line six, then. *Hello*, darling. What you got for *me*?'

Kate closed the Prussian blue door to her flat behind her and instantly felt the day's frustrations free-float into the ether. She gazed lovingly at the creamy pine floors and the rose-embroidered rugs – picked up for a song in Bermondsey – and wondered what Roberto would make of its dimensions. The flat was minuscule – one bedroom, a tiny cubby-hole she used as an office, and a sitting room with a galley kitchen which she'd partitioned behind an old screen she'd found in a skip. But it had good light and, despite the property developer's worst intentions, pleasing proportions. She pulled off her Cossack boots and coat, arranged them neatly in the little Swedish armoire she had filched from home, and padded over to the kitchen. Pity the contents of her fridge didn't match up to the contents of the flat. Twenty-six years old and here she was scraping the remainder of a jar of pesto on to a half-tin of Alphabetti spaghetti. She lit all the tin sconces on the walls and poured some of Sadie's home-made essence of fig into an oil burner. It smelled so much better than the pesto that she was tempted to eat it. By the time the candles were all flickering merrily against the pale green walls, she even felt ready to tackle Mark Lacy's buff file.

Martha trudged up the Holloway Road and turned into Tollington Way. The one silver lining to these dark wintry evenings was that she could no longer see how unremittingly bleak her neighbourhood was. The reek of oily bikes in the hallway mingled with the stench of Mrs Kossov's pig bones which she vaporized dutifully for her dogs every Friday. She climbed wearily up the stained porridge-coloured stairs and fiddled with her keys. The bloody lock never seemed to work properly and she wasted hours of her life trying out various keys from a bunch of relics that dated back to her days at Balliol.

Eventually, through a combination of force and cunning, she managed to coax the door open and practically fell on to more stained carpet. She was exhausted. It was all very well for Donna — her megalomania was the reason they all had to adhere to a punishing schedule of six morning shows a week. But it was killing the rest of them. She got to the office at five every morning and hardly ever got away before six o'clock at night. She felt for the switch, but only one of the wall lights was working. What had made her even think that buying a flat around the corner from BSR was a good idea?

Come to think of it, what ever made her think anything about BSR would enhance her life in any way? Whenever Martha ran through the thought processes that led her to abandon the BBC course, which she did approximately eight times a day, it was with an increasing sense of disbelief. She had been mesmerized by Jack. Fair enough. So had all the other females on the course. He had a dazzling interview technique – particularly when it came to chatting up anything with a pulse, and that included their appalling lentil-chewing vegan visiting lecturer. And equally scintillating keyboard skills, notably when it came to locating the G-spot.

Sadie would say it was because subliminally she didn't want to be a serious journalist. But then Sadie hadn't actually ever finished her psychotherapy night classes. Martha smiled ruefully. Cooking and an inability to complete courses were the two things she'd inherited from her mother. Not the radiant, fragile beauty. And certainly not the talent for interior decorating that had always made their home such a welcoming refuge, even if the mood swings of the incumbents left the odd emotional scuff mark.

Thank God for her parents. When all was said and done, she loved them to distraction. Sadie might have her neuroses – her passionate hatred for Prue Leith, Fay Maschler and Delia Smith, women who had carved sparkling careers for themselves despite having inferior talents to her own, for example. But all in all she had been a pretty okay mother. Even her father could be relied on in an absolute life-or-death crisis.

Martha looked vacantly at the brown stain spreading across the Artexed ceiling in her sitting room and wished some *deus ex machina* would take control of her life, though with her luck the bloody *machina* would blow a fuse. She was jogged out of her reverie by the phone. She stumbled into the darkened sitting room and groped for the receiver. It was Jem.

'Don't ever go so close to the wire again. We need you at that station. I can't face it if you go. So get your act together and come in at four tomorrow morning and I'll run through part one of Jem Parsons' survival guide.'

'It's sweet of you, Jem, it really is, but I honestly don't know if there's any point.'

'I bet your dad does. What is it you still owe him for that course – two and a half grand?'

Martha sighed. All she wanted was to sleep. Since starting on Donna's *Cookin' Breakfast*, she'd averaged four hours a night. She'd worked her way through the entire cornucopia of natural sleep remedies in Tufnell Park's only health food shop to no avail. She was considering shifting to vodka.

Before she could switch on the answer machine, the phone rang again.

'It's me. Family summit. At my place. In half an hour.' Kate sounded winded.

'What's wrong with sensible conversation. On the phone. Now?' asked Martha wearily.

'Fine,' snapped Kate, wondering how anyone lacking such a sense of occasion ever landed a scoop. 'Won't happen again. Only Mum called. She tried you but you were endlessly engaged. White House again, was it? Anyway, just wanted to let you know, Dad's finally left her and she's on the verge of a nervous breakdown. So sorry to bother you.'

Chapter Two

Martha awoke with a guilty start and struggled out from under a hirsute arm to get a better view of the alarm clock. It was 6 a.m. Somehow even the knowledge that she didn't have to face Donna for another twenty-four hours didn't assuage her panic. Her schedule was so tightly sardined with Things To Do that even a rogue phone call from a friend could throw her out for the rest of the week. She grappled with the arm again. Even asleep, Jack was proprietorial.

Jack. What the hell was she doing? It was Kate's fault for being so vile on the phone. And her mother and father for splitting up. She still couldn't take it all in. One minute she had been staring morosely at the remains of some spatchcocked Bresse pigeon and raspberry sorbet – when in crisis Martha cooked – and the next the phone had gone again. This time it had been Jack. Charming, blithe, seductive as ever. And back briefly from New Orleans to film an interview with Paddy Ashdown and, for some reason, Tony Patterson, the Right Honourable MP for North Seaton. And desperate to see her. Or so he said.

He'd put up a pretty good performance, she'd give him that. In fact he'd put up a pretty good everything. Her brain went fuzzy again as she remembered the way he'd worked his way energetically up and down her body with the true zeal of an expert investigative reporter. Finally escaping his embrace, she slipped out of bed and contemplated his slumbering figure as dispassionately as she could manage. She hated him, of course. Which was why she could appraise his stocky, sunburned body without embarrassment. Definitely not her type. He was so swarthy, he had five o'clock shadow by half past nine in the morning. The gleaming black hair sprouting from his head like newly drilled oil and bushy eyebrows were the only bits about him she found irresistible. That and the searing blue eyes. And the dramatic cleft in his chin. And his sense of humour. And the metal-rimmed spectacles he wore when he was being serious. And probably the fact that he was a contemptible shit.

She tried looking at him with the blinds wide open. Talk about the luck of the Irish. Celtic colouring *and* a suntan. And no bloody conscience. Jack's family had lived in Putney for at least three generations. But that didn't stop him from putting Donegal down as his place of birth when he'd applied for the MBC job. The Americans, of course, loved him. Hence the pay packet that had enabled him to invest in Château Docklands. He was so proud of it that she almost couldn't resent it, not even his circular extractor fan. He'd given her the complete tour, from the blameless, stainless steel Bulthaup kitchen he'd had installed (untouched by human hand, she thought bitterly), complete with island counter which she'd christened by rustling up steak au poivre and crème brûlée, to the *bateau lit* which he'd christened by comprehensively seducing her.

She padded over to the window and gazed up at the stern edifices at either end of Tower Bridge. Trust Jack to have two gigantic phallic symbols bang outside his bedroom. The view was mesmerizing, intoxicating and almost worth the inevitable pain she was about to endure. It was all so very different from Tufnell Park. Already feeling disconsolate, she wandered across to the Corbusier chaise-longue in the sitting room, where she was horrified to see an empty bottle of Jack Daniel's that she vaguely remembered being full at the start of the evening's proceedings, and began collecting the clothes she had abandoned there the night before. She ran a hot shower and, needing a news fix, crept into the kitchen to switch on the radio while she made some fresh coffee.

Things were getting pretty bad in Romania. Nicolae Ceaușescu and his Lady Macbeth of a wife had been brought back for trial and the crowd were baying for blood. But the soothing voices of Radio Four's newsreaders made the whole gory saga sound like another edition of *The Archers*. Donna's DJ italicese, on the other hand, could make a bulletin about Princess Diana being served with a parking ticket sound cataclysmic. And now she was talking about getting Jem to read the weather in the nude.

There had to be a way of injecting some sense of authority into Donna's *Cookin' Breakfast* news bulletins. She turned back into Radio Four. David Owen was in the political wilderness following his resignation from the SDP. Welcome to the club, thought Martha morosely, zoning out again as the newscaster read sombrely on.

'*It is an ill wind that blows nobody any good, however. One MP who stands to gain from the political fall-out is David Crawford, shining light in the New Democratic Party ...*' She came to with a start when she heard her father's voice floating emolliently across the airwaves. The words so beautifully rounded, the pauses so fecund: anyone would think he'd been to RADA.

Oh God, thought Martha guiltily. Sadie. She'd be surrounded by open recipe books with her best Sabatier hovering perpendicular to her breast by now. And Mata Hari, her mother's Persian-Siamese which had dominated the Crawford household ever since Martha could remember, would be hysterical. She adored David and left thoughtful traces of matted fur all over his Gieves and Hawkes suits as a constant reminder of the fact – another source of friction between her parents.

In the aftermath of Jack – and a bottle of whisky – Martha had managed to forget about the impending apocalypse of her parents' marriage. Now it came flooding back in a sickening tidal wave. How dare her father sound so suave when the family was in a State of Emergency? She lit one of Jack's Marlboros. Bastard. He hadn't once asked her how she was – at least not in a way that suggested he was interested in a full and frank disclosure. Well, she wouldn't bloody wake him. Just slip out without leaving a message. The way he'd left her the last time. She was meant to be in Bath in three hours anyway – plenty of time in a normal car, but the Escort was pathological. She'd just finish her coffee.

She was on her second cup before Jack finally roused himself. Naked – she couldn't help contrasting the luxurious warmth of his riverside palace with the arctic wasteland of her own ecological disaster area – he crept up from behind and ruffled her silky brown hair. 'Sexiest smell in the world. Fresh coffee the morning after,' he mumbled, nuzzling into her neck. He hadn't even showered. Wordlessly she handed him her mug. 'I was just leaving,' she said lamely.

'In my bathrobe?' His mouth twitched. 'Oh, Martha,

sweetheart ...' He launched expansively into his Donegal twang, which she always found irritatingly appealing. 'Don't go all belligerent on me. I know I'm a congenital scoundrel, but I am very fond of you. And we do have fun together, don't we?'

She looked at his spiky hair and the ridiculously blue gaze, ran her eyes crossly down his endearingly squat body and found herself twisting her fingers through his pubic hair. He reacted predictably and she began stroking his penis. Shit, even semi-hung-over she still found him attractive.

'It's over,' she said flatly.

He pretended to digest this for a moment. 'Can a condemned man have one last request?' he pleaded.

She looked at him expectantly.

He bent down on one knee and took her hand. 'Can it at least be over this island counter? It's my ultimate culinary fantasy.'

Kate's heart began to pound. Tiny beads of sweat spontaneously evolved above her top lip, despite the freezing early morning air.

'You all right? You look terrible.'

Kate stared coldly at the sulky teenager minding the stall. She had been out for dinner with Eliza – a civilized girls' night out, she had thought, and a chance to share the family calamity. But then Podge, Eliza's sex toy – there was no other term for it; she certainly refused to believe that Eliza could be in love with someone possessed of such an abundance of nasal hair – had turned up. Instantly the talking had ceased, before they'd even broached the matter of David and Sadie, and the drinking had begun.

It was all right for Podge, who had an obscene expense account and an obscene hairstyle to match. If only he had the imagination, he could have trained his nasal hair to trail over his thinning patches. He must be brilliant in bed. It was the only possible excuse for Eliza's lapse in taste.

'How much?' she asked in her best down-at-heel voice. The teenager ignored her. She could hear Talking Heads thumping away in his Walkman speakers and made a half-hearted attempt to remove one of his earphones. The wire got tangled up in his turban, which was so tatty he ought to have qualified for a Turban Renewal grant. 'Thirty quid,' he said petulantly.

She looked at the set again. Russell Wright, if she wasn't very much mistaken, and worth ten times that. Kate collected 1950s china as well as Swedish furniture and French pieces from the 1940s. Actually she collected anything cheap, and was always so certain the bits she loved were about to be discovered by the rest of the world at any moment that whenever she saw a bargain she experienced all the symptoms of extreme stress. The teenager hawked into a Kleenex and rolled a cigarette. She waited until he began fiddling with his volume control before picking up a saucer nonchalantly and looking at the underside.

Halfway back from Jack's shiny flat, Martha remembered to call Kate. It was stupid for them both to drive separately to Bath. If she could get herself to Kate's flat in Shepherd's Bush they could go together, sharing the driving and the cost. She got out at King's Cross and made her way past a gang of fat goths and a gaggle of drug pushers to a phone box. The phone rang for what seemed an eternity, clattering ound the void of Martha's numbed head. Damn. Kate had obviously already left. The journey would be endless – her radio was broken and she'd have to take the ghetto-blaster. A tattoo of heavy footsteps echoed eerily behind her on the concourse. One of the drug pushers edged up to her and tuck his handsome bullet head into her airspace.

'Hi, Rembrandt,' she said distractedly. 'I'm in a bit of a rush just at the moment.'

He tutted disapprovingly. 'That's a pity, Martha, 'cos 've got a bit of a scoop for you this morning.' He pushed his large hands into the capacious pockets of his white puffy jacket.

'Tomorrow? I'll meet you straight after work.'

He laughed mirthlessly. 'Twenty-four hours? That's a ery, very long time on Fleet Street, Martha.' He swaggered off.

Damn. Rembrandt's leads were always of the highest quality and had provided her with several tasty BSR stories. t was no good; Kate would kill her if she didn't make the ummit. Reluctantly, she strode away across the concourse efore she could change her mind. She got back on to the platform just in time to hear the announcer introducing passengers to the possibility of a thirty-minute delay on he Northern Line. Which just gave her time to catch up vith Rembrandt and phone whatever titbit he'd come up vith over to BSR.

Kate dragged herself reluctantly from the battered stall. The old was beginning to seep through her 1930s astrakhan oat into her bones. The teenager tapped his foot. 'It's a omplete set.'

'Fifteen. Cash,' said Kate.

He snorted. 'You 'aving me on?'

She shrugged. This was the best part and also the most foolhardy. The set was worth at least £300. She'd be furious if she didn't get it. On the other hand she couldn't really afford 15p.

'Twenty-five and that's my last offer.'

He tried not to smirk.

Triumph made her reckless.

'Twenty and that's all I've got.'

Blimey, there was one born every day. He looked at his watch smoothly. 'Go on, then.'

Barely restraining herself from kissing him, she fumbled in her bag for her purse. It wasn't there. She'd removed it to try to stop herself spending any money. She didn't know the stall-holders at Brick Lane as well as she knew those in Portobello. She fixed him with her sweetest smile. 'You couldn't hold it for me, just for a few hours?'

'Look, d'you want this or what? 'Cos any minute now, right, I'm packing up.'

'Er, hang on,' said Kate, casting around desperately for any familiar passers-by who might lend her some money. You never knew.

The teenager began wrapping up his merchandise. Kate wanted to weep. 'Please wait.'

''Ow long?'

Kate did some rapid mental calculations. Thirty-five minutes at least to get back to Shepherd's Bush – *if* she was lucky enough to find a taxi that would wait while she ransacked the flat for her purse. Twenty minutes to locate cash cards. Thirty-five minutes back. 'An hour and a half,' she said hopefully.

'You what?' He sniggered sarcastically. 'Listen, I been 'ere since four. It's now nine-firty, right? So that makes five and a half hours and two frozen bollocks. I'm off.'

Nine-thirty. The painful realisation that she was meant to be somewhere else dawned on her. It looked extra bad because she was the one who had declared the State of Emergency in the face of Martha's overwhelming apathy. She had two and a half hours to get back to Shepherd's Bush, find her purse, track down the car which she'd left at a party, fill it with petrol and herself with self-righteousness, and hotfoot it to her mother's.

Sadie's. Already home had become her mother's and not her parents'. She pulled off her fedora and handed it to the teenager. 'Deposit. I'll be back at dawn next week to collect it.' She smiled sweetly. 'Sorry, got to run.'

In a state of shock, he gazed at the intricately embroidered fornicating snakes decorating the back of Kate's coat in disbelief. 'It's not even as if it's a nice yellow,' he thought scornfully. And if she thought he wasn't going to offload it on to the next person who came along and offered him a tenner . . . Kate returned, panting. 'And I forgot to say that if you don't keep your word, your bollocks, frozen or not, will be history.'

Their parents had certainly recognized an idyllic rural spot when they saw one, thought Martha, gently bumping the Escort through the elegant stone gateposts that flanked the gravel drive leading up to Tithe House. A small but serenely symmetrical Georgian rectory, it seemed to Martha always to have been suffused in golden light, although she now realized this may in part have been a trick of a clever architect who had built it from Bath's famous biscuit-coloured stone and positioned it so that it always seemed to catch the sun.

Just being in the driveway somehow calmed her. She stopped the engine – or rather it juddered to a worrying halt – and revelled in the silence. This was precisely the weather she loved best; the clotted winter mist that had hovered above the frozen ground for most of the drive, like Miss Haversham's old veil, had finally lifted, and, now, at just past one o'clock, the sky was a miraculous, clear blue, with hard stabs of unforgiving sunlight piercing the occasional white cloud. She climbed out of the passenger door, taking a spray of gaudy pink carnations and purple helleborus – her mother's favourite colours – from the seat, and walked through the open front door. The hall, with its burnished parquet, smelled faintly of rosemary and hand cream – a deliciously comforting blend she always associated with her mother.

Sadie was in the kitchen bent over a haunch of chargrilled lamb that would have fed twenty. 'I know that recipe,' said Martha, flinging down the carnations. 'Sophie Grigson—'

'Don't talk to me about that bitch. I was chargrilling lamb when she was still pulverizing rusks,' said her mother bitterly. She stood up and wiped the perspiration from her brow, leaving a slight trace of cinderized meat above her eyebrows. Martha looked at her, trying to assess the emotional depredations of the past few days. Even with the black smudge, Sadie's dark exotic looks, most of which had been siphoned off into Kate, took her breath away. The years had dealt lightly with Sadie Crawford. At fifty she was supple and slender, vivacious and delicate; with only a smattering of grey hair and blessed with the kind of small, fragile features which lent themselves superbly to tragedy. After her outburst, she smiled bravely at her eldest daughter. 'Oh, darling, you brought me flowers.' She eyed the carnations suspiciously. Was Martha being ironic? Sadie looked at her daughter's hideous jumper. Probably not. 'How sweet.'

'They're not great, but I know you like the colours.'

Sadie looked at her daughter, mystified. Martha had absolutely no aesthetic discrimination whatsoever. It was amazing, given her genes. But she was a marvellous cook, terribly clever, and quite a wonderful human being, albeit in a rather serious way. Sadie had even given up falling apart every time Martha introduced her to one of her dreadful boyfriends. Anything was better than Martha's Barren Patch, when they'd all had to suffer the traumas of watching her get to grips with how to put up shelves and use a jigsaw because she refused to find a boyfriend who could do it all for her.

'How are you, Mum?' asked Martha cheerfully, helping herself to a plateful of warm orange and cinnamon biscuits.

'Suicidal,' said Sadie, pouring them both some wine from a dusty-looking bottle. 'So I suppose things are improving. At least now you're here we'll both get through your father's precious cellar that much faster. I was having a hard time drinking any of it, to be honest. Chin-chin.'

'How's Dolly?' asked Martha, moving on to safer ground.

'Blooming,' said Sadie morosely. 'Inasmuch as Dolly can bloom. She's started coming to night school with me. We're doing a Marxist reading of *Moll Flanders*.'

Martha gazed at her mother sceptically. The only

left-leaning tendencies Dolly had ever shown were when she placed most of her weight on Sadie's precious Victorian broom to pontificate about her son Kevin's latest girlfriend. Dolly was without doubt the world's worst cleaning lady. But she made a splendid scapegoat and somehow stopped them all from rowing with one another most of the time, so they had kept her for twenty years.

'Don't look so supercilious, Martha,' admonished Sadie as she sloshed half a bottle of Château Lafitte into the gravy saucepan. 'I thought you were supposed to be a communist.'

'That was years ago,' said Martha indignantly. Jack had introduced her to Glenys Kinnock last year and now she was a more or less fully paid-up member of the Labour Party. Or at least she would be when her father got round to signing the standing order.

'Anyway, I've got Dolly enrolled in my Women's History course. She wrote an excellent paper on Shirley Bassey, although frankly I didn't think the subject matter was strictly relevant, but the tutor's very intent on being inclusive—'

There was a histrionic scrunching outside as Kate swung her Alfa Spider through the gateposts. Martha looked up from her mug of wine to see Kate striding up the driveway, a huge bunch of calla lilies in her hand. Her face was the colour of putty and – this was the clincher – her hair was particularly verdant and ringletty – a certain sign, in Martha's experience, that she was hung over.

Kate looked up at the inscrutable sash windows of Tithe House – and felt miserable. A solitary robin hopped on to the bonnet of the Spider and leaned its head on one side quizzically. It seemed an apt metaphor for her poor benighted mother. How could Dad leave her?

On the other hand, what the hell had her mother done to prompt this crisis? The pair of them needed their heads banging together. All these blessings – Tithe House was an absolute gem – and they were prepared to jeopardize the lot. And on top of everything else, she'd been dying to ask her mother the name of the colour she'd had the Aga custom-sprayed. But what with the State of Emergency, it might seem a bit heartless.

'Thanks for the lift,' she snapped, striding into the kitchen.

'I could say the same to you,' replied Martha evenly.

'I did try ringing.'

'What time?' asked Martha guardedly.

'About nine.'

'I must have gone to get some milk.'

Kate looked at her accusingly. Martha was never without milk. It was one of the characteristics she shared with her mother – a well-appointed and beautifully stocked fridge. Martha was obviously trying to hide something – bloody Jack must be back.

'God, those flowers are hideous,' she said hurriedly, fingering Martha's spray as if she might contract leprosy from it. 'They look like something from *Carnation Street*. Dolly is a scream, isn't she, the way everything has to be colour co-ordinated?'

'*I* bought them actually,' said Martha stiffly. 'They may not be in *The World of Interiors*' top ten of chic blooms but they happen to be Mum's favourite colours.'

Kate looked at her sister pityingly and dropped the subject. 'Sorry. I've had a disastrous week.'

'Join the club.'

'Not work?'

Martha nodded miserably. Any residual hostility Kate might have been feeling evaporated. She knew nothing about the ethics of journalism but the one time she had run into Donna she'd been appalled by her dress sense and the massive amounts of Obsession she hosed herself with. It was amazing she hadn't been arrested years ago for vandalizing the ozone.

'Oh, Martha.' She went to put her arms round her sister. 'Don't tell me, the prodigal bum's returned?'

'It's all right,' said Martha stoically. 'I really think this time I'm well and truly over him.'

'That makes a change. I thought he was a loyal member of the Missionary Society. I suppose you had a fantastic night. Last throes of passion and all that.'

Martha giggled. 'It wasn't bad ... You?'

'Fabulous, if your idea of heaven is listening all evening to Podge deconstructing every single political manifesto since Magna Carta.' She shrugged resignedly. 'He gatecrashed mine and Eliza's girls' night ... Oh my God ...' She watched Martha's ghostly expression.

Eliza. They had forgotten to tell Eliza.

Neither Sadie nor Kate had much of an appetite. Martha, who was ravenous after last night's gymnastics with Jack, tried to distract them both from the number of times she helped herself to Sadie's crispy roast potatoes by asking plenty of *In the Psychiatrist's Chair*-type questions.

'You don't think Dad's little peccadillos are really just a cover? Maybe it's a cry for help. Perhaps he just wants some attention,' she suggested, reaching for the gravy.

'Well, if they are just a cover, then all I can say is three's a shroud,' said Sadie crossly. 'And they are not just peccadillos, Martha. They're affairs.'

'But Mum, I'm sure they don't mean anything. He's devoted to you. Everyone knows that.'

'Funny way of showing it,' snuffled Sadie from the depths of an antique hankie.

'You don't think perhaps, subconsciously, you goaded him into it?'

'Why would I do that?' sobbed Sadie.

'Maybe it's your way of bringing things to a head.' For a moment, Martha engaged her mother's full attention. Years of night school had made Sadie highly susceptible to a bit of cod psychoanalysis. Martha ploughed on. 'It's so difficult to get Dad to react sometimes—'

Sadie looked at her daughter intently, before blowing her nose loudly. 'You think this is all about me trying out some childish ploy to get him to look at me? Oh, darling, do I really seem that foolish to you?' She began weeping softly again. Kate looked at Martha in accusation. Sheepishly, Martha began clearing the plates, secretly glad of the opportunity to help herself to some more roast lamb. God knows how they'd get through Christmas.

'Now,' began Eliza, parking herself on a pair of lips, 'the crucial thing is that you mustn't in any way blame yourselves for what is happening between your parents.'

She was trying not to allow the knowledge that there

had already been one family summit to which she had not been invited to prejudice her in any way. After all, why should they invite her? Strictly speaking, she wasn't family. Just because she had spent most of her school holidays since the age of thirteen at Tithe House; just because she looked on Martha and Kate as the sisters she had never had; just because she had even deluded herself that Sadie and David regarded her as a sort of surrogate daughter didn't mean any of them felt the same. Obviously.

'But why?' asked Kate plaintively, feeling like a child as she settled herself on the gleaming floor of Eliza's immaculate flat, and leaned her head gently against Eliza's glossy brown legs. 'I mean, it doesn't make any sense. Not now. A few years ago, when they were rowing all the time, and we could have understood, but they seemed to have got over all that.'

'Well, of course, one never knows for sure what goes on in other people's lives,' began Eliza gently, 'but Sadie was very young when she met your father, you know. Perhaps she feels it's a phase of her life that is over.'

'But we thought it was Dad who wanted it,' said Kate, confused.

'*I* didn't.' Martha looked at her indignantly.

'Oh, he's always been happy with the status quo,' said Eliza. 'But it was *his* status quo. I think your mother has been feeling frustrated for some time. Not just with your father, who is, of course, a wonderful man in many ways, but with herself.'

'Has she spoken to you about it?' asked Martha, suddenly.

'Not since this happened,' said Eliza. In fact no one from the family had bothered to contact her about it. As if it didn't affect her as well. 'But over the years we've chatted.'

'It seems a bit feeble, to break up a marriage of thirty years because you're feeling a bit unfulfilled,' said Kate, marvelling at the way all the sleek pale wood and Perspex furniture in Eliza's flat managed to be as angular and polished as she was.

'I think there's a bit more at stake than that,' said Eliza, refilling all their wineglasses. 'And I don't think it's feeble. I think it's rather brave. I think your mother never quite got over giving up her career to marry your father.'

'She was a house model, for heaven's sake,' said Kate.

'That was quite something in those days. She was bloody good at it too. There was talk of her going to New York to work with Richard Avedon.' Kate and Martha looked at her in astonishment. 'I don't think she told many people,' said Eliza quickly. 'Anyway, she married your father instead. But her work wasn't only glamorous, you know. It provided her with an independent income, and an identity, which she subsequently, and through no deliberate fault of either of them, subsumed completely and utterly in your father's. Imagine how it must have felt. One month a bright, beautiful young woman about London, the world at her feet, self-determination in her grasp, the next a wife and mother, albeit a decorative and highly successful one. You can see, can't you, how it might deeply affect one's sense of oneself?'

'You're right, I suppose,' snuffled Kate. 'How horrible to be middle-aged.'

There was a silence while they all reflected on the tragedy of not being born into their own generation.

'Well, let it be a lesson to us not to squander our opportunities,' said Eliza, opening another bottle of wine.

'Talking of which,' said Martha slyly, 'how's Podge? I hear he's turned into a bit of a sexual samurai.'

Kate and Eliza both shot her outraged looks.

'Oh, come on, Eliza, why not just revel in it?' Martha giggled, relieved of a chance to change the subject.

'I think you're both jolly lucky to have any sex in your lives at all,' said Kate. 'The closest I get to being frisked these days is when I try and smuggle an original idea into work.'

'Anyone would think he was a total pervert the way you're both carrying on,' said Eliza primly. She stood up and smoothed her immaculate French pleat before plumping up the cushion on her Jasper Morrison suede sofa.

'Tell Martha about Podge and the nose fixation,' beseeched Kate.

'What's to tell?' said Eliza. 'Don't all men have a thing about licking a girl's nasal hair?'

After prevaricating over the tortellini, Roberto finally revealed that he had discovered the name of the solicitor dealing with Horrowitz's lease. 'Is very complicated, but is a start,' he said, handing her a scrap of paper with a telephone number on it.

Suddenly energized, Kate snatched the paper and kissed it. 'Thanks, Roberto. You're a sweetie. I could almost kiss you.'

He grinned expectantly. When he opened his eyes again, she'd disappeared. He felt strangely despondent. Somehow, when he'd envisioned this scenario over the weekend, he'd foreseen a more dramatic conclusion. And she'd forgotten to take the cappuccino.

✳   ✳   ✳

Donna behaved so badly to Martha that week, calling her the Mighty Moaner and finally hurling a bottle of her Revlon Vixon nail polish over Martha's new jeans, that by Friday Martha felt fully justified in calling Jack. Not that she wanted to see him in the least – but just in case the red jumper she'd mislaid had turned up at his place.

'Nope,' he said, pretending to cast his eye around the spare lines of Château Docklands. 'Can't see it. But then you weren't wearing it that night.'

Damn.

He'd relented, of course, as she'd hoped. And proved to be a sympathetic listener, ladling endless helpings of Scotch into her tumbler and bestowing on her the occasional flash of insight and sensitivity. 'It'll be the best thing for them in the end, you'll see. And it certainly won't do you and Kate any harm. You need a bit of shade in those sunlit lives of yours.'

She marvelled at Jack's interpretation of her life. And wondered just how miserable the childhood he only occasionally referred to really had been. She was about to ask him, probe into corners of his past that she'd never dared approach before, when he suddenly pulled her on to him, running his fingers up and down her smooth thighs, twisting her hair round his stubby fingers and kissing her strong, aquiline nose. 'Well,' he began cheerfully, nuzzling his stubble into her neck, 'you wanted to be over me, and now you really are.'

Chapter Three

Kate hugged a mug of her mother's delicious coffee on the terrace. In the background, George Michael was whingeing about new decades on the radio. Well so far 1990 was proving a bloody disaster. In the foreground, Sadie was digging what looked like a trench across two corners of her beloved ornamental lawn. It was part of a plan she had suddenly conceived the night before to extend her vegetable patch in a drive towards complete self-sufficiency. Probably reliving her youth as a Land Girl.

The disparity between what Kate felt for her mother when she was at a safe distance – the hundred and sixteen miles that separated them when Kate was in London, for instance – and what she felt now, when she was cooped up at home with her and having to work her way through her father's best burgundies, struck her with a more chilling urgency than ever. At least she'd managed to get two days' compassionate leave from work, which had given her time to map out a business plan for Horrowitz's. Sort of. And even in the depths of sorrow, Sadie made a dynamite Parmesan and basil soufflé.

These delicious meals were something their friends, even when they'd been quite young, had always noticed. It wasn't just food. There was a degree of comfort about Tithe House, a sense of luxurious largesse, that was apparently uncontrived and wholly beguiling. In summer the doors always seemed to be open on to the gardens, ushering in a sense of lush bountifulness and the scent of Sadie's roses and jasmine. In the winter, the fires crackled away in most rooms, the lamps were kept on at all times, and the air smelled of cinnamon or myrrh. The conversation usually crackled too. They might all have disagreed with each other on just about everything, but life had never been dull. Gazing up at the tiny Swedish glass wall fittings Sadie had had installed in the kitchen, Kate couldn't help thinking that pleasant surroundings definitely helped ease life's pain.

That was half the problem with eastern Europe, thought Kate. And Martha. No taste. If only they all had access to pure linen sheets and decent light fittings they wouldn't be so resentful. It was incredible that Martha could be such a fantastic cook and live in such a grotspot. Kate, who had fantastic taste – and culinary skills that made most prison kitchens seem like Le Manoir aux Quat' Saisons – never ceased to marvel at her sister's inability to have clean laundry in her flat while being in full possession of a state-of-the-art coffee-maker. Nature might abhor a vacuum. But Martha definitely hated a vacuum cleaner.

She gazed blearily at her mother again. There was something poignant about seeing Sadie's slight figure engaged in brutal combat with the land, even if the land in question was a slice of highly manicured prime real estate. The whole vignette was made doubly touching by the fact that

Sadie had to pause every few seconds to inhale deeply on a cigarette. Even Mata Hari found the sight pitiful and wandered off, swishing her tail in disgust.

Misty-eyed, Kate decided to retreat back into the oasis of her bedroom – a very successful duck-egg blue that she and Sadie had been especially proud of – so that she could more objectively contemplate her mother's future.

Sadie Crawford was attractive, intelligent and, despite her superficial fragility, one of life's survivors. She might be in turmoil now, what with the single event that she had most dreaded, always suspected and, perhaps in her way, deliberately navigated towards, having finally come to pass. But in the last thirty-six hours Kate had noticed her mother veering between blind panic and a certain sly euphoria.

Sadie had numerous untapped talents. She could open a shop, run a hotel, launch a range of frozen gourmet dishes. She'd get herself a career, restore her tattered self-confidence and, in time, even find a replacement husband. Kate could think of any number of her own boyfriends who'd commented admiringly on her mother's charms. Sadie would be all right. In which case it was perfectly okay for Kate to spend what was left of her compassionate leave working on a profoundly compassionate leaving speech for when she waltzed out of Morton's.

Feeling cheered and somewhat heroic, she padded over to the window and gazed across the verdant green at her mother, who, in between digging and puffing on her cigarette, was now intermittently weeping.

Against all her better instincts Martha was once more sitting across a candlelit table from Jack Dunforth, although to give the situation credit, for once they weren't in his favourite wine bar but revelling in the plush surroundings of Bibendum – Jack's treat in recognition of Martha's long-suffering good nature.

So far he'd done all the right things – told her she looked wonderful and complimented her on her new leather jacket, which he said accentuated her athletic figure. Martha wasn't sure whether he meant Sharron Davies or Sebastian Coe but she let it pass. The jacket certainly made a change from her usual grey T-shirts. Her Live Aid one was so old that bits of typography kept flaking off and it now simply said 'L Aid', much to Jack's amusement.

Over the seared monkfish and sun-dried tomatoes, he regaled her with an hilarious account of his weeks trailing Paddy Ashdown. Halfway through, he reached across and took her hand in his square, all-encasing one. 'I have missed you, you know,' he said tenderly.

'You certainly kept missing my phone calls,' she said, trying not to sound truculent.

He squeezed her hand.

'I know I'm a reprehensible reprobate,' he began. She loved the way his brogue made 'reprehensible' sound like artillery fire. 'But it's just a load of macho braggadocio taken in with my mother's milk. Or it would have been if she'd given me any,' he added with mock self-pity.

Martha smiled sympathetically. Jack's childhood, when he could be prevailed upon to talk about it, which wasn't often, sounded like the worst form of child abuse. Well, not the worst perhaps, but the slow drip-drip effect of indifference and neglect which Jack and his four brothers had suffered at the hands of overworked and under-educated parents had had a damaging long-term effect. As Jack remarked in his bleaker moments, if his father had only had the energy to beat them all up occasionally, they could at least have got taken into care.

As it was, the authorities left them alone and the family had limped on, grappling with accommodation that wasn't quite grim enough to be demolished, lives that weren't quite painful enough to end, ultimately defeated by mankind's most commonplace enemy – the depressing dreariness of everyday life. 'That's why,' he told her during one of his many self-justifications (generally just before he was about to ask a sexual favour), 'I crave excitement now. I can't help it. I'm a congenital risk-taker.'

He was certainly popular in Ladbroke's. Jim Dunforth, Jack's father, had initiated him into the rites of greyhound racing – Wimbledon dog track was the only ground they'd ever had in common. And university had educated him in just about every other form of gambling.

She had agreed to have dinner on the pretext that they would discuss what she laughingly called her career. But as usual they were mired deep in tales of Jack's magnificent journalistic feats.

'I do seem to get on with Americans,' he was saying smugly. 'I like the vigour of their political campaigns and the professionalism of the news-gatherers.'

'Their ability to gather advertising revenue, don't you mean?'

'If it's the difference between getting six million to tune into a congressional hearing and sixty million I'll go for the commercial option every time.'

'So you wouldn't object if the institutionalized news networks here were dismantled?'

'If you mean doing away with compulsory news slots

at nine and ten, no, I wouldn't. Look, the days when the nation sat down as one to watch the Queen's speech or the moon landings are drawing to a close. People get their news in all sorts of ways now – satellite, faxes ... within five years we'll be sending all kinds of data to one another on our computers. We'll have to lure our viewers the best way we can ...'

'So you don't find them a bit slick, a tiny bit vacuous and totally uninterested in anything happening outside their fifty shining states?'

'That's what's so great about them.' Jack chuckled. 'Seriously, when it comes to weighing up the pros and cons of American news reporting, I think you'll find their account pretty fit.'

Martha sighed. The only account Jack was really interested in was the one pertaining to his expenses. And that, she had no doubt, was in the rudest of health. She changed the subject slightly.

'Eliza says there's something going on at *The Late Shift*, Radio Four's ten o'clock news programme. Jenny Stewart, the producer, is looking for a researcher. The pay's terrible, even worse than Bog Standard Radio, but it might just save me a fortune in shrink's bills.'

'Is BSR really so awful?' he asked. His voice suddenly sounded so gentle and concerned that she could feel the tears pricking behind her eyes. Damn. She had to get a grip.

'Put it this way, did I really spend three years researching the fiscal policies of the Tudors and Stuarts in order to debate whether it's Sting's Tantric sex that put that irritating perma-grin on Trudi Styler's face?'

'Never mind about them – and incidentally, I can tell you the Tantric sex thing's a load of bollocks. Not literally, of course – more's the pity. Tell Uncle Jack what exactly is so vile about this job.'

She loved his eyebrows. They were so adorably mobile. 'For one thing, Donna believes that BSR listeners are only interested in events that affect their wallets and the TV schedules—'

'Crude, but she has a point.'

Martha frowned. '—and she really feels that BSR has a moral duty to talk down to its audience at all times. As a consequence, our bulletins, in which incidentally no sentence may contain more than nine words, or twenty-two syllables, make the *Python* look like Proust. Do you know, she actually thinks she's invented a new kind of iambic pentameter?' She paused while the waiter silently refilled her glass.

'Is that based on speaking three or four words a second, do you think?'

Martha looked at him venomously. 'Don't tell me you think she's on to something?'

'There's no point in pitching above your audience. That's just bad journalism,' said Jack smoothly. 'Anyway, who's to say that taking an interest in whether George Michael might be gay is any more prurient than getting worked up about some famine footage from Ethiopia? News is in the eye of the beholder.'

'Donna said something along those lines. Perhaps you should meet her,' said Martha coldly.

'Perhaps I should. She's starting to sound like a rather entertaining light at the end of a tunnel.'

'Lightweight, certainly. And she's about as entertaining as a piece of effluence,' said Martha, 'only not as wholesome.'

Jack laughed. 'Oh, get off your high horse, Martha.' He

reached for her hand again. 'You'd suffer from a lot less vertigo down here. So, she's a populist. And,' he conceded, looking at her outraged expression, 'very possibly a bully. But so far you haven't given me any evidence to suggest that she's the polluting influence you maintain.'

Martha was well and truly cornered. If she gave the litany of the many and varied ways in which Donna made her life a misery, she would sound pathetic. If she didn't, she was still pathetic. But at least she was pathetic and dignified. Another waiter appeared to sweep away their breadcrumbs. Furious, she stalked off to the cloakrooms to rethink her strategy and apply some of the Chanel Rouge Pure lipstick Kate had given her last Christmas. She marched back into the restaurant to find Jack reading the menu inaudibly to himself, while his fingers drummed a backtrack which sounded dangerously like Donna's new iambic pentameter.

'Jesus, it's freezing in this flat.'

Jack shivered. Needless to say, Martha's lacklustre bathroom didn't actually run to any dry towels. In fact just about the only thing it did run to was seed. He'd been reduced to warming his hands on her toaster before it exploded.

She decided to ignore him. 'So – you never got round to telling me what you thought of my plan?'

'Which one was that?' he said maddeningly, rubbing himself down with a crisp tea towel that Martha handed him. He wrinkled his nose fastidiously.

'The one about applying to Jenny Stewart,' she said, trying to squash her exasperation.

'Ah.' He sucked on his teeth thoughtfully and shook his head. 'She's pretty infamous, Martha. Well known for her impossible demands, ridiculous hours, unbridled criticism when people don't come up to scratch ...'

'High standards, in other words. Sounds like the nursery slopes compared with Donna.'

'It's a savage little fiefdom, that programme, what with Jennifer Stewart presiding over everyone like a rabid autocrat. I couldn't let you do it to yourself. Real dog eat dog.'

'Better than being humiliated daily by a rabid bitch.' She handed him a steaming cappuccino.

'Do you want me to be honest?'

She scowled at him. 'Actually I'd like you to lie through your teeth.'

'Well, personally I think you'd be mad to leave BSR at the moment.'

She snorted.

'You should stick with that show. It's a hell of a lot more challenging than working in an ivory tower. Donna's bloody good at what she does. She's generating quite a bit of heat in the industry. I'm not saying she's not a monster, but you've got Jem there and Donna obviously rates you—'

He overrode Martha's howl of protest. 'Of course she does, you ninny, otherwise she would have fired you months ago. Within six months you could be joint-producing that show at the very least. Okay, so it's a small pond, but you'd be a huge fish. Whereas you'd be plankton at the Beeb.'

'I've always wanted to be a proper researcher,' persisted Martha, wriggling out from his grasp and heading back into the kitchen.

'Proper? If you consider researching telephone numbers

for Le Caprice for Jenny Stewart's infernal lunch appointments to be proper, then fine. My advice is to forget it. Radio's about to undergo a massive shake-up over the next few years. The opportunities, provided you don't harness yourself to some monolith, will be mind-blowing.'

Something in Martha fizzled. Possibly it was the last few embers of her desire for Jack. Seeing him there, wrapped in a tiny, stained tea towel, risible and thoroughly, transparently selfish, she could only wonder at her previous gullibility. As soon as she could, she ushered him off to another hard day's slog of late breakfasts and long lunches, and set about her application letter to Jenny Stewart.

The cherry-coloured ottoman started to swim before Kate's eyes like a huge, vengeful blood clot. It was a beauty, or at any rate a Sleeping Beauty. The Dralon was a travesty, but there was no disguising its art deco origins. She hadn't seen such a bargain since the Russell Wright china tea service. She would cover it in the mint-green stripe with the rose sprigs that she'd brought at a bring and buy last year.

'That'll be thirty-five quid, love,' said Reg through an eclipse of cigarette smoke. That meant a week of Tesco's own-brand baked beans. Portobello would be the downfall of her. As would Brick Lane and Bermondsey. But she couldn't resist them. She supposed that was what they meant by market forces. She snapped out of her calculations. A girl with frizzy red French lieutenant woman's hair and a little embroidered Indian bag was sniffing the ottoman. Nasal inspection finished, she rummaged in a silk drawstring bag for some money. Hurriedly, Kate brandished two twenties.

'Looks like you've been gazumped, dearie,' said Reg to Kate, scrupulously fair as ever. He was fond of her but she couldn't expect to snaffle up everything. She looked so disappointed he almost reconsidered. 'That would have looked lovely in your flat,' he said wistfully. 'Gone a treat with that little chaise-longue you got. Shame.'

The Meryl Streep double counted her change, pulled up the collar of her long Victorian-looking velvet coat and fixed Kate with turquoise, staring eyes the colour of a Portuguese man-of-war. 'Do you collect nineteen forties?'

'Some,' sniffled Kate. 'Generally I seem to end up with more from the fifties.'

The man-of-war eyes took in Kate's dark ringlets springing out from her fedora, the lace petticoat, just peeking from the double-breasted military coat, and the polished men's riding boots. A wisp of interest flickered within them.

'Have we met before?'

'I don't recall,' said Kate coolly. She was still smarting over the ottoman. Things evaporating in a puff of smoke seemed to be the story of her life lately.

'What do you do?'

'Apart from shop, you mean? I design hideous clothes for the over-nineties. Size ninety, that is.'

The man-of-war eyes gazed back unblinkingly beneath thick, pale red eyebrows that almost met in the middle à la Frida Kahlo. A large grin stretched her dainty bow lips halfway round to her ears, revealing an unexpected gap between her two front teeth. Years later, when Kate came to consider the unlikely basis of their friendship, she decided that it wasn't discovering that Magda Marakeepski was editor-at-large on *A la Mode*, or the fact that she knew everyone who was anyone, or even her stunningly original way with paint colours, but the huge, gappy smile which had started it all.

'Okay, so I got the ottoman. In return, let me take you to my favourite shop in the world,' said Magda.

Kate looked at her watch doubtfully. It was already a quarter to ten. Or eleven. Mark Lacy's buff files weighed heavily in her Gladstone bag.

'It won't take long,' coaxed Magda. 'And in my experience, if you're going to be late, you might as well be chronically late. That way you can think up a really cracking excuse.'

The traffic was a disgrace – something else her father and all his political cronies seemed incapable of sorting out – and Magda's driving was horrific, like being in a slow-motion multiple pile-up. She made no attempt to park, but shunted her bashed-up Uno on to the pavement, almost colliding with Rupert Cavendish's plate-glass windows. The shop – Guinevere's – on the King's Road, was crammed with gorgeous pieces that were way out of Kate's price range. Nevertheless, she spent a blissful couple of hours waltzing round, pointing out her favourite objects, while Magda sniffed them – that way she could get a sense of their history, she said – and duly noted them down on a list which she handed to the manager as they left. 'Could you have them delivered to the office by tomorrow?' she said sweetly. 'The shoot's on Tuesday.'

'You have a good eye,' she remarked, turning to Kate as they strolled towards the Uno. 'You spotted one or two things I missed.'

Kate was on cloud nine. During her tour of Guinevere's she had discovered that Magda was the editor responsible for all her favourite pictures in *A la Mode*. She was a stunningly creative stylist. Praise from Magda Marakeepski was praise indeed. Or just possibly a raise indeed. Not that she wasn't going to leave Morton's any minute and open her shop, just as soon as the lease got sorted out and she raised some cash . . . but in the meantime it was about time Mark Lacy upped her pittance of a salary. This could be just the incentive she needed to badger him about it.

'At least let me buy you brunch, in return for keeping you so long,' said Magda illogically, casually sweeping a parking ticket off the windscreen and into the gutter.

They headed back to Notting Hill, and Magda screeched up outside 192. This time she more or less managed to miss any shop windows. Inside, she seemed to know everyone.

'Darling,' cooed an exquisitely chic girl whom Kate recognized as the actress Phoebe Keane, 'it's been ages.' She puckered her lips against both of Magda's cheeks.

'At least twenty-four hours,' purred Magda. 'I'll call you later, angel. I'm a bit rushed at the moment.'

Phoebe wafted back to her table, where she seemed to be holding court to about six actor types, any one of whom could have played Adonis convincingly.

'*Elle est tellement chic, n'est-ce pas?*' said Magda admiringly.

'Er, *oui*. Is that Nick Wilde?' asked Kate, trying to sound nonchalant.

'Mmm,' said Magda, waving at the table in general. He's totally mad about her, of course, which is just as well. Phoebe, much as I adore her, can be so insecure. We used to work together,' she added, ordering a bottle of champagne. 'I was a stylist on some of her films. Absolutely appalling, each and every one of them, but such a hoot. I don't do clothes any more. Furniture's much more rewarding, don't you think? Now, what about you? I want to get to know you, but I really ought to get into work before three. Tell me about your work. What's it like?'

'A bit like being in prison,' sighed Kate, scanning the menu nervously – she had five pounds in her purse and her Switch card had been swallowed by the cash dispenser that morning. 'But without the variety.'

'I had a job like that once,' said Magda, 'for incontinence brochures. It's a big challenge making a nappy look chic – but I think I can honestly say I managed it.'

It was such heaven finding someone who cared as much as she did about 1950s prints and French eiderdowns, and felt the same way about Wenge wood and Alessi kitchenware, that the hours flew past. Kate even considered telling Magda about Horrowitz's. But she decided it might jinx things. Reluctantly, she said she really should be getting into Morton's and signalled the waitress to bring them the bill. Magda intercepted it and refused to let Kate go halves, which was just as well, as Kate would have had problems stumping up one nineteenth of the tip.

'Absolutely not,' she said magnanimously, as Kate made a feeble attempt to pay. 'I get to keep the pouf – and your telephone number, I hope. *A la Mode* can get this. I'll say I was interviewing an assistant. God knows I need one ... come to think of it, you wouldn't like to come and work at *A la Mode*, would you?'

Before Kate could answer, Magda caught sight of Kate's watch. 'What time did you say you had to leave?' she asked, wrapping the remains of some lemon cake in a napkin and shovelling it into her bag – it was the exact colour she'd been trying to paint her kitchen. 'Only it's almost four.'

'Or maybe even five,' said Kate, blenching. 'You can never quite tell with my watch, I'm afraid—'

'Oh well, makes life that bit more exciting, I suppose,' said Magda calmly, taking their five – or six – hour brunch in her stride. Kate, heart soaring despite the circumstances, could have kissed her.

Martha swung up the Holloway Road feeling strangely inviolable. She hated Jack. That had to be some kind of result. She burst through the BSR chipped double doors feeling almost happy. Samantha, the receptionist, half-heartedly twiddled the dial on her radio back to BSR when she saw Martha approach. But Martha didn't even seem to notice.

'Well, look who it is, *Martyr Crawford*. Nice of you to pop by,' smirked Donna. 'You've missed the main news conference, which is a pity given your *abiding passion* for seeking out the *Higher Truth*. But just to recap, I've had a *brill* idea for a *new* slot.'

As of that second, Martha had decided not to rise to a single one of Donna's taunts. She would be dogged, determined – and devious. She would take what she could from Donna's sleazy, but undeniably slick, repertoire of broadcasting tricks, surf onwards and upwards through the sordid ripples of media pond-life at BSR, and proceed to make a new life for herself working for Jenny Stewart.

So she didn't blink when Donna said she was going to have to do on-the-spot traffic reports from now on, starting tomorrow at the Hanger Lane gyratory system. She didn't demur when Donna announced that they were going to introduce a gong that would sound whenever the news got too boring. She didn't mind because she wasn't listening. It was all curiously disappointing as far as Donna was concerned. So she decided to up the ante.

'It's called *zoo* radio. It's *mega* in the States. That means you and Jem have to chip in with *witty, provocative* comments *all the time.* Spot the fatal flaw in *that* plan. *Hah hah!* Still, you're the best I can come up with. For the *moment.* Anyway, once you've done your six-thirty slot from Hanger Lane you're going to *race* back to the studio in time to do the *Knickers Slot.* It's *genius,* though I say it myself.'

Martha looked at her blankly, hoping that she'd remembered to put a stamp on the letter to Jenny Stewart.

'Oh, come on, *Martyr* – you always said you wanted to be an *undercover* reporter,' she sniggered. 'The idea is that the listeners call in *all* week to suggest *which* pop star they'd *most* like to see with no *underwear* on. The crudest suggestion wins a bottle of champagne. Jem's fixing a sponsor. It's *perfect.* Because, on Fridays, we call the celebrity we *all* agree we'd most like to see *knickerless* for a live *on-air* interview. And as a final, *totally brilliant* finishing touch, I thought they could *donate* a pair of *their* knickers to the *winning* caller. It'll be called *Briefs* Encounters.'

Martha looked at Jem and Donna stonily. Talk about rock bottoms.

'It's going to be *wicked. Historic.* And if doesn't *double* the listening figures, *I'll eat Jem's balls.* It's got *continuity,* suspense, *sex,* glamour and, er, *suspense.*'

'In fact the only thing it doesn't have,' said Martha frostily, 'is anyone who'd be stupid enough to take part.'

'That's where *you* come in, Martyr, you *lucky, lucky* girl. You have been *unanimously* elected by *moi* to be the *roving* reporter who tracks down the *celebrities.*'

Martha stared at Donna's lip liner in disbelief – honestly, the girl must have more ink on her face than an entire transcript of all Neil Kinnock's speeches put together – and fervently prayed that Her Majesty's mail workers would overlook the small matter of an unstamped letter.

It was just typical that at the exact moment Magda had been about to confirm her offer of a job to Kate, fate should have stepped in in the shape of a clapped-out old watch. If it hadn't jumped forward an hour, Magda wouldn't have rushed off and the style assistant's position would have been hers. Perhaps it was all for the best. There clearly wasn't going to be any white knight rushing to her rescue – not even one in a dented Fiat Uno. She would just have to make her own destiny. Which meant somehow scraping the deposit together to buy Horrowitz's. She decided to sell her flat.

In their different ways, Tatty and Eliza both tried to tell her this wasn't the wisest decision. 'Not that it's any of my business,' Tatty began gingerly in the lift one morning, 'but it's a buyer's market at the moment. As a matter of fact I've just bought a house in North Kensington. It's a bit of a wreck but Daddy thinks I'll get five flats out of it. I'm going to rent them out till things turn. Daddy thinks the economy's bound to pick up in two or three years.'

But Kate had already glazed over.

'You're stark, raving mad,' said Eliza crisply when Kate told her the plan to sell her flat over a delicious supper Martha had rustled up in her flat for the three of them.

'We're in the middle of the longest recession since the last longest bloody recession and you want to strip yourself of your biggest asset.'

'It probably isn't that sensible,' agreed Martha, wondering if Jenny Stewart had read her letter yet. She was thrilled that Eliza and Kate had deigned to trek up to Tufnell Park. Kate was normally too chaotic to make it up there and Eliza always said that she got culture-shock.

'Christ, Martha,' exclaimed Kate as she carried the plates into the kitchen and came face to face with the peeling paint, bare light bulbs and mountains of unwashed crockery. 'It looks like Julian Schnabel's been doing your housework.'

'It's not that bad.'

'Yes, it is,' said Eliza, getting out her new Pentax zoom which she was trying out before taking on the account, and pretending to photograph a rare breed of leaf mould on one of the dishcloths. 'Has David Bellamy seen this?'

'I don't see why my using the proceeds of a flat to open a shop is so barmy,' said Kate huffily, raising the issue again after supper. 'It's not as if I'm planning to blow the lot on a leg wax. In case you hadn't noticed, I'm trying to start my own business.'

'In retail,' pointed out Eliza. 'And retail's flat on its back.'

'Well, something in my life ought to be. Anyway,' grumbled Kate, 'this is precisely the kind of negative talk that drives this country into the ground. Why the government can't encourage wealth creators like me I do not know.'

'By handing out wads of cash, you mean?' chipped in Martha.

'Well, I know one member of the government who

might hand a bit out,' offered Eliza. Martha and Kate grimaced simultaneously.

'All you have to do is swallow your pride and ask him for a loan in return for some equity,' persisted Eliza.

Kate looked at her, mystified. 'Eckie Who?'

'Honestly,' said Eliza, heading for a tea towel before thinking better of it, 'you two don't know how lucky you both are to have a father who's got some spare money.'

'I'd rather swallow a bottle of Donna's Obsession than swallow my pride,' said Kate stubbornly.

The subject was closed and they spent the rest of the evening getting pleasantly tipsy. Eliza and Kate trashed the plot of *When Harry Met Sally* and Martha, who never had time for the cinema, trashed the plot of her life. And they all took it in turns to take pictures of one another with Eliza's snazzy new camera while they each pretended to be David Attenborough finding new forms of insect life in the rainforest. The next day, Kate, with the heaviest of hearts, put her flat on the market.

Chapter Four

Nick Wilde's career may have been going from strength to strength, but it was a different matter for his wife. It had been fine, thought Phoebe nostalgically, while they'd both been struggling in rep, laughing their way through a succession of disgusting digs. But in the past year, Nick had shone in the RSC's *Richard II* at Stratford, on the back of which he'd been cast in *Something about You*, a low-budget Britflick which against everyone's expectations had been a sleeper hit in America, and which had culminated in the acquisition of a horrific new agent. Gloria Morgenstern, as far as Phoebe could see, had all the charm of Pol Pot without the latter's strong humanitarian streak.

What made things doubly galling about her situation, Phoebe decided, was that it was such a sodding cliché. Nick couldn't put a foot wrong; she couldn't get one through the door, let alone on to the casting couch. Not in LA at any rate.

There were always her Euro-pudding bodice-rippers to fall back on. For some reason, the French, Spanish, Germans and Hungarians couldn't get enough of her. She'd just been offered the part of Marie Antoinette in *The Milkmaid Queen*. Sponsored by Deutsche Bank and an Italian TV station, it was absolute drivel. But the pay was terrific and the rest of the cast – all of whom she'd worked with on other Euro-messes – were all old comrades-in-yarns. In addition, the melodramatic script would certainly allow her to trammel the hills and valleys of her emotional range. Hollywood hills, however, they were not.

'Thanks but no thanks,' said Phoebe.

An hour later her agent rang back to say the Italians had upped her fee to £50,000. In a weak moment, Phoebe capitulated. She was dreading her next Amex and Access bills – her statements were so spattered with debit signs they looked like Morse code. It meant three weeks' filming just outside Prague, which was doubling as eighteenth-century Paris, and lying to Nick. He disapproved violently of Phoebe squandering her talent in Euro-puddings.

Partly as a sop to his feelings, and partly because she was an inveterate present buyer and the promise of money made her even more financially reckless than usual, she set about tracking down the very first car he'd bought when he'd got to England. It was an old Karman Ghia. It had been a wreck and he'd lovingly restored it. But it had leaked money and in the end he'd reluctantly got rid of it because he'd been behind with the rent and had refused to compromise his integrity by doing a Marmite ad. It took her two weeks to track it down, and it would take another two months to persuade the owner to part with it and then get it restored to its former glory. But he would be thrilled when he finally got it, and part of Phoebe loved making him happy.

✳   ✳   ✳

It wasn't until she listened to Martha's first traffic update in the shower that Eliza remembered the phone call she'd had the night before from Donna Ducatti begging her to take her on as a client. Donna was unhappy with the way her TV career wasn't going and had decided to increase her exposure in the tabloids in a bid to get the commissioning editors interested. She had managed to track down Eliza's home phone number with a view to barracking her into agreeing to represent her.

'I was thinking of checking into the *Betty* Ford clinic, or is *that* a bit *passé*?' she squawked.

'Are you an alcoholic?' asked Eliza, trying to sound businesslike while Podge stuck his tongue in her ear.

'*Excuse me?*' said Donna, sounding affronted.

'Well, it's just that I was going to suggest somewhere a bit closer to home. It's terribly high-profile at the Betty Ford. I don't even know what its success rate is like these days – most people just seem to come away with Elizabeth Taylor's home number . . .'

'But *surely* that's the *point*,' said Donna, now sounding exasperated.

The truth began to dawn on Eliza. 'So you're not addicted to anything?'

'Only *Twixes*. But there's not a lot of *mileage* in that. Although I could get *really* obese, I s'pose. And then go on a *diet*. Actually that's not a bad idea. There'd be the book and the exercise tape – *To Diet For* . . . On *second* thoughts, it all sounds a bit *time-consuming*. Whereas if you could organize a few *pictures* of me looking *wrecked* at parties, followed by weeks of *tearful denial*, we could get the whole thing *sewn up* inside two months. Then I thought we could try for the *full confession* in *The Python*, then there's the rehabilitation in

Hello! . . . by which time that *jerk* Charlie Pitch-For-It should be *gagging* to sign a contract with me.'

Signing a contract to gag her was more likely, thought Eliza. The last thing Charlie Pitchcock, the new honcho who had been brought in to raise standards on BBC 2, needed was a foul-mouthed jock on his glittering new roster. Even if Donna did keep trying out visual routines on her show in a bid to prove that she was made for television. The breakfast slot was getting smuttier by the day, and though the audience loved it, the Broadcasting Standards Authority were making noises about fining her.

Regretfully Eliza had had to turn Donna down. Not that the challenge didn't intrigue her, although she suspected the only thing Donna was realistically likely to get sewn up in the next few months was her mouth. Anyway, Martha would never have forgiven her for taking on Donna. And although Eliza was still tingling from not being invited to the original family summit, she had decided that their friendship was too precious to be jeopardized by one little oversight. It wasn't as if they hadn't included her since. Sadie had taken to calling her so often for pep talks and advice that Eliza was starting to feel emotionally drained.

She took a ferocious loofah to her blue-veined skin and began sandpapering away at the green gunk that had worked its way down her legs. Podge's food fetish was getting out of hand – or rather it was getting in hand, in hair and between her toes.

It was all very well when he'd confined himself to coating her with chocolate spread – Eliza had insisted on it being Bendicks; what was the point of spending a fortune on Origins if she then allowed her skin to be covered in any old additives? But in the past few weeks he'd begun working his way through Sainsbury's chilled cabinet. Last night he'd reached the guacamole. She shuddered in disgust. Through the open sash she could see across her dear little roof terrace with its tubs of white hydrangeas, which matched the white towels in her sleek white bathroom, to the elegant rooftops of the surrounding Georgian terraces, and felt mildly appeased.

Eliza loved her flat. Every last angle and architrave. She revelled in the luxury of having white walls, white furniture and anaemic concrete, even if Podge said that it was like living inside Julia Roberts' mouth. She relished being a stone's throw from the restaurants and shops of Upper Street in Islington, where she bumped into Stephen Fry or Ben Elton or one of Podge's friends from the City. And she adored the fact that she herself had paid for every last bowl and picture. Not that there were many of them. Eliza didn't believe in clutter — it reminded her of her mother.

With a pang she thought of poor Kate having to leave her flat. Though why she didn't just ask David to lend her some money was beyond Eliza. He wasn't that bad. In fact, as fathers went, he was pretty good. Suave, handsome, clever and well-off. How very different from her own dear pater, who was so tight-fisted Eliza was amazed he didn't suffer from constant cramp.

Sadie and David had seemed the most glamorous couple when Eliza first set eyes on them. Still were, really. She'd been thirteen, newly moved into Bath from Weston-super-Mare with her parents. They had scrimped to send her to Bath High — to them it was the apogee of five generations of genteel social mountaineering. For Sadie and David, of course, sending Martha and Kate to Bath High, with its relatively modest fees, was a stab at egalitarianism.

She and Martha had become instant friends, each of them recognizing a strong Calvinistic self-improving streak in the other – though their grails were somewhat different. Eliza had quickly discovered that being friends with Martha meant being friends with Kate, even though she was eighteen months younger. Not that it mattered. At eleven and a half, Kate was already miles more sophisticated than most of the girls Eliza had left behind in Weston-super-Mare.

As she had grown older and more successful in her own right, Eliza half expected the glamour of Tithe House to diminish in comparison with her London experiences. But it never did. Even now, Eliza found herself imitating Sadie's ways – laying a table with the elegant simplicity that Sadie always favoured, choosing the seemingly haphazard mixtures of peonies and roses that Sadie loved, ordering with her stationery supplies the same aubergine ink that Sadie always used.

To her gratification, they seemed to like her too – they'd practically adopted her. And now it was all disintegrating and, for some reason that she couldn't fathom, Eliza couldn't bear the idea of David and Sadie being rent asunder and rendered mortal just like everyone else.

Through the drumbeat of her power shower, she could hear the phone ringing. Reluctantly, she stepped out of the pounding heat and picked it up. It was Rosie, her ultra-efficient secretary, reminding her that she had an 8.15 breakfast meeting with Newton Foods.

Eliza slathered herself in caviare extract and smiled like a Persian cat. Chris Newton-Evis was the most truculent, pompous man in her life at the moment, and that was saying something. He was also number 132 on the *Sunday Times'* rich list. She was hardly likely to forget any meeting with him.

*   *   *

'Gosh, they're really cool,' cooed Tatty admiringly over Kate's shoulder at her drawing board. Kate looked up, scowling.

'They're also private,' she said ungraciously.

'Sorry,' said Tatty, blushing. Her eyes looked wounded.

Kate was feeling sensitive to emotional wreckages at the moment. 'I'm sorry. It's just that I'm supposed to be working on this brief – a new range for the fifteen- to twenty-five-year-olds—'

'Goodness, how exciting,' gushed Tatty, her cheeks pulsating.

'Yes, well, forgive me if I don't hyperventilate,' said Kate sourly. 'Knowing Morton's the fifteen to twenty-five bit probably refers to their size, or the extent of their annual spend. Anyway, this clearly doesn't fit the brief.'

'I think it's lovely,' began Tatty cautiously, looking at Kate's elegantly wiry black illustrations. 'It's a capsule wardrobe, isn't it?'

Kate looked at her, surprised. The only capsules she'd have thought Tatty would have known about were of the laxative variety.

'Yeah. I got the idea from an American magazine. Donna Karan's very big on them apparently.'

Tatty nodded sagely. 'She was just starting on them when I was working for her.'

Kate nearly dropped her pen.

'Oh, it was just for a few months. Bloody good laugh, actually. I *love* New York, don't you? Anyway, Donna had done this body thing, and then she wanted all these pieces to go with it. You know, five items that take you through life.'

It would take more than a leotard to get her through life, thought Kate sourly. And it would probably take a leoTardis before Tatty could fit into one. 'Yes, well,' she began, somewhat winded, 'this is a bit different. I mean, it's only loosely based round the concept . . .'

'Oh, I can see that. I love the hooded top and the skirt that can be worn as a mini or a maxi. Freddie's mad on hoods at the moment. Lycra and fleece, is it?'

'Actually, it's sweat-shirt, but fleece might work quite well, I suppose,' conceded Kate graciously.

'Have you thought about accessories?'

'I thought a huge over-the-body sack, like a messenger's bag, but in canvas – or maybe a rucksack, or both.'

'It's economically more viable to keep it to the one, tempting as it is to do lots of styles. Rucksacks have a longer life in them. They're only just starting to catch on. Mailbags might have peaked—'

Kate looked at her in wonderment. Until now she had always considered that Tatty's fashion flair made the chimpanzees from the PG Tips ads look like the Duchess of Windsor. Perhaps she'd misjudged her. 'But, as I said, it's totally inappropriate.'

'I don't see why.'

'Too stylish.'

Tatty hooted like a ship's foghorn. Laughter, Kate presumed.

'Oh, Kate, listen, if you're really worried about that, you could do them in some brighter colours. But I don't think we're supposed to deliberately design hideous things, even if they sometimes turn out that way.'

The previous minutes' camaraderie evaporated like watered-down Chanel No. 19. How could anyone be so naïve?

Martha's hand rested hesitantly on the telephone while she allowed her eye to be caught by a fascinating-looking article on Georgian crop rotation in the *New Statesman*. Telling herself it might come in handy for when she went to work on *The Late Shift*, she replaced the mouthpiece and struggled womanfully through the first paragraph. Twenty minutes and none the wiser later, she ran out of displacement activities and dialled Kylie Minogue's number again. Engaged. Thank God. She got up and visited the coffee machine for the seventy-sixth time that morning.

'Yup, it's still here,' said Jem waspishly, helping himself to some chocolate sawdust. 'Nice of you to keep checking, though. Managed to do any work this morning?'

He had spent the last week trying to cajole a sponsor into donating them crates of champagne for the Knickers slot. Given that it wasn't an obvious marriage of product and placement — most vineyards preferred their champagne to be associated with more up-market programmes — it had been an uphill slog. But he had finally persuaded Madame Hermione of Hermione & fils that Donna's *Cookin' Breakfast* was a cutting-edge cult, and Madame Hermione, whose son Jules was on a media course at Warwick University, had finally capitulated.

Martha looked at him contemptuously. 'If you had actually had the guts to say something at that infernal so-called meeting you and Donna had without me, I wouldn't have to waste my time on something that so obviously isn't going to work.'

'Oh, for heaven's sake, Martha. I thought you'd be grateful.'

'What!' She exhaled so hard that the froth and sawdust from Jem's instant cappuccino detached themselves from his cup and began parachuting gracefully down towards the carpet tiles.

'If you weren't so narrow-minded you'd see this for what it is — a bloody good opportunity for some investigative journalism on what's going to turn into the most talked-about slot on commercial radio,' he retorted impatiently.

'Oh, and this is your idea of educational populism, is it?' snorted Martha, who was coming to the conclusion that as far as Jem was aware, Paxman was probably a form of stuffing, balance was a sign of the zodiac, and ethics a county outside London where idiotic blondes came from.

'And I suppose you'd much rather be working on something terribly worthy with about two and a half listeners,' said Jem.

'At least their combined brain cells would run into double digits.'

'Oh, Martha, why are you in such awe of Radio Four? They put out as much crap as we do. It's just that their crap is boring and ours is entertaining.'

Martha blushed. 'Why do you persist in bringing up Radio Four all the time?'

He waved the letter from Jenny Stewart, which he'd found sandwiched between a pile of *Vogues*, inviting Martha to meet her at Le Caprice.

*   *   *

'They're fantastic. Really. Slick, novel and commercial.'

'But?' said Kate guardedly.

'There is no but. I really like them.'

She wasn't convinced. She had surprised herself by showing the sketches of the capsule wardrobe to Mark Lacy in the first place. But he'd caught her off guard when he'd asked her if she'd like an after-work drink. Since she hadn't produced anything else in the fortnight since he'd set her the project, she thought she'd better take along the ones she'd shown Tatty.

The Pet Shop Boys whined away in the background. Appropriate really, thought Kate, given that the unappetizing wine bar around the corner from Morton's, where she seemed to spend half her life, was called Your Place or Wine. It was a dismal dungeon, next to the Tube station and decked out to look like an old French wine cellar when everyone knew it was a former Tube depot. In fact the only thing whinier than the music, the decor and the name was the manager, Vince.

Kate gazed distractedly at the mock-Gothic candlestick on the table and thought how dated it looked. They were sitting under one of the arches and the acoustics were appalling. Every time Mark Lacy cleared his throat, which he did frequently, Kate kept imagining a Tube was about to smash through the wall. 'The thing is, Kate, I can't help noticing that you still seem a little restless—' Nervously, he took a sip of Sauvignon. 'So I was wondering if it might help if I outlined where I see you heading with Morton's.'

Not the One Day a Vauxhall Could Be Yours Too pep talk, thought Kate.

'Because I do see you having a really bright future. I know it all seems a bit dreary to you now, but once you start seeing your stuff being worn in the street, on real people – well, the bottom line is that nothing beats it for satisfaction.'

She tried to block out the bottom line that hove into her mind at that moment.

'I know it's not exactly couture,' he continued valiantly, 'and probably not what any of us imagined we'd be doing when we were at art school—' Kate nearly choked trying to picture him at art school. She'd always imagined that he'd been born brandishing a Woking Poly business degree in cost-cutting instead of an umbilical cord. '—but it's pretty exciting working at the grass-roots ends of things, rather like shooting the rapids.' He crossed his legs uneasily. 'You know the sort of thing – will the four hundred thousand striped track-suit-style skirts we've ordered arrive in time, and if so, will we shift them? It can get pretty nail-biting . . .'

The suspense wasn't exactly killing Kate. They sat in silence for a few moments while he took two more gulps of Sauvignon and peered round desperately, hoping that Vince would bring them some Twiglets.

'Anyway,' Kate began lightly, anxious to get the pep talk over and done with so that she could go and meet up with Eliza, who was taking her to a new restaurant she was handling, 'I don't suppose you've invited me here just to praise me.'

'Actually, I have. I mean, what's really terrific about these sketches is the way you've handled a pretty sophisticated concept in a manner that's so broadly appealing. Making them in fleece is a masterstroke. And I love the colours. As for the rucksack—'

Vince slammed another bottle of Sauvignon on to the table and an avalanche of cigarette ash blew out of the dirty ashtray on to Kate's customized mini-kilt and bounced on to her brogues.

'Really?' Kate was flabbergasted. And appalled. What if she were coming round to Morton's way of seeing things?

'Anyway, I think the board will love these. I wouldn't be at all surprised if they wanted to get cracking on them immediately. So as a precaution, I thought you should join the buyers on a trip to source some fabrics.'

'Are you sure?' Kate looked at him saucer-eyed. For once the blasé tone of voice had been silenced.

'Don't look so surprised.' Mark chuckled, delighted by her evident pleasure.

'But no one under the age of fifty-five ever gets to go on those buying trips,' she blurted tactlessly. Morton's was notoriously mean about sending its staff abroad. In two years, Kate's only trip had been over the loose lino tiles in the women's loos.

'Not everything at Morton's is set in stone,' he replied, smiling.

Just polyester, thought Kate. She hugged her knees excitedly. Not hearing from Magda had been a bitter blow, but perhaps her luck was changing.

'So, to sum up,' purred Christopher Newton-Evis, eyeing Eliza's smooth, silky thighs over his Armani bifocals, 'do you think you can satisfy our needs, Eliza?'

Eliza looked up from her orderly notes and smiled queasily. During the past hour and forty-five minutes, Christopher Newton-Evis's patrician vowels had stretched and squirmed their way round so many euphemisms that in the beginning she hadn't been entirely sure what the crisis was. Eventually the penny had dropped. Or rather the millions of pounds Newton-Evis stood to lose if the situation deteriorated any further.

The truth, particularly about what went into Newton-Evis products, as Eliza was discovering, was pretty disgusting. The discarded animal tissue, the chemicals, the severed genitals and the bulking agents – and that was just in the baby food – made haggis look like the ultimate detoxification programme.

What had begun four days earlier as a minor incident – an isolated case of sabotage perpetrated by mindless thugs in a Midlands supermarket on a consignment of Newton-Evis Doggy-Dog dog food, was threatening to escalate into a catastrophe. Far from aimless troublemakers, the saboteurs had turned out to be a group of articulate protesters who went by the group name of POISON, or Positive Organized Insurrection against Secretive and Opaque additives to Nutrients.

The name really bugged Eliza. Not just because it was also the name of one of her favourite perfumes but because the acronym didn't work at all. She found herself thinking that POISON could do with some professional PR help.

They certainly seemed to have a valid point, even if their tactics lacked subtlety. They had injected dog faeces into Doggy-Dog, which they'd rechristened Dodgy-Dog, and bombarded supermarkets with leaflets explaining that the new addition was just as palatable and certainly no less nutritious than Newton-Evis's other ingredients.

The initial public outcry against POISON had been tempered by the release, yesterday, of some highly confidential and – to anyone who didn't work in the food industry – shocking information regarding the ingredients in certain other of Newton-Evis's tinned ranges. According to this document, not only did Doggy-Dog contain traces of canine tissue, but there was evidence that everything from Newton-Evis's baked beans to its home-made fish pie (*'when you haven't got the time, we have,'* simpered the blurb on the box) contained toxic levels of additives.

'A right dog's dinner,' screamed the *Python's* front page above a list of ten things it suggested readers could do with Newton-Evis foods, which included donating them to a nuclear reprocessing plant and sending them to the entire West German football team.

'Heaven only knows how POISON came by that information. Those papers were highly confidential,' Christopher Newton-Evis said urbanely, examining his flawless cuticles with no more visible signs of anxiety than if he were having to deal with a tantrum in the nativity play. 'When I find whoever was responsible for the leak I'll crucify them,' he continued smoothly. 'But now is not the time for witch hunts, don't you agree, Eliza?'

It probably made no difference what she felt, she thought. Christopher Newton-Evis was one of those sublimely self-confident men who believed their very existence was ample justification for anything they might do. He was fluent in sound-bitese. Watching his soft features emote sympathy for ten whole minutes on *Newsnight* the previous evening, while he argued that Newton-Evis Foods had a moral obligation to continue providing millions of British families trying to feed themselves on a stringent budget with cheap, wholesome food, Eliza had been mesmerized.

'How about persuading John Selwyn Gummer to get his daughter to eat one of Newton-Evis's crinkled faggots for the press?' he suggested, flashing a wolfish smile in the direction of Eliza's legs. 'A nice fat donation to party funds should do it, don't you think?'

What Eliza thought was that he had to be kept away from any more television cameras and journalists, at least until she had had a chance to groom him in the basic tenets of civilized behaviour. With the social conscience of a mass murderer – from a professional point of view he was irresistible. He was so odious, in fact, that he had the potential to rule the world, thought Eliza. And when he did, she wanted to be damned sure that she, and none of her rivals, was there to assist him.

Chapter Five

'Hi, Kate.' Tatty beamed, heaving a gleaming Louis Vuitton case into the hold of the National Express coach. It was about minus six degrees, despite being July, but Tatty was already glowing and her cheeks were throbbing. 'What a gorgeous blouse.'

Kate looked at her stonily. When Mark Lacy had first mooted the possibility of a buying trip she knew they wouldn't be going on a first-class round-the-world tour. But she hadn't envisioned a coach trip to Bradford either. And even that had taken weeks to get off the ground. And to make matters fifty times worse, it looked as though she was stuck at Morton's for the foreseeable future. Tatty and Eliza had been right; it was a terrible time to be selling property. In any case, Max Horrowitz's will had turned out to be an even bigger tangled mess than his selection of antique wools. Even if she had the money it was doubtful whether they'd ever find out who actually owned the place. She was going to have to revise her twelve-month plan. At this rate her father would be in an old people's home – probably one overlooking Monte Carlo – before she ever got her business off the ground.

'But it's where all the best fleeces are. Freddie loves fleeces. And I've heard they do brilliant sari fabrics,' Tatty had pointed out equably. 'You could get some seriously lovely things for your flat. And just think how much we'll learn from seeing round all those mills. It's all happening up there, apparently.'

A veritable Mills and Boom, thought Kate darkly. She looked out of the window as the rest of the Morton's buying team – mostly cheerful men and women in their fifties with a fatal taste for V-necked tank tops and elasticated waistbands – filed on to the bus.

'I don't know how you manage to look so amazing on such a cold day,' said Tatty, wedging her Lycra-insulated bottom on to the seat next to Kate's. Kate felt marginally appeased. She was rather pleased with her outfit, considering it was freezing. Fraying white trousers that Reg promised her had belonged to John Lennon, a gold cummerbund from an antique textile gallery, pale oyster-coloured embroidered Chinese slippers, and a cream sheepskin jerkin Sadie had picked up in Shepton Mallet.

Tatty rustled around in her wicker basket and produced two mini-tubs of Weight Watchers' ice cream and two squashed Mars Bars. 'Fancy one?' she asked Kate kindly. 'They're a bit battered but that makes them easier to spread on the ice cream.' Kate shook her head and slumped miserably into her seat.

It was an interminable journey, what with the singalong at the front of the bus, and Tatty's constant wittering. Somewhere around Manchester, she had produced a bag of wires and needles that Kate had initially mistaken for knitting, but which turned out to be the innards of an old Bakelite telephone. It transpired that Tatty collected them.

'I've got all kinds, from a 1918 wind-up one to those funny little Triniton ones from the sixties. It drives Nigel, my boyfriend, absolutely bonkers. But I get it from Daddy. He's got hundreds. He must have every novelty phone ever made, including one shaped like a penis. The cradle's the testicles. It's hysterical. Not very good reception, though. A right bloody balls-up, he calls it ...' Tatty giggled appreciatively at her father's joke.

Kate didn't know whether she was more surprised by Tatty's ability to assemble a 1920s telephone or the revelation that she had a boyfriend. Not that Tatty was unattractive. It was just that she'd always seemed more interested in puppies than men. But perhaps in her circle they amounted to much the same thing.

Tatty giggled. 'When Daddy and I get together we usually spend most of our time taking them to bits. Apparently when I was five I took every phone in the house apart and they couldn't get an engineer in for a whole week. I'm a bit better now – I can usually put them back together. But it drives Mummy mad.'

'I can imagine,' said Kate in her least encouraging tones. The last thing she wanted was a discourse from Tatty on the internal workings of the telephone.

'Actually, to be honest,' Tatty continued, warming to her subject, 'what really interests me is computers. You'd be amazed how fascinating they are. Inside, they're works of art.'

Kate stuck on her headphones but it was no good. She couldn't block out Tatty's eulogies about the word processor, or the snatches of Kajagoogoo that floated unbidden from the front, no matter how loudly she turned up U2.

*   *   *

Martha arrived outside Le Caprice breathless from a close encounter with some over-zealous Tube doors that had swallowed up half her linen interview jacket as she attempted to disembark at Green Park. It was her own fault. She had been up much of the night brushing up on the Middle East and had been half asleep by the time the train got to her stop. She had only just woken up in time to get off at all.

The coat-check girl eyed her torn outfit distastefully and Martha tried to arrange her shoulder bag over the worst of the damage as the maître d' ushered her towards Jenny Stewart's table. She was so busy trying to sidle towards the table sideways that she completely missed the Princess of Wales sitting at her favourite table with Clive James.

Jenny Stewart held out a roughened hand. 'You must be Martha,' she said in a voice that sounded as though it had been marinading in several cases of vodka for twenty years. 'How nice of you to come. Now, before we go any farther, what can I get you to drink?'

'Er, Perrier would be lovely,' said Martha nervously. She needed all her wits about her. She had to get this job.

'Perrier.' Jenny beamed at the tall, disapproving waiter. 'And another vodka martini.' Unimpressed by Martha's attire and Jenny's slurring, the waiter stalked off. 'Honestly,' husked Jenny, 'the youth today are so po-faced. Now, what would you like to eat? I tell you what I fancy—'

Jenny Stewart's idea of lunch turned out to be thirty-eight different kinds of lettuce leaf, washed down with several litres of vodka and martini. Talk about high spirits, thought Martha. It was a miracle she was still sitting by the end of lunch, let alone in any condition to contemplate standing up.

Not that it seemed to affect her brainpower. Even with two bottles of Cinzano inside her, Jenny Stewart's thought processes were razor sharp. She must be painful when she was sober.

'So what do you think of Radio Four's competition?' she asked Martha probingly.

'I don't really listen to any of it,' said Martha. It was true. Three days earlier she had tuned her transistor to Radio Four and wrenched the dialling knob off so she wouldn't be tempted to reset it. Not that she needed any encouragement. She was addicted to practically all of Radio Four's output, even the really dreary bits that went out when no one else was listening. And she couldn't begin to get ready for bed until she heard the closing strains of Wagner's *Tannhäuser* which opened and closed each edition of *The Late Shift*.

'Oh dear, you are disillusioned. Still, my advice is to keep up with some of the popular stations. There's a lot of vitality and ideas there we could learn from.'

'Really?' said Martha, too nervous to digest what Jenny was saying beyond the required niceties. Jenny Stewart was one of those people who spoke in clipped, elliptical sentences that would have been equally at home in an obedience school for repeat offenders. Sometimes she was so cryptic no one understood what she was talking about, but her general air of distracted, earnest intelligence meant that she was always given the benefit of the doubt.

'As a matter of fact, I'm a big fan of what you've done at BSR. Post-modern self-knowingness. Going to be a driving force in nineties media, don't you think?'

'I've always tended to regard BSR as a bit of post-modern tragedy actually,' said Martha, in a tone she hoped reverberated with post-modern irony.

Jenny laughed. 'Why d'you want to leave, by the way? Cracking little station.'

'Tabloid burn-out, I suppose you could call it,' said Martha, summoning all the gravitas she could while trying to ease a bit of lollo rosso out of her teeth with her tongue. 'Actually, I've always really wanted to do old-fashioned reporting. BSR was a diversion.'

'Not too old-fashioned, I hope,' said Jenny breezily. 'We're on a bit of a modernizing quest ourselves. Make it more digestible to the listener. Shorten the slots, add more human interest. First thing to go, that bloody dirge that opens and closes the show. Always makes us want to slash our wrists in the studio . . . you might be able to help us come up with something more contemporary. Along the lines of "Spirits in the Material World".'

Martha looked at her aghast.

'By the Police,' added Jenny helpfully, misconstruing Martha's look of stunned amazement. 'We can be quite radical too. Not the whole thing. Just the first few bars, of course . . . Anyway, digression. CV and demo tapes – most impressive. So tell me a bit more about life at BSR.'

'Well,' began Martha uncertainly, 'it's a bit like *Hedda Gabler*. Only not quite so soothing. There are lots of ideas – Donna's very creative, to give her credit – but you have to keep a tight rein on them sometimes. Two weeks ago she decided to organize a national Blind Date phone-in. The idea being that since it was on the radio it would literally be blind. Now she says she's got this new competition she wants to launch. Out a faggot and win a holiday on Mykonos. She got sponsorship from an 18–35 travel company and everything. It's all a bit gratuitous for my liking.'

'Ratings shooting through the roof, however,' said Jenny admiringly.

'Not very PC though,' said Martha pointedly. 'Fortunately we're a bit bogged down with our other new slot at the moment so we managed to postpone the faggot one.'

She could have kicked herself because Jenny Stewart insisted on hearing the full gory details about Knickers.

'Brilliant,' she roared, when Martha finished telling her how many celebrities' agents had so far told her to get lost. 'Be an absolute hoot. They'll all be dying to get on it in the end. It's just securing the first one. Oh my God, look at the time.' She beckoned for the bill, sending a glass of martini flying over Clive James's suede brogues. 'Shame,' she murmured lovingly, eyeing the wasted luminous liquid. 'Been lovely meeting you. Have a think. We'll be in touch.'

Before Martha had retrieved her napkin, she had disappeared into a cab. And that was it. No questions about the Gulf. No piercing examination of Martha's reporting techniques. Just a worrying acceptance of her credentials based on her brilliant contributions to the hallowed output of BSR.

'It *is* you. Thank God,' sighed Magda as Kate opened the door of her flat. 'I've been looking everywhere for you. For six months. I'd just about given up. Then I saw a picture in Foxton's property magazine that looked just the way you'd described your sitting room. So I made an appointment.'

She paused triumphantly before pushing past Kate into the tiny hallway, knocking half the framed little silhouettes that lined the walls skew-whiff with her hat.

Kate didn't know whether to laugh hysterically or weep. After dreaming about bumping into Magda for weeks, she had eventually given up hope of ever seeing her again and instead had begun dreaming that one of the many potential viewers from Marsh and Parson's would walk into her flat and actually make an offer.

'What a divine shade of green,' cooed Magda, peering into the kitchen. 'John Oliver?'

'No, Chanel No. Five. You add a few drops to a tin of Dulux,' said Kate. It was an old trick of Sadie's, who swore by it.

'I knew you were a marvel,' sighed Magda, settling down on a little Swedish sofa Kate had just finished painting pale blue and smoothing out her ruffled skirt. Kate winced inwardly. She couldn't swear the paint was completely dry. 'That's why I've been searching high and low. I even tried to reach you at Marks and Spencer. They put me on hold for about four months and then said they'd never heard of you. What happened? Did you leave under a cloud?'

'Morton's — that's where I've been. I never worked at Mark's,' Kate began to explain, and then gave up. 'Never mind. Where've you been?'

'Oh, here and there,' said Magda, who always spoke as if she were halfway through a yawn. She had left *A la Mode* not so much under a cloud as swaddled in a pea-souper following a disagreement about her expenses, and had subsequently spent three months in Colorado styling Virginia Slims ads.

Her sacking still rankled. 'While I enjoy a bit of creativity as much as the next person,' the head of the accounts department had told her, 'I draw the line at paying for every item in your flat on the pretext that you used it in a shoot. Haven't you heard of borrowing?'

'Well, forgive me for pointing this out, but most souks don't have press offices,' said Magda, flouncing out. 'And I live in a house,' she had added as she cleared her desk.

'At least I managed to get all my garden furniture out of it. I would have returned the hammocks if *A la Mode* hadn't been so aggressive. As it was I sold them and bought this skirt instead.' She stroked the lace flounces lovingly. 'It's sixties couture, you know.'

Kate made them both some honey and ginseng tea and lit her jasmine candles. In the dying summer light, with the wall sconces flickering away, and the new blinds she had made out of the Bradford saris fluttering at the windows, the flat looked beautiful, she thought wistfully.

'Well, Kate,' said Magda, after an enjoyable hour or two in which they had destroyed the contents of every interiors magazine on the market, 'delightful as all this has been, I didn't just drag over here for fun. I have a proposition.'

Kate looked at her with trepidation. Perhaps Magda wanted to move in. She blanched at the thought. Much as she liked her, she didn't think there was room for her, Magda and Magda's skirts.

'To cut a rather tedious business story short, the funding for *Domus* finally came through. I did tell you about *Domus*, didn't I? Ah. Well, it's this blueprint for a magazine I've been working on for years — a stylish, glossy interiors magazine for people with more dash than cash, but done in a witty, urban way. Bernie Higginbottom thinks it's an excellent idea.'

Kate looked bemused.

'Don't tell me I didn't tell you about Bernie either? He's

big in cement and caravan sites. And his wife Nancy's just big. I met her at the Chic Home summer exhibition. She was looking at window treatments, as she calls them. Anyway, I stopped her walking home with several miles of moire taffeta and introduced her to Roman blinds. There was no stopping our friendship after that, I can tell you. And of course it was just a hop, skip and a jump from blinds to getting her hubbie to set up a publishing house. Nancy seems to think it's a guaranteed route to respectability. Anyway, it's all worked out brilliantly for us.'

'Us?' asked Kate, surreptitiously fingering the woodwork on the sofa to see if it was dry. Her finger stuck to it ominously.

'I need an editor-at-large and I thought you'd be just the ticket. Not sure about the salary. Bernie's still working out the finances. But tons of perks, kudos and the chance to be blindingly creative.'

Kate, trying desperately not to kiss Magda's feet, groped for something sensible to say.

'How many in the team?'

'Three, counting you, me and the art director.'

'Who's that?'

'I haven't actually found one yet. But I'm very close.'

'When does it launch?'

'November.'

Kate nearly spat out her tea. 'Magda, that's less than three months away.' Inexperienced as she was she knew that was no time in which to launch a magazine from scratch. Especially with no art director.

'It is a bit tight. But that's half the challenge. Please say you'll think about it.'

'Er, fine. When would you like me to let you know?'

'This morning. By eleven. I've got a meeting with Bernie at quarter past and I'd quite like to say I've got the team together.'

Kate giggled. It was twenty past ten already.

Seated behind her newly installed Perspex Philippe Starck desk, Eliza pressed the remote control and waved it in front of the equally newly installed television, a flicker of contentment curling across her blue-pink lips. Chrome sweet chrome – her office was starting to look very impressive, she noted with satisfaction. Moving from Soho to Covent Garden had been the right decision, even though the rents were astronomical and she'd had to forgo a salary increase in order to secure her sixteen hundred square metres. The WC2 postcode had put her on the right bit of the map. It was where all the advertising agencies she admired were stationed, and Eliza, although she hadn't yet quite formulated how, was convinced that over the next few years Cody Associates would be appropriating some of their techniques, if not their clients. She wasn't ready to compete with the big boys, but at least now she was in the same arena.

John Major was droning on about the economy for *Channel Four News* on the television screen that was permanently on in a corner of Eliza's office. It must be gone seven. She ought to be getting home, especially as Podge had been threatening all week to prepare something special to smear over her. She gazed in wonder at John Major's upper lip. If only he'd let her do a makeover. Paddy Ashdown was on next, vaunting the moral probity of his party – clearly a recipe for disaster. She wouldn't be in the least surprised if a

Lib Dem got caught with a rent boy in the next twenty-four hours. When would these leaders learn?

What attracted David Crawford to politics? she wondered idly. Clearly not power, otherwise he wouldn't have joined the New Democratic Party. Perhaps he really was altruistically motivated. It was funny — although he was charming and even kind, she could never think of him as anything other than entirely out for himself. Perhaps that's why she found him so appealing.

Her musings were interrupted by flashing lights on the switchboard on her desk. Rosie had gone home and it took a few moments before Eliza got the right line, by which time she'd managed to flick Channel Four up to volume thirteen.

'Eliza?'

She started at the mellifluous deep tones. She'd recognize that voice anywhere. It was David Crawford. 'Speaking.'

'Am I interrupting something? It sounds awfully high powered in there.'

'It's the news. I can't seem to get the volume down.'

'Thank the Lord. I've been trying to track you down for hours. I think I've got a project that might interest you a great deal. It's quite a hot potato, as a matter of fact.'

Eliza was getting to like spud missiles. 'I don't know whether you feel ready for Westminister yet,' he continued, 'but after what you did with Doggy-Dog I thought you might be ready for bigger stuff. That's if you're not feeling too ruff-ruff.'

Eliza smiled at the feeble joke. 'That's not very original, David.'

'You're right. You've probably had more than your fr

of canine jokes recently. Terribly impressed with the way you managed the whole thing, though. Absolutely spot on to get Chris Newton-Evis to remove his ghastly dross off the shelves.'

'Only the stuff that was directly named in the report. And he didn't think so at the time. Said he'd never lost a million pounds so quickly or efficiently.'

'It was nothing compared with what he stood to lose if you hadn't made him see the necessity of restoring public confidence so quickly. Anyway, I didn't ring to discuss Chris Newton-Evis, much as I admire your handling of him, but because I thought you might be interested in taking on another challenging client.'

She said nothing.

He continued smoothly, 'Look, I think it would probably be easier – and safer – if we met in person. Shall we say Wilton's, at eight-thirty?'

Prowling through the cosy, narrow vestibule of Wilton's, Eliza looked as exotic as a tube of crimson Dior lipstick in a shaving kit. On into the warren of low-ceilinged Edwardian rooms she strode, creating quite a stir – not surprisingly, as she was sporting little more than a gleaming Alaïa black leather jacket and legs, which, David Crawford immediately decided on spotting her, could only be described as rapacious.

She really was a striking girl, he thought appreciatively. Her hair, swept back into a disciplined, sleek chignon, was exactly as a woman's should be, he felt; deceptively prim. Just from looking at the unblinking concentration of her pale blue eyes, he could tell that she was up to the job. And so glacial she looked, as though your fingers would freeze stuck if you touched her. He was in for a good evening. As she sat down, he poured her a glass of Puligny Montrachet. He had rehearsed a little introductory dinner speech about neither of them wanting to waste their time, and bushes, the futility of beating about them and so on, but just as he was about to launch into it, he thought better of it. This was a bush about which, he rather fancied, he might enjoy beating.

Martha drained another glass of the Hermione et fils champagne that was now arriving at BSR by the crate and poured herself another slug. Since the idea of Knickers had first been mooted she'd put on half a stone through stress – and champagne. At this rate they'd have to hospitalize her before they got a single guest on to the slot. She looked at the studio clocks. It was 9.30 p.m. Or 6.30 a.m. in Tokyo. Either way she'd been in the studio for sixteen hours. In that time she had visited the coffee machine twenty-nine times, read eight back issues of *A la Mode*, filed all her *Hello!*s in alphabetical order according to who was on the cover, checked her answer machine at home twelve times to see if Jenny Stewart had left a message, and – finally – called a total of nine people.

One of them had been Kate, who told her she mustn't degrade herself another second by remaining in Donna's orbit; another Argos to see if they had her toaster in yet; and twice Eliza to see if she'd had any luck persuading some of her clients to do Knickers. But Eliza had been out.

In despair, she navigated her swivel chair – the room was too minuscule to warrant getting out of it – back towards the tower of champagne crates in the corner as Jem poked his head round the door. He briefly surveyed the day's emotional fall-out, most of which seemed to have landed on Martha's hair, and said in the cheery manner of a front-line nurse speaking to a soldier who'd just lost most of his limbs: 'If it's any help I've compiled a list of a few more celebs who might take part in Knickers.'

She looked at him despairingly, her hands raking through her hair like a bunch of Fagin's boys steaming through Harvey Nichols. 'Jem, I've called everyone in London. All the anyones who are anyones; all the anyones who *used* to be someones, and even the anyones who are no ones. I might just as well start going through The Yellow Pages.'

'What about Amanda de Cadenet?' he asked brightly.

'I tried her last week. It's gone way beyond that. The daytime soaps don't want to know. Even Kilroy's declined.'

'Blimey, that really is scraping the barrel. The thing is, Donna is not going to let this one die. She thinks that if Paula Yates could get all those rock stars to pose in their knickers, the least we can do is persuade them to send them in. We just need one yes, from the right person. Then it will become a cult. A year from now, Arnie Schwarzenegger will be begging to send in his jockstrap.'

Martha blenched at the thought and yanked angrily on the cork now wedged between her knees. 'In case it escaped Donna's attention, there was a certain nepotism acting on Paula Yates's side. I'm sorry I'm not related to anyone famous, but it wasn't part of the job description when I applied.'

'That's not strictly true ...' began Jem tentatively. 'About not being related to anyone famous.'

He paused, swallowed, and relieved Martha of the half-opened champagne. Martha looked at him befuddled.

'Your father,' he blurted.

Martha began to laugh hysterically. 'Oh yeah. Given that ninety per cent of our listeners don't know who Margaret Thatcher is, I can see that an obscure NDP MP is the perfect choice to catapult her listenership into double figures.'

'Not that obscure – he does have his own *Spitting Image* puppet, and ever since he did that Harry Enfield special ...'

'*No*,' said Martha, appalled.

'It would get us loads of coverage in the tabs. Frankly, Martha, I think it might be your last chance.'

'Note the brisk switch from us to you. Whatever happened to us both being in this together?'

The phone on Martha's desk rang, its insistent trill reverberating around the matchbox. Martha's heart lurched. Perhaps it was Jenny Stewart. But before she could get there, Jem picked it up. 'It's Trevor Kay. For you.'

She snatched the phone from him. 'Martha Crawford here,' she hiccoughed. 'Who's that?'

'Trevor. I just said.' The voice sounded muzzy.

'Yes, but what do you want?'

'I represent Darren Dennison.'

'Darren,' said Martha befuddled. A noxious cocktail of cheap champagne, nerves and exhaustion had slowed her brain to the pace of a caravan.

'You called about the celebrity slot,' said Trevor, sounding peevish. 'Darren's thought it over, and having juggled his dates has agreed to take part.'

The penny finally dropped. Darren Dennison was the star of a series of cheap British films that included the illustrious *Secrets of a Toilet Attendant* and culminated in the disastrous *Secrets of a Funeral Undertaker*. Martha had read about them in the *TV Times* when Channel Four had run a themed Seventies Dross Evening. Tracking him down had been surprisingly easy. According to the *TV Times* article, Darren was now working as a Tarzanogram. Presumably his dates weren't all he'd had to juggle.

'That's very sweet,' said Martha, panicking. If Jem thought Kilroy was the bottom of the barrel, Darren represented the creosote. 'But I don't know if we're still running the slot. If we are, tell Darren we'll be back to him straight away . . .'

Jem was frantically mouthing something, but the room was spinning. Eventually he snatched the phone from her.

'Is that *the* Darren Dennison?' he gushed.

'No, you tosser, it's Trevor Kay. His bleeding agent.'

'Well, Trevor, I want you to know it's an honour. An absolute honour. Those films of Darren's were seminal in the birth of alternative British comedy. Without Darren there would have been no Julian Clary. No Vic Reeves. Possibly no Ben Elton . . . we're just thrilled to have him on the show.'

It took another five minutes of abject sycophancy and a promise of three crates of champagne and the top ten CDs before Trevor was finally won round again. But Jem seemed to think it was freebies well spent.

'He's absolutely cult,' he beamed when he'd put the phone down. 'You sly old thing, Martha. You really had me worried for a while there. But with Darren on board, Knickers is going to be the coolest thing on the airwaves, you mark my words.'

*   *   *

'So, as you can see, Laurence Patterson's little tax problem isn't exactly a mortal sin – more an oversight,' said David Crawford, lovingly cradling a Cognac in both hands. It was getting late and he was feeling decidedly expansive. Eliza wondered idly whether he'd ever been that demonstrative with his daughters. He was impeccably spruce, from the clearly expensive haircut to the almost too shiny, hand-made Lobb brogues. She wondered how his colleagues in the House viewed him – and whether he cared.

'But we mustn't be complacent,' he continued. 'It could so easily all blow out of proportion.'

'Especially as he was the one, if I'm not mistaken, behind your party's campaign to put a penny on income tax.'

He looked at her approvingly. She was sharp.

'Quite so. Though I don't think we'll be emphasizing that particular historical aspect.'

'So what will you be stressing?' Eliza was distinctly amused.

'I rather thought you might supply us with that. The divine one has put me in charge of troubleshooting this one, and I thought you might be interested in being enlisted.'

Eliza tried to contain her shock.

'But I do PR for hair gel, department stores, the odd TV show and dog food. I don't do politicians.'

'Not yet.' He pressed his fingers together and rested his face against the steeple. If he weren't English, she would have sworn he'd had a manicure. 'But the way you handled Chris Newton-Evis was most impressive. Your media contacts are invaluable. And of course, if you did as good a job with

Laurence, it would have a most impressive effect on your business.'

'I can see that,' she said sharply. She wanted to ask him why he had chosen her. Why not some experienced army of Whitehall mandarins long practised in the nefarious art of cover-ups?

'The world of politics is changing,' he said, reading her thoughts. 'It's increasingly important to get the look of things right rather than the thing itself. An external eye is crucial for that. And with your television experience, coupled with the Doggy-Dog stuff, I think you're ready for a big challenge.'

She decided to overlook his condescension and contented herself with calling the waiter over for the bill instead.

'Would you care for another brandy?' David asked, looking slightly taken aback for the first time that evening. 'By the way, I've a file on Laurence – compiled by party office. It makes interesting reading.'

'When can I meet him?'

'I thought tomorrow morning.'

'Why not now? After all, an hour is a long time in politics. You should know that, David.' She reached for the bill. He put out a smooth, almost hairless, hand to stop her, but she had already signed the slip.

'How very ungallant of you not to allow me to be gallant. I was going to pay for that,' he said almost petulantly.

Don't worry, thought Eliza. One way or another, you will.

Chapter Six

'So you see, it's an offer I can't refuse,' said Kate, tugging on a tendril of hair until her scalp felt as though it were splitting. Vince was excelling himself with excruciatingly depressing music. He had obviously taken Morrissey's Meat Is Murder stance to heart, since there was no danger of finding any in his lasagnes. And Mark Lacy, it was fair to say, was not taking her resignation speech well.

'But your future at Morton's was really starting to look rosy. The board even approved your presence on the buying trip. Not many novices get to go on those, you know.'

'Oh, Mark, it was a trip to Yorkshire, not the Yucatán,' said Kate, both touched and appalled that he'd had to go to the trouble of getting special dispensation for her to attend. 'And I've been with Morton's two years, so I'm hardly a rookie.'

'Look, I know this magazine seems like the answer to your dreams,' he began desperately, a flush creeping across his pale cheeks like fire across a wheatfield, 'but have you really thought it through? It's a completely different direction, you know — more like journalism than design.' He tried to make the word journalism sound despicable but he couldn't make anything sound awful. 'And what about Xtra? It's all going so well and it's got your name written all over it. Any minute now I think the board's going to approve it,' he pleaded.

Kate beamed at him beatifically. She couldn't help it. Since Magda's offer her endorphins had been somersaulting.

Vince slammed another warm bottle of Chardonnay on the table.

'I suppose journalism has its place,' Mark continued, brushing away some wine that had splattered in his face, 'but it's not terribly creative, is it? I mean, when all's said and done, it's just documenting other people's achievements.'

No one ever seemed to get round to documenting Morton's achievements, Kate thought savagely. 'And Morton's is creative?' The words were out before she could stop them. His translucent tobacco-coloured eyes seemed to withdraw into their sockets like shock-absorbers.

Mark Lacy's hypersensitivity was another reason she had to leave Morton's. The number of times she had noticed him flinching when she made a thoughtless remark didn't bear thinking about. One of these days she was going to lose it completely and launch into some fully fledged sarcasm, and then where would they all be? Probably standing round Mark Lacy's bed in Accident and Emergency.

Typically, he began stammering to cover up her rudeness. 'W-w-well, of course, if you're set on it—'

'I am.' Everything But the Girl were singing about broken hearts. '*I don't wanna talk about it,*' they wailed. Nor did Kate. She had a meeting with Magda at eight.

'Then I wish you the best of luck,' Mark said miserably, helping himself to a stale Twiglet.

Twenty minutes later, as she bounded up the steps from Your Place or Wine, Kate was peeved to find that, along with the small knot of excitement swelling in her stomach, there was an additional kernel of something she recognized as a Mark Lacy causal-effect speciality – guilt.

'I have to hand it to you, Martha,' said Jem, gingerly picking his way to her desk across a wasteland of empty champagne bottles, overflowing ashtrays and decimated plastic cups. 'In a perverse way, Darren Dennison was quite superb.'

'And which particular perversity would that be?' She folded her arms across the desk and laid her head on them. It was nine o'clock at night and she ought to have been out having a life. Instead she was in the matchbox, as she had been for the past six nights running. She hadn't consumed anything for two days other than crisps and Hermione et fils champagne, and she felt exhausted. 'Are you referring to his diatribe against gays, Pakistanis and feminists? Or the moment when he said he'd quite like to roger Mrs Thatcher?'

'Controversy's what the ABC1 youth segment wants, Martha, sweetheart,' said Jem cheerfully, dodging a sliding pile of old *Spectators* that weren't so much yellowing as decomposing.

Martha sighed. She hated it when he lapsed into his jaunty pop-culture-speak. It was becoming futile even trying to argue the finer points of anything with Jem, who by now probably thought Media Responsibility was the name of a song by Elvis Costello. If only Jenny Stewart would actually confirm her offer in writing. But she was at home feeling under the weather, according to her PA.

She had been off work for two weeks, as a matter of fact, and Martha was beginning to fret that Jack might have been right all along and that Jenny wasn't so much under the weather as under a table somewhere sleeping off a hangover. Still, Eliza kept telling her to chill out and to call her every time she felt like ringing Jack. For four months she had managed to resist 'phoning him – an unprecedented achievement that probably owed less to willpower than to Hermione's fermenting skills, which generally saw her comatose by the time it was a godly hour in Atlanta. She sighed. Darren Dennison indeed. When Donna had asked him if it was a relief to be able to go around incognito these days he had angrily retorted that all the rumours about him not being able to have children were completely untrue.

Jem wittered on, spectacles blinking like a spaceship. 'By the way, I almost forgot. It's Boy George's direct line. Apparently he thought the Darren Dennison interview was hilarious and wants to take part.'

Martha lifted her head a few centimetres from the table, all she could manage, and looked at him mutely for a few moments. He was serious. Perhaps Knickers was about to take off after all. She allowed herself the luxury of sinking into the deepest possible gloom.

In normal circumstances David Crawford would have thoroughly enjoyed seeing Laurence Patterson crucified by the press. He found Patterson insufferably pompous and endowed with an ostentatious amount of hair for a man of his advancing middle years.

Worse still, Patterson's tawdry little misdemeanours threatened the honour of the party and that, as far as

David Crawford, the Right Honourable MP for West Fordingshire, was concerned, was unpardonable.

The problem was that Patterson had his uses, as even the most self-righteous member of the NDP had to concede. For one thing he was a terrifically successful businessman, steering Northern Star TV from near-bankruptcy to glowing profitability when he was still only in his early thirties. He was deeply disliked by certain old-school politicians in the House, but his leader, along with many of the political commentators whom Patterson so assiduously wined and dined, had always put that down to snobbery. Laurence of Suburbia, as the press referred to him, was the sort of man who resorted to buying his own monograms. His oily charm was bad enough on television, but in private he was so politically incorrect he made Benny Hill look like New Man.

'Well, hai-llo,' he had crooned at Eliza's pale cleavage as he poured her a whisky she hadn't asked for. And 'Charming' as she arranged herself as demurely as she could – which was difficult since his L-shaped leather sofas had obviously been designed with maximum leg rumination in mind. He sat opposite her, his puny bejeaned legs stretched out in front of him, openly appraising her from beneath his droopy fringe as if she were a cigar in a particularly fine case from which he was allowed to choose just one. David stood behind him, fiddling with his crested cuff links.

'Look, David,' he began emolliently, 'I'm as dismayed by the discovery of this as anyone else, but it's hardly front-page stuff – a petty oversight, committed by an overworked accountant.' He paused to imbibe a slug of whisky.

'That's where you're wrong, Laurence,' said David dryly. 'The *International Gazette* has got hold of this and they certainly seem to think it's front-page stuff. They're not going to let it drop.'

'Oh, spare us the sanctimoniousness of badly paid journalists,' drawled Laurence, flashing Eliza a conspiratorial look that she chose not to reciprocate. Without consultation, he poured them all a drink. 'I certainly don't imagine this little hiccough is worth your bother, nor, I imagine, my dear, your expenses. You look rather costly to run.'

It was probably meant as a compliment, she decided. But so thinly veiled was his contempt for women, and with such difficulty did he manage to squeeze out the words either side of the absurd cigar he had placed in his mouth in the absence of anything more interesting to put there, that it came across as profoundly offensive. As did just about everything else he said.

'If she doesn't bother, we might find the party set back five years by this little oversight.' David was even more disgusted by Patterson's lack of humility than he was by his appalling tasselled loafers. He'd lay bets on Patterson never having played the Steinway grand squatting at the foot of the curving staircase that swept up to an absurdly theatrical mezzanine.

'Oh, come, come, it's human error. Even those sanctimonious hypocrites on Fleet Street can understand that.' Laurence tossed his hair as if he were a starlet auditioning for a part in *Charlie's Angels*.

'Difficult, when the human error worked so enormously in your favour.'

Lulled by the unexpectedly convivial evening with David Crawford and the two bottles of Puligny Montrachet, Eliza was curious rather than riled. She looked round the penthouse. With its soaring columns – more bionic than

Ionic, she decided — it was a bit like Trafalgar Square, only larger. What with acres of dark wood panelling and the ghastly furniture which his cleaning lady must have to spray with eau de leather every day, there was no trace of a feminine hand. Presumably his long-suffering wife, Zena, who always looked ill at ease in front of the camera, was kept safely away from this monument to Laurence Patterson's bulbous ego. Probably chained to their country seat.

'Now, Ms ... er ... what would be really helpful to all of us would be to break up this jolly little gathering and get some sleep. Otherwise you'll have no energy left to tend to your hair gels and chat show presenters.' He smirked at Eliza. On cue, an estuarine twang floated across the columns. 'Laurie, are you comin'?'

'Soon, my angel. Or at least, I hope so.' He winked at Eliza. David looked at him in disgust.

'Oh, don't be such a stuffed shirt. At least I don't try to pass my mistresses off as political consultants. How seriously do you expect me to take this little incident when you present me with someone whose troubleshooting thus far consists of finding last-minute guests for *Celebrity Squares*?'

For the first time that evening Eliza, perched on the edge of Patterson's enormously long, tan leather sofa, felt a flash of anger. Patterson, crossing his legs in a surprisingly effete gesture, lightly brushed her ankle.

'What precisely are the qualifications required for your line of work, Ms, er, Coady, apart from deliciously slim ankles? GCSEs, or is it more dependent on low cunning?'

Eliza focused on the bare tanned feet that had clearly been shoved hurriedly into his tanned tasselled loafers, and felt her icy composure return. She said nothing.

'Look,' said Laurence Patterson, his florid good looks

starting to distort beneath a very thin film of sweat, 'you and I both know, David, that this could easily be swept under a handkerchief if needs be. Don't think I don't understand your tactics. You'd quite like my job yourself, wouldn't you? Only you hate having to ask people for funds. I, on the other hand, will happily ask anyone to donate to our beloved party. The old bags with their blue rinses, the young single mothers on welfare. The insufferable smug arseholes who are the backbone of golf clubs the length of this green and pleasant land. And that's what makes me rather good at what I do. It's called social inclusion. It's what the New Democratic Party is about, in case you'd forgotten. And without my fund-raising abilities, there wouldn't be a fucking party. Now I would offer you both another drink, but as I've already said, it's late.'

'Sorry if that seemed to be an appalling waste of time,' said David Crawford as the glass lift whooshed them down to the Embankment. 'He'll see the error of his ways. I just hope it's not too late.'

'Too late for what?' asked Eliza, looking vainly for a taxi.

'To save his skin. Not to mention the party,' he said sharply. The cold pierced their lungs like a bullet.

'Oh, I think the party's easily salvageable,' she said airily. 'Laurence Patterson, however, is probably a lost cause. But does that matter?'

'Of course it matters. He might be an insufferable shit but the old bags, the arseholes and the single mothers, unfathomable as it might seem, love him. And, regrettably, he's the best fund-raiser in the business. If this gets out in the open it could put us right back in the wilderness.'

'Surely he's not the only person who can organize a

whip-round. My PA, Rosie, can rustle up a mean collection when she puts her mind to it.'

'We're not talking about raising fifty pounds for some-one's leaving present, Eliza.'

'Now who's being patronizing? As a matter of fact, one of our clients, unpaid, of course, is Save a Child. Since we took over the publicity, donations have increased by three million pounds.'

He looked at her intently, his purple-grey eyes – the exact colour of sharkskin, thought Eliza – bore into her in a most unsettling manner. 'I appreciate what you're saying, Eliza. But I reiterate, the party cannot afford to lose Patterson.'

A taxi pulled over and she stepped in, quickly closing the door behind her. She had the feeling he might otherwise have followed her in. It was probably the wine blunting her intuition or Laurence Patterson's crude innuendo.

'I'll call you in the morning. Thank you for an interesting evening.' She reached through the open window and kissed him lightly on the cheek. It was, she reasoned, the only fitting response to someone who was, and always had been, an avuncular figure. Why then, she wondered, sinking back into the ridged leather seats, did she get the distinct and rather shocking feeling that he'd like to become something more?

Somehow, thought Eliza, gulping a second espresso *en route* for the shower, she needed to convince David Crawford that Laurence Patterson was dispensable. For most of the night her mind had teemed with stratagems to rescue his reputation, since that was what David clearly wanted. But by 5 a.m. she'd read about the mistresses, the petty cases of sexual harassment, the semi-neglected children, the overseas investments in companies that had long since been proven to use child labour, the tax evasions, falsified accounts, and failure to pay National Insurance contributions for at least three of his domestics. She was so disgusted that she decided to ignore the party panjandrums. Little tax problem indeed.

Besides, she was convinced that he wasn't actually as popular as the NDP obviously thought he was. She had a feeling for these things. If only there were time to commission a poll. Grabbing a towel, she stepped out of the shower, reached for the phone and dialled Pete Ruthers' home number.

'How quickly could you package together a survey on a politician?' she asked, excitedly.

'I don't know,' said Pete, scratching his head doubtfully on the other end of the line. 'I've never done a politician. Consumer polls are more my thing, as you know. Who's the unlucky subject?'

'Laurence Patterson.'

There was a startled silence at Pete's end.

'I'm asking you because you did such a brilliant job on Doggy-Dog. The questions were very lateral and very telling — and had an incredible accuracy score. And I think you'd give this a different approach from Mori.'

'What's he meant to have done?'

She gave him a brief résumé.

'Your average politician, in other words,' said Pete.

'They're not all that bad,' said Eliza, thinking of dinner the night before.

'Ah, the naïviety of youth,' said Pete.

'You've got two days.'

'Thanks.'

✳   ✳   ✳

Kate slipped out of Morton's, ostensibly on a coffee run, and sprinted over to 79 Wardour Street in Soho. Magda was waiting for her in the street, her red hair whipping around her face like an exotic cashmere scarf.

'I didn't want to go over the threshold without you,' she said, looping her arm through Kate's. 'This is a momentous day.' Immensely flattered, Kate took a step back and looked up at the rather wonky town house.

'We're on the top floor. No lift, needless to say, but think what it will do for our thighs,' burbled Magda ecstatically, struggling to turn the key and simultaneously heaving against the chipped brown door.

'There's a knack to this, and I haven't quite got it yet,' she said breathlessly as the door unexpectedly fell open and a corpulent, balding man in a cheap blue suit sidled past them sheepishly.

'*Charmant, non?* I was tipped off about it by one of the work experience at *A la Mode*. I think he and some friends had been squatting in it. The neighbours are terribly sweet, apparently.'

Kate could think of more appropriate words to describe the grimy chipboard in the entrance hall and the slimy, dirt-encrusted red carpet that more or less ran up the full six flights. Chargrilled, for instance, since most of the interior looked as though it had been fire-bombed. Never mind tip-off; rip-off would have been more accurate. She wondered if Bernie had seen the offices of his new publishing empire yet. The missing length of banister between floors four and five added a certain *frisson* to the journey too. But once inside the two smallish attic rooms and kitchenette that were to be *Domus*'s headquarters, she too was utterly beguiled.

'Of course, the whole place needs redecorating,' said Magda, as one of her legs disappeared through a loose rafter. 'I thought Jacobean meets Cecil Beaton.'

'You mean Jack the Lad, don't you?' volunteered Kate, giggling excitedly. 'The place is obviously a brothel.'

Magda looked at her uncomprehendingly. 'What I had in mind was the minimalism of Jacobean married to the flamboyance of Beaton. Can't you just see it?'

Kate couldn't exactly. But how thrilling to learn from a genius.

'You see, it's contrasts that excite me,' said Magda, her violet eyes narrowing dangerously. 'I like things to be airy, but with a touch of heaviness. New but old. Light but dark. Fresh but somehow stale . . .'

The impenetrable babble was interrupted by a trilling phone. Magda scowled so violently Kate thought her eyebrows might become fatally entangled. 'Who put that bloody thing in?' she said, stomping into the kitchenette whence the ringing emanated. 'I certainly didn't organize it. Who is it?' she barked into the mouthpiece. 'Bernie,' she mouthed silently to Kate, who stood in the middle of the rotting floorboards, gazing out at the rooftops of Soho.

'Bernie, did you order this phone to be installed?' she asked accusingly. 'Only I'm not sure that we're ready to be constantly pestered at the moment. It's important for us to have some contemplative time before we launch into the frenzy of producing a magazine.' She held the phone at arm's length from her ear. There was a pause while Kate made out a garbled Brummie accent that could slaughter pigs at fifty paces.

'I see,' said Magda darkly. 'Very well. But I warn you, I draw the line at a fax machine.'

'Well, really,' she said, slamming the phone down. 'Anyone would think he owned us. Just because we work for him doesn't mean he should be able to contact us at all hours of the day and night.'

Kate refrained from pointing out that since it was half past eleven in the morning, a phone call from their employer didn't exactly constitute a human rights abuse. Nor was it her place to explain that since they were meant to be producing their first issue in less than four months, the odd phone line might come in handy.

Personally she thought the combination of Magda's creativity and Bernie's deeply pragmatic approach to life (not to mention his deeply lined pockets) was most encouraging. She was doing the right thing, coming to work at *Domus*, she told herself for the thousandth time. Horrowitz's would definitely have to wait, or given the rate the solicitors were going, indefinitely wait. Overcome with excitement, she felt like hugging Magda.

'It's not just charming,' she said, breathless, 'it's perfect.'

Pete Ruthers did a brilliant, compelling job with his poll – not least because his findings corroborated Eliza's hunch about Laurence Patterson's unpopularity.

But that wasn't all. By an amazing coincidence, one of the women canvassed turned out to have been a former secretary of Laurence Patterson. She had left him after he'd raped her. After years of suppressing that fact – and the secret knowledge of all the documents he'd asked her to shred – she had gone up to Pete at the end of the session and quietly talked to him. She had even kept copies of the papers he'd asked her to destroy – documents that showed that Patterson was up to his neck in at least four scams that involved DTI seed money and that he had taken a large number of shares in two notoriously dodgy pension companies and a ten per cent stake in a company selling arms to Iraq.

It was these files that Eliza handed to Jim Allwater, leader of the NDP. Their contents weren't so much toxic as completely carcinogenic. And while the atmosphere was suitably polluted, she delivered her speech about Patterson being precisely the kind of politician that alienated the precious under-forty voter. If the NDP made a stand on this, she told Jim Allwater, it wouldn't just be showing the country it could keep its house in order, it would be making a stand about moral values in general.

Reluctantly, Jim Allwater conceded her points, thanked her and then thanked his lucky stars that Mrs Allwater wasn't anything like such a ball-breaker.

David thought she could break his balls any time she liked.

'So, if it's all right with you both,' said Eliza, snapping the buckle of her black patent trenchcoat, 'I'd recommend you delay the announcement until five. You'll miss the lunch-time bulletins, but it will be so much fresher for the six o'clock news – and that's the one the audience really tunes in for.'

Mentioning Boy George's name brought about an extraordinary transformation in people's reactions. After months of being unavailable, Wanda Devlin, agent to numerous soap stars, finally returned Martha's call and told her that yes, she might have some names on her book who would be interested in taking part. Her phone didn't stop ringing. The tabloids loved the whole thing, of course. 'Donna pulls it off,' sniggered the *Python*. 'The Bum Deal that got the ratings soaring,' trilled the *Digger* above a photograph of Donna in a flowing white silk dress that made her look like Richard Branson's missing balloon. The *Independent* ran a full-page article claiming that Donna Ducatti had an unerring instinct for popular entertainment that was almost highbrow in its sweep.

'I'll give them highbrow,' fumed Martha, as she waited another week for Jenny Stewart's letter. 'The only things capable of plunging lower than Donna's brow are her breasts.'

Laurence Patterson could take comfort in one thing, decided Eliza the following morning, luxuriating in Podge's absence and spreading the newspapers across her pristine linen sheets: his sacking dominated all the front pages, apart from the *Python*'s, which had given equal weight to Boy George's Knickers interview.

'The divine one's terribly impressed,' said David, lifting his wineglass in a discreet toast. They were having a celebratory lunch at the Savoy. 'He's very keen to get you on board as an adviser in some kind of official capacity.'

Eliza looked startled.

'He thinks you have your finger on the female pulse. I hope you'll think about it, at least.'

'I'd be rather foolish if I didn't.'

He leaned across and laid a proprietorial hand on hers, and she blushed to match the hue of the very expensive claret they were cheerfully working their way through. Despite her tiredness, the evening had been surprisingly relaxed.

'And one day,' he said conspiratorially, 'I hope you'll tell me exactly how you got hold of those documents.'

And then again, perhaps not, thought Eliza. She smiled enigmatically. She liked to keep him guessing. She hugged her knees gleefully. Never mind divulging Deep Throat. Just at this minute she was happy enough to indulge in a deep gloat.

At two minutes past five, Donna emerged triumphantly from Studio 1, a bottle of champagne in one hand, a sheaf of faxes from the tabloids in the other. *The Word* had been calling all day, desperate to get her on the show. Unsteadily she weaved her way over to Jem and Martha's matchbox. Boy George had been brilliant: witty, frank and just the right side of bawdy.

'Actually, I think the *underwear* leitmotif may *well* turn out to be one of the great interview devices of the *late* twentieth *century*,' she declaimed to the room. 'Who's Martyr got for *tomorrow?*'

'Janet Jackson,' said Martha, unable, despite her better judgment, to keep the satisfaction out of her voice.

Donna leaned tipsily against the door frame and fondled a hair extension, while pretending to ponder the choice of guest.

'Another *bloody* singer,' she said dismissively. 'Still, I suppose she'll *have* to do.'

Chapter Seven

Magda wasn't sure who was more irritating: Saddam Hussein for inciting the Gulf War or Bernie Higginbottom for delaying the launch of *Domus* which he had postponed from November until the New Year, to see what Saddam decided. 'War, of course,' snarled Magda, as if he'd done it to spite her. 'Surely,' she had argued, 'people will value their homes even more if there's a threat that they might be blown up at any second?'

Although normally Magda couldn't be bothered to get cross about anything, in this instance she was so incensed that she persuaded Kate to drive down with her to Bernie and Nancy Higginbottom's very own suburban sprawl in Berkshire for a summit. In retrospect Kate decided this inclusion had more to do with the fact that she had a car than anything else, since Magda barely let her get a word in edgeways.

To make matters worse, she only just avoided scraping the Spider on the gateposts that flanked Salam Walaykoom, the rambling stone house that Bernie had built when he came back to England from a fortnight in Morocco in the 1960s.

They bounced along the tarmac drive, coming to a halt by Nancy's personalised number plate, BIG N.

It was a house which even Bernie's most ardent admirers – and there were quite a few – had to admit wasn't a total aesthetic success. The garden, which had originally been surrounded by rolling meadows, was gradually being encroached on by Reading and what looked like a thousand rockeries. This, together with Nancy Higginbottom's habit of calling in the builders every time one of their increasingly grand friends came to stay, had given the whole place a rather haphazard appearance. The local planning department had given up objecting. It was such a jumble, they had decided that their best hope was to wait until it evolved into a fully blown folly, which the Higginbottoms could then bequeath to the nation.

'My God,' said Kate, shocked, even though Magda had prepared her on the journey for the worst. 'It looks like a geological eruption.'

'Wait till you meet Nancy,' muttered Magda as she rang the doorbell, setting off a jollied-up version of 'Greensleeves'.

Nancy Higginbottom was waiting for them in what she called the drawin' room, the pair of them a symphony of apricot ruching. 'I'm so pleased to see you again, Magda,' she said graciously. 'I can't tell you how much I'm looking forward to the publication of *Domus*. And you must be Kate.' She held out a chubby hand, and for one alarming moment Kate thought she was expected to kiss it.

Magda stared at Nancy with incomprehension as they were served clotted cream and scones amidst several acres of paper doilies. She couldn't understand a word of her strangulated Received Pronunciation. Kate didn't find it that easy either, which made conversation somewhat stilted.

'They're low-fat scones, girls.' Nancy beamed amiably. 'So gobble away. Cream or milk in your tea, by the way?'

Somewhat dazed, Kate gazed round the peachy planes of Nancy's drawin' room, which had clearly suffered a thousand deaths by rag-rolling. Magda's lessons on Roman blinds had evidently come to nothing. A stack of Herbal Life leaflets bearing the catchline 'Lose Weight Now, Ask Me How' were curling up next to the *Encyclopaedia Britannica*. The smell of sizzling dripping floated in aromatically from the kitchen.

'You will stay for lunch, I hope,' said Nancy, getting out a miniature set of Weight Watchers scales to weigh out her portion of low-fat chocolate biscuits. 'I was so looking forward to a little chat about sponging.'

Magda, as Kate was beginning to grasp, was a past mistress of sponging, especially when it came to Bernie's wallet, though she doubted that was quite the sponging Nancy had in mind. She couldn't help but warm to Nancy. She was clearly so eager to please. She seemed devoted to her family – there were framed photographs of unattractive children all over the place – and although *Tatler* had described her social skills as lacking in subtlety ('She has a propensity for bursting into rooms as enthusiastically as she bursts out of dresses,' it had sneered), Kate found her rather appealing.

And it wasn't her fault that she was on the plump side. Kate thought of Tatty and her all-encompassing knowledge of the calorie contents of the entire stock of Marks and Spencer. Fat lot of good it did her. Still, for Nancy and Tatty scrupulously adhering to the latest diet as well as some of the classics was a passion, diligently maintained and assiduously fanned. If only they could have managed not to follow them all simultaneously, they might even have lost some weight.

'I would love to talk to you about paint effects, Nancy,' said Magda in a contralto which lent itself perfectly to the sorrowful pitch at which she was now aiming. 'But I am so *distraite* at the moment, I can't really put my mind to anything much except this poor, benighted magazine of ours.'

'Oh dear, I'm so sorry to hear that, Magda,' clucked Nancy, pouring them all some more tea. 'Whatever is the matter?'

'It's Bernie,' said Magda tearfully. 'He wants to delay the publication. Because of some silly war. I'm afraid he's got cold feet. At this rate it'll be 2001 instead of 1991 by the time we launch this magazine.'

'Over my dead body.' Nancy sounded outraged, all her dreams of bumping into Princess Michael at the next Decorex exhibition disappearing in a cloud of Bernie's cowardice. 'Now, my dear.' She leaned over and patted Magda's knee. 'I can't think where Bernie could have got to. He's awfully fond of riding to hounds of a weekend, you know, but I wasn't aware he was riding to them today. Anyway, my dears, we'll hear no more about delays. I'll sort it for you. And now, tell me, have you seen any good window treatments lately?'

At two minutes to one Bernie strode noisily into the room, kissed his wife lovingly on her podgy shoulder, and took in the two girls, who were busy taking in his plus-fours and Pringle diamond-patterned sweater. He had been on the golf course and was glowing puce.

'Now then, Magda,' he said briskly, 'to what do we owe this pleasure?'

'Er, shall we withdraw to the dinin' room?' said Nancy tactfully.

All through lunch, Nancy steered away from talk of business with the delicacy of a sheepshearer who finds himself suddenly asked to do a bikini wax. Kate had to admit that she did it efficiently, however. Magda was practically incandescent with impatience. She crossed and uncrossed her fisherman's wader boots so violently it was like having an electric fan under the table. Over pudding – a reduced-cholesterol Stilton, walnuts and 'as an afterthought', said Nancy, cheesecake – Magda cracked nuts so loudly in her bare hands that Nancy, who flinched every time she did so, was in danger of becoming a nervous wreck.

'That's quite a gift you've got there, Magda,' remarked Bernie.

'It's the least of my talents,' she retorted, her voice steeped in Brechtian sorrow. 'But at the moment it's the only one that is getting an airing. I do hope, Bernie, that you're not wavering.'

'Shall we withdraw to the drawin' room?' butted in Nancy, sensing a storm brewing.

'It's only for a few months,' Bernie resumed later, when Nancy was out of earshot. He shifted uneasily in a snug peach velvet Parker Knoll that was several inches too snug for his girth. 'I promise.' He leaned over and patted Magda's crenellated fist, practically impaling himself on her new Solange Azagury ring.

Not remotely appeased, Magda split another walnut, dearly hoping that Nancy would find Bernie equally easy to crack.

❋   ❋   ❋

That same afternoon the long-awaited letter confirming Jenny Stewart's job offer arrived by messenger at Bog Standard Radio.

'Blimey, are you up the duff or something?' said Samantha, sauntering over to Martha with the recorded delivery.

Martha smiled vaguely. It wasn't Samantha's fault if the only letters that came special delivery where she lived were ones from the bailiffs or clinics. She took the letter as casually as she could and then rushed to the loos to gloat.

The salary wasn't quite what she'd hoped for, but then they'd never really discussed it. Anyway, what did money matter when job satisfaction was at stake? She reread the letter several times – Jenny sounded genuinely thrilled that she was joining – and then stuffed it into the top of her jogging pants. It made her feel inviolate, like armour – not least because it was scratching like mad. Never mind. She couldn't wait to tell Donna, and marched back to her den to prepare her leaving speech.

'The thing is,' Mark Lacy began tentatively, as Vince slammed some smeary glasses in front of him and Tatty, 'business is a bit slack at the moment. It's very tough out there on the retail front line.'

Tatty sat before him expectantly but non-judgmentally. Her good spirits were as bouncy as her pneumatic thighs and breasts – attributes Mark Lacy valued deeply because, he had correctly guessed, it meant Tatty wouldn't complain about having to design for size 16-pluses.

Her creamy skin flushed delicately, as if a bowl of strawberries had leaked into it. Her nose, blotchy from hayfever, added a raspberry ripple effect which set off her pink-and-orange Arabella Pollen suit rather sweetly, thought Mark.

'It must be very stressful for you,' she gently prompted. 'Still, I'm sure that whatever you decide, we'll all understand. I do anyway.' She fumbled around with the cork. 'I'm not that worried about losing my job, actually. Golly, I hope that doesn't sound arrogant. It's just that my father always says everyone should be fired once. Good for the fibre.'

Mark thought fibre was the last thing he'd need if anything as awful as redundancy ever happened to him. He was just pondering what kind of a father could encourage his children to get sacked when it occurred to him that she must have thought he was hinting at getting rid of her.

'I-I-I didn't mean you, Tatty,' he stammered. 'In fact, I didn't mean anyone. At least, I hope not. There are lots of cutbacks we can make before we start eating into the workforce. Oh gosh, that would be terrible.' The thought of having to fire anyone nearly brought on one of his migraines.

Tatty beamed. She could think of half a dozen workers in her office alone who couldn't be described as an asset by any stretch, but felt it probably wasn't the time to point this out. Still, she'd have to find the moment sooner or later.

'Cutbacks?' she said softly. 'You mean like reorganizing the invoicing system? It is rather antiquated. Or did you want to bring the PR office in-house first?'

'Er, the jury's still out,' mumbled Mark, blushing. He had been so busy the past fortnight chasing numbers across spreadsheets, searching vainly for anomalies and oversights into which the smallest saving could be accommodated, that the jury was about the only thing that had been out. His social life was so dead it made downtown Eastbourne look positively throbbing. 'Tatty, you wouldn't like to put some suggestions down in writing, would you? I think it's important these things are tackled in a democratic fashion, don't you?'

Flushed with pleasure, Tatty said she would simply adore to. Then she told him about an idea she'd had to launch an in-store magazine to go with Xtra, the teenage capsule collection Kate had inaugurated which she had since taken over. 'And if that works,' she said, her eyes shining as brightly as her underused credit cards, 'we could launch a magazine for the bigger woman. I've already done a dummy, actually. It's called *Buxom*. You'll probably think it's rubbish,' she added shyly, 'but it's the kind of thing I know I'd like to read. Lots of useful tips. I thought it might give us an edge over the competition. And I thought maybe we could do an Xtra bigger-sister range called Xtra Too.'

Mark listened to her babble on, thrilled that at last someone who worked for him was exhibiting some enthusiasm that wasn't the result of antidepressants. His wine cup veritably overran with happiness, which was just as well because it wasn't going to be filled by Vince. Brimming with an inexplicably festive sense of collaboration, he and Tatty threw caution to the wind, and asked Vince for another bowl of Twiglets.

Tatty practically floated out of Your Place or Wine, which was no mean feat considering she and Mark had each polished off a portion of Vince's chilli con carne. She was so relieved that she wasn't about to lose her job. It meant she could finally plan the rest of her life. And she would start by buying a flat of her own.

It was all very well being a property mogul, she told herself, but not if you still lived in your parents' pied-à-terre in South Ken. It was lovely of them to have given her the free run of it for so long – not that she had used it that much lately, having spent so much of her spare time round at Nigel's.

But now that Nigel had decided that Tatty was just one ball too many for him to juggle in his hectic, successful life (funny that, Tatty had thought miserably at the time, she hadn't noticed he had any balls at all), it was definitely time to move on. Mummy was in tears, of course, especially when Tatty had explained that not only was she boyfriendless, she was looking for her own place in Shepherd's Bush.

She hadn't told Kate that she was going to look at her flat. Not that she'd seen Kate or even heard much from her since she'd gone to work at *Domus*. Morton's didn't really make the kind of things that might be called in for shoots. She did it all strictly through the estate agents, visiting the flat when Kate was out.

It was every bit as gorgeous as she had imagined. Kate's bedroom, with its white fairy lights round the little Victorian fireplace, and muslin-shrouded bed, was idyllic. Like something out of a Dickens novel. Tatty wanted to buy the whole thing then and there, lock, stock and Christmas carol.

She couldn't for the life of her work out why Kate wanted to sell it, especially now that her plans to open a shop appeared to have been put on hold. But then she bumped into Kate one day in Portobello, and Kate told her that she wanted to consolidate her money so that she wouldn't be dependent on her father any more. She was moving in with Magda, who lived in part of a converted theatre in Spitalfields which, according to Kate, was riddled with ghosts, lots of original dry rot and hot and cold running damp.

'The great thing is,' Kate told Tatty cheerfully as she haggled with Reg shamelessly over a rickety spinning wheel that looked as though it would collapse the next time anyone sneezed, 'that I've finally found a buyer. They want to buy the lot. All that ghastly old Swedish stuff. That look is so passé, don't you think? And they're paying the full asking price.'

Tatty gazed after Kate's receding cloak wistfully. How was she ever going to find the courage to face Kate once she discovered that the poor sucker who was buying the flat was her? She tried to imagine what the house in Spitalfields must look like. It sounded very exotic, she thought, resolving to inject a little more atmosphere into her next capsule collection for Morton's.

As predicted by Nancy Higginbottom, Bernie soon relented on his decision to postpone the launch of *Domus*. Not only that, but the magazine's budgets were ridiculously generous. Magda, used to the clamp-fisted approach of most British publishing companies – which was why she could never stop moonlighting – had basically tripled her initial estimates in preparation for an almighty financial battle, only to have Bernie green-light everything.

Even so, it wasn't easy furnishing the offices of *Domus*. Magda had changed her mind about Jacobean and decided on Zen instead. She had already installed half a dozen tatami mats, and liked the empty effect so much that she was having problems co-ordinating anything else.

'Do we have to have desks?' she asked Kate plaintively, her voice echoing ominously around the bare walls.

'Yes,' said Kate firmly. 'And we'll need computers, faxes and a few more phones too. Now don't look so disappointed.'

In between trying to get hold of some white desks that Magda had heard about which had apparently been made by a collective of blind Buddhist monks, Kate began drawing up short lists for the other members of staff from the vague descriptions Magda had given her.

'You've simply got to get hold of this divine-looking girl I bumped into at Lachlan O'Hennessy's primal poetry reading the other night. I think she'd be perfect as a features assistant.'

'Where is she working at the moment?' asked Kate with a sinking sense of hopelessness.

'Dunno.' Magda shrugged. 'But she's got oodles of style. If you hang around 192 long enough you're bound to run into her. Ruby, I think her name was. She's got the voice *d'un ange*. I'd ring Lachlan but he's gone off to the Bahamas to find inspiration for his second volume of poetry. You wouldn't believe the way his publishers are hounding him.'

Kate was beginning to get used to the way Magda peppered her conversation with names of the rich and famous. Or, in Lachlan's case, infamous. It wasn't so much stealth bombing as wealth bombing. She knew everyone. Kate, despite having grown up in a household where politicians and guests from *The South Bank Show* regularly dropped in, was deeply impressed. Her parents' friends seemed distinctly old-school compared with Magda's set, who probably hadn't been to school at all. Certainly Lachlan O'Hennessy, notorious for his raw, empty view of life, had set new standards of illiteracy with his first slim volume of poetry. The publishing world had naturally suffered a collective hernia in the stampede to sign him up for his next *thinus opus*. After an unseemly scrum, Vickers & Snood had snagged him for a cool million, which he was evidently putting to good use on some raw, empty golden beach.

In the end Ruby had tracked *them* down. It turned out that Magda had accidentally swept off from Lachlan's primal poetry reading with Ruby's vintage Pucci scarf and, after some investigative work in which Ruby had managed to locate Lachlan via ship radio on some glass-bottomed boat just off Glitter Bay, she had dropped into Wardour Street to collect it. They heard her voice first, coming up the stairs, the same voice, thought Kate, spirits plummeting, that all posh girls adopt when they're trying to sound as though they graduated from borstal rather than Bristol.

To Magda's eternal disappointment, her name wasn't actually Ruby but Trudy. Still, she was as stunning as a cattle prod in her crimson, laddered fishnets and a short black velvet miniskirt that had probably served time as a choker in another life. Magda offered her the job there and then.

Trudy, or Ruby as Magda persisted in calling her — and insisted that Kate address her in the contract they drew up together — had been trying to break into journalism for ages. She had even penned the odd piece for the *Face*, but the money was so bad she had been supplementing her work by waitressing at 192. So Magda's hunch about Kate finding her there had been right. As had her gut reaction that Ruby would be plugged in to every zeitgeist in London.

Despite Bernie's lavish budgets, which Magda was doing her best to burn through by flying all over the world to shoot precious objets – even though the original idea had been to have everything photographed against plain backgrounds of fuchsia, turquoise and yellow – she wanted to keep the staff small. She said it was more creative. So Ruby had to double as editorial assistant and Senior Feature Writer, depending on Magda's mood – and Kate had to do just about everything else. As a huge concession to reality, Magda drafted in her old mucker Fenton Wigstaff. Fenton was a brilliant art director who had made his name five years ago on account of his dazzlingly original layouts for the highly acclaimed launch issue of the *International Gazette*'s classy Sunday supplement – and the fact that he had moved into one of the desks there.

'You mean he worked long hours?' asked Ruby, stapling together the ends of a Lurex Missoni napkin that had been left lying around to make a miniskirt, allegedly in preparation for her monthly 'Why Don't You?' feature but in reality for a party at the *Face* that night.

Magda looked at her, uncomprehending. 'No, I mean he lived in one of the desks,' she repeated slowly, as if living out of a filing cabinet were the most natural thing in the world.

For a while Fenton had been the talk of the Groucho, although lately he hadn't been seen around much owing to his unfortunate inability to remember to pay his taxes. As a consequence he'd spent the last couple of years living between two bookcases at the *Sydney Herald*.

'The taxmen absolutely harassed him,' said Magda,

moist-eyed. She'd just returned from a boozy lunch with Fenton at Kensington Place, during which she'd signed him up. 'You'd think they'd at least have some respect for genius. Fenton's a god where graphics are concerned. There's nothing he can't do with Times Roman Bold.'

With the main components of the *Domus* masthead in place, it remained for Kate to track down the Buddhist desks which, alas, turned out to have been a dream Magda had after one of her high-paying all-night freelance styling sessions for Homebase. In desperation, Kate ordered some interlocking units from Ikea on to which she spent three weeks gluing little mirrored mosaic tiles because Magda was having a Moroccan phase.

Unfortunately a phase was all it was. By the time Magda got back from shooting a load of loofahs in Mauritius against plain fuchsia, turquoise and yellow backdrops, she was in love with Cretan style. But it was too late to get rid of the desks. Fenton, whose unfortunate run-ins with Her Majesty's fiscal officials had left him with an otherworldly view of possessions, had moved in under one of them with his freebie Versace sleeping bag and, with the launch date of *Domus* looming, Magda didn't dare upset his delicate equilibrium by suggesting he relocate.

Martha was listening to the Russian election coverage on Radio Four through her Walkman headphones and was so stirred by Boris Yeltsin's acceptance speech that she almost forgot about her leaving speech. And the phone next to her had rung at least half a dozen times before she heard it. She picked it up guiltily, half expecting Donna to bawl her out for missing a cue. Ever since Donna's favourite tan-coloured Versace leggings with the blue swirls had shrunk, her moods had been more volatile than an evening with Marco Pierre White.

'I was about to give up on you. I thought you must have gone on strike.' The voice on the other end was attractively resonant, with a slight break in it, and the faintest echo of an accent that Martha couldn't quite put her finger on.

'Who is it?' she asked suspiciously. She had forty seconds to get the nine o'clock bulletin into Donna — and she hadn't written it.

'Nick Wilde.'

Unable to process this shocking information, her brain went on strike.

'Returning your call. About the knickers slot,' he said helpfully.

'Oh, piss off, Jem,' she retorted good-naturedly, putting the phone down. Glancing at the clock, she typed in two rather spiky comments about the government's attitude to British businesses, which were going bust at a rate of eighty-six a day, and a ghoulish tidbit on street crime from Rembrandt. Thirty-four seconds to go. She punched the print key. The machine whirred feebly, choked and began flashing histrionic Out of Ink warnings. Martha felt her top lip melting. The phone rang again. She ignored it as long as she could until her journalistic instincts got the better of her.

'Is that how you treat all your guests?'

'*Fuck* off,' she fumed, slamming the phone down before frantically rummaging in her drawer for some ink. Five seconds. She rammed in the cartridge and the machine juddered into action. She skidded into Studio B five seconds late. Donna appeared not to notice. And Martha's digs about the government passed too.

'That's ten—six to me,' said Martha jauntily, poking her head into Jem's control room.

'The trouble with your so-called political digs,' said Jem, looking especially owlish, 'is that they're so subtle absolutely no one picks up on them. You're about as provocative as a *Tammy* annual.'

'And your impressions are about as convincing as Dick van Dyke's,' she retorted. He gazed at her blankly.

'Have it your own way,' she said, sauntering down the corridor to their matchbox. Back at her computer she opened a new file for her resignation speech. She had decided on a dignified Churchillian tone. Instead the list of celebrities lined up to do Knickers flashed at her spitefully. It was really quite impressive. Ever since Boy George, people had been queuing up to be on it. It was a terrible indictment of the bankrupt state of modern culture, mused Martha, distracted from her speech by the new cover of *Hello!* Amanda de Cadenet was not looking her best. She sighed and typed: *'Never in the history of broadcasting has so much been suffered by so few'* (that was meant to be her).

It wasn't quite right. She began again, but everything kept coming out sounding a bit pompous. The phone rang again. This time the line was crackly.

'I'm calling from LA on behalf of Nick Wilde, you piece of snot,' said a bleary voice that sounded as though it were coming from the bottom of Donna's tube of Helena Rubinstein Extra Cover. 'For some reason he wants to be on your radio show. He thinks it's cult. And some little asshole keeps putting the phone down on him. Deal with it, will you?'

Then seconds later the phone went again. Whoever it was did have a lovely voice, now Martha came to think about it, full of sincerity and veiled intensity.

'You're not going to put the phone down on me again, are you?' he said. Martha's knees went wobbly. It was a voice that could sell modern architecture to Prince Charles, the joys of modesty to Donald Trump, and the art of low maintenance to his ex-wife.

'I thought you were a prankster,' she said weakly.

'So I gather.'

'It's just that I can't quite work out why you want to do it.'

'I think it's funny.' His laugh was one part honey, two parts gravel. 'It can be a little draining just doing Shakespeare and thrillers, you know.'

Martha didn't know. The last time she'd had a spare minute to go to the cinema, *Chitty Chitty Bang Bang* had been top of the box-office ratings. 'So you'll do it?' she asked disbelievingly.

'Pleasure. It'll be some light relief,' he drawled.

Martha practically bounced back into Studio B to inform Donna of her catch of the day, only to hear Donna firing her. The ungrateful witch, fumed Martha, all thoughts of dignity and Churchillian structure crashing about her trainers.

'Sorry to disappoint you, Donna,' she extemporised, 'but my letter of resignation is already in your locker. I'm finished with casting pearls before swine. Talk about swill party. I'm off to work at a place where the audience IQ soars above double figures.'

Donna looked at her blankly. 'Frankly the only reason your audience gets into multiple digits is because most of them are so stupid they don't know how to reset the dial. I know you like to think this dross is pioneering, but the only groundbreaking that goes on at BSR is when you put on weight. And the only thing that remotely resembles a zoo around here is your hair. Frankly I can't wait to go. Pity about Nick Wilde, though. Oh, and by the way, I've been meaning to tell you, those Versace leggings with the stems on? They make you look as though you've got terrible varicose veins. Don't bother to see me out!'

As speeches go, it hit its mark. Martha was so astonished by her own catty fluency that she didn't register the ON AIR sign until she heard Donna mellifluously crooning into the microphone.

'Why don't you tell us what you *really* feel about our loyal audience, Martyr? *Seriously*, folks, you heard it here *first*,' she said, without missing a beat. 'The truth *hurts*, but at least you got it *straight* from the *horse's* mouth. And if you could see what Martyr was wearing today, you'd know I do *mean* horse.'

Chapter Eight

The downside of Kate's life at *Domus* after eight months was that despite her best attempts to maintain a Zen-like oasis of space and calm, the clutter kept on accumulating. Since she had arrived she had received more mail – in the form of press releases – than during her entire life. It bulged out of the buff files that were stacked round the outer reaches of her desk like sandbags.

Mountains of English crockery, Swedish picture frames, German cushions, Italian ergonomic kitchenware, Japanese light fittings, Austrian throws, Sri Lankan chrysanthemum-flavoured tea bags, Irish linen, French tea towels and American Shaker-style Christmas tree decorations kept arriving with relentless regularity. As, for reasons no one had quite worked out, did batches of smoky bacon from the Danish tourist office and crates of two-hundred-year-old extra-virgin olive oil from Languedoc.

'Does extra-virgin mean it has to be kept in the frigid?' Fenton asked, eager to find new ways to cook his smoky bacon. They weren't just suffering from bacon overload. They had more candles than the Vatican. And because they never had time to send anything back the office now looked like the first day of the Harrods sale. So Kate should have known she was asking for trouble when she borrowed half a dozen dogs from the Battersea Dogs Home to liven up a tartan throw shoot. Sure enough, by the time she finally persuaded Fenton to help her return them they seemed to have acquired an extra one.

'Not ours, love,' said the warden.

'Well, it's not mine,' said Kate, ignoring the pleading eyes of the warden, only to find herself staring into the chocolatey irises of the dog.

'We're overcrowded as it is,' said the warden, scratching his head despairingly.

There was no way Kate was going to get landed with a dog on top of everything else. Especially an ugly one that looked like a cross between a Jack Russell and a Rottweiler.

'No,' she said firmly.

The dog whimpered. 'No,' said Kate again, and turned round resolutely. The dog pattered after her pleadingly.

'Sod off,' hissed Kate.

'You're a hard woman,' said the warden, scratching his head sadly.

Indeed I am, thought Kate contentedly. She didn't care if yuppies were as relevant these days as Curiosity Killed the Cat. She was finally about to become one.

'Strays are very easy to look after,' said Fenton helpfully, as they squeezed in on either side of Nibbles in the taxi on the way back to the office, the warden having promised them that there was absolutely no trace of Rottweiler that he could discern in the animal. 'Just chuck 'em a bone from time to time and, when they need exercise, tie them to the back of your car.'

Eventually, what with all the late nights Kate put in at the office, she grew to appreciate Nibbles' company on her journeys back to Spitalfields, although she didn't remotely appreciate imperfect strangers stopping to tell her she ought to muzzle her Rottweiler.

She'd given up all hope of a social life. Not that she minded. *Domus* was her life and family rolled into one – a state of affairs Eliza and Sadie complained about bitterly. Martha, on the other hand, was so busy herself she barely seemed to notice that it had been months since they had shared a proper heart-to-heart. Still, Kate consoled herself there was nothing she didn't now know about *How to Turn Your Broom Cupboard into Versailles, How to Make a Moroccan Souk in Your Bedroom,* or *How to Transform Your Garden into Sissinghurst.*

There was nothing like the thrill of going through the new issue before it hit the news-stands. The sense of satisfaction, the air of tremendous camaraderie, the immense fulfilment would probably have been overpowering, if they weren't so exhausted. 'What we need,' yawned Ruby one night, her lightly consonated voice floating in through the kitchenette where she was opening another bottle of vermouth, 'is a celebrity pad. Some big, fuck-off venue that everyone will talk about over their sun-dried lentils.'

Magda, who was sniffing a pile of Balinese bamboo night-light holders, shot her a withering look. Since *Domus* had launched eight months ago, the love affair between Magda and Ruby had dimmed, not least because Ruby's ring of confidence had grown so much it was now blinding.

Magda just about put up with her because she was very good at her job; so uncannily spot on at predicting the next big thing that Magda was beginning to suspect she might be taking night classes in astrology – except that she didn't see when Ruby could possibly have squeezed them into her schedule, which was even more tightly-packed than her Wonderbra.

The whole team was marvellous. They worked harder than galley slaves, but without the moaning. And the simmering rivalry that Magda had done her utmost to fan between Kate, who supplied a good deal of the magazine's most striking visuals, and Ruby, who provided its words, was proving to be a creative furnace. In its last seven issues, *Domus* had been first among the glossies to tackle *The New Lava Lamp*, *The New Tidy*, *The New Rattan*, *The New Ethnic*, *The New Stripy* (Kate got particularly emotionally entangled over that one), *The New Toile de Jouy* and *The New Messy*.

'We've got Phoebe Keane,' offered Kate helpfully. It was eleven o'clock and she and Fenton were sprawled over his sleeping bag.

'Yeah, but you haven't really done Phoebe's *house*, have you?' persisted Ruby, cupping her left breast in a quilted Hermès oven glove to see if it could be adapted into a bikini. 'It's more those rug thingies she designs.'

'Kilims,' corrected Kate pedantically. 'And they're rather beautiful,' she added admiringly. Phoebe Keane had turned out to be multi-talented.

'That's hardly going to wipe the floor with the competition, is it?' sniffed Ruby.

'An actress who starts fiddling around making knick-knacks is an actress whose career is knick-knackered,' said Fenton puckishly as he attempted to set light to a box of snuff Magda had given him. She'd told him it was the New Marijuana.

'She makes them on set to pass the time,' said Kate defensively. She had been very taken with Phoebe when she'd visited her at home in Canonbury Square. Whether this was down to the opium they had polished off, the fact that Phoebe was wearing the most gorgeous antique emerald lace dress that set off her saffron-coloured bob and pale skin to a tee, the handcuffs Kate had spied hanging from Phoebe's very cool four-poster, or the fact that her bathroom was painted the exact shade of lilac Kate had been trying to get for ages, she wasn't sure. But Phoebe was definitely Kate's new crush. She could even act – Kate and Sadie had watched her on TV at Christmas in a German-Hungarian modern-day version of *Hamlet*. It had been a very loose version, with Hamlet cast as a bus-driver and Ophelia as his conductress, but Phoebe had been brilliant.

'What about something really provocative, like *Why Fishing Is the New Sex*?' suggested Ruby.

'Your plaice or mine?' sniggered Kate.

Fenton, who hadn't suggested a single idea so far, raised his eyes. 'Oh, *puhlease*. Whatever happened to glamour? What about doing a retro piece on Bette Davis's house?'

'Now that really would be going for old trout,' snapped Ruby.

'If we're going to do a celeb, then it has to be really vulgar, so people realize we're being ironic. Irony is the New, um—' said Magda, removing a box of matches from Fenton.

'Sarcasm?' offered Ruby helpfully.

'What about Troy la Finet?' asked Fenton, suddenly rousing himself from the depths of his Versace quilting.

'They're planning a huge retrospective of his work at the Tate next autumn, so he's very much *au courant* again.'

Magda's eyebrow shot up. The last time Fenton had visited Troy's villa in Tangier, the two of them had run through £12,000 of expenses in a weekend, and Michael Croft, the *International Gazette*'s lawyer, had ended up flying out to extricate Fenton, Troy and two fifteen-year-old Moroccan boys from prison.

'I'll make a note of it,' she said dryly, duly jotting it down and then setting light to it, 'and perhaps we could get Kate to go out and do him a bit closer to the show.'

'Scorcher Morehouse has a manor house in Devon which is incredible, apparently,' said Ruby.

'That's true,' said Magda, knowing everything and everyone as usual. 'Since his most recent session in rehab he's given up heroin and become addicted to Chippendale instead. But the last time I visited Meadowlands it wasn't finished. What do you think, Fenton?'

'If it's anything like his old place in Chelsea it could be okay,' said Fenton grudgingly. He prided himself on being rock-chick-in-chief, and was annoyed that he hadn't suggested Scorcher. 'But he's a bit raddled, isn't he?'

'Lived in,' sighed Ruby, who had another successful parallel career as a groupie and had hankered after Scorcher ever since their one-night stand at Knebworth. 'The wounds of his life are present on his face, yes, but the wrinkles and lines are simply the contours of history. And I for one find them very beautiful.'

'That's settled, then,' said Magda spitefully. 'I'll give him a call and Kate can pop down and do the story on Friday.'

*　　*　　*

Two days later, a nervous Kate, who wasn't used to doing interviews, settled gingerly back into the polyester depths of a railway compartment as the forlorn suburbs of Reading gave way to promising glimpses of lush green Berkshire countryside. She was accompanied by Fenton, who was trying to get another career as a photographer off the ground and had bullied Magda into letting him shoot the story and put a massively complicated new camera with more controls than the flight deck of Apollo 19 on expenses.

They were met at Torquay station by a vintage silver-blue Bentley and Douggie Kenwood, a dapple-cheeked pixie with marmalade tufts of hair shooting out of his ears, a good-natured squint, and more freckles than Kate had ever seen, apart from the time she had accompanied Martha to a Fergie look-alike convention for BSR. A former jockey, he was so small his head barely reached the top of the Bentley's dashboard. He also had a habit of screwing up his eyes so tightly against the dazzling late winter sunshine that she doubted whether the Bentley, having magnificently survived four decades, would reach the end of the next journey intact.

'Mr Morehouse likes to feel the elements,' confided Douggie ruefully, cigarette ash scattering to the four winds as he twisted round to talk to Kate, who was huddled in the back seat. 'Even in January. It's elements this, elements that. I once said to him, "Wouldn't you prefer to feel the filaments?" It was a hint, like, to get the radiators fixed.' Douggie chuckled until Kate thought he might choke on his rollie. 'But I don't think he got it. He doesn't even like to have the heating on. Says it's bad for the complexion.'

It was a little late for Scorcher to be worrying about the effects of central heating on his skin, thought Kate. Judging by recent photographs, not even moving into an igloo would save him. Still, at least his nose appeared to be intact, unlike one of the other Stenchies who had shoved so much coke up his nostrils he was rumoured to Sellotape his septum in place every time he went on-stage.

Douggie pressed the accelerator, as if speed would somehow warm them, and switched on Bog Standard Radio, while Rizlas flew out of the glove compartment like a jetstream of confetti.

As they ricocheted round the tiny lanes, twigs snapping and scraping against the Bentley like over-enthusiastic percussionists, Kate breathed in the damp air, filtered by the rich russet Devon soil. Above her soared the moist, creamy-coloured sky. She gazed up and thought wistfully of the lavish picnics Sadie used to prepare and of her father, who always turned up — albeit at the last minute — looking like a classic English squire by way of *L'Uomo Vogue*. She had loved those outings.

Fenton shivered theatrically while Douggie and Kate chatted. He had never got the point of the countryside except as a backdrop to a fashion shoot — and even then he thought foliage should be kept to a minimum. The rest of the time it bored him rigid, and he couldn't understand how Scorcher could bear to sequester himself away in all this soil and hedgerow, unless of course he was still secretly imbibing copious amounts of illegal substances.

But even Fenton had to admit that Meadowlands was ravishing. A classic Elizabethan manor built in the shape of an E, with a trail of eighteenth-century thatched outbuildings, its tawny brick exterior glowed in the sunshine like a radiant red setter who had just given birth to a litter of puppies.

'Welcome, travellers, to my manse,' boomed a voice so cracked it sounded Palaeolithic. A familiar yet shockingly skeletal figure in black skittered across the sweep of gravel drive to meet them. As he neared, flanked by three enormous Irish wolfhounds and what looked like a geriatric poodle, she could see that the dyed raven hair had been woven into plaits and threaded with what looked like budgerigar feathers, so that he looked as though he had some ancient farmyard gate swinging from his head.

'Here, Velasquez. Come on, Ingres and El Greco. And you, Frou-Frou, you old bugger.' He whistled to the dogs, swivelling on his pixie boots and looking like a spider who'd been involved in a caffeine experiment.

Kate gazed up at Meadowlands' glorious display of mullioned windows. 'At least one of them's aged well,' she muttered under her breath to Fenton.

'The good news as far as the ratings are concerned,' said Jenny Stewart, leaning back in her favourite chair at the Caprice, 'is that it's all looking absolutely appalling in Bosnia. If things carry on like this, we'll be so desperate for reporters you'll be drafted out there in a few weeks.'

Martha's eyes practically flipped into her salmon fishcakes with excitement. But Jenny thought she'd insulted her.

'No offence, Martha, but you're not exactly experienced on the war front.'

No point denying that, thought Martha. Cindy Crawford's front, however, was another question entirely. In fact, what Martha didn't know about supermodels' mammaries could be written on the back of their G-strings. Ever since she had arrived, Jenny had pigeonholed her as the reporter who could put a highbrow spin on trash – and all because the audience figures for Donna's Cookin' Breakfast had shot through the roof since Martha's first and last on-air performance at BSR.

At first Martha had tried to kid herself that Jenny Stewart's insatiable appetite for trivia was just her way of testing her out on lighter stories before she put her on the Westminster beat. But for eight months, until this moment, there had been no sign of the floodtide of drivel abaiting. And the veneer of respectability which Martha had given her first few drossy stories was now wearing thinner than Arthur Scargill's hair. She had even drawn up one of her lists of World Events for 1992. While Labour had marched to another defeat, riots erupted in LA and America prepared for its elections, Martha had been chatted up by Peter Stringfellow in the middle of a supposedly serious interview about the bankruptcy of his nightclub empire; conducted a vox pop in which she'd canvassed most of Oxford Street to see whether they preferred Demi Moore as a blonde or a brunette; ridden through Oxford on Clive Sinclair's new Zike, to hoots of derision from the students; gone on a wine crawl to retrace Norman Lamont's steps round his favourite branches of Oddbins; camped all night outside Books Etc on Charing Cross Road with all the other ghouls waiting for Madonna's *Sex* book to go on sale; and covered a mini-conflagration on the set of *Eldorado*. If she ever wrote her autobiography she could call it *Bonfire of the Inanities*.

It was during the Madonna investigative assignment that she had shamingly bumped into Jack, as he was returning victorious from a late night interview with Andrew Morton about his Diana book. He was in high spirits, not to mention beer and wine.

'Well, well, well, if it isn't the Kate Adie of Bond Street,' he said, practically tripping over her Thermos, as she huddled on the pavement taking down her interviewees' names with a leaky Biro. She hurled him what she hoped was a lacerating scowl and pretended to adjust the sound levels on her tape recorder.

'Oh, now, don't look at me like that, Martha, my sweet,' he cooed thickly, sounding for all the world as if he'd just this minute stepped out of a Bailey's ad. 'It's lovely to see you.'

Four hours later, he told her how it was even better to see all of her.

She blamed her appalling lack of self-discipline on the fact that she'd been freezing her ballpoints off – Jack's exceedingly warm flat had always been her undoing, or at any rate her undressing. As penance she forced herself to listen while he rhapsodized on about his coverage of Black Wednesday and how his reports on the Kevin and Ian Maxwell court case and the European single market were up for an award. No surprise there, thought Martha bitterly. If there was one subject Jack was world expert on it was the singles market.

'You look great, Martha, by the way,' he mumbled as she got dressed. 'New wardrobe?'

As a matter of fact, she had been shopping – in Joseph – but only to while away the time while she was waiting for Princess Stephanie of Monaco to come out of the changing room so that she could interview her for an item Jenny had asked her to do about celebrities and their bodyguards. Inspired by Jenny, whose favourite reading was *American Vogue*, she had blown two months' wages on a capsule wardrobe that consisted of a black leather jacket, a pair of leggings and two T-shirts. Together with all the unguents and expensive make-up that came her way via Kate from the magazine, she was dangerously close to looking glamorous.

The one positive outcome of the whole evening was that she was no longer remotely attracted to Jack. He was getting distinctly paunchy, and if it hadn't been for his boiler she would never have spent the night.

'When will I see you again?' he asked, catching hold of her wrist as she was about to swing out of his front door.

In the dock, when I'm being tried for your attempted murder, she thought. She mumbled something inaudible.

'I'll call you,' he said.

Don't bother, she thought.

'You didn't actually eat a raw goldfish?' giggled Kate, appalled. She was seated beneath the minstrels' gallery in the vaulted dining hall where they had been served a delicious lunch of sea bass, fresh vegetables and fragrant wild rice while Scorcher Morehouse regaled her and Fenton with a volley of outrageous anecdotes. Even Velasquez, El Greco and Ingres, the three wolfhounds, wagged their tails appreciatively, while Frou-Frou treated the room to a series of increasingly noxious emissions.

'Actually it was a koi,' said Scorcher with mock pomp. 'I had to. It had a gram of heroin in it. I was a bit desperate in those days, you see. I got the chef to make a mornay sauce for it. Sorry about Frou-Frou, by the way.' Aware that she was being talked about, the mottled poodle attempted a mournful flutter of what remained of her pom-pom tail. 'She was me mum's. Must be about a hundred and three in dog years. She stinks – it's the goitre, you see, and the vet can't do a thing about it. Crying shame. Douggie washes her in Rive Gauche three times a week. It was me mum's favourite. But nothing seems to do the trick. Story of my life with women, I'm afraid – can't live with them, can live without them.'

'What about your niece?' asked Kate, enthralled.

'Oh, I bought her a whole aquarium of tropical fish to make up for losing her koi. The note on it said, "Sorry for all the fishy business". She was not amused. And do you think we could find a bleeding goldfish anywhere in the whole of Hawaii? So of course, being clever clogs, I went deep-sea diving, to try and find her some, only the gear I took down with me was faulty – the oxygen thingy was only half full. I was so bloody high when they reeled me up I needn't have bothered with the heroin. But even the fact I was half dead didn't appease her. So when we got back to Britain I dropped her off back in Dagenham and bought her a pet shop. She's been happy as Larry Lambton ever since. Thank Gawd. Not that she actually saw me eat it. I mean, even then, I drew the line at inflicting such a horrific sight on a child. Not that she was that young, of course – only slightly underage. I've never felt the same about fish an' chips since she dumped me. I think she'd quite like to have battered me as well. Actually, Katie, I'll let you into a little secret ... she wasn't actually my niece.'

He hooted wickedly, the bottomless gullies of his face breaking up like the ripples in a turbulent river. 'We concocted that detail for the newspapers. Well, I had to preserve some semblance of moral rectitude.'

Lunch, much of which had been harvested from Scorcher's new pride and joy, his organic vegetable garden, meandered on enjoyably into the afternoon. Kate and Fenton ate and Scorcher forced down about three grains of rice and an eighth of an organic pippin, and when Douggie wasn't looking distributed the rest to the dogs. Afterwards he escorted them round the grounds. The Elizabethan knot garden and the maze which had been built in the seventeenth century, and which now served as a cunning shield for the helicopter launch pad, saw him grow especially misty-eyed. By the time they reached the fountains she thought he was going to have another nervous breakdown.

'Hold it there, Scorcher,' twittered Fenton while he twiddled frantically with his knobs, and Scorcher stood forlornly in the centre of the maze surrounded by dogs.

'Shit, I've forgotten the walkie-talkie,' he said. 'That's normally how Douggie guides me out.'

'Isn't there a map?' asked Kate helpfully.

'Yeah, but I never bring it. Can't ever read the bloody things.'

Three-quarters of an hour later, as Fenton was beginning to hyperventilate, Scorcher waved a crumpled piece of paper in front of them.

Kate looked at the scrumpled napkin on which the words 'just kidding' were scrawled. Scorcher looked at her perplexed expression and cackled.

'Blimey, you didn't really think I didn't know my way round this by now, did you? My little way of getting you to extend your visit.'

'This is my real love,' he said, leading them out of the maze and into the rose garden, his marmoset eyes fixing on the skeleton of a Rambling Rector like searchlights.

'Designed by Rosemary Verey and lovingly tended to by Phillips here.'

An ancient gardener nodded to them. 'Good stuff, Phillips. The roses are looking lovely,' said Scorcher cheerfully.

'Yes, they're not coming along too bad, sir,' said Phillips. 'We should have a decent show this summer.'

''Course, some think Penelope Hobhouse was the true innovator of gardens,' continued Scorcher, wheeling them past the beds, 'but I'm not so sure. Anyway, look at this crazy little bundle of sticks and thorns. In six months' time it'll be bursting with life and filling our senses with its gorgeous aroma – one of the most beautiful, generous sights in the world. Beats stripagrams any day.' He grew wistful. 'I think it was smells I missed most when I was in prison.'

Back in the house he showed them his collection of African tribal headwear, his library of ecclesiastical manuscripts, the roomfuls of Chippendale, Beidermeier and – a more recent passion – Rennie Mackintosh, and his cellar of vintage wines. 'That's the big five in there, that is: Châteaux Lafite, Margaux, Mouton, Latour and Haut-Brion. Six if you count the Château Ribena. 'Course, I can't drink the alcoholic ones. I'm TT. Given up sex too. Going the Tantric route, so the collection of eighteenth-century porno's not much use either. I keep meaning to get Sotheby's to come and collect it.'

She was amazed at how much he knew about the house and how respectful he was of its heritage. He showed her into his study, which was the one bit of the house where Douggie wasn't allowed and which was consequently in total chaos, with teetering piles of paper, books and old magazines wobbling all over the place. Fenton photographed some of the porn, while Kate took notes.

'Actually I'm writing a history of the house,' said Scorcher shyly, settling himself into a huge old leather chesterfield which looked almost as beaten up as he did. 'Well, of Devon actually. To be honest it's turning into a bit of a panegyric, but it might be interesting to some people . . .'

Then he played them some snatches from a libretto he had been writing with Ambrose White, the country's leading playwright. Entitled *Marionettes*, it was a searing diatribe against political and sexual hypocrisy, loosely based on *Cosi fan tutte*. Scorcher's music was surprisingly haunting – far more mature and resonant than any of his work with Stench.

'It's Ambrose,' he said modestly. 'He's really inspiring to work with. He's a lovely bloke too. Do you know him?' Kate shook her head. 'I met him at some Prince's Trust do,' continued Scorcher. 'He was the only non-pompous git there, 'scusing HRH, of course. Trouble is he's always rewriting. Gawd knows if we'll ever get a complete version of *Marionettes*.'

He pointed to a state-of-the-art computer, clearly unused, next to which was a teetering mountain of papers spattered with spidery writing. 'What about you, Katie. What's your bag?'

'Oh, nothing very interesting. Just revelling in the transient world of fashion and style. Deeply shallow, I guess.'

The unblinking eyes fixed on her probingly. He was half annoyed at himself. He had told only Douggie about the history he was writing, which was proving to be so consuming, so all-encompassing, that he sometimes fretted he might die before it was complete. He had never imagined one county could be so fascinating, although he was dramatizing certain events just a teensy bit, but only to further his own point of view, which had increasingly come round in favour of devolution for Devon.

'Not quite the picture of the demotic rock star, is it?' he said, gesturing towards the walls of leather-bound books and the silver tea tray Douggie had just clattered in with.

Kate looked at his hedgehog hair and castratingly tight black jeans. 'You've certainly got an extensive, er, library,' she said.

'Perils of an autodidact, I'm afraid. Can't stop reading. I got five A-levels when I was inside and I was gonna start an Open University course in English literature — I swear to God I'd never had so much peace and quiet before — but they bloody well went and released me early for good behaviour. After that it was tour, tour, tour. Anyway, now that I've gone and half baked this book, I'm thinking of skipping the BA and going straight for a PhD. Trouble is, the other Stenchies keep nagging me to go on tour, shag a few groupies, drop a few tons of acid, make a few million . . . you know, the usual tedious crap.' He smirked impishly. 'Groupies. Who needs them when you can go to bed with Charlotte Brontë?'

They ended up staying the night, finally departing after lunch the next day, laden down with brilliant anecdotes, sumptuous photographs and some of Fenton's wickedly accurate illustrations of Scorcher scampering through the grounds, love beads and bangles flying, dwarfed by an aureola of frazzled black hair and Velasquez, Ingres, El Greco and Frou-Frou. Most touchingly of all, Kate had been presented with a cutting from the Rambling Rector and several small pots of lavender from the herb garden.

'Send her my love – Magda, I mean,' said Scorcher, sounding wistful. As they drove off, Kate peered out of the rear window at the small forlorn figure in his self-enclosed universe. For a split second he seemed the essence of loneliness. He waved and she smiled, even though he wouldn't see it from there. For a famous person, he was almost okay.

Keith's ambition, he says, is 'to go on enjoying science'. He has achieved his first specific goal – to clone a pig – but the cloning of pigs is only a starting point.

Chapter Nine

More than eighteen months after its launch Magda was thrilled to be selling only twenty-five thousand issues of *Domus*. Fenton agreed with her one hundred per cent, since the low figure meant he could tell everyone at the Groucho that he was working on an underground art magazine. The paltry figures proved they were reaching the crème de la crème – and to give Magda credit, the magazine was a huge *succès d'estime*.

Unfortunately the advertisers were more interested in *succès de* wallet, especially since Bernie had recklessly promised them a circulation of a hundred thousand. Magda wasn't remotely inclined to speak to the masses, however. She had once gone on hunger strike when her old boss at *A la Mode* had banned her from running any more profiles of obscure cutlery designers. Unfortunately everyone had simply assumed she was on the Grapefruit Diet, and when she finally emerged from her sick bed two stone lighter, they all congratulated her on her massive weight loss.

So as far as its staff was concerned, *Domus*'s achievements were not going to go unmarked, especially as they'd all been too tired and emotional to organize a proper launch party. After a tearful evening out with Phoebe, who was rapidly approaching her twenty-ninth birthday and whose knick-knacks and witty opinions on taste had become a staple of *Domus*, Magda declared they would throw a joint party for which, naturally, Bernie would foot the bill. Strickly speaking that meant *Domus* would be almost two years old on its first anniversary, but Magda felt it was worth waiting for. With Phoebe's endorsement, they could be sure of a good quota of celebrities, which would mean some useful coverage in the press. Heaven knew, thought Magda, they could all do with a change from the constant diet of stories about Charles and Diana's separation.

'Magda, that is so sweet of you,' fibbed Phoebe, when Magda turned up in Canonbury Square to tell her about the planned party. Magda was meant to be *en route* to see some graduate from the Royal College of Art who made dinner plates out of yak hair but was all too easily distracted by Phoebe's offer of a cup of ginger and ginseng. 'Next to having your ovaries removed, my colonic irrigationist swears it's the most invigorating, cleansing treatment you can give yourself,' she babbled. 'But then he is a colonic liar.'

Magda looked at Phoebe adoringly. How she managed always to be so ebullient was a mystery. She made Dawn French look like a manic depressive. And a not very stylish one at that. Whereas Phoebe was so stylish Magda was considering putting her level pegging with the Duchess of Windsor in her personal list of all-time favourite icons. Today, for instance, Phoebe was wearing a mint silk antique Schiaparelli narrow tunic over a couture chiffon beaded flesh-coloured skirt that Christian Lacroix had given her.

Magda could hardly believe it when Phoebe told her she'd worn it to rustle up a 5 a.m. fry-up for Nick. There wasn't a speck of grease on it.

'I do think he should see me looking nice, especially as he sees me so rarely at the moment,' said Phoebe.

'We'll make it a New Year's party to welcome in 1993. I thought we'd hire a magician and serve supper after,' Magda said, broaching the subject of the party again.

'It sounds lovely, but Nick can't stay out very late at the moment. He's got to be at Pinewood by six,' said Phoebe wistfully. A party was the last thing she felt like throwing. She was so depressed she was more likely to throw herself into the Thames. The only decent role she'd been offered lately had been covered in mascarpone and served in Pont de la Tour. It was all very well the Queen whingeing on about *her annus horribilis*, thought Phoebe savagely. At least she was guaranteed a regular slot on TV. Even the BBC couldn't commit to Phoebe. One minute Ambrose White, the writer who had adapted their sumptuous production of *Vanity Fair*, said she was his dream Becky Sharp. The next moment they were talking about scrapping the whole thing in favour of a new so-called art-show quiz format where audiences had to guess which celebrity 'artist' had drawn the squiggles that were projected on to pieces of fruit that looked like genitals.

'It'll be at my house,' continued Magda, 'so if you and Nick need to leave early, you can. We'll do everything. You just need to provide us with a guest list.'

Phoebe fixed Magda with her arresting emerald gaze; her narrow eyes somehow managed to be predatory and timid at the same time. 'Are you sure? I mean, you must be so frantic with the magazine and everything.'

'You know what they say,' said Magda stoically. 'When you want something done, ask a busy person to do it.'

The busy person Magda had in mind, of course, was Kate. In between organizing a shoot in Donna Karan's beach house, persuading five fashionable architects to design a cat basket, and selecting a hundred essential items for the bedside table, she now had to organize a dinner for forty of London's most difficult-to-please guests. But she did as she was told. Magda was a truly brilliant people manager, not least because she waxed on at such length about the sanctity of her staff's creative spirit and their need for total freedom that she got them all doing precisely what she wanted.

Two weeks before the event, Phoebe suddenly flew to Egypt to film an advert for Negroni diamonds. 'They're hideous and I look like an Egyptian tart, but no one outside Japan will ever see it, thank God. And the fee will put a down payment on a place in the country.'

Or pay off half the Manolo account, thought Magda indulgently. She entirely approved of Phoebe's tireless dedication to looking good.

Ten days before the party, Magda was summoned by Bernie to a Higginbottom Inc. bonding weekend at the Birmingham Hilton. Spending forty-eight hours with middle-ranking construction engineers and caravan site managers left her so traumatized that she was totally incapacitated for the remaining eight days leading up to the party – which left Kate on her own to deal with everything. From then on, temperamental caterers, premenstrual florists and Starlight Mystere, a cult hypnotist who had levitated Donna Ducatti live on-air during a Knickers slot, all directed their problems at Kate.

Starlight wasn't so much levitating as livid because Kate

had asked her to wear a bright colour. 'Well, why did you do that?' demanded Magda sharply.

'Because you said this was the Back of Black party,' said Kate wearily.

'I said it was the Back *to* Black, *Annus Horribilis* Party.'

'No,' said Kate staunchly, 'I've got the fax.' She rustled through a pile of papers in her party filing cabinet.

'Anyway,' said Magda hastily, 'it doesn't matter, because I think the whole thing should be white now.'

'But you said all that New Age stuff was passé,' pointed out Kate, panicking. Half of London's caterers had competed to win the commission for the colour dinner party. Graham de Castellet, the most up-and-coming of the new wave of florists, had been up three nights running dyeing his tulips day-glo and individually gluing sequins on to them to make them look like cosmic triffids.

'Scrap it,' said Magda grandly.

'What?'

'White's the only way to go,' continued Magda, casting her eyes distastefully over a pile of fuchsia Maryse Boxer china.

'What about Graham?' wailed Kate. 'He's got most of Dylon on stand-by.'

'You're not using Graham? God, Kate, he's so *l'année dernière*.'

Kate spent the next few days in a living whitemare, wading through menus for angel-hair pasta with white truffles; sea bass with lemon-grass and coconut dressing; meringue with white peaches and lychees; and mopping Graham de Castellet's brow, which was anything but white by now.

She yearned to call Eliza, but in the last few months Eliza had been completely wrapped up in all her new political work. Even Podge seemed to have got elbowed out. Eliza was so busy setting up think-tanks and chairing her various all-women committees it was a miracle she had time to sleep, let alone think. Still, at least she'd sent lists of ideas for guests to Kate, complete with addresses and phone numbers, postcodes and suggestions of favourite haunts where they might be tracked down if they weren't at home.

You had to hand it to her, thought Kate, even rushed off her stilettos, Eliza was still one of the most efficient people she knew. Which was more than could be said for Sadie, who was currently orienteering up the Matterhorn. She had been on so many character-building outward bound courses in the last eighteen months it was a miracle she wasn't suffering from multiple personality disorder by now. At least it took her mind off her financial situation, which thanks to some catastrophic investments with Lloyd's was plummeting faster than a sailor's zip on shore leave. With Eliza preoccupied, and Martha talking about going to Bosnia all the time, Kate felt utterly alone.

It had been a most trying week. Kate's phone hadn't stopped ringing, with guests who suddenly found it necessary to reveal previously top-secret entanglements as well as the internal workings of their colons.

'So you see I can't possibly sit next to Ian Novak,' drawled Magda down the line from Milan, where she'd disappeared to style an ad for Mangealotti pasta sauces. 'I'm not sure I can bear having him in the same city. Let alone my house . . .'

'But I didn't even know you knew him,' wailed Kate.

She was very proud of having persuaded Ian Novak, the famed eco-warrior from the Exeter bypass incident, to agree to come to anything as bourgeois as a dinner party. Actually it had been Eliza's suggestion. He was a new client of hers, and she had not only lassoed him on to one of her think-tanks but secured him a lucrative and witty campaign for No Sweat's new biodegradable deodorant and skincare range for men.

'Fucked him at Greenham,' said Magda. '*Très* well endowed, I'll say that for him. Ten feet away from a cruise missile. I'm amazed I didn't get them mixed up. I can't tell you how erotic it was.' She sighed. 'But that was then. Before I discovered what an arrogant, self-centred, self-absorbed bastard he is. Never mind eco-warrior. Ego-warrior would be closer to the truth. And I can tell you, there was no question of deodorants then, environmentally friendly or not.'

Kate was not disinviting him, however unJolly a Green Giant he turned out to be.

It had been thanks to Eliza too that she had snagged Philip Lane, the man most widely tipped to be the next Shadow Chancellor. And it was no thanks to Magda, who had accidentally invited him when she had mistaken him for Lionel Blair, that Laurence Patterson was also expected.

'You do realize that Philip Lane is giving evidence against him if his case ever gets to trial?' stormed Kate.

'Oh, don't be such a pessimist,' said Magda dismissively. 'We can always tell everyone he *is* Lionel Blair and they'll think we're terribly clever for having such an ironic guest.'

'Kate, sweetheart.' It was Phoebe on the phone. 'You haven't forgotten that I'm only eating alfalfa at the moment.'

'But it's your birthday,' protested Kate.

'I know. Normally I wouldn't be so fussy, but I'm up to play a supermodel in a made-for-TV movie and I need to lose a stone by next week. They'll have to put me on stilts if I get it, but it's worth a go. You won't seat Nick next to any politicians, will you? He's liable to get a tad aggressive with them. Oh, and Lachlan will be coming with us. He's written some epic poem about Thor. Actually I'm not sure whether it really is an epic poem or just called "Epic". Anyway, Hollywood's desperate to make it into a movie and I think he wants me to co-star as a cloud. Oh, and he wants to know if he can bring Max Clifford. By the way, Tarquin has irritable bowl syndrome.'

Not knowing who Tarquin was, Kate began to lose the will to live. She certainly didn't have the energy to explain to Phoebe that she deliberately hadn't invited Lachlan at the request of Ruby, who had had a distressing fisticuffs incident with him in front of the paparazzi at Heathrow, where she had gone to welcome him back from his trip to the Bahamas, only to discover three other devoted girlfriends there too. It turned out he'd dedicated his second anthology to them as well.

The guest list was now so long that they'd had to erect a marquee to fit everyone in. They may have been living in an eighteenth-century theatre, but it was one that could only have ever seated about twenty-five people.

On the plane back from Milan, Magda had sat next to someone who knew someone who specialized in custom-designed marquees made from scraps of holy fabrics that had washed up on the banks of the River Ganges. As usual, she couldn't remember their name, but after three days of detective work, Ruby and Kate had tracked Sereta Katel down in the metal utensils department of John Lewis, where she worked during the day. It was short notice, Sereta told them, and she wasn't sure whether her stock of scraps would accommodate the size of tent they had in mind. But after a spot of gentle coaxing from Ruby (who offered to double her fee) she decided that she probably did have enough — and promptly skipped off to Southall to stock up at her Uncle Bibi's discount sari store.

'You won't put me next to any celebrities, will you?' said Martha disdainfully.

Kate counted to ten and ignored her. Her head was splitting from all the banging going on in the back of the house, where Sereta's saris were proving most uncooperative. They would keep splitting when she tried to nail them. Kate had been rather surprised when Sereta had arrived to put up the marquee on her own, but Sereta said she couldn't have clumsy hands interfering with her blessed bits, and Kate supposed she knew what she was doing. Besides, she had plenty of other things to worry about. Martha's increasing self-righteousness, for instance. It was a bit rich, considering she seemed to be turning into Radio Four's answer to *Hello!*

'As a matter of fact I had you down between the Pope and Princess Di,' she said.

'By the way,' Lachlan called to say, 'I've gone vegan.'

'You do know he has a wheat intolerance,' enquired Ian Novak's new PA.

Kate revised her plans for the ninety-ninth time. In a weak moment she even invited her father after he called her for one of his bimonthly chats. It was getting beyond a joke. She now had thirteen different menu options. Thai for Magda, who had just discovered she was allergic to Western food. Yin and yang for the kitchen staff, who insisted on eating afterwards chez Kate and Magda. Laurence Patterson was on the Montignac diet and Chloe Capshaw, the journalist

Magda had invited from the *Probe*'s women's pages, would only eat alternate courses entirely composed of one food.

'It's very simple, really,' Chloe had explained on a crackly mobile from Old Street, where she was supposed to be filing a piece about the aftermath of the IRA bomb for the *Probe*'s women's editor. 'You have one entire course of pineapple; then one of steak tartare. Then you wait fifty minutes . . .'

Kate turned off and waited for Chloe's battery to do the same.

The next time the phone rang, two hours before all the guests were due, it was Ruby. Kate braced herself while Graham worked round her with a bottle of Evian that he was spraying on to his drooping triffids.

'I don't know how this affects your seating plan,' began Ruby, 'but I've just discovered that Fenton is a rabid anti-environmentalist. He regards them all as superstitious Canutes. At least I think he said Canutes. It's the one thing he gets really worked up about, other than Copperplate Gothic Light. He launched into this whole big tirade this afternoon about how ecologists were pathetic vandals attempting to hold back the tide of progress when we should just let everything be concreted over and allow civilization to follow its inevitable course.'

'So next to Ian Novak or not?' asked Kate wearily.

'Depends how explosive an evening you want. Fenton was waving his fists in the air just talking about it this afternoon. He thumped his light-box so hard it smashed. I think there's a whole side to him that's about to break free.'

Arm's length it was.

* * *

After Starlight Mystere made all the *placement* cards disappear, the seating plan degenerated into chaos, especially as Lachlan O'Hennessy had arrived with half a dozen of his miniskirted female groupies, who had all turned up to hear him première his new poem. 'PuKe' was a savage satire on America which, unbeknown to Kate, he was planning to read over dinner. Kate asked Fenton to write out some new *placements* in his best Gill Sans Condensed Bold, but then Magda had told him that Gill Sans Extra Bold looked more modern and he had stormed off in a huff.

Scorcher had arrived hot — steaming, to be precise — off the plane from Karachi, where he'd been visiting an ashram, and went straight into the kitchen to tell Kate that he couldn't eat anything because he'd picked up a worm.

'I'll tell you about worms,' muttered Kate darkly as Scorcher and Ian Novak proceeded to get in everyone's way by reciting ancient Druid and Yogic incantations over each other. In the dining room Graham de Castellet and his two assistant florists had nervous breakdowns because in the furnace of a kitchen the wilting triffids now looked more like trifle. The theatre looked gorgeous, however, although the central miniature dome, beneath which they were eating, sucked up warmth, and in order to fend off the cold they had imported several mega-heaters. The problem now was that inside the house it was about 110 degrees, and in the marquee it was minus 50. Sereta had nearly blown a fuse when they suggested putting heaters next to her extremely un-flame-retardant drapes.

Thanks to Starlight, the table plan was all jumbled up. Martha, whom Kate had deliberately placed away from all the celebs between Philip Lane and the eco-boffin, had instead landed up between Phoebe and Jason Donovan, who was telling Ruby that he hadn't meant to nearly bankrupt the *Face* by suing them. To make matters worse, she was bang opposite Sharon Weiner, a Hollywood starlet who was back in London publicizing her new line of jewellery on QVC.

And that wretched Chloe Capshaw was so politically clueless she actually thought Laurence Patterson was Lionel Blair and had plonked herself right next to him. Until she had seen that Philip Lane, the Shadow Chancellor, was sitting on the other side, at which point she announced she wouldn't mind shadowing him, and promptly switched her *placement* with Martha's, mumbling something obscene about the Right Honourable's member.

Not that any of it seemed to matter. 'You're a genius,' giggled Phoebe, dodging Graham de Castellet's Evian spritzer as she sidled up to Kate, who was fortifying herself with a white Bellini – her fourth – in the kitchen.

'I can't thank you and Magda enough. And don't think I can't see who's put in the hard work,' crooned Phoebe, nuzzling her little butterfly mouth against Kate's neck. She was wearing a blue-and-yellow Sonia Delauney flapper dress and stilettos that Manolo Blahnik had dyed specially to match. 'I'm seated between the most heavenly people. Charlie Pitchcock, the new controller of BBC2, is very sweet, if slightly dim. And your sister's a honey.'

Kate scanned Phoebe's eyes, which gleamed like emerald chips, for signs of sarcasm, and discovered none. In which case Martha must be behaving herself. She had certainly perked up since joining *The Night Shift* and jettisoning Jack. She'd cut her hair to a sexy shoulder-length crop which gleamed like melting tar, and taken to wearing eyeliner again, which looked amazing against her creamy skin. And thank God, she'd finally chucked away her Support the Miners T-shirts. The dress she had bought specially for the evening — a black, clingy wraparound from the Ben de Lisi sample sale Kate had taken her to — showed off her taut figure amazingly. Even Kate was surprised at how sexy she looked. But she still couldn't imagine Phoebe and Martha being soul mates.

'Oh yes,' continued Phoebe blithely, 'she's been regaling us with anecdotes about Donna Ducatti. How clever of Martha to spot her potential.' She sauntered back to the dining room, plucking a half-dead tulip *en route*. Kate, not daring to see if Graham had spotted her, stayed in the kitchen with a tray of creamy-white feta cheese soufflés which she would happily have thrown at Magda, who hadn't so much as exercised her eyelashes all evening.

Eliza, looking incredibly sphinxlike in a black Calvin Klein halter-neck, had swapped her seat next to Melvyn Bragg for one by Max Clifford, in the hope that she could pick his brains. Meanwhile, across the table from Martha, Nick Wilde was squashed between Martha and Sharon Weiner's new breast implants and had the whole table in fits with a brilliant impersonation of Jim Allwater.

'Allow me to reassure everywun present tonight that impropriety and moral turpitude of any kind will not be tolerated by t'party. Furthermore, let me assure you all that we shall be tekin' draconian measures of t'severest, most terrifying, horrific, wretched, goot-wrenching kind to ensure that only candidates of t'ootmost propriety apply ...'

Martha, slightly abashed by Nick's wide-reaching general knowledge, and Phoebe's grasp of the artistic scene, laughed. She decided she liked them both immensely. They each had the knack of making whoever they talked to feel slightly more colourful. Nick, she was faintly mortified to discover, actually remembered talking to her on the phone at BSR two years earlier.

'I still can't believe you were up for it,' she said shyly.

'You sounded desperate. And I was getting a bit bogged down with serious parts at the time.' His dark blond hair flopped into his intense green eyes — the same colour as Phoebe's. 'There's only so much Shakespearian tragedy you can take. I never did it in the end, though. The show lost some of its integrity after you left. Seriously. Did you really get Lulu to sing down the microphone during the Knickers slot, by the way?'

Martha blushed and turned round to tell Phoebe how much she enjoyed contemporary theatre — a shameless lie since her last trip to see any show predated even the one to see *Chitty Chitty Bang Bang*.

When everyone had been served with something — Kate had given up trying to pander to everyone's food fads, especially as they all kept moving around, and decided they could bloody well eat what they were given — Lachlan, who had spent most of the evening graciously allowing his groupies to feed him figs from Graham's centrepieces, cleared his throat majestically and stood up. He rubbed his hands to rid them of any fig juice. The effect, together with his undertaker's suit, which looked at least a hundred years old, made him look like Uriah Heep. An expectant hush fell over the room.

'He wrote this last January after President Bush's trip to Japan,' Phoebe told Kate *sotto voce*, 'but he's been editing and polishing it ever since.'

'You PuKed / I PuKed / We all PuKed / The World's

NuKed,' boomed Lachlan. The whole table stared at him in stunned anticipation, but Lachlan sat down again, apparently creatively drained. He had agonized for months about the punctuation before deciding to abandon it. But what had really left him an emotional wreck was having to decide whether the K should be upper case or not.

'Look's like he polished it off,' said Magda.

'Lengthwise, it's not exactly a threat to *The Rime of the Ancient Mariner*, is it?' mumbled Nick to Martha under his breath.

'I call it sick,' tittered Chloe.

Martha looked at the steak tartare in front of her and was inclined to agree. But then everything seemed to make her feel nauseous these days. Including the thick waves of perfume that were wafting from across the table. 'I do hate the smell of Fracas,' she announced to Phoebe.

'Whoops.' Phoebe grinned. 'I'll remember to wear something different next time.'

'Oh God,' said Martha, blushing, 'I didn't think it was you. I thought it was coming from Chloe Capshaw.'

'Don't worry,' laughed Phoebe, 'it is a bit strong. Nick thinks it smells like Domestos.'

'I think, judging by that overblown piece of nonsense,' said Philip Lane, 'we can assume that satire really is dead.'

'Nick really wanted to be a satirist,' Phoebe said proudly. 'But he's so talented as an actor and so deliciously gorgeous that it was just never going to happen. He's totally clued up about current affairs, whereas I'm afraid my topical knowledge ends in about 1811.'

'That's my favourite historical period,' smarmed Laurence Patterson, helping himself to another carafe of port. 'Napoleon is my hero.'

'Really?' butted in Chloe adoringly. Phoebe raised an immaculately arched eyebrow. Laurence Patterson was precisely the kind of pompous, self-regarding man she most despised — and found most dangerous. She made a mental note to flirt with him later and get his number — for a rainy day.

'I'm surprised,' said Phoebe. She had played Josephine in a pudding two years earlier and, thanks to copious amounts of Georgette Heyer and an historical partwork she had picked up in her local newsagent's, could bluff for Britain on the subject. 'People think of him as the archetypal working-class role model, but frankly he's utterly bourgeois. The sort of man who has to invent his own crests.'

Laurence flared his considerable nostrils, thereby giving the Dartford Tunnel a run for its money, and turned his back on her. He wasn't used to women as attractive as Phoebe questioning his judgment. Martha, however, was intoxicated by Phoebe — everything about her. She especially liked the way a tiny scar cut through her right eyebrow, leaving a jagged little bare patch, as if lightning had struck there. She had never come across a couple like Nick and Phoebe — witty, intelligent, dangerously attractive, although fortunately, from the point of view of temptation, they were clearly both mad about one another. She could almost imagine being friends with them. By the end of the evening she heard herself agreeing to accompany Phoebe to the Clerkenwell Mummers' all-female rendition of *Damon and Pithias*.

'I thought you despised celebrities,' said Kate crossly, when Martha found her in the kitchen, where she had the temerity to criticize her for inviting David.

'It's not fair — when you didn't ask Mum.'

'Oh, for God's sake,' said Kate crossly. 'Don't pretend you're still not talking to him. Listen, just because Mum wants to kill him doesn't mean we shouldn't rise above it. A bit.'

'Okay, you're right,' said Martha. 'It's just that Mum has a way of making me feel treacherous for even mentioning his name.'

'Well, no one's saying you have to spend all your time with the man. Anyway, Eliza's got stuck with him, thank God – or thank Starlight and her bloody seating cock-up,' snarled Kate. She knew she wasn't looking her best. Her wavy hair had gone completely emotional and huge in the heat of the kitchen; her mascara was probably halfway down to her navel by now; and her face was the same colour as her bank statement. And when she wasn't in the kitchen, she seemed to have got stuck with the uninvited Tarquin, who turned out to be one of Magda's obscure cutlery designers and had bored on all evening about the purity of his forks. Kate hoped to God that Starlight would finally stir herself and levitate Tarquin out of the room.

She was still fuming about her seating plan when Starlight re-emerged looking tragic and wrecked (an effect she had spent hours achieving in front of Magda and Kate's bathroom mirror) and announced tearfully that the force wasn't with her. She then went and rudely plonked herself next to Nick and tried to hypnotize him into bed with her.

None of it mattered by now, thought Kate dejectedly. In any case, Martha was meant to be sitting next to the unJolly Green Giant, who instead had landed Sharon Weiner. Not that he had any right to complain. Sharon's hills and valleys might be a bit built-up, but at least the view to them was unimpeded.

Two weeks later Martha surfaced into the smog of the Holloway Road. The good news was that after a year and a half Jenny Stewart had at long last taken her off the celeb beat, from which she had apparently graduated *summa cum laude,* and posted her to Bosnia for a month.

'Now you're sure it's what you want?' said Jenny, managing to sound motherly while she poured some gin into her mug of lapsang. 'Getting your brains blasted out isn't all it's cracked up to be, you know.'

'I know,' said Martha, so excited she could hardly concentrate. She was already planning the contents of her flak jacket.

'I'm going to miss your wonderful take on popular culture,' said Jenny. 'But if it's what you really want ...'

'It is,' sighed Martha gratefully.

'Well, just look after yourself. Oh, and look after Tim O'Mara, will you? He's an old chum of mine from when I was a foreign correspondent. Done more wars than I've had hot toddies. Knows everything and everyone. Got masses of awards. I've told him to take you under his wing, but frankly he could do with a bit of hand-holding too. Bit fond of the hard stuff – and I'm not talking about front-page news.'

Martha was deeply touched. Tim O'Mara must be more pickled than a Damien Hirst if even Jenny saw fit to comment on it. But Martha knew his work and it was brilliant. She couldn't wait to learn at the feet of a master.

It would be the making of her career, she reflected,

scurrying past the Limonia kebab takeaway before she had a chance to retch. At last, she would be taken seriously. She leaned against the grimy glass of a bus shelter to catch her breath. She would work night and day to impress Jenny and convince her that out in the field was where she belonged. She took some deep breaths, catching the bountiful emissions of the number 42. It was extraordinary how much better pollution made her feel. She must be like the toughest urban cockroach. This thought was curiously comforting. She had to concentrate on her inner strength. Because the bad news was that she was two months' pregnant.

Chapter Ten

She was all alone. Blissfully so — peace and quiet being hard to come by in Bosnia these days. Actually, she wasn't quite alone. There were two sultry-looking waitresses crashing through several tin mines' worth of cutlery. That was fine by Martha. It meant she couldn't think too hard. Ever since she'd left London in that terrific hurry — all to show Jenny Stewart that, after all her hints, she was truly serious about coming — she'd avoided thinking. Thinking hard hurt Martha these days. Which was funny, because the abortion itself, with all its frightening, half-understood procedures, had been quite painless. For a few days she had thought she had succeeded in tiptoeing over all her emotional tripwires without setting a single one of them off. It was as if someone had taken a pair of pliers to the circuit that connected her heart and emotions to her brain. What with the flurry of getting everything sorted out for work, she had hardly had a moment to reflect. The journey itself had taken days. She'd had to fly to Rome, get a train to Brindisi, and then make her way via a succession of rickety buses and vans, over the border into the traumatized remains of former Yugoslavia, where she had made one final stopover to get rid of her and Jack's unborn baby before meeting Tim.

True to his word, Tim O'Mara had met her in Srebenica off an arms convoy on which she'd managed to cadge a lift from Sarajevo, after an uncertain, jagged journey along heavily mined roads. All in all, the trek from London had taken her almost a month. She had to lie to him about why she looked so worn out already, which was hardly a good start to their working relationship, but she couldn't exactly turn up saying, 'Hi, sorry I was late, I just had to stop off for a quick termination.'

'Welcome to paradise,' he said, sweeping his eyes over her anaemic pallor, pristine flak jacket and the Prada nylon rucksack Kate had lent her from the *Domus* freebie mountain, out of which was poking a copy of the collected war reports of Martha Gellhorn.

The Prada rucksack hadn't scored very highly on *Domus*'s 'Open and Shut Case' feature on account of Magda snagging one of her nails on its zip. And it didn't rate much with Tim O'Mara either. 'Well, well, well, I didn't realise they were sending out the fashion editor.'

He could talk, thought Martha, following him out to a battered brown Volvo. Eccentrically dressed in pale linen trousers and a bright pink silk (despite the biting cold) shirt, he looked as though he'd stepped out of a Versace ad. As far as appearances went, he wasn't what she'd expected at all. She'd imagined an addled old soak of about fifty who reeked of beer. But Tim was about forty, with curly brown hair that was attractively too long, wicked blue eyes and the biggest dimples Martha had seen since she'd covered a story on celebrity cellulite for *The Late Shift*. And the only reeking he did was of YSL Kouros aftershave.

'I s'pose Jenny told you I was a total piss artist,' he said, steering the Volvo over potholes and round corners with reckless abandon. 'Haven't touched a drop since dear old Reggie Bosanquet passed to the other side. I'm talking about death, by the way, not the Beeb. It was a bit of a wake-up call, I can tell you. How's Jenny's consumption these days, by the way? No, don't answer that. Too compromising. Tell me all you know about Bosnia instead.'

Reluctantly, Martha tore her eyes from the views outside the mud-spattered windows, where hundreds of people appeared to be living on the streets, and began to regurgitate from all the cuttings she'd been poring over for the past six weeks. She was pretty up to speed on the siege of Sarajevo, alarmed that the Serbs had taken two-thirds control of Bosnia, dismayed that Lord Owen had got nowhere with his negotiations, and in total awe of General Morillon, the UN commander in Bosnia.

'Yeah, yeah, yeah,' said Tim, narrowly avoiding a tank. 'They still don't teach you anything useful on these courses, do they? Listen, here's what you really need to know. One, your first instinct must always be to protect yourself. Two, always insist that you have a hotel room overlooking the courtyard and not the street – that way there's less chance of being shelled. Not that we've had what I'd call any decent shelling here so far, mind you. And three, never ever hand in your expenses without multiplying them by at least five. It makes it look very bad for the rest of us.'

Martha was appalled at the turn the conversation was taking.

'Oh, *please*.' He chuckled. 'How d'you think these war hacks pay for their new swimming pool and patio? One of them's even got a plaque that says "Gulf War Memorial Garden" next to his barbecue.'

Martha looked blank, which was how Tim liked his receipts, not his women. He shook his head in disbelief. 'Dear oh dear oh dear.' They fell silent for a while, and Martha leaned out of the window again, lost for words, her breath freezing in the snowy air. All the swotting in the world couldn't have prepared her for the real-life results of ethnic cleansing. Spluttering puddles of diesel, the Volvo dodged ragged little donkeys laden down with sodden mattresses, young mothers walking alongside with their babies bundled in Puffas; old women in headscarves huddling round fires, their sharp eyes glinting pitifully out of careworn features that were cracked and crevassed with emotion and the wear and tear of a hard life.

He watched her concentrating on the devastation around them. 'Welcome to Srebenica 1993. Fifty years after Europe was almost obliterated . . . haven't we done well?' They finally juddered to a halt by the Imperial Hotel. Tim said something to a stern-looking receptionist that made her break into a huge, gold-flecked smile. Then he showed Martha to her room, next to his and overlooking the courtyard, and took her down the corridor to a makeshift newsroom that had been sealed off from the rest of the hotel with sheets of clear plastic – not that they were necessary. The only people left in the hotel were journalists and soldiers. The place was a flurry of activity and combat uniforms, yet at the same time surprisingly orderly.

She still felt sick all the time, but at least the bleeding – a seeping wound that seemed to go on much longer than they had warned her – had stopped, more or less. Over the next few weeks she clung to Tim more tenaciously than his Kouros aftershave. For all his swagger he was a dedicated war reporter. He had an unerring instinct for where the story was and a deep-seated kindness that meant he was always happy to share a hunch with other, less talented journalists, provided he thought their intentions were honourable. As far as he was concerned honourable intentions meant giving a story everything he had so that the bastards on the news desks back in London had no excuse not to run it. Where his colleagues were content to gather second-hand reports from videos and briefings from Nato or tales told by fleeing refugees, he would insist on getting out there and seeing events at first hand. It made for an exceptionally tough apprenticeship, especially as he took Martha's insistence that she be treated as one of the boys at face value and started off as he meant to go on – by making her carry the satellite phone, which weighed practically more than she did.

'It's a tough world out there,' he would say to Martha as they bounced along behind a UN convoy. 'And I'm not talking about the Serbs. We're fighting a running battle with the Genifer Flowers story at the moment. The papers would much rather run six pages on Clinton's extramarital sex life or the Duchess of Fergiana's new diet than show another mass grave in Vukovar. It's our moral duty to keep this war on the front pages.' It was nearly spring, not that you'd guess from the freezing weather. And hundreds of thousands of Muslims had been flooding into Srebenica, despite the fact the city was under siege by the Serbs.

Little by little, she got used to the syncopated rhythm of shellfire. And the fact that sometimes a change of clothes and a bath were very low priorities. After one field trip she got back to the hotel and was appalled at how much she smelled when she took off her flak jacket. She found herself begging Tim for a splash of his Kouros. Kate had already sent her two large Red Cross parcels stuffed with Aveda and six back issues of *Vogue*, but she'd had to give practically everything away as bribes and tips and Tim had absconded to his room with the *Vogues* and she hadn't liked to follow him there.

She still slept fitfully, but she was no longer terrified. She stopped noticing the fronds of wallpaper hanging off the walls, or the stale food, because she realized how privileged they were to have any in a city that was under siege. She never got used to the odour of dead bodies, however; it would haunt her all her life. And she found it difficult to adapt to the notion that, even in the middle of a war, journalists were censored, though this time the police weren't PRs and celebrity agents but the UN.

'Don't worry about it,' Tim told her. 'It's the price we pay for access. If you want to be a free spirit, fine – I've been there and it's great for the ego – but be prepared not to get the story half the time.'

Gradually she found herself making friendships – with the other correspondents, with their Bosnian translators – and in a few weeks her old life started to seem like a dream. She found herself hardly ever thinking about Jack but marvelling instead at the beauty of the thickly wooded hills surrounding Srebenica and the courage of the people who were slowly being starved into submission. There was no way she could ever agree to go home when her month was up.

On the few occasions she had caught one of Martha's reports, Sadie fretted terribly and slept even worse than usual. The one time she managed to get through to her on Tim O'Mara's satellite phone, she had sounded blissfully happy — which was all to the ill, as far as Sadie was concerned. She had heard all about war euphoria.

What with Martha and her new neighbour, who insisted on practising his drums until three in the morning, Sadie's nerves were shot to pieces. Everything made her cry, even watching the repeats of the sheepdog trials, which she found herself doing at three in the morning. In a way, she thanked God for her neighbour, who, rumour had it, had been in prison and thus constituted a diversion of sorts. He certainly looked in need of some rehabilitation — occasionally Sadie caught the tail wind of his dreadlocks, heavily doused with Patchouli oil, as he pedalled past her driveway, trailing his little cart of organic vegetables which he sold in Shepton market every Wednesday. But she'd never actually got close enough to tackle him about the drumming.

Dan Hammond wasn't the only reason she couldn't sleep. She had had a row with Kate — the first since they had quarrelled bitterly over a boyfriend Kate had brought to stay the night when she was sixteen. She couldn't even remember what it was about now — something to do with her fretting over the amount of time Kate spent in the office and Kate accusing her of being jealous of her career and living in 1893 instead of 1993.

'I wouldn't quite say that,' said Sadie, for once wishing she hadn't been raised to be so discreet. But she had been, and so her daughters would never know about her close encounter of the slurred kind with Johann, the brawny ski instructor she had met halfway up the Matterhorn.

Still, the row, together with a brisk tramp through the

meadows surrounding Tithe House, finally goaded her into action. The early spring sunshine was so invigoratingly bright and the foliage so verdant after all the rain they'd had that the fields looked like giant lime powder puffs, and she found herself thinking that maybe Kate had a point. It was about time she resumed her career. It was too late to be a model, but she could capitalize on her other talents. Everyone was always telling her what a brilliant hostess she was. Well, she would turn Tithe House into a small country hotel. It would be very secluded – strictly word of mouth – and she would offer a very individualized service. It would be special and personal. And it would irritate the hell out of David.

To say things weren't as buoyant in the *Domus* offices as they had been was a bit like saying Slobodan Milosovic had a teensy problem with image. Bernie's attentions were otherwise engaged with a massive brewing company he'd taken over. Ruby was spending half her time at the *Face*. Even Fenton had decamped, finally putting the deposit on a broom cupboard in Knightsbridge and his notions about all property being theft behind him. 'To celebrate becoming a respectably paid-up art director again,' he announced, toasting himself in Ruby's Cinzano.

The problem was, he wasn't paid, fully or otherwise. None of them was. Magda had so overshot all her budgets she was in danger of dwarfing Third World debt. Of course, Fenton hadn't bothered to check any of his bank statements but had used them to make an installation for the ICA's Seditious Art exhibition.

The truth was that, having hotly pursued Magda for

the best part of three years, Bernie was now playing hard to get, especially when it came to Magda trying to extract any more money from him.

'The only extract she'll get from Bernie,' remarked Ruby one day when she deigned to drop in to check her post and rifle through the freebie pile, 'is yeast. Apparently this beer factory he's buying produces so much of it he's thinking of setting up a chain of bakeries.'

Magda was getting so desperate she'd even considered driving up to see Nancy again, but Nancy had been very cool on the phone when she'd suggested it.

'I'm rather busy these days, Magda, you know,' she mumbled. She sounded as though she was munching something – probably a catering pack of low-sugar mini-éclairs. 'I've become rather chummy with the editor of *Simply Splendid*. She was so helpful when I needed some help with my murals. And she had a delightful party to celebrate *Simply Splendid*'s twenty-fifth birthday. I sat next to Princess Alexandra,' she finished proudly.

It was then Magda remembered, with a terrible sense of impending catastrophe, that they had forgotten to invite either Nancy or Bernie to *Domus*'s first birthday – an oversight that wouldn't have seemed quite so appalling if they hadn't been quite so efficient in remembering to send Bernie the enormous bill.

Kate stared intently at the layout in front of her. It was no good. Try as she might to get enthusiastic, her job just didn't excite her the way it used to. Ruby came and perched on her desk, displaying a huge expanse of fishnets and the most trashed pair of Shelley's platforms Kate had ever seen.

'We ought to commission a piece on shrimping,' she

said nonchalantly. 'Apparently in Norfolk shrimping is the new golf. And you do know that Norfolk is the new Cornwall?'

Kate looked at her mutely, willing her heart to soar the way it used to when Ruby spouted her sociological predictions. But the only things soaring these days were their overdrafts.

She was starting to rue the total disintegration of her private life, which meant that, even though it was nearly six o'clock and she'd done most of her work, there was nothing much worth leaving the office for. She was just debating whether to walk Nibbles all the way back to Spitalfields or let him run behind the bus for half the journey when her phone rang. She picked it up to hear a vaguely familiar, lubricious voice on the other end.

'Finally I got hold of you,' Roberto crowed triumphantly. He'd called to say that Max Horrowitz's messy last will and testament had finally been sorted out and that there was a For Sale sign up outside Horrowitz's. He gave her the telephone number on the board.

Kate was standing to attention in his shop in less than half an hour.

'This is posh,' she said, surveying the gleaming expanse of his new chilled cabinet.

'Bloody EU regulations,' he grumbled, not quite able to hide his pride in Spiga's, which had expanded into the shop next door and was opening a second branch in Pimlico. He frowned, remembering that he'd been in a sulk with Kate for the past two years. 'And we're not allowed bloody dogs either. Especially Rottweilers.'

'Nibbles is not a Rottweiler,' hissed Kate. 'Look, sorry I've been a bit hopeless about staying in touch,' she resumed, more emolliently. 'But things have been very hectic. Anyway, I wanted to thank you in person for letting me know.'

'You still want that dump, then,' he said, looking at her reprovingly. A bumptious young fogey in a loud tweed suit glared at Roberto impatiently and took a call on his mobile from Wall Street.

'More than ever,' said Kate. 'And this time I'm really going to do it.'

'Look, just because I told you about it doesn't mean I approve. I still think you're gonna have big problems with lack of passing trade. Then there's the initial cost of stock. And probably an overvalued lease—'

Kate had thought of all that. Well, some of it. Well, she'd stopped off in WH Smith's on the way to Roberto's and bought a DIY entrepreneurial starter pack, at any rate.

'How do you know the lease will be overvalued?'

'Stands to reason. With the economy poised to come out of recession, the lawyers will be gambling on a bull market—'

'Oh, spare us *The Money Programme*,' barked the banker in the tweed suit. 'Any chance of some service round here?'

'I've made an appointment to see it first thing tomorrow morning,' said Kate, ignoring him.

'Just don't say I didn't warn you,' said Roberto, ladling some of her favourite chicken-and-pepper salad into a plastic container.

'I've got the money from my flat to get me going.'

'You know your problem?'

'No, but I've got a feeling I'm about to learn.'

'Oh, for God's sake,' snarled the banker. Kate gave his Rolex a withering look. The rest of the queue was agog.

'You don't live in the real world.'

'And what world would that be?' Kate snapped. 'The one where all women are madonnas in the kitchen and whores in the bedroom?'

'Look, what does a person have to do to get served round here?' demanded the banker, pretending to strangle himself.

'No,' said Roberto, waving his slicer around animatedly. 'The one where the proceeds of a one-bedroom flat in Shepherd's Bush sold in the depths of recession won't begin to cover what you need.'

Kate's eyes filled with tears at the sudden realization that he was right.

'I'll lend you the money.'

'What?' she said, dazed.

'I could be a sleeping partner. Strictly business,' Roberto added somewhat reluctantly. He looked so earnest that even Mrs Cowie was moved. She'd only come in for some grated Parmesan but this was much better than *EastEnders*. 'Go for it, dearie,' she said to Kate.

'Look, for the last time, any chance of a cuppuccino?'

Kate, Roberto and the rest of the queue looked at the banker disapprovingly. 'Shut up,' they chorused. As if in agreement, Nibbles brushed against the banker's lichen-coloured tweeds and, mistaking them for a particularly prickly bush, cocked his leg.

In August Nick Wilde, in his new role as a goodwill ambassador for Save a Child, arrived in Sarajevo. The organizers of Save a Child had been astonished when he'd agreed to be one of their patrons but it had only taken one 'phone call from Eliza to get him on side. They never expected him to accompany their field workers out there and had scrupulously explained to him just how dangerous it was. But he insisted. He took his position very seriously and, besides, he wanted to see for himself what Martha's excellent reports, which she had filed from Tuzla, Zep and Gorazde, had been telling him for months.

He had been there about two hours when he bumped into her. She was on her way with Tim to visit a school that was supposedly protected by the Geneva Convention but had apparently been under constant fire. After Martha had got over her shock at seeing him there (and her blushes) she introduced him to Tim, who asked if Nick wanted to come with them.

The three of them became inseparable after that. When Nick wasn't observing the field workers he was working like a trooper with Martha and Tim. He had an impressive grasp of what was going on and insisted on being treated the same as everyone else, which included immediately relieving Martha of the satellite phone. Like them, he was quickly coated in dust and mud – although unlike Martha he didn't try to sneak off with the satellite telephone to ask Kate to send out some Chanel Cristalle. He went on several dangerous expeditions with them – and was bemused and angered to discover that all the so-called safe zones were in fact among the most profoundly unsafe places on earth. And his admiration for Tim and Martha and everyone else working out there rocketed.

When he was being completely honest with himself, he also had to admit that being in Bosnia was a way of dealing with his guilt over Phoebe. Each new tangible proof of his growing success only exacerbated his niggling sense that it was she, and not he, who should be succeeding. It was Phoebe who, at drama school, had been the student most likely to succeed. They had all – students and teachers – marvelled at her ability, not just to play, but *become* anyone.

He had watched, quietly and passively to begin with because he had been going through his taciturn rebel phase (i.e. he had been painfully shy), as she had set off on her personal reinvention, transforming herself from a rather hard, brassy-looking hustler into a far more sophisticated creature. By the end of their third year she was perfect. He could hardly believe it when she'd agreed to go on that first date with him, let alone move in. They had found themselves a sooty little bed-sit on the Cromwell Road. They could hear the buses roaring past and the rumble of the Tube and they couldn't afford to pay the electricity bill half the time. But it had seemed so romantic. The jobs had started to roll in slowly. He had been so excited in the beginning he hardly noticed there were more for him than there were for her. He was so sure that she would be a star that his main concern was not to disgrace her by being a total failure. But life wasn't turning out like that. And it was hard to deal with the new reality.

Escaping to another world, where his fame and success counted in a different way, helped, especially when he was with Martha and Tim. The three of them camped out, sleeping and walking in the same clothes for days, although in his case it just made him look more rugged than ever, and sometimes Martha rustled up makeshift but miraculously tasty meals over a fire. He was kind and thoughtful and both Martha and Tim completely forgot he was a celebrity in another life. But only Martha began to think about him in any kind of context outside their present one.

He told her about his family in South Africa and his early acting days as a drama student and asked her all about her family and her life at BSR. Before long their conversations were spattered with more pregnant pauses than an oversubscribed prenatal class. Much to her horror, Martha began preening herself every morning in what remained of her hotel mirror. Shaved and showered, Nick looked impossibly handsome and smelled delicious. Martha kept reminding herself that he was married. She told herself that her crush was war madness. Ever since she'd been out in Bosnia she'd felt everything a hundred and ten per cent more keenly than she ever had at home. The highs she felt when he was near were like being on drugs. And the downs, she told herself every morning, sternly, contemplating her reflection in the battered, chipped mirror in her room, would be just as scalding. But she still bitterly regretted giving away all the shampoos and moisturizers Kate had sent as bribes, and found herself visiting the reception desk twice a day to see if any more SOS parcels had arrived from Kate.

'I still can't quite work you out,' Nick said softly one night. They were sitting back to back, cross-legged, on the roof of the hotel, looking past the smoking ruins of the city towards the dusty hills, swigging from bottles of beer. Discreetly, whenever possible, Tim had increasingly left them on their own together. The night was stiflingly hot and eerily still, apart from the televisions flickering through a chink in the curtains in the building opposite.

'Why?' Martha asked. She was uncharacteristically clean. Her gleaming hair swung over her jutting cheekbones like curtains blowing against an open window. Leaning against his back, she could feel his heart beating.

'Well, now that I know you, that whole life of yours

at BSR doesn't seem to fit in. I keep thinking I imagined your voice on the end of that line.'

Just the thought of Nick remembering her voice or bothering to analyse her made Martha blush to her roots in the greying light.

'It was the only job I could get at the time,' she lied. She didn't want to go into the whole sorry Jack saga. But something about Nick hypnotized her into telling the truth. 'Actually, that's crap. I had a boyfriend who thought it would be a good idea.'

'Didn't like the competition?'

Unnerved, Martha twisted round to look at him. 'How did you know that?' she said, horrified to find that she was pursing her lips. She didn't really care about the answer, she just desperately wanted him to kiss her. Not that she would make the first move. But if he did . . .

He looked at her affectionately and smiled; his crinkling blue-green eyes looked like sapphires that had been thrown into a pond and were making ripples. There was another of their pregnant pauses in which enough electricity to restore light to the whole of Yugoslavia crackled between them. To her disappointment he answered her instead of grabbing her in his arms.

'I'm an actor, sweetie,' he replied in a mock-luvvie accent. 'It's my burden in life to sympathize, empathize and synthesize. Actually, to tell the truth, I know what it's like to have career envy. When we first left the Old Vic, Phoebe practically had to fight the offers off. I was the one who couldn't get arrested. Deservedly so. I was such a ham I could have kept the Harrods food hall going for months. I wanted to be a method actor, but I just ended up method resting.'

'I don't believe you.' Martha smiled.

'It's true. I'm not saying I haven't improved. But I've really slogged at it, whereas Phoebe's a natural.'

'What happened?' asked Martha, and could have bitten her lip as a frown passed across his brow.

'Why does everyone assume something's happened? Phoebe's doing fine.'

'I'm sorry. I didn't mean to imply—'

'Oh, it's all right. I'm just hypersensitive, I suppose. Phoebe gave up a lot to help me in the beginning. The RSC desperately wanted her to join them but she turned them down to be with me while I made a film in Australia. In the end, of course, it bombed, and by the time we got back the RSC had found their Juliet.'

'And you've felt responsible ever since?'

'Yeah – in a way I suppose I have. I haven't thought about it like that before. It's funny, isn't it, how one decision can prove to be such a turning point? I can still see her sitting there with the letter from the RSC. She had such a strange expression on her face. It was one of total triumph, and yet I think her mind was already made up. She wasn't going to do it. She just wanted the confirmation that she was good enough.'

Martha smiled wryly, disappointed that he hadn't made a move and disappointed too that she hadn't. She knew all about small decisions that could be turning points. Why didn't she just lean over and kiss him? What was the worst that could happen? It seemed that all her life she was destined to be an also-ran.

By the time he was due to go back to Los Angeles, where he was taking a break from filming, they felt as if they'd known each other for ever. She had even found herself one wine-sodden night confiding in Nick about the abortion, which she hadn't been able to discuss even with Tim. He was so sympathetic, so non-judgmental, so tender, it made her even more sad in a way.

'You poor, poor thing,' he kept murmuring as he hugged her against him so that she could smell the skin on his neck.

'I hate myself — for getting pregnant by Jack in the first place and for not having the guts to keep it,' she said, the tears she hadn't been able to shed for so many months finally spilling down her cheeks.

He smiled his soft, slow smile. 'Why would you hate yourself? It might just as easily not have happened—'

'But you can't approve of what I did. You work for Save a child, for God's sake—'

'I'm not crazy about the idea of abortion, it's true. I once thought that—' He trailed off. '—that Phoebe was thinking of having one and I begged her not to, I must admit. But that was different. There was no need in that case. I was with her and I wanted to stay with her. I would have loved to have had a baby. Anyway, it turned out that it was a false alarm. In any case, I don't really think any man has the right to judge . . .'

Martha felt much more at peace with herself after she had unburdened herself to Nick, although it made her dread his eventual departure even more. She saw him off in what remained of her old bottle of Cristalle and the scrapings of her Rouge Pure. Irrationally she felt betrayed by his departure, even though she told herself he wouldn't have gone if it weren't for the fact that he was due in Hollywood to make his first American film, a clever little indie thriller called *A Lighter Shade of Black*.

'Bloody nice for an actor,' was how Tim described him, after they'd seen him off.

'Quite nice for a human being,' agreed Martha.

'Yes, I thought you were rather smitten.'

'I don't know what you mean,' she said defensively. 'He's married. I see him more as a brother.'

'Oh yeah. Incest your thing now, is it? Your filial regard was perfectly obvious from the way you both kept accidentally brushing against one another whenever you thought anyone wasn't looking. Or the way you couldn't keep your eyes off him. Or the way he clearly had problems keeping his hands off you.'

'Oh, shut up,' she said lamely.

'Why are you out here, Martha?' asked Tim, suddenly sounding serious.

'The same reasons you are. In search of truth, history – and a good suntan,' she added, anxious not to sound too pious.

'The difference is I'll be moving on to another war soon. And you're supposed to have gone back months ago.'

'You think I should be covering the catwalk shows or tracking down the latest cure for PMT?'

'Oh, please, anything but a fashion show. At least here the explosions start on time. But hasn't it ever occurred to you that if you're not careful you could turn into one of those war junkies?'

'Like you?'

'I'm no role model, Martha. And I never pretended to be.'

'Well, what's our problem, then? We're a good team, aren't we?'

'Excellent. I've seen the way you've blossomed since you

came here.' It was true, and not just because ever since Nick had arrived Martha had started wearing the Bobbi Brown blushers that Kate sent out. 'The kick you get out of filing your stories,' Tim went on. 'Not to mention the lows when they get cut. It's giving you a sense of purpose you didn't get from your other jobs I suspect.'

'You're as involved as I am – and it's not a bad thing. It's better than being some dried-up old stick who's jaded by the whole thing. I've seen you deeply moved in the past few days.'

'Signs of humanity don't mean you're getting too involved ... But the way you're carrying on, you'll end up drained of all feeling. Why didn't you go home when Jenny Stewart offered you leave?'

Because Jenny had told her she was doing a brilliant job. And for the first time in her life Martha had felt valued for doing something that she valued. She didn't say anything. She suddenly felt pathetic for not having wanted to go home. For not wanting to break the spell. For not wanting anything to intrude on the perfect little world of anarchy and imperfection in which she had so thoroughly immersed herself.

'Look,' he said gently, turning to face her, 'I know what it's like. You get an assignment that seems to be filling this big void in you. But it doesn't last. The void comes back. And then you'll have to move on, somewhere even more terrible, to stop up the hole. You don't need this, Martha—' He gestured to the shrubby landscape that stretched out blackly around them. '—to make you feel good about yourself.'

She stood up abruptly, her eyes stinging. 'If it's okay by you, I'm rather tired,' she said. She had desperately wanted

Nick to take her in his arms the night before when they had been up here on their own. 'Here endeth the lesson.' Confused, she stumbled past him down the concrete flight of stairs, to the narrow, lumpy bed, where she tossed and turned until daybreak.

Martha wasn't the only one tossing and turning. Hundreds of miles to the north-west, and halfway through the seventh reprisal of Van Morrison's 'Bright Side of the Road', Sadie's patience finally snapped. She had been working like a demon to get Tithe House ready to receive paying guests. She'd already commandeered David's old study and his dressing room and turned them into bedrooms. And as if dealing with a set of builders who had the worst problems with closure Sadie had ever come across wasn't stressful enough, she was having to coax Dolly into actually doing some work. She needed her sleep more than ever.

Blearily she reached for the alarm clock. It was 2.35 in the morning. In a fit of rage she grabbed a feather-trimmed La Perla negligee, trudged downstairs to the utility room, where she thrust her feet into the first wellingtons she could, and grabbed a sou'-wester and Mata Hari, who could look pretty fierce when the chips were down. Halfway across the two sodden fields that separated Tithe House from Dan Hammond's cottage, she began to feel slightly less incensed. But it was too late to turn back now.

Only the clinically insane or an estate agent would have described Dan Hammond's cottage as chocolate-box. Vaguely taking in the dilapidated fence that straggled round his vegetable garden and the ramshackle thatch that dripped moss into the brim of her sou'-wester as she waited impatiently for someone to come to the door, Sadie wondered how much it would cost to get its current incumbent out. Done up a bit, it would make an excellent addition to her country hotel. It was only after she'd knocked sharply on the front door – the bell had expired aeons ago – that she noticed the disconcerting silence that had descended on the black, mysterious-seeming landscape. The rain seemed to have seeped into the cavities of the wall and was now emitting a mulchy smell that, in the darkness, seemed to Sadie vaguely sinister. No, the only box it resembled was a coffin. She was tempted to scurry back home to her warm lavender-and-rosemary-scented bed. But she knew that if she didn't tackle Dan Hammond now she was doomed to more sleepless nights.

She was about to rap again when the door opened and a massive, damply pungent Labrador jumped up at her. Mata Hari screeched her disapproval and leaped over Sadie's shoulder into the night, taking some marabou trim from the negligee with her and leaving a little trail of blood trickling into Sadie's cleavage.

'Down, Horace, you disgusting animal,' said Dan Hammond, surveying Sadie's get-up with amused brown eyes and taking in the delicate aroma of her rosemary body lotion. 'Sorry about that. His manners are as bad as his master's, I'm afraid. We get a bit stuck for company, you see. It's awfully dark round here.' He gazed up at the starless sky. 'Venus must be angry. Pleased to meet you. I'm Dan, by the way.'

'It's three in the morning,' said Sadie, stiffly. She was thrown off guard by his sorrel-coloured eyes.

'Really?' he said, running his hands through the dreadlocks.

'I'm not very good with clocks. Too much electricity in my body. They always go haywire. Er, would you like to come in? You must be freezing.'

'No, I would not,' said Sadie, shivering. She was finding it almost impossible to regain her composure while the rain turned her negligee into seaweed. 'I just came to say that these midnight rock concerts have got to stop.'

'Ah. Yes, I can see that. I'm terribly sorry. It's just that I lose all notion of time. Oh, look, you're bleeding. Listen, you really should come in.' With that, he bundled her into the tiny hallway and through to a cosy flagged candlelit kitchen where a drum kit – the source of all the Van Morrison – sat in one corner. A log fire was roaring away in the other and a delicious stew was bubbling away on the stove.

'Are you hungry?' he asked. 'Supper's almost ready.'

Was he mad? she wondered. She certainly must be, dripping on to a strange man's flagstones at three in the morning. 'Let me get you something for that cut.' He disappeared into what looked like a pantry and resurfaced with a little glass phial of clear amber liquid.

'It's a herbal recipe I developed myself,' he said modestly. He poured a little on to a surprisingly clean tea towel and handed it to her. Awkwardly she dabbed herself. 'And you must get into some dry clothes.' With that he bounded upstairs and returned with one of his fisherman's sweaters and a pair of faded combat trousers. They smelled, Sadie noticed, as she slipped into his bathroom to change, pleasantly musky. Like the tea towel they were clean – or at least as far as she could make out. Dan Hammond might have electricity sparking through his body but he was the only thing in the cottage that was plugged into the national grid. Elsewhere it was strictly candlelight. Not that she minded, since it cast flattering shadows which made her already impressive cheekbones look like the biggest calcium deposits this side of the Alps.

The liquid she'd put on her wound, which was delicately scented with rosemary, sage and what Sadie thought was probably a twist of canteloupe, seemed to be doing the trick. It already looked less angry. Perhaps he wasn't crazy after all. She decided to stay and try some stew. It was always sensible to promote good neighbourly relations. And if he was a decent cook, she might be able to give him some work at the hotel.

All Kate could think about was Horrowitz's. This time she was determined not to let it slip through her fingers. She began drawing up lists of ideas for stock, sourcing suppliers and, most pleasurably, planning how to decorate it. What with the money from her flat and Roberto's contribution, she'd just about have enough without having to ask her father for a penny. Her biggest problem was how to break the news to Magda.

At the beginning of September, Sadie received a dinner invitation from Dan Hammond. Actually invitation was overstretching it, she thought, as she slipped into a pair of Kate's cast-off embroidered jeans. What he had actually said, when she had bumped into him outside the NatWest in Bath, was that he had been experimenting with some organic meat pies which he wanted to try out, and perhaps she might pop round next Thursday. She wouldn't make the mistake of overdressing, but a little care and preparation, she thought, as she soaked herself in David's Floris geranium bath oil, never went amiss. Mata Hari looked at her reprovingly as she soaped herself with Camay.

By the time she stood beneath the thatched porch again – not dripping this time, but exhibiting advanced stages of mildew – she began to regret the whole venture. But before she could turn back he had opened the door and bundled her in again. He was an excellent cook, and surprisingly talkative. And he loved the Beatles and the Rolling Stones as much as she did, could play seventeen instruments, including the sitar, and seemed to know everything about organic food. By the end of the evening she was so tickled at the idea of being entertained alone by a former convict that she was reluctant to ask him about it in case it wasn't true.

As she made moves to leave, he announced that he had something to confess to her. 'I've been to prison, Sadie,' he said, his sorrel eyes spilling over with remorse. 'For the most sordid of crimes.' She didn't want to hear this. Her mouth went dry.

'What was it?' she asked, alarmed. What if he was a rapist? At the very least she pictured him having blown up a fish-finger factory or organizing a violent demonstration on behalf of plankton.

'Fraud,' he said flatly. 'When I was twenty-three, and a very different person from the one you see in front of you today, I embezzled sixty thousand pounds from the company I was working for.'

'Oh,' was all Sadie could say. It wasn't the kind of thing that was going to win him the *Today* programme's Man of the Year award, that was for sure. But it wasn't unforgivable.

'Was someone in your family ill? In need of an operation?' she offered encouragingly.

'No, I was just desperate for a Porsche.'

'I see.'

'But that's not the worst of it,' he said, penitently. 'You see, Sadie, I was a stockbroker.'

He walked her home and, as they stood by the door, he pecked her on the cheeks and told her how much he had enjoyed himself. For one heady moment Sadie felt that, had she asked him in, he would have stayed. She was about to take the plunge when Horace caught wind of a fox and scarpered across the garden at ninety miles an hour.

In the event, Kate never had to break the news of her elopement to Magda. *Domus*'s death was surprisingly painless. Not least because Kate was the only one in the office when Bernie called to say he was putting it out of its misery. Ruby was moonlighting at the *Face*, Fenton was twiddling about with his installation, and Magda was styling a fitted-wardrobes ad in New York.

'I've decided regretfully to close it,' said Bernie, fidgeting nervously in his Parker Knoll. He was expecting a tantrum. 'It's been haemorrhaging money, love. Not that I don't appreciate your hard work, Kate. In fact, I'd like to give you a bonus. But I never really did feel comfortable in your world.'

By the first week of October Sadie felt sufficiently chipper to suggest meeting David so that they could at last talk over the divorce rationally.

She reached the sixth floor of Dolphin Square and took a deep breath in front of the solid mahogany door before letting herself in. Nothing about it had altered, and yet everything had changed in the way she now looked at it. It had never felt like home but, before, she had always felt some proprietorial kinship with it.

Typical David, she thought, almost fondly, gazing around the handsome room with its fine if overly grand Louis Quinze furniture. Everything immaculate. Everything just as it always had been. Perhaps if he hadn't been quite such a perfectionist or quite so dedicated to his work, they wouldn't be in this sad situation.

From the lofty vantage point of all her therapy, Sadie could now see how hard it must be to be David, a man so repressed that his idea of being in touch with his emotions was to allow himself a minute's silence when Dolly had mistaken a bottle of his one-hundred-and-sixty-year-old burgundy and used it to spice up one of her Cook-In sauces. A man with all the spontaneity of a preset oven (he too switched off after fifteen minutes). But in spite of everything, and even with the faint aroma of Dan's patchouli essence lingering on her skin, Sadie still wondered if she and David might not be able to patch things up.

She sank down on a chaise-longue, kicked off her heels, sipped her gin and tonic and began to relax. A hot breeze ruffled the curtains in the drawing room. She must have dozed a little – it was still very hot. There was laughter coming from next door. She didn't remember the walls being so thin. She began to perspire and padded down the long, twisting corridor towards the bathroom to take a shower. The laughter was in the flat. Sadie froze. David was home, with another woman. She began to feel sick. She wanted to get out of the flat without disturbing either of them. She began to tiptoe back down the hall, her heart pounding. It was too late. The bedroom – their bedroom – door burst open and David emerged naked, a skimpy black dress in his hand.

'Give it back, you bastard,' giggled the woman, lunging towards the dress from behind him.

'And surrender my only guarantee of getting you to stay the night?' he said, making for the bathroom. The woman raced after him, gloriously oblivious to her nakedness, slapping straight into Sadie. The collision was so violent that for a moment Sadie almost lost consciousness. When she recovered her breath, she saw that not only was the woman Eliza, but that there was no sign anywhere of her husband's precious ministerial briefs.

Chapter Eleven

Donna cast her eye over the morning's front pages with a mounting sense of fury. Not a glimpse of her anywhere. Not so much as a dimple, a pore, a hair shaft. And after she'd gone to all the trouble of paying for a drop-dead tasteful dress from Armani. Mean bastards. She'd told them it was for a première, but the PR had muttered something pathetic about not having a sample in her size. And now frigging Liz Hurley had nabbed all the headlines with that walking black hole of a publicity stunt. She'd give her safety pins. One thing was for sure, *Four Weddings and a Funeral* could kiss goodbye to her vote. She swivelled back to the microphone, cutting off her Kurt Cobain memorial medley with unseemly haste, and proceeded to maul *Four Snores and a Coma*, as she had dubbed it, as only she could.

'Now you're sure you understand *exactly* what's meant by a sleeping partner?' Kate snuffled anxiously. She had decided to make a prototype scented duvet that smelled like Sadie's linen and was up to her knees in lavender, rosemary and goose feathers.

Roberto, who had been gazing at his sideburns in his patent moc-croc loafers, looked at her fondly. Kate knew she shouldn't boss him so mercilessly – he had already told her she was like Mao Zedong only without the compassion. But she couldn't help it. It would be horrific if Roberto started slipping his hideous marble statuettes and World of Leather armchairs into her stock. He'd already scared her to death by suggesting she stock loo mats, doilies and some lookalike terracotta pots he'd seen in the Innovations catalogue. Fortunately, just as she'd been wondering if she hadn't made a hideous mistake getting involved with Roberto, Scorcher had called her out of the blue. Or rather out of the ultraviolet, as he was having a tanning session in order to dissipate his ghostly white pallor for a *GQ* photo shoot.

'The fashion editor insisted on it, the raving poofter,' shouted Scorcher above the roar of the fan. 'Said I'd end up looking like a blank page if they shot me as is. Still, it's all good publicity for the new single. Now what's this I hear about a shop?'

Kate told him. 'I didn't leave *Domus* until after it was closed,' she added defensively.

'Oh, that's not what worries me,' he yelled cheerfully. 'And don't worry about Magda. She's making a mint with her Virginia Slims ads again. Loving it. In fact she's thinking of going back into fashion. No, what upsets me is that here's a nice little business opportunity and you didn't invite me to take part. Magda tells me you've been having to raise a bit of dosh.'

How Magda had gleaned any of this was a mystery to

Kate, but not exactly a surprise. 'Now, I don't want to get involved with the maths – not my thing at all – but I'm happy to bung in a few quid. I'd hate to think of you not being able to do things the way you want to.'

Scorcher's equity – which Kate never disclosed to Roberto, attributing her extra funds to a windfall – made all the difference to her psychologically and very probably prevented her from murdering Roberto.

As the opening drew closer, she was beside herself with excitement. She was born to have a shop. Where other girls had doodled their signatures in the margins of their school books, Kate had designed door signs.

She stayed up half the night sewing antique beads on to tiny slivers of silk velvet ribbon, and when she finally collapsed into bed it was to dream of all the other products she wanted to sell in the shop. Muslin sachets of lemon-grass, lace-trimmed cardigans, lampshades made from all the old scarves she had collected over the years ... She was racing frantically up and down the country checking out the samples in the factories and tracking down bits and bobs. She was determined to succeed. Ever since Sadie had broken the news about David and Eliza's affair she had broken off all communication with both of them. The thought of them together still disgusted her. It would be supremely satisfying to triumph without one bit of help from the pair of them. And when she was a hugely successful businesswoman she would not be using Coady Associates to do her PR.

'You realize you're going to have to call this shop What Katy Did Next, don't you?' said Sadie over the phone one day. She was standing in Dan's kitchen, where the two of them increasingly whiled away enjoyable afternoons trying out new organic recipes for the hotel and listening to demo tapes of Dan playing seventeen different kinds of instruments, including the spoons, to a background of whale moaning. He was expecting approval for his home-made Wensleydale any minute now. He popped a sliver in her mouth.

Kate thought for a moment. 'Of course. It's perfect. Thank you.' She told Roberto the new name.

'I don't get it,' wailed Roberto.

'You don't have to,' Kate told him.

On the way back from the solicitor's one day, where they had signed the contract legally binding them together – as business partners, but it was a start, thought Roberto – Kate had stood on tiptoe to kiss him.

'Thank you so much. You don't know what it means to me not to have to ask my bastard father for any money. I don't know how I'll ever thank you, but whatever happens you'll get your thirty per cent.'

He looked at her dark curls flapping in the wind, and thought that if she would only marry him he'd let her off at least ten per cent.

Careful not to splash any chlorine on her face or the enormous Philip Treacy sunhat balanced precariously on her glossy red bob, Phoebe swam up and down the rooftop pool of the Beverly Hills Peninsula, breathing in the heady sent of the jasmine that spiralled in luxuriant tendrils round the walls of the terrace, and tried to think positive thoughts.

Thirty-one wasn't that old. But the problem was that actress years were a bit like dog years – they just kept piling on too quickly. After two months in California, she could do a flawless Los Angelino accent, as well as a pretty impressive Texan and Waspy East Coast one. If she devoted enough time and energy to being seen in the right places in Hollywood, sooner or later someone might even cast her in a Kentucky Fried Chicken ad, she thought morosely.

She tried to think positively again, just as Nick had suggested. It was easy for him, she thought rancidly. Since the release of *A Lighter Shade of Black*, his career had gone stratospheric. After an almighty scramble, Artists Incorporated, LA's hottest agents, had secured him, fighting off awesome competition. The bait that Nick had been offered to go with other agents easily surpassed Phoebe's income for the past three years. Artists Inc. had also taken on Phoebe, enthusing about her quirky Britishness. The same quirky Britishness that seemed to deter anyone from actually casting her in anything.

And now, here they were – the talk of the sodding town. Or at least he was – inundated with scripts and social invitations. Not that he appreciated any of it. It drove her insane listening to him moan about the downside of fame when there were so many perks as well. Perks she fully intended availing herself of – except that it somehow wasn't nearly so satisfying being the *wife* of someone famous when she had always imagined she would be the star in the family. The truth was, Phoebe had never been more bored. She had thought her cult of the body beautiful was pretty rigorous in London. But since coming to LA she had taken up reiki, reflexology and running, as well as yoga and psychic yodelling, aromaceuticals and ayurverdics.

Then there were the weekly enemas to cleanse her colon, the fasts to cleanse her system, and the wax to cleanse her of all bodily hair. What with her personal growth trainer calling her every two hours to remind her to drink more water, her days had become a dizzying round of depilation, irrigation and deprivation. If Nick travelled any more, she'd have to add masturbation to the list. At least she seemed to have kicked her taste for one-night encounters with unsavoury characters. The thrill of getting into dangerous situations with utter creeps seemed to be wearing off for her – probably because there were just too many of them in LA to choose from. Thank God she and Nick had left London before she'd had time to disgrace herself with the ghastly Laurence Patterson.

Phoebe had never understood what motivated the disturbing desires that overtook her sporadically – for someone so keen on self-improvement she was surprisingly terrified of serious analysis. But she'd been experiencing the weirdest sexual impulses ever since she was about thirteen. Back then she'd reasoned that sleeping with the odd sinister character for money gave her some economic power. But even when she'd found a far more salubrious way to earn money, she'd never given up her old habits entirely.

She didn't know if Nick knew – and she didn't want to. She would hate to think he did know and turned a blind eye. On the other hand, he'd have to be a complete cretin not to suspect something. Or perhaps he just needed to be a really self-centred actor. God knows, he was distracted. As if his film commitments weren't enough, ever since that weird month he'd spent in Bosnia for Save a Child he'd been different. She couldn't quite put her manicured finger on it. War syndrome, she supposed idly. Or maybe he was method acting for his next role. It was hard keeping up with all his many and various parts.

She hated feeling bitter. But it was increasingly hard

not to when everything seemed to go Nick's way. The funny thing was, back at drama school, *she'd* been the girl who could be anyone and have anyone. For the first year she'd barely registered him. But when she finally started to notice, she recognized a kind of philosophical doggedness that complemented her own desperate ambitions. She found herself falling in love – for the first time in her jaded nineteen years. He had a strength and a vulnerability that made her feel safe – and a million miles from the dank, urine-soaked corridors of the Chaucer Estate, where she'd grown up.

A righteous pair of pilgrims her parents had turned out to be. Her mother had left home when she was nine. You couldn't blame her, Hartley always told her (Hartley – what had her parents been thinking?). But then Hartley was a bit older than Tanya (she'd changed her name shortly before applying to drama school). He could remember their mother before the gin and their father's beating had sent her half demented. She would have taken them both with her, Hartley said, but it just hadn't been possible, and in the end the safest thing had been to leave them with their father.

She used to joke that she was Nick's Eliza Doolittle. He was so middle-class. But sometimes, when she was low, she fretted that the gulf between their two worlds could never really be breached. Perhaps that was why she had retreated into retail therapy with such a vengeance. It was difficult sometimes to know which was more frightening – the increasingly manic amounts of Nick's money she was spending, or the increasingly manic smile that was permanently plastered across her face like a giant SOS.

Not that Nick seemed to mind about the spending. But she knew it must be getting out of hand when rumours of her blow-outs on Rodeo Drive reached the British tabloids. 'Phoebe goes Wilde' was one headline. British *Elle* nominated her as one of its top fifty stylish people and *Allure* magazine photographed her closet. It wasn't exactly Judi Dench territory.

Deep down Phoebe knew she wasn't right for Hollywood, where keeping track of her laps in the pool was about as intellectually stimulating as things got. She was too old and too European to scrape in on the new wave of grungy actresses currently rising through the ranks. But she wasn't conventional-looking enough to be part of the establishment either.

She had two choices, she thought, stepping out of the pool and noticing a rogue hair on her bikini line that she'd omitted to pluck the day before. She could allow what was left of her career to be totally subsumed in her husband's, which would mean following him everywhere on location and might drive him mad. Or she could try to save some face by carrying on working in Europe, which might mean they never saw one another at all. She looked at the clock on the wall. Another twelve hours to kill until Nick got back and fell asleep over dinner.

To give her credit, Kate felt marginally guilty ringing Mark Lacy after months of assiduously failing to return any of his calls. She had decided that if anyone could tell her where to source raw materials, teach her about costings and point her in the direction of a couple of reliable factories, he was her man.

He was waiting for her beneath the far vault in Your Place or Wine when she rushed in, breathless from having left her taxi in a static traffic jam. He looked different. His hair was no longer parted flat against his head but was cut into expensive-looking layers. Very Nicky Clark, thought Kate, noting that he was also wearing a suit that looked suspiciously like a Paul Smith. Someone had clearly taken him in hand. There wasn't a trace of a V-neck tank top in sight.

'You look wonderful, as ever,' he sighed. How to begin? thought Kate, casting around desperately. Where was Vince when you needed him?

'How are things at Morton's?' she asked tentatively. It seemed a bit rude to launch straight into her own problems. Half an hour later she realized she'd never really had any until she'd had to listen to Mark droning on about Tatty.

'... enthusiastic, absolutely brimming with ideas, so clued up about *everything*, from where to find the cheapest interlining to how to achieve the best market reach.'

'Incredible,' said Kate, who would quite liked to have reached out and strangled Tatty.

Things at Morton's seemed to be going horribly well. Tatty had been promoted.

They'd upgraded his Vauxhall for a convertible Audi. Tatty loved it.

Xtra, the capsule collection, had exceeded all its targets. All thanks to Tatty, of course.

Its customers had probably exceeded all theirs as well, thought Kate spitefully.

She was right.

'Tatty suggested doing a capsule range for larger sizes called Xtra Too and it's been our most successful launch in a decade. I didn't think I'd ever be able to replace you, but . . .' He trailed off when he saw Kate's thunderous expression.

'Yes, I seem to remember you said Xtra was the project that was meant to have my name all over it,' she said.

He looked sheepish.

'Don't worry.' She smiled graciously. 'Outsize is so much more Tatty's thing.'

It all floated blissfully over his Nicky Clark hairdo.

'It turned out Tatty was doing more than any of us thought,' he continued rhapsodically. 'Not just designing Xtra but editing this magazine she dreamed up. It's called *Buxom* and it sells in the shops next to the Xtra Too.'

'Super,' said Kate tonelessly.

'The really impressive thing,' Mark pressed on obliviously, 'is that the management originally vetoed *Buxom* for being expensive. But she went and did it anyway, borrowing the money from her father. It's proved a terrific marketing tool. The other chains are green with envy. Look.' He produced a copy of the *International Gazette*'s City section and handed it to her. Page three contained a pin-up of Tatty and Bernie Higginbottom above a caption that read: *Keeping it in the family. Concrete and caravan tycoon Bernie Higginbottom takes a substantial stake in* Buxom, *his daughter Tatty Hatfield's new publishing venture.* Despite the muzzy colour reproduction, Kate could see that Tatty's cheeks were vermilion.

Kate scanned the article in disbelief. *'I look forward to this being the first of many successful magazines,' said a proud Bernie Higginbottom. '1994 is turning out to be the best year of my life. It is terribly exciting having my father back me,' commented Tatty Hatfield 'Knowing that he has faith in me is very inspiring. It means I'll be able to take on some more staff, so I'll still be able to do some designing at Morton's. I plan to work day and night not to disappoint him.'*

If she hadn't been so astonished, Kate would have been twisted with jealousy at this picture of filial devotion. As it was, she couldn't tear her eyes from the photograph of them both. Talk about a dark horse. Or a colt out of the blue. Why had she never spotted the family resemblance until now? They were like peas in a pod or, to judge from their cheeks and their waistlines, plums in a pudding. It was the name which had thrown her off the scent. Nancy must have made Tatty change it when she went to that Swiss finishing school of hers.

'The first issue of *Buxom* sold out in three days flat,' Mark informed her. 'She's even been approached by WH Smith's who want to stock it, and now the management are tearing their hair out because they want to carry on doing it exclusively in-store, but Tatty's got the copyright. That's where she is now, at the printers, putting the latest issue to bed. If you wait, you might be able to see it hot off the press.'

Kate could scarcely wait – to leave, although she would have loved to have known how exactly Tatty flirted with Mark. She was so unassuming Kate couldn't imagine her fluttering anything more suggestive than a batch of freshly signed invoices.

'I'm thinking of opening a shop,' blurted Kate disingenuously. She would have told him she was opening a brothel if it would steer the conversation away from the Tatty love-in. 'Just a tiny one. I've done a business plan and got my profit margins sorted out and, er . . . Seen any good factories lately?'

Of course, he had masses of helpful information about factories and suppliers. And of course, he was far too nice not to share as much of it as he could with her. After about forty minutes of frantic note-taking, she noticed Mark looking at his watch. He peered over her shoulder and suddenly his face split into a radiant smile as Tatty, a vision in purple and green bouclé, clattered down the steps with a pile of the latest issue of *Buxom* under her arm.

At first Phoebe had visited Nick on the Mexican border every Friday night. He had bought her a dark green Saab convertible to match her eyes, so that she could drive the two hundred miles to the set, which was twenty miles north of the border. She had said she didn't mind the journey and insisted it gave her a break from the vapid torpor of LA. It certainly saved him the burden of coming home at weekends. But after their first few forays into Mexico, they were hard pressed to find things to do. And if they stayed near the rest of the film crew Phoebe became distressed by the lack of privacy. So increasingly she stayed alone at the Peninsula.

He couldn't blame her. She wasn't cut out to be an appendage. It was all so unfair. Phoebe was an exceptionally talented actress – more original and a bigger risk-taker in her work than he was. Yet he was the one who had, so far, struck lucky. And all because he had landed a role in a quirky low-budget black comedy which just happened to have caught the eye of somebody influential in Hollywood – and because he, of all the cast, had been blessed with the dark blond, regular features of the classic leading Hollywood man.

Phoebe's sharp little face and exotic couture tastes, on the other hand, were considered a little too hothouse. Gloria Morgenstern, his agent at Artists Incorporated, had told him as much when she had signed Phoebe up.

'She's a lucky lady,' she drawled through the froth of a

cappuccino. Gloria, an X-ray vision in Armani whose blond came not so much out of a bottle as an industrial-sized vat, had no time for hangers-on.

'How's that?' asked Nick politely, wondering if Gloria ever took off her Armani sunglasses. Perhaps they were implants. If not, they were the most natural thing about her. Even her beige wrap-on nails were an elaborate work of fiction. She really ought to rename herself a talons agent. She sank back in her vanilla leather Eames chair, and drummed on the desk with what sounded like several tons of acrylic. They were meeting in her penthouse office, ostensibly to discuss the welter of scripts he had been sent. Gloria had some exceptionally astute things to say about them – which was one of the reasons why he was prepared to put up with her brittle manner and insular contempt for anything that existed outside Hollywood.

Gloria looked at him steadily across her cappuccino and weighed her options – diplomacy versus honesty – and plumped for her usual. Nick Wilde had superstar stamped on his forehead, but he also needed to realize that the only reason his wife was on the list with Artists Inc. was because Gloria had recognized that she was part of the package. She would not be diverting too much energy into Phoebe's career which, as far as Gloria was concerned, was about as dead as Mary Pickford's. Deader, in fact – there was a big demand for Mary Pickford on cable.

'I'm sure Phoebe's blessed in many ways,' she began evenly, 'but I was thinking particularly of her good fortune in having you to kick-start her career.'

Nick had been so incensed he had almost torn the contract up then and there. 'It's actually more like the other way round,' he said politely.

'How so?' Gloria enquired nasally.

'Well, Phoebe's actually got a lot more theatre experience than me.'

'Really,' said Gloria, sounding bored. She sensed there was a much deeper and darker cause for Nick's defensiveness than common-or-garden marital loyalty.

'Yes. She was nominated for an Olivier for best newcomer.'

That must have been a while back, thought Gloria. 'Is he the guy who did those Lexus ads?' She yawned.

Nick ignored her. 'She's done masses of fringe, and quite a bit of TV.'

'Well, TV's a start,' said Gloria, swivelling her chair away from Nick so that it faced the willow trees that brushed against her window. Perhaps she could put Phoebe up for one of the daytime soaps.

'Anyone would think her career was in decline,' said Nick sharply, 'instead of in its prime.'

Gloria sighed. At this moment, decline would be a big improvement on the true state of Phoebe's career, which was non-existent.

The meeting, like so many he went to in Hollywood, left Nick sliding precariously between euphoria and depression. On the one hand the work he was being offered was, for the moment, stimulating and extremely flattering. It looked as though his next project would be a big-budget romantic comedy based on Noël Coward's *Blithe Spirit*, opposite Julia Roberts. He had never done comedy, or at least not since drama school, but Gloria had convinced him he could do it. And in return – and not without a battle – she'd agreed that he could do *The Meaning of Loss*, to be directed by one of Nick's heroes, Lars von Doren, the cult Swedish director who went in for what the critics called neo-naturalism – and lots of shaky film footage. Lars was revered in Cannes and completely misunderstood in Hollywood, which made everyone there feel completely inferior and overcompensatory. To give her credit, Gloria was one of the few brave enough to say that what Lars's heightened naturalism amounted to was heightened boredom. Everyone else took about two hours to say something similar without actually admitting to it. And then to make themselves feel better they always gave him an award and invested a stack of money in his so-called indie oeuvres.

But Nick was adamant. He had seen Lars's early work, which had indeed shown signs of genius, and he loved the script of *The Meaning of Loss*, which was loosely based on *Love's Labour's Lost*. To add to Gloria's distress, *The Meaning of Loss* featured more hand-held video cameras than Dixons, one decapitation, and very little in the way of budget, although, thanks to Nick's involvement, Liggers Pictures had agreed to invest a few million.

On the other hand, for the first time since arriving in LA, Nick was beginning to doubt if Phoebe *would* make it there. The first few months after they had arrived, he had been so consumed with his own success that he had failed to register the polite indifference that greeted her wherever she went. Other than the store assistants on Rodeo Drive and Melrose, who fell on her like Rock stars falling on groupies, she existed in an anonymous vacuum in a town where anonymity was regarded as a particularly antisocial virus.

In London, when Phoebe walked into a première, or what they both called a works outing, the flashbulbs burst into turbo-driven action and all eyes swivelled in her direction. In Hollywood, she was just another unfamiliar face. They were all too dense, he thought angrily, to recognize her talent and style. At first he hoped she wouldn't notice – it would be much more convenient for him if that were the case. But after a while he knew she must have. The brittle energy that had always been one of her hallmarks became all the more fragile, burning incandescently when they were on show together, and extinguishing the moment they got home. The wit, without its appreciative audience, grew sharper and sourer.

'The thing about Tatty,' began Mark Lacy jovially, pressing his foot gingerly on the accelerator of the Audi, 'is that she's absolutely brilliant at distilling the essence of a trend for a mass market.'

The prospect of being subjected to yet more Brilliant Things about Tatty had almost put Kate off the journey to Wales altogether. But her conversation with Mark the night before they set off convinced her that the excursion to see a couple of factories there would be invaluable. He had been helpful beyond the call of duty, she had to admit, introducing her to fabric suppliers and manufacturers who wouldn't mind dealing with the small quantities she had in mind.

It was the kind of September day Kate adored. Pale cornflower-blue sky stretched endlessly, berries audibly ripened, hay had been rolled into thick, crunchy barrels, small, succulent-looking clouds sailed serenely above, and twigs snapped beneath the Audi. Mark had rolled back the roof and turned up Classic FM. Kate, who couldn't bear jingles, asked him whether he'd mind if she just tuned into the news, and twiddled the knobs frantically, accidentally retuning to BSR.

'... and *another* thing,' belted Donna, revving up her bid to become Generation X's sharpest spokeswoman, 'the *first caller* who can tell me what's so *great* about opening a *tunnel* that brings us closer to the *French* wins a *magnum* of *champagne* ...'

It was hard to decide which was worse: Mark's hagiography on Tatty or Donna's rant. She returned to Classic and decided to rise above the jingles and let Chopin float over her instead.

It was a very nice car. She pulled her collar up over her ears. Things might almost be decadent, thought Kate drowsily, if Mark would only venture above fifty miles an hour. Covetously she fingered the walnut veneer glove box which promptly fell open, unleashing an avalanche of Barbara Cartlands and a packet of low-fat chocolate waffles. Bloody Tatty!

The factories weren't at all like the satanic sites she'd visited on the infamous buying trip to Bradford, but small, chatty places where the people seemed genuinely interested in trying something different. While she explained about the velvet and satin trims she wanted to put on the laundry bags, showed them her duvet prototype and the beaded necklaces and photograph albums she had designed, Mark negotiated frantically on her behalf. Tatty, he said, had taught him to become really tough and had bought him Donald Trump's *Art of the Deal* for his birthday.

They stopped for lunch at Chepstow, near the race-course, and tucked into a delicious meal of roast lamb followed by strawberries. It was an almost perfect day as they basked in the gentle heat, despite the fact that by now Kate could probably win Mastermind of the Year; special subject: Tatty.

But it was their last stop, on the way back to London through Herefordshire, which changed Kate's life professionally. Until they scrunched up the driveway of a spruce stone farmhouse where Mark introduced her to a tall, imposing woman with gleaming blond, shoulder-length hair and the fiercest blue eyes Kate had ever seen, a little worm of self-doubt had been gnawing away at her confidence. After all, what did she know about business? And how could she be sure that there were enough people with similar taste to make What Katy Did Next a success? It certainly hadn't worked for *Domus*.

But Tor instantly got the point of everything she said, so that all her anxieties disappeared. It was a perfect scene of rural domestic bliss, thought Kate, overlooking how hard Tor must work to keep everything together. Two of Tor's four children were bent double over the homework that was spread out on the scrubbed-oak kitchen table. A third, Sky, Tor's eldest and a shinier, less careworn nineteen-year-old version of Tor, made them all some supper. Tor scribbled away on Kate's original designs, crossing through the ideas that wouldn't work, embellishing (and, Kate could see, improving) the others.

Tor Delaney, as Mark explained in the car when they finally left, was a talented knitter and seamstress who had long ago trained at the Royal College of Art, before being swept off her feet by Edmund Delaney, a pig farmer from Hereford who had later disappeared in the Solent in Mysterious Circumstances.

'According to Tor, he was a terrible swimmer and it

was all dreadfully unlucky. But why he would then choose
to go swimming in the Solent in November is something
she's never addressed,' he shouted above the grinding roar
of an articulated lorry as it overtook them. 'But I'm afraid
poor Edmund was a terrible businessman. The farm was in
hock up to its haunches and Tor was left in an awful state
– financially as well as emotionally. She's much too loyal
to say anything, but I'd say she's done a phenomenal job
of pulling herself out of things.'

Thanks to phenomenal organizational talents and aggressive bullying, Tor had drawn together a team of skilled
women scattered through the local villages to make all
manner of local crafts – which Tor modified for sophisticated metropolitan tastes. Mark had come across her years
before when he had been looking for outworkers to make
up the elaborate knits he had planned to produce under his
own label. The project had never come off, but they had
stayed in touch. Kate snuggled up in the passenger seat in
a blissful daze, marvelling at Tor – and the idea that Mark
Lacy had once dreamed of starting his own business.

To Nick's relief, Phoebe's mood was transformed completely the moment they moved into the house on Coldwater
Canyon. Although he had dreamed of them buying a house
near the ocean (which he found himself missing more with
every year that passed since he'd left Cape Town), and of
maybe buying himself a little boat, Nick was thankful that
Phoebe had found a project for her frustrated talent. And
one that she was clearly equipped to bring off beautifully.

The house, a turreted Gothic folly that had been built
in the 1920s and briefly inhabited by Jean Harlow, was a

little gem. Set in an acre of densely wooded hillside, it had a crumbling pool that glimmered mysteriously in its lush, overgrown setting, like an abandoned sleeping beauty, and a captivating air of secrecy. The price, of course, despite the slump in property caused by the LA riots and the recent earthquake, had been exorbitant. Far more than he had originally envisaged spending. And the penalty of finding somewhere so unspoiled was that it was a wreck. But Phoebe had set her heart on it.

She made it exquisite, of course, tearing out the plaster-board walls that had sprouted up over the decades, ripping up worn carpets and grubby tiles to reveal original parquet, replacing the hideous open-tread staircase with a delicate curving oak one. And when the structure was restored, Phoebe set about filling it with furniture. She travelled to Clignancourt in Paris for old French armoires and chandeliers. In London she tracked down huge, comfortable, overstuffed sofas and armchairs, bolts of original Colefax and Fowler chintzes, and gorgeous little nineteenth-century oil paintings that shone mysteriously in the LA heat. From Stockholm, she returned with a pale yellow dresser for the kitchen, a dainty little escritoire for the study, and an eighteenth-century summerhouse that she found in an auction at an old hunting lodge. The garden had to be relandscaped to accommodate it, but it made a perfect fairytale retreat.

When Nick had confessed one night that he'd always fantasized about having a pool that looked like a souk, she had got on a plane to Marrakesh to search for some authentic green and cream tiles which she brought back in vast quantities to decorate the terrace and steam room that dovetailed round the pool.

For months she worked like a dervish, sourcing, superintending – and for the first time since they had arrived in LA the smile seemed less like a huge SOS and more like a genuine expression of happiness. She set up a charity, networking all Nick and Gloria's contacts shamelessly. Her first fund-raising lunch, held by the pool, was a sell-out, not least because practically every successful female in Hollywood wanted to see the new couture collection that Phoebe had persuaded Karl Lagerfeld to bring over from Paris.

It didn't take a genius to see that the house had given Phoebe a *raison d'être*. Even Gloria had remarked on her exquisite taste when she had come to one of the series of dinners they held to celebrate their moving in.

'I mean it, Nick. This house is fabulous,' she had said as he led her down to the pool, which glinted like an emerald in the flickering candlelight, while Phoebe regaled the other guests on the terrace with tales from one of her Euro-puddings. 'I'm huge in Bratislava,' she giggled loudly, mixing double-strength vodka martinis for everyone. From below, Nick could hear the tinkle of her laughter, gradually growing louder. She never used to talk about her Euro-puddings. It had taken her ages to confess even to him that all those trips to retreats and spas and *nouvelle vague* acting seminars had been covers for a series of highly successful Catherine Cookson adaptations. Yet hearing her discuss them so openly this evening made him nervous. The wit was too self-deprecating, the laughter too brittle.

'It's divine,' Gloria cooed from inside the summerhouse, where she had sunk into one of the downy chaises-longues. 'So original – totally unlike anything else here. Maybe she should think about doing it professionally.'

'I'm sorry?' said Nick distractedly, following her into the pool house.

'It's just that it would save Phoebe so much heartache in the long term. She's a very accomplished woman. There are people in this town who would pay a fortune for this degree of panache and taste. If she quit acting now there'd be no humiliation. It's not as if people even know she's an actress. And let's face it, papering and painting haven't harmed Ali MacGraw or Candice Bergen.'

Nick looked at her, horrified. How dare Gloria give up on Phoebe's talent like this, before she'd even given it a chance? She had more ability in her dear little left eyebrow than the entire podium of winners at that year's Academy Awards.

'Darling, don't go all petulant on me,' said Gloria, twirling the cherry in her cocktail. 'Let's face it, Nick, it's not going to happen for her here, acting-wise. But she could have a very big career in interior decorating. Surely it's better to excel at your second choice than fail at your first?'

'She's not failing,' he replied. 'Now, if you'll excuse me, I'd better get back to my other guests.' He stalked back to the house.

Gloria shrugged. 'Honey, think about it. I know I'm a bleached dragon, but I really don't mean her any harm. By the way,' she called after him, 'let me know when you decide to do *Green Cover*.'

On the rare nights they were alone – Nick was either away filming or they were both at home entertaining the dizzying number of new friends Phoebe seemed intent on acquiring for them both – they would sit back to back on the huge windowsill looking on to the garden. Nick would read to her from the bound set of first-edition Hemingways she had given him for their tenth anniversary. Or they would gaze up at the stars, toasting themselves in Californian pink champagne and giggling about the grandeur of their new home. Only once, when she presented him with a bill for eight hundred new saplings, did he blench. Money certainly didn't grow on these trees.

'A lot of the roots were destroyed in the earthquake,' she said, looking up from the copy of a script Gloria had sent him. *Green Cover* was a slick eco-thriller that had box-office hit stamped all over it and meretricious nonsense stitched into its ending. Gloria was desperate for him to do it. They were swaying gently on an upholstered swing that Phoebe had designed to fit under a dark green canopy that overlooked the pool. The scent of rose petals, which Phoebe scattered over the water every day, wafted over them.

'Mmm, but eight hundred trees does seem rather a lot,' he said idly. She said nothing, but flicked idly through the script for *Green Cover*. She had been very quiet for the last two hours. Perhaps she had noticed that *Green Cover* required three months' filming in Uganda.

'It takes a lot to fill out an acre,' she replied eventually.

'What are they, bonsais?' he said teasingly.

'You want your precious privacy, don't you?' she said sharply. Her eyes narrowed, she snapped the manuscript shut, slid off the swing and thrust her feet angrily into her spiky mules, knocking over a glass of mint julep as she did so. Without stooping to retrieve it, she marched towards the house, grinding shards of broken glass beneath her as she went. Nick stared after her. It was as if a squall had swept through their little idyll. The harmony of the last few weeks now seemed very fragile. He shivered, suddenly cold.

'I'm telling you, I need the new windows in by Friday.' The workman made a show of studying the hole overlooking the tiny terrace at the back of the shop, where Kate had planted an old enamel Victorian bath with herbs, and scratched his head in bemusement.

'You've got the wrong carpenter, love. I don't do miracles.'

Kate looked at him murderously. With only three days to go before What Katy Did Next was due to open, she was still waiting for Tor to send her all the bright felted blankets and cushions that were meant to provide the colour along the whole of one side of the shop. Also half the wall area was missing at the back. She had asked Sadie to get her an electric saw for her birthday but Sadie had dissolved into tears at what she saw as another sign that Kate had renounced men.

Kate was beginning to wish she'd renounced Roberto, who was harrying her mercilessly over his spreadsheets and flow charts. He had made her list every product she planned to stock, along with a complete breakdown of what it cost to make, including all the cups of tea and ginger biscuits Tor gave her outworkers and the time it took to boil the kettle. He said this was a crucial factor in ascertaining the profit margin of What Katy Did Next. Kate sighed. All she had really hoped for was to make enough to live on from the shop. Roberto, on the other hand, seemed to believe it set him on the path to being the next Mohammed Al Fayed.

✳   ✳   ✳

Phoebe woke up the morning after her row with Nick filled with remorse. Once or twice in her sleep she had reached out for him across their huge *bateau lit*, but he had already left for the studio. By the time the alarm went off — she didn't need to wake up at seven-thirty, she thought bitterly; she didn't need to get up at all, but it was a pretence she kept up to make herself feel busier — she was tense with pent-up energy and frustration. Skipping the pool and the gym for once, she jumped into the Saab and headed straight for Malibu, her copper bob fluttering like a banner in the bright sunshine. She needed to talk to Starlight, who, in the absence of any kind of sensible, professional analyst, had become Phoebe's confidante. Phoebe had a fear of proper analysis, fearing what they might find. She resided in an almost permanent state of guilt over the way she had treated Nick over the years — alternating with a sense of outraged resentment at his undeserved success. But worst of all was the sense of inadequacy she felt at having lied to him over the abortion that time when they'd gone to Sydney.

It had happened five years ago: the same time she'd got that terrible letter from Adrian Noble at the RSC turning her down for the part of Juliet. She had kept it. She kept everything — every last scrap and memento. She took the letter everywhere, carrying it inside her clothing like a hair shirt. Of course, she hadn't been able to face telling anyone, not even Nick — *especially* not him — about the rejection. So she had told him that she didn't want to do it because she wanted to be with him in Australia. She knew it would make him feel bad — and she knew he'd be too weak to argue. The worst bit was that she'd been so confident of getting the part that she'd had the abortion in anticipation – she could hardly play Juliet five months gone. She told Nick she was going to do it so that she could come with him and he'd gone mad – that was the bit that had surprised her. Who would have thought Nick was capable of such moral outrage? She had never seen him so angry. He almost frightened her. So she pretended it was a false alarm, that she wasn't pregnant after all. And he'd pretended to believe her.

Well, she'd got her comeuppance in Australia, hadn't she? Tom Wately, the pretentious shit of a director who was nominally in charge of the film, hated her from the word go, probably because he was in love with Nick. People nearly always were. He certainly made sure he hijacked as much of Nick's time as possible, insisting on endless reshoots and loading Nick down with pseudo-intellectual notes so that even when he did get home he was up half the night rereading the script. So she had got her own back. Tirelessly copying out Wately's notes, she perfected his tiny looped handwriting, and when she was satisfied that even he wouldn't be able to tell their writing apart she had written a letter to herself in which Wately told her how much he was in love with her and how it was because of her that he'd cast Nick in the lead role. And then she had placed the letter between the leaves of a book she'd been reading and pushed it under the sofa, where she knew Nick would eventually find it.

Since heading West, things had flourished spectacularly for Starlight Mystere. She had become astrologer to the A-list or, as Nick put it, a double-whammy star-fucker. In the old days Phoebe would have agreed, but since arriving in Hollywood she had become dependent on all the mumbo-jumbo she could find, even if she could never manage to remember whether she had been born with Venus or Neptune rising. It didn't really matter, she grimaced, as she pressed the dial on her radio to find a station that wasn't playing Whitney Houston; what was really rising was her sense of self-disgust.

Starlight was calm and said all the right things as usual. Since moving to LA she had renounced colour, dyed all the hair on her body white, and filled her beach house with bits of bleached driftwood she had found along the Pacific shores and in the Ikea flat-pack section. The scent of white arum lilies was so strong Phoebe almost passed out. Starlight poured her a wheatgrass and oatmeal smoothie and reassured her that of course she had a future with Nick.

'But I'm such a bitch,' wailed Phoebe, trying to extract some oatmeal that had got stuck between her teeth. 'I don't know how he puts up with me.'

'He loves you,' cooed Starlight, smiling her bewitching smile, 'and he knows you love him.'

'Do you really believe that?' snivelled Phoebe.

'Of course,' said Starlight. 'Now you know you mentioned the other day that you wanted to buy Nick a little boat but you hadn't found anything pretty enough? Well, I think I might just have come up with something.' She wriggled her non-existent bottom – the result of four hours of yoga a day – in her white velours track suit and giggled triumphantly. 'You won't believe this but my mate Flip works on the keys and he's tracked down this little beauty that once belonged to Ernest Hemingway ...'

Phoebe gasped. 'But he's Nick's favourite—'

'I know. So how about we go and check it out?'

Starlight omitted to tell Phoebe that the keys in question were in Florida and the little beauty a forty-four-footer in dire need of reincarnation as a boat. However, that *The Stingray* had once belonged to the great Papa Hemingway was proved incontrovertibly by the appearance of a logbook that Flip, in the rare moments when he was comprehensible, presented to Phoebe the following evening over dinner in South Beach.

Purchasing the boat proved relatively straightforward and only slightly beyond Phoebe's means. Transporting it to California and renovating it to its former glory, or rather to a gleaming picturesqueness that met with Phoebe's rigorously high standards, was another matter — and one that almost cost her what little goodwill remained between her and her bank manager. However, she needed another Project, and this answered her prayers. She would just have to sneak off and do some more Euro-puddings at some stage to pay for it all. The morning she drove Nick out, blindfolded, to Santa Monica and led him aboard *The Stingray* was one of the most rewarding of her life. Nick, completely taken by surprise, was almost overcome by Phoebe's thoughtfulness and persistence.

The fact was that life had been getting him down a little. *The Meaning of Loss* was proving more laborious than he'd anticipated — in his worst nightmares. He was beginning to see why the tabloids called Lars von Doren Lars von Snoren — and why Gloria had been less than keen on the project. Lars wasn't so much a control freak as an out-of-control freak. He was such an anal retentive that he had made the entire cast spend the first two weeks of their precious shoot in silence, so that they could learn the meaning of loss of sound. By week three, not a single frame had been shot — even shakily. The 98 degree temperatures on set were unbearable, tempers frayed, and the leading lady, Hiroko

Reiku, Japanese cinema's biggest name, suffered from heat exhaustion and collapsed in her trailer, although thanks to Lars's draconian ban on talking it had taken a whole afternoon before anyone had discovered this catastrophe. *Variety*, which had been monitoring the film's progress, or rather lack of it, ran a disturbing front-page article headlined 'The Meaning of Box-Office Loss'. Marty Shicker, the head of Liggers Pictures, who had previously been too cowed by Lars's formidable reputation to interfere other than by shovelling an extra couple of million dollars his way every so often, began to threaten mutiny.

Meanwhile, over in London, the *Python*, which didn't normally interest itself in affairs of the avant-garde but because of Nick's involvement had been following events avidly, was more direct. 'The Meaning of Toss,' it screeched halfway through week four. To add to the pressure, Nick was due on the set of *Blithe Spirit*, which was to start filming with Julia Roberts in four weeks, and Gloria, who could foresee an almighty battle ahead with Marty Shicker if Nick left *Loss* early, was on the phone to him every morning pleading with him to go down with sunstroke.

So the arrival of *The Stingray* touched him beyond words. He couldn't wait to take Phoebe out on it. Whether or not Lars liked it, he made sure he got two or three free weekends in the coming weeks. As for Phoebe, rushing around fiddling with bits of rigging on a cramped yacht wasn't necessarily her idea of heaven, but in years to come she would look back on those precious weekends with Nick as some of the happiest days of her life.

*　　*　　*

It had almost been worth the nearly five-year wait, thought Kate wryly. The instant What Katy Did Next opened it was mobbed. Something about the decor, which had been kept deliberately simple, seemed to strike a chord. *Vogue* called it the opening of 1994. Within weeks, the whitewashed room, with the little glass chandelier she had found in Bermondsey market dangling above the tiny staircase, and the chunky square shelves which were filled with bottles of honey-coloured bubble bath and giant slabs of French soap, were being copied in the style supplements. Kate hardly had time to unpack the clothes – little slip dresses trimmed with marabou, velvet, flowers and scraps of Chinese silk – and hang them on the eau-de-Nil and violet silk padded hangers before they were snapped up. Tor's collective was working so hard she had renamed them Tornado.

Kate was busily unpacking another cardboard package while a knot of customers clustered around her anxiously when she realised it was addressed to her personally. Carefully wrapped in several layers of brown paper was a first edition of *What Katy Did Next*. She looked at the inscription. It was from David. With tears in her eyes, she called his office. For once, Elaine Fletcher put her straight through.

'It's beautiful,' said Kate shyly. It was four and a half years since her parents had first split up and yet she still felt guilty – for speaking to her father behind her mother's back and for not giving him a chance to put his side earlier.

'I'm glad you like it. I ...' He trailed off awkwardly. '... I'm very impressed, Kate. I want you to know that, whatever happens. You've got up and done something for yourself.'

He was off to Brussels again, but they arranged to meet after that. It wasn't the most uproariously entertaining evening Kate had ever had. David was subdued and uncharacteristically hesitant as to how to behave. The fact that they both avoided all mention of Eliza made conversation stilted, and it was with some relief that they both realized at a quarter to eleven that they could call an end to the evening without too much loss of face on either side. Still, at least she'd done the right thing, thought Kate. Eliza, however, she couldn't forgive.

The What Katy Did Next groupies couldn't get enough of whatever Kate put in there. Roberto didn't understand any of it, although he was sufficiently businesslike to make sure that Kate kept the stock levels up. His personal preference was for the kind of obvious glamour of the marble Versace palace on Bond Street, and some of the better gadgets in Innovations. But he supposed that What Katy Did Next had a certain charm. And on the rare occasions Kate ever gave her arid sex life a thought, she had only to look in the pages of the glossy magazines, none of which could get enough of her products on to their pages, to get all the thrill she needed.

Phoebe sipped her spinach-and-wheatgrass cocktail and wondered when she would pluck up the nerve to tell Nick about the offer she had had from London. It had been sitting on her writing desk for days.

Sometimes she thought she must be insane even to be considering a job as a chat-show host. But Charlie Pitchcock, controller of BBC2, had made it sound so tempting and classy. She looked again at the letter.

London, June 1994

Dear Phoebe,

I hope you'll forgive me for writing to you out of the blue. But ever since Magda and Kate's dinner nearly two years ago, I've been puzzling about how to harness your unique blend of wit and glamour.

As you may or may not know, we've been undergoing a bit of a shake-up here — under that great umbrella of modernizing. The missing jigsaw in our schedule is a modern, sophisticated talk show. I've racked my brains and can only think of one perfect candidate: you.

What would set the show apart would be the fact that you can go and talk to A-list guests anywhere in the world, spend weeks with them if you like, in as zany a situation as you like.

Please do think about it. I can come and talk to you if you don't have time to come to London.

I await your response.

Yours excitedly,

Charlie Pitchcock

Controller, BBC2

Nick crept silently into the room and put his arms round her waist. She jumped, dropping the letter guiltily.

'You startled me.'

'I'm sorry, darling.' He looked at her apologetically. She seemed so fragile.

'Phoebe, we have to talk. I've been offered a part in *infidelity*, Ambrose White's new play. It's the first time he's going to direct as well. It's at the Almeida. It's brilliant and they're holding it for me so that I can do *Blithe Spirit*. The money will be the Equity minimum and Gloria thinks I'm mad—' Too late he realized that he had just revealed that his agent knew more about his life at the moment than his wife did.

Gloria sick bloody mundit, thought Phoebe bitterly. 'What about *The Meaning of Loss?*' she asked carefully, her heart pounding. She mustn't show Nick how keen she was to leave LA.

'Gloria's managed to get a moratorium on it. Lars has had to take a break anyway to get more funding. I think he's trying to raise some of it personally. At any rate he's going to London to shoot a BT ad, so he'll be marginally appeased if he knows I'm there too. It'll make him feel he's still in control . . . Oh, Phoebe, I know that you're making a fantastic go of things here. But I just feel I have to do it. The script's amazing. Of course, I want you to see it before I sign anything – and you wouldn't have to come if you really couldn't bear to leave. I'd miss you like crazy, of course, but if you really couldn't face it—'

She narrowed her green eyes and smiled sleepily. 'Darling, how exciting! I'd love to read it, though I'm sure it's absolutely brilliant. Of course you must do it. And I'd love to come.'

After his initial doubts, Nick had been extraordinarily encouraging about Charlie Pitchcock's proposal, partly, though he only vaguely acknowledged this to himself, because it dovetailed very nicely with his own plans. While Phoebe was packing up the house in LA, he went to New York to shoot *Blithe Spirit* which, as predicted by Gloria, had all the hallmarks of a smash hit. By the time filming had to all intents and purposes finished there, she was ready to come back to London, just in time for Nick to make the rehearsals of *infidelity*.

Shortly before Christmas, they arrived back in London. Nick suggested they both meet up with Charlie Pitchcock to finalize details of the show, which was actually Charlie's wife Charlotte's idea. Boyishly enthusiastic, Charlie had elaborated his plans for the show. Or rather Charlotte's plans. Secretly, she was the brains behind all his successes, but because she was so busy having babies she let him take all the glory – and do all the work. As a result, he never did anything without her approval, which was why he'd had such staggering success in attracting high-spending, intelligent female viewers – just like Charlotte, in fact.

'What would be really brilliant is if Phoebe could visit them *in situ*,' gushed Charlie. 'Then, when we've filmed that for a few days, we would invite them to the studio in front of a celebrity audience and you would chair a question-and-answer session.'

'Would Phoebe have veto over the guests?' asked Nick.

'Absolutely.' Charlie beamed. 'The DG is very anxious to make this work. He sees it as a flagship for the new kind of up-market popularism he wants to introduce throughout the BBC. Europe has already expressed an interest in taking it. With Phoebe on board I'm sure the US would too, and most of the Far East. It goes without saying that budgets and remuneration would be extremely healthy.'

It was really rather nice being back in London again, thought Phoebe, even if for the first few weeks Nick was still going back and forth to California to finish internal scenes for *Green Cover*. She and Nick were seen as the all-conquering couple, even if the only things she'd managed to conquer in Hollywood had been a couple of particularly hideous *en suite* bathrooms. Nick, who had initially been cautious about the chat-show proposal because he believed in Phoebe as a serious actress, was won over by the format when he met Charlie, who seemed a thoroughly decent and intelligent man. Phoebe, while moaning that she'd never met such a pair of Charlies, was secretly delighted at Charlie's enthusiasm, and the generous contract, which by BBC standards was huge.

Both she and Nick were also taken aback by what a big deal the press clearly thought this show was going to be. 'Charlie's Secret Weapon in the Ratings War,' trumpeted the *Guardian*. 'Phoebe's Keane as mustard and twice as sharp,' chirruped the *Python* in a very positive piece which suggested that Phoebe was so well connected that she not only had the direct telephone numbers of Jesus Christ and the Holy Spirit but Steven Spielberg's as well.

She signed and within weeks was having fittings, script meetings and consultations with Charlie over the line-up of guests for the first few episodes – and feeling a fully-paid-up member of the glitterati once more. It was just as well because Nick was working like a dog.

'You won't believe the state Ambrose is in,' Nick told her when he got back from rehearsals one night. 'He's about to direct for the first time and it's his first new play in four years. And do you know what's panicking him most? What to buy all the cast for their first-night gift. You haven't any ideas, have you? You're always so brilliant at presents.'

'Tell him to send his secretary into What Katy Did Next,' said Phoebe drowsily.

'It's terribly fashionable,' she told Nick the next morning. 'It's bound to solve all Ambrose's present worries — although God knows it's his past and that bloody leech of an ex-wife of his that's his biggest problem. All the women will love it, and the men won't care either way.'

She had recently been introduced to it by Charlie Pitchcock's wife Charlotte, and was extra taken with the place because Kate herself had been serving the first time she'd gone in and had looked gratifyingly pleased to see Phoebe again. Phoebe had taken to calling in so often, and had been so helpful in recommending the shop to all her friends and dropping its name into every article that was written about her, that Kate had shyly taken her to lunch one day at Julie's, just opposite, on the pretext of 'customer service'.

'I can't offer you a loyalty card, but I can offer you a menu card.' Kate grinned, her confidence surging after a particularly gratifying encounter with the till that morning. Phoebe had been charmed and charming, regaling Kate with just the kind of anecdotes she loved to hear — lifestyles of the kitsch and famous.

The two had got along so famously that Phoebe had reciprocated by asking Kate out for a girl's night, after she'd finished at the studios. Phoebe won Kate over all over again, as they giggled their way through a tipsy dinner at the River Café. 'Whoops. Talk about cheap frills.' Phoebe shrugged as she accidentally tipped a bottle of their most expensive wine over her new ruffled Lacroix. 'Oh well, I'll just tell everyone tie-dye is the new black.' Kate was dazzled. Which was all very satisfactory as far as Phoebe was concerned. She needed a friend who wasn't in the same line of business, and Kate, she decided, fitted the job description very well.

✲   ✲   ✲

Ambrose White was in the enviable position of being one of the country's most critically and commercially acclaimed writers, while still being considered, at the significant age of forty-five, one of its premier *enfants terribles*. Naturally, as befitted a man of impeccable left-wing credentials – Maggie Thatcher had actually lambasted one of his plays on *Question Time* with Robin Day in the last but one election, which had ensured it an extended run at the National – he had no intention of delegating the very personal process of buying his cast presents to his PA. When Nick relayed Phoebe's suggestion, he was all the more anxious to execute the task himself, particularly as he had read about What Katy Did Next in all of the Sunday supplements and was desperate to investigate for himself.

The shop was bristling with small, slim women wearing Gucci clogs and Prada rucksacks. As predicted by Roberto, they were all so indecisive that all Kate had to do was make sure she had everything in at least three different colours to send sales rocketing, since they all ended up buying each version.

Above their heads, Ambrose's eye was immediately caught by a tall, graceful girl at the back of the shop. Deep in some intensely private reverie, Kate was bending over one of the small glass counters she had designed, her long curls tumbling over her saffron peasant shirt. Ambrose, who recognized an artist in any field when he saw one, watched intently while she rearranged some delicate crystal bracelets across an olive silk rice bag, her long neck tilting forward as she stood back to examine her work.

Oblivious to the hum around her, she made a few

adjustments and smiled her satisfied cat smile. It was, he would always tell her later, the smallest, most secret fleeting smile — and one of the most erotic things he had ever seen. He turned immediately on his heels and made straight for Julie's, the wine bar round the corner from the shop, and waited there, watching out of the window until he saw her usher out the final customer. Only then, just as she was approaching the door to lock it, did he return, confident that she wouldn't turn away someone about to buy thirty-five overpriced presents.

PART TWO

———◦◦◦◦◦———

Chapter Twelve

For all her delirious happiness, Kate recognized that her two recalcitrant stepchildren were probably not the best things about being married to Ambrose.

For weeks she told herself that Marcus, *'fifteen and a budding action man, seen here kayaking down the River Dart, and his lovely sister Cressida, left, thirteen, a pupil at St Catherine's in North London'*, as *Hello!* had helpfully described them, weren't completely horrible.

But after Cressida (*'already the image of her curvaceous, beautiful Italian actress mother Allegra Brandolini'*) had locked herself in her bedroom and sobbed for two weeks when Ambrose told her about the engagement, she began to have doubts. Then when Cressida 'accidentally' put two of Kate's favourite dresses — an oyster-coloured velvet one Ambrose had bought her in Voyage and a pale pink silk bias-cut dress from Phoebe — in the washing machine with a tub of acid-yellow Dylon, her worst nightmares began to be played out in reality. Life might have thrown Kate a few curves in the shape of her parents' failed marriage and her tribulations at Morton's and *Domus*, but really, as she was later to realize, until she became stepmother to Cressida and Marcus, she hadn't known what problems were.

Cressida had pleaded delirium in the instance of the destroyed Voyage outfits. But there were too many accidents of this nature to be entirely coincidental – even with the best, most blissfully post-connubial will in the world. They had begun even before Kate moved into Ambrose's *'gracious Queen Anne home in Vanbrugh Terrace'*. Marcus and his *'brooding aquiline features'* had 'accidentally' let off a fire extinguisher in the kitchen two days after Kate had had it redesigned. Cressida had accidentally set fire to a pile of 1920s cloth-bound books Kate had bought in Hay-on-Wye as props for the shop (and for her bedside table, to impress Ambrose). Marcus had accidentally left the handbrake off Kate's beloved Spider and watched it slide down Highgate Hill. Cressida had accidentally watered the rose beds she had planted with creosote. And they had both told her that the way to all their hearts would be to reunite them with comforting, homely dinners every evening.

This shamelessly bathetic ruse had spurred Kate on to some dangerously ambitious culinary heights. Every night she attempted three courses and elaborate table settings that made Merchant Ivory's efforts look skimpy. Not that anyone noticed. Cressida was always threatening to go on a diet, Ambrose could barely tear himself from his study for more than twenty minutes, and Marcus would have been just as happy with a pressure cooker full of Pot Noodles.

One particularly humiliating evening, while they were all foraging through the candelabra and foliage for their knives and forks, Kate went to fetch the slow-roasted Barbary duck and minted potato mash only to discover that she had forgotten to switch the oven on. The following day Marcus had set off pointedly on his rusty, squeaking push-bike and returned two hours later with a cash-and-carry-size pack of Birds Eye ready meals.

But Cressida was definitely worse. Cressida had borrowed Kate's white Prada sandals and accidentally polished them with her Lancôme self-tanner. Cressida had accidentally mistaken Kate's favourite deconstructed Comme des Garçons cardigan for a cast-off in need of resuscitation and painstakingly hemmed it – wonkily – with a staple gun.

To top it all, Cressida had cut herself on one of Kate's beaded curtains and then almost bled to death all over a pile of cashmere baby blankets for the shop. After Cressida passed out – the only time she'd ever gone quiet – Kate conceded that the bleeding might have been a genuine accident. But she wouldn't swear to it. And that was the problem. They were turning her into a suspicious, vicious parody of a stepmother.

Kate felt so guilty during Cressida's convalescence that she stocked up on a pile of self-help books to foster better relations with her stepchildren – not that she need have bothered. Her life was spattered with people bursting to give her good advice, from Sadie and Dolly to the regulars in her shop.

Sadie thought Kate should introduce Cressida to a Chanting for Pain course, which Dan had found very helpful for counteracting aggression when he'd been in prison. Dolly thought Cressida should be encouraged to empower herself through education rather than tantrums.

Phoebe suggested that Kate take her on a bonding shopping session.

Dan sent one of his experimental aromatherapeutic

soothing candles but the wax wasn't set quite right and it ignited Cressida's Wet, Wet, Wet poster.

None of them seemed to hit the right note.

'Cressie's just staking her emotional territory,' offered Charlotte Pitchcock, who had become such a regular in What Katy Did Next that Kate had installed a nursing chair in the corner specially for her. She was pregnant again and oozing emotional support and empathy for anyone with what she called Junior Problems. 'Think yourself lucky,' she added unenlighteningly. 'Cats poo everywhere when they do it. Anyway, all you have to do is build some time for her to be alone with Ambrose into the family schedule. And try and show her you can be a comforting presence, not a threat. Now ... should I have the blue one, the yellow one or the white one – or the blue, yellow *and* white one?' she asked, holding up four velvet and Chantilly lace babies' bibs, the last of a successful batch Tor had sent up from Herefordshire. She couldn't decide and took the lot.

Kate was having enough problems building some time for herself to be alone with Ambrose, who was frantic with rewrites of *infidelity* for an American audience, but she resolved to give Charlotte's suggestion a go. She spent every spare moment when she wasn't attempting to be alone with Ambrose trying to rustle up nourishing, comforting soups for Cressida, who was using her convalescence as an opportunity for a quick spot of sanctioned dieting. Sadie had sent her thirty foolproof recipes that had all, without exception, failed. She was just trying to rescue some alleged minestrone with a tub of Marcus's Pot Noodles when the police arrived at the door. Cressie had daubed HELP ME, I'M STARVING on one of Kate's best antique linen sheets – completely wrecking Kate's François Nars Red

Wine lipstick in the process — and hung it out of her window.

Then, for a while, it seemed as though the war of attrition might be on the wane. This was probably due more to lack of application on Marcus's and Cressida's part than any real victory, but Kate was in no position to be picky. So when Marcus had told her that he could see — at a stretch — what his father found attractive in her, she had smiled encouragingly.

And when he had added that good sex was never the basis of a lasting relationship, she had restrained her itching fist from making contact with his distinguished aquiline nose. The good news was that, after the visit from the police, Cressida had departed for Capri to plague her mother. Allegra wasn't entirely thrilled to see her daughter, as she had been planning to seduce Brad Haven, a young American journalist who was ghosting her memoirs, but she was always happy to lend a motherly ear whenever Cressie wanted to badmouth Kate.

It was only after Nibbles had endured a week of debilitating diarrhoea, some of which inevitably found its way on to one of Ambrose's rewrites, that she finally managed to get things under some sort of control.

It was the dark before the dawn — and in Nibbles' case it was very dark.

Kate had been curled up with a copy of *How to Talk So Your Stepchildren Will Listen* when Ambrose had emerged ashen-faced from his study, brandishing the offending documents. Marcus had breezily suggested getting Nibbles put down; Kate had finally given way to tears; Nibbles had licked them dryish; Kate had smelled prune juice on his breath, put two and two together — and found a consignment of prune concentrate lurking under Marcus's bed among the copies of *Penthouse*.

'Don't you ever pull another stunt like that again, you little fucker,' she said the next morning, after she had got up extra early to catch him red-handed as he poured the syrup over Nibbles' breakfast. Taking in the flowing hair, the clenched fists and the billowing silk negligee, which made Kate look rather fierce – and a bit of a babe – Marcus had turned first white and then pink.

'Like what?' he said innocently. He knew the game was up and was simply playing for time.

'You've caused an innocent animal considerable pain,' shouted Kate angrily, thwacking him on the shoulder with her *How to Talk* book. She grabbed his hand, and twisted his little finger back almost to a right angle until he winced.

'I don't want your grudging apologies, Marcus,' she said coldly, releasing him. 'I've given up on hoping you'll like me. I just want to be left in peace with your father. Whether you like it or not we're married. And in love.' She sounded far more convinced than she felt. 'Don't mess with me, Ambrose or Nibbles. Do you understand?'

It had all been such a blur since that Thursday in late September when Ambrose had walked into the shop. She had just been putting the Closed sign on the door. But he had looked so crestfallen that she hadn't had the heart to turn him away. She was glad she hadn't when he informed her that he needed thirty-five presents. In the event, it took them about two and a half hours to decide on exactly the right gift for everyone.

Kate insisted Ambrose give her a résumé of the entire

cast's characters and the roles they were playing so that she could help him decide what to buy. It was half an hour before she realized that he had both written and directed the play, and not until the end of their transaction, when Ambrose wrote a cheque for three thousand pounds and she gave him a six-hundred-pound discount, that she ascertained his name. Even then it rang only the faintest of bells.

Of course, as she later explained to the diarist from the *International Gazette*, when he'd called her after the wedding for a quote, she *knew* who Ambrose White was. She'd always been a huge admirer. (She hoped that he wouldn't ask her which of Ambrose's plays was her favourite, as she was still wading through them.) It was just that the theatre hadn't been top of her list of priorities lately.

That was the understatement of the decade, since it hadn't been anywhere near her list of priorities. Ever. In fact the nearest Kate came to enjoying theatre was once when she'd sneaked into a John Galliano fashion show at St Martin's. On a good day Kate could giggle over the irony that saw her ending up with the country's foremost left-leaning playwright. In the past decade, Ambrose White had been garlanded with more honours and praise than any other living British writer for his thought-provoking work, which culminated in a coruscating trilogy about social hypocrisy and the breakdown of religion and other institutions, the final instalment of which was *infidelity*.

On bad days – when she let Cressida get to her – this strange alignment made her feel desperately insecure. But for the moment, she was deeply, desperately in love.

Anyway, after Ambrose had spent that amount of money in the shop, she had felt obliged to gift-wrap every single item in her lilac and green layers of specially dyed What

Katy Did Next tissue paper. It had taken so long that she had offered him a cup of jasmine tea while he waited. He had settled on one of the little fisherman's stools she had painted denim blue, and asked her about the shop.

He seemed so charmed and interested that Kate, who always became nervous around intellectual types, forgot her qualms. Instead she told him how she had tracked down the linen in Paris and how she'd found the basket-shaped 1950s chairs which had been made by the inmates of the local asylum at a school fête near Tor's. 'Is that why they call them basket cases?' she asked him, as she disappeared into the stockroom to look for some more tissue paper. Then she told him how, from the age of about seven, she used to help Sadie redecorate the house, even coming up with her own colour schemes. 'Then when I was thirteen my father let me redesign his flat in Dolphin Square. I stuffed it with all this ghastly Louis stuff because that's what I thought a barrister's home should look like ...' At this point he'd even got out his notebook – a yellow Sainsbury's book with curling corners – and started scribbling notes.

She described Tor's farmhouse and how her bossiness was producing the most beautiful workmanship. 'Workwomanship, we ought to call it, I suppose,' she said, pausing to slice some more raffia ribbon, 'since most of Tor's stuff is unsullied by the male hand.' After a while, she worked in silence. With her head bent in the utmost concentration, hair curling round her neck in sticky tendrils, little beads of perspiration on her skin, Kate was nonetheless aware that he was watching her intently.

When the last bottle of lime, lavender and oyster extract bath oil had been wrapped, it had seemed the most natural thing in the world to accept his invitation for a drink.

Which had turned into supper. Which, eight weeks later, had turned into marriage.

Their wedding, in Kensington and Chelsea Register Office, was simple and romantic. Just her, Ambrose, Marcus, Cressida, Sadie, David, Phoebe, Nick, Tor, Fenton, Ruby, Magda, who was back in London with a vengeance and a new passion for Amazonian tribal costumes, Roberto, Scorcher, who had helicoptered up from Meadowlands with Frou-Frou, who had clung to his leg as he was leaving in a most undignified fashion, the entire cast of *infidelity*, plus a few old theatrical buffers — and most of the British and American tabloid press, who had conceived an insatiable passion for Ambrose's work ever since they had discovered that there were copious amounts of nudity in it.

They only had four days to plan it, which was just as well, otherwise Kate would have had a nervous breakdown trying to style everything into perfection. As it was, the impromptu posies of roses and peonies that Sadie brought up from her garden looked gorgeous. Kate looked delicious in an olive-and-gold Empire-line dress, run up from old Indian fabrics by Tor, that set off her tawny skin magnificently and which *A la Mode* immediately elected to their 1995 Hall of Fame, prompting Kate to stock a collection of embroidered muslin Empire-line dresses in the shop. Ambrose, in a creamy Nehru suit, looked knee-knockingly glamorous. And when Dan, who at Sadie's suggestion had taken along his sitar, struck up 'Morning Has Broken' as the couple signed the register and the guests sipped lime-blossom-and-mint tea, there was barely a dry eye in the very full house.

After the wedding they all went back to Vanbrugh Terrace, where Dan and Sadie had rustled up a delicious feast of quail stuffed with berries, cheese stuffed with nuts, meringues stuffed with ice cream, and cocktails stuffed with alcohol. And the guests, who were all stuffed with food and David's best white burgundies, wandered increasingly tipsily among lines of tables piled with antique linen, crumbling glassware, petals, vine leaves and the odd clod of compost that Dolly, drafted in for the day to help and somewhat confused by the event's theme, had left behind by mistake.

Kate's only sorrow was that she hadn't been able get hold of Martha until the day before the wedding. She and Tim O'Mara had been sent by Jenny Stewart to Sierra Leone and then on to Chechnya, and by the time Kate got hold of her they were, as usual, up to their eyes in mud and shelling.

The conversation did not go well. For one thing, Martha was so stunned at the news that she thought she'd misheard, and it took Kate three attempts to convince her. Then Martha explained that there was no way she could get back in time, even if Jenny gave her permission to return at all.

'I see,' said Kate coldly, while Tor tried to make her stand still so that she could take up the dress. 'Well, it is only your sister's wedding, I suppose.'

'Don't be like that,' said Martha, sheltering from the wind behind a tank. 'It is quite short notice.'

'And getting shorter all the time,' snapped Kate. 'And I don't see why it took so long to convince you I was actually getting married in the first place. Anyone would think I was the last of the free world's spinsters.'

'Oh, pull yourself together,' said Martha, crossly. The line crackled ominously. 'Kate – are you still there? Kate?'

But it was too late. The lines were down and Martha was in the dog-house.

She wasn't the only one. If Kate had more or less forgiven David his transgressions, Sadie had not. And she was not happy to see him looking quite so suave and pleased with himself. He roared up in his silver Mercedes convertible and a purple NDP rosette and proceeded to deliver party political broadcasts to anyone who would listen. The luvvies loved it, of course. What with the Tories so low in the polls, there was genuine optimism that they might finally be routed in the next election. Consequently anyone who offered an alternative was fine with them, especially when David rashly promised to look into theatre subsidies if the NDP were ever in a position to do anything about it.

At least Dan looked outrageously handsome and sexy in his dishevelled turquoise silk shirt and faded corduroy trousers, she thought. And very young.

All in all, it seemed to pass off rather well, even if Cressida, dressed in a micro-mini and an *I must not chase boys* T-shirt, sobbed most of the way through, which wasn't entirely a bad thing as it helped cover up Roberto's snivelling. Poor Cressie was completely grief-stricken — not just because she was hacked off about the wedding but because she had only remembered that Nick Wilde would be there after she had begun her crying fit. She had the most enormous crush on him — along with the rest of her school — and now, here she was, about to meet him and looking dreadful. She had already repaired to the loo three times to try to disguise the damage with a ton of Kate's Stila concealer, but to no avail. What with the tears and the swirls of eyeshadow that had collided with some rouge on her cheeks, it all just ended up looking like a huge marsh. Her only hope was to keep on crying and get completely smashed until her eyes were so swollen she looked unrecognizable.

'Pity she forgot to finish getting dressed. Talk about brief,' remarked Ruby as Cressie lurched past on one of her trips to the loo. Ruby, who never knowingly overdressed for anything, was miffed to find someone wearing an even shorter skirt than she was. 'Her smudged mascara rings are bigger than that T-shirt.'

'I rather like it,' said Bunty Leigh, the *International Gazette*'s camp art critic and raconteur. He was feeling extra perky because after years toiling on Fleet Street and Radio Four he'd finally been given his own arts show on Leviathan TV. 'I was rather hoping for a brief encounter myself.'

Ruby lobbed him a scathing look. 'Hardly your type, Bunty. And young enough to be your great-great-granddaughter.'

He peered at her short-sightedly through his pince-nez while a juggler accidentally fired one of his balls down the front of Ruby's skin-tight shirt. 'Grand*daughter*, did you say? Dammit, I thought she was a boy.' He wandered off to drown his sorrows over the androgyny of modern youth with all the other buffers.

Bunty wasn't the only one who liked the look of Cressie. Old habits died hard with Scorcher, and he tended to like his girlfriends the way he liked his racehorses – young and frisky. Desperate not to offend Kate, however, he steeled himself to remain on his best behaviour, taking copious swigs from the bottle of ginseng and honey he had secreted in his inside pocket, and reluctantly giving Cressie, who spent most of the afternoon propping up the bar and flirting with the minstrel band, as wide a berth as possible. He must have allowed his eyes to stray for a bit, however, because he lost Frou-Frou and a histrionic (as befits a crowd of thespians) hue and cry went up until she was eventually discovered under Magda's Philip Treacy hat in a compromising position with Nibbles.

There hadn't really been much time for a honeymoon, as there was talk that *infidelity* might transfer to Broadway and required a few changes for American audiences. Instead Ambrose had whisked Kate off for a week to a ghostly but blissfully well-heated castle on the shores of Loch Lomond, where she cursed herself for not having paid more attention at Bath High to the works of Sir Walter Scott, until Ambrose informed her that he thought them sentimental.

There were times, that week, when Kate fleetingly wondered whether she would be able to live up to Ambrose's ideal of her. He seemed to find everything she said and did fascinating. Sometimes she would drift into wakefulness to discover he had been sitting by the bed gazing at her. Or she would find him watching her do the simplest chores and was mystified – unable to understand that he was simply captivated by her grace. But she was pretty intoxicated by Ambrose as well.

On the few occasions they had roused themselves from the cocoon of the baronial suite – once to tramp round the lake in the ever-thickening mists, another to flirt outrageously with one another through a banquet served to them beneath the minstrels' gallery in the great hall – she had been shocked to discover butterflies performing what felt like *Riverdance* in her stomach in case Ambrose suddenly began testing her on German declensions or asking her to recite the first paragraph of *Ulysses*.

But he never did. Instead he listened intently as she babbled about the glorious slate colours of the wintry Scottish skies, quizzing her gently about her designs for the next collection, chuckling whenever she told him about life on *Domus* and jotting things down in his Sainsbury's notebook. Every so often he would toss the huge mane of peppery-coloured hair that framed his face like two giant commas, his grey eyes would crinkle humorously, and he would pick up one of her feet from under the table, nestle it between his thighs and begin slowly, tantalizingly, to untie the ribbons of her ballet slippers.

When she got home, she asked Sadie to rustle her up a reading list. As Sadie had never actually completed her English A-level evening classes, the list didn't have anything more up to date on it than John Webster and Milton. Kate dutifully ploughed her way through *Westward Hoe*, *The Duchess of Malfi* and *Paradise Lost*, but what with Listening to Her Stepchildren she was having problems finishing *Paradise Regained*.

Annoyingly she found herself missing Martha. What with that, the rift with Eliza, the fact that Sadie was busy trying to run Tithe House as an up-market B & B (which was becoming increasingly booked up) and a nagging feeling that the rest of her life might be spent under siege from Marcus and Cressida, she was a bit low on the friend front at the moment. Even Roberto had inexplicably taken himself off on an extended tour of Club Med resorts shortly after the wedding.

'I think it's for the best,' he had said, looking at her with sorrowful, knowing eyes. She didn't know what had got into him. It certainly wasn't his thirty per cent, which was still well and truly wrapped up in the business, despite

the surging turnover. He claimed it was better that way
– she needed the money for the business to expand and
the delis were doing so well he could afford to let his
investment sit with her a little longer. Anyway, he said,
hoping desperately for a contradiction from Kate, he was
sure she would be fine without him.

Kate was sure too. But weirdly, she was going to miss
him. After the first few weeks of their marriage, when
Ambrose could barely tear himself away from her, and
they had spent long, languid days in bed, just him, her,
Nibbles and Ambrose's notebook, he had thrown himself
back into his work with a flourish. He also happened to
fully approve of her work – not least because he felt it gave
him *carte blanche* to spend all day and night writing.

It looked as though *infidelity* was definitely transferring
to Broadway, and he was busy with the rewrites. Moreover,
if it was a success there, there was a strong possibility it
might be made into a film, particularly if Nick Wilde
stayed on board, as looked increasingly likely. Ambrose,
who affected to despise Hollywood, was so excited by
the prospect he seriously considered taking some Prozac
to calm himself down.

Kate, meanwhile, toiled like a dervish. The problem was
that while Ambrose cherished her talents for homemaking she
also seemed to expect her to be a publicly listed entrepreneur
as well. He kept saying how much he admired independent
women and, Kate got the distinct impression, he despised
those wives of his friends who stayed at home to run the
family. So she threw herself into her work even more.

No wonder she increasingly turned to Phoebe, who was
sick of renting and had begged her to go house-hunting
in London with her. 'After all,' she said, looping her arm

through Kate's as they set off after lunch one day to the estate agents, 'we're both the victims of *infidelity*.'

'*There is just one star of Cannes '95 that anyone cares about. At the age of thirty-two, Nick Wilde is hip, hot and happening.*' Chloe Capshaw broke off from this masterpiece and looked across from her vantage point on the Carlton Hotel terrace to the palm-fringed Croisette where Nick was about to go down for the second time in a scrum of paparazzi. Talk about paphazard, she thought, pityingly. Thank God she did something dignified for a living, unlike those horrid men who spent every waking hour harassing celebrities, making their lives a misery and wearing horrendous clothes. It must be hell being famous, she thought, ordering another bucket of Buck's fizz.

If she could only get a one-to-one interview with Nick, she was convinced she could bring him succour. Hadn't Pierce Brosnan fallen in love with a journalist? Hadn't Harrison Ford? Hadn't ...? Chloe couldn't think of anyone else. Anyway, Nick didn't seem in the mood for close encounters with the fourth estate. No one could accuse her of not trying – she'd shoved endless messages under his door *and* rung his phone *and* dressed up as maid, before the Carlton manager had had her intercepted and escorted down to the police station. She'd soon had him put in his place when she'd flourished her gold Amex at the chief of the Cannes police, although she might have some problems getting the thirty-thousand-franc bribe past the accounts department at work. It was disgusting, really, the way the police in France operated. Thank God. The Buck's fizz arrived and she girded herself for another sentence.

Just to show how hip, Quentin Tarantino has been wooing him on a palatial £10 million yacht with a view to getting the South African-born hunk to star in his new project. Right-on Nick, who has been earning just £235 a week in the smash hit infidelity, *which is about to transfer from the luvvie hangout of the Almeida to Broadway, is said to be more interested in working again with leading leftie playright Ambrose White. 'I'm really into work that has integrity,' says gorgeous Nick. You can get inter my grity any time you like, Nick.*

Chloe closed her laptop, exhausted by the effort of concentrating for a whole ten minutes. Nick hadn't said any such thing – not in so many words. But she was sure he would have if he would only grant her a bloody audience. In a way it was his own fault if he was misquoted, thought Chloe self-righteously. She looked at her watch, a gold-plated Gucci number she'd bought on expenses after she'd mislaid her Swatch. Eleven a.m. Almost time for lunch.

Such was the buzz about the screenplay for *infidelity* that a number of Hollywood studio executives, none of whom ever went to the theatre, had greatly increased the likelihood of their succumbing to a coronary meltdown in an unseemly scramble to nab the film rights. Nick and Ambrose were determined to maintain a majority stake, however. Each night, Nick had to fight his way into his suite at the Carlton past great rainforests of tropical flowers that had been flown into Cannes, sometimes on private jets.

'They haven't even read the script,' he complained to Gloria one night on the terrace of the Carlton, as he sipped a neat vodka and she sluiced her mouth down with a triple espresso. Cannes didn't do decaf, so Gloria was even more aggressive than usual.

'It's better that way, believe me,' rasped Gloria, gingerly crossing her legs on a wicker chair after a particularly thorough Brazilian bikini wax She still wasn't convinced by the whole theatre experience. 'It's your involvement that has got them salivating.'

It was getting ridiculous, he told Phoebe on the phone. The flowers were taking up valuable script room. 'I could probably sue them for invading my olfactory space,' he said morosely. 'I'm not joking. I'm going to have to get a bigger suite.' As soon as the words were out, he cursed himself for being so tactless. He sounded like the worst kind of spoiled movie star. And to cap it all, Phoebe hadn't been sent a proper script in months. Even the Euro-puddings were sinking.

But she had giggled good-naturedly, told him to just say nose in future and to be sure to grind up the stamens of the African lilies, which, she told him, were the world's most powerful aphrodisiacs. It seemed to work. She arrived in his suite two days later hotfoot from the BBC studios in White City bearing an antique silver-embossed knife, to hack his way through the flowers with, and they didn't get out of bed for the entire weekend. On her last morning, she made a disgusting infusion out of the ground stamens and made him drink it all, after which she informed him that he would have an erection for three days. 'My special gift,' she said as she was leaving. 'The world's longest session of floral sex.'

The gifts didn't end with flowers. Nick was inundated with jewellery, open invitations to spend the rest of his life on various yachts, in beachside villas and luxurious rainforest compounds. By the end of his first week, he was the proud owner of six Cartier Tank watches, one Porsche and several wardrobes of designer clothes.

It was fun. But it meant that, far from getting to see some of the more recherché films on the schedule that he had been hoping to catch, he spent almost all his time on the terrace of the Carlton among a haystack of Cuban cigars and mobile phone antennae. It was no wonder that he just wanted to crawl into bed at night, or that he could barely focus on the questions he was asked during the blurry round of press conferences.

They were all the same, anyway. He was tired of having to explain his motivation for Guy Swanson, the darkly anarchic character trapped inside a successful barrister whom he played in *infidelity*; bored with being asked how LA compared with London; sick to death of the sound of his own voice. He had used up all his jokes, run dry of anecdotes and no longer knew the difference between spontaneity and slick, over-rehearsed repartee, largely, he suspected, because it was so long since he had experienced any of the former. Someone was getting short-changed in the whole process. And he had a nagging suspicion it was all of them.

'So if this production deal goes ahead for you and Ambrose White—' Nick gazed blankly at the doe-eyed journalist earnestly asking questions from the front row and felt faintly disorientated. '— does that mean you might set up your own company to start producing for your wife?'

Chloe was rather pleased with this question. Actually her features editor had thought of it, but the readers would never know. This could be the question that moved her on to a whole new round of interviews. Watch out, Lynn Barber. Nick narrowed his eyes suspiciously. What was she implying? That Phoebe would only get parts through nepotism? She beamed, revealing small, even white teeth and a cleavage that seemed to expand with her smile. She looked innocent enough, but you could never tell with the press.

'Er, look, Carrie—'

'Chloe,' she corrected him, edging her knees a little farther apart. The split in her pencil skirt began to tug across her thighs, like two waves waiting to part. He looked at the open mouth again and remembered that Gloria had told him back in LA, when the first weekend's gross had come in on *A Lighter Side of Black*, that he could have any woman he wanted. The thought revolted him and humiliated them all.

At the end of July, Roberto had returned from his travels with a tan that would have made a World of Leather sofa proud, a wife called Berniece and an eleven-year-old going on thirty-one-year-old stepdaughter called Serenity, who made Cressie look like Anne of Green Gables.

He had, he informed Kate, been profoundly invigorated by his rest, deeply moved, not just by the Roman remains he had explored at Ephesus and the fondant sunsets he had watched in Hawaii, but by the way Calvin Klein underwear had made inroads into all these places.

'It's the future, Kate. Globalization. This—' He nodded towards the gridlock of Gucci rucksacks belonging to a gaggle of women who were sharing a collective orgasm over some bags Kate had designed from some vintage Fortuny fabric. '—is all very well. But to make money you have to have economy of scale. We must expand. I want you to look at these properties I've found . . .'

*   *   *

Charlie Pitchcock raised a glass of tepid BBC champagne. 'To *Friday with Phoebe*,' he said jovially. 'And all who sail in her.'

Phoebe executed a mock-curtsy and sipped some of the champagne before clutching at her throat as if she'd been poisoned. It was an uphill struggle civilizing the culture at White City. To think that Charlie had suggested they conduct their first meeting over lunch at a wine bar in Chiswick. She had soon put him right. It wasn't as if the BBC couldn't afford it, charging whatever it was they did for a licence fee.

Before long she had put him right about a number of issues, not least of which had been her mode of transport into the studio. She would not be using the BMW convertible which Nick had given her, or even the normal BBC black cab service – the colour depressed her, she explained cheerfully, and would bring her performance down – but expected a lilac limo. The clothing allowance he had suggested was, she assumed, per show and not, as the wording on the contract seemed to suggest, per series. Charlie had gulped his Kir Royale and manfully mumbled that of course it was. To give him credit, he was a fast learner.

'Speech,' cried some of the members of the crew, clustering round her protectively.

She grinned impishly. 'Unaccustomed as I am to speaking in public,' she began, and they all roared appreciatively, 'being more what you might call a professional listener these days—' This met with more cheers. 'I have this inexplicable urge to tell you how much I love you all. Even Charlie, without whose indefatigable support over many lunches at the Ivy I would still be a size two (American admittedly).

And Will, the most adorable, patient, wonderful director in the world.'

Will blushed to the waistband of his donkey-coloured corduroy trousers. He had been so terrified of working with Phoebe that the stammer he had finally conquered at the age of fifteen, at considerable cost to his mental health and his father's bank balance, had returned with a vengeance. It took him so long to complete a sentence that by the time he had expressed himself Phoebe had invariably tripped off for lunch with Charlie and thus failed to hear him disagreeing with her. It caused him endless sleepless nights, but the upshot was that they got along famously. In fact, thought Will, it was the happiest set he'd ever worked on.

'And,' continued Phoebe merrily, 'Phil, without whose lighting I would look a lot older – I am forever in your debt. Seriously, I just want you to know that even if *Phoebe* is the biggest flop in television history and Charlie becomes hard to reach on the phone – well, you know what they say about clouds and silver linings—'

There were more cheers. Phoebe milked the applause before resuming. '—I will have loved every minute. I have made so many new friends who I trust implicitly. Hell, I'd even cash some of your cheques. So here's to you all and at the very least a BAFTA award for the set.'

She raised her glass again to Charlie, who flashed back an indulgent smile. 'To Phoebe,' he said magnanimously, tilting his glass, 'who has proved not just to be the most delightful comrade-in-arms but a comrade-in-charm.'

The set had, on Phoebe's insistence, been designed by Zaha Hadid and had been ferociously expensive. It had almost breached what was beginning to look like a fruitful friendship between Phoebe and himself. But she had been right. The flecked, royal blue swivel chairs and abstract walls with fishbowl-effect swirls on them that the BBC's own set designers had come up with – gruesome, provincial English dreck were the words she'd used – hadn't really worked. He could see that now. Zaha Hadid's glittering set, with its sliding glass screens and their infinite reflections of Phoebe's guests, was much more appropriate. Much more transatlantic.

It was all he could do to prevent himself igniting his hands in a rubbing frenzy of anticipation of all those international television awards. All in all, he thought smugly, £250,000 was a small price to pay to reverse the tide of American chat-show imports. Game, minimalist white set and match to Phoebe.

He had to hand it to her. She had surpassed all his expectations. Not only was she right about most things, but her name was an undoubted honey-trap when it came to reeling in A-list interviewees. And for the past two months she had been working tirelessly, complaining only when she thought his decisions would hurt the show, winning the undying devotion of the crew and proving to be a sensitive and charmingly probing interviewer. Sharon Weiner had broken down in tears when she had gone elephant-riding with her at Whipsnade.

'My daddy was a dedicated animal rights activist,' said Sharon tearfully. 'He always banned us kids from going to the zoo and beat our mother whenever he suspected her of defying his wishes.'

'And did she do that often?' asked Phoebe gently, praying that her elephant's flatulence wouldn't break the bond she was establishing with Sharon.

'Never,' sobbed Sharon. 'He was a lunatic who suffered

from crazy paranoid delusions. Everyone thought he was such a great guy, sticking his neck out for all those giraffes – if you'll excuse the pun.' She blew her nose loudly on a floral-edged handkerchief Phoebe recognized from What Katy Did – Kate must be making a fortune – 'and mortgaging his house to build that monkey sanctuary. But he was just a brute. He used to drag my little brother and me out fund-raising. All those times we'd be on the streets waving our flags or collecting door to door when we should have been doing our homework. And we weren't allowed to come home till we'd gotten our targets.' She shuddered. 'It was pitiful.'

'Is that why you were so keen to play the prosecuting lawyer in *Green Cover*?' persisted Phoebe.

'No, that was because they offered me eight million dollars,' snuffled Sharon, 'but it's probably why I have such a thing about wearing fur.'

'You mean you can't bring yourself to?' asked Phoebe, wide-eyed. Surely Sharon wasn't going to try to pull that one. She had seen her in at least six different Dolce and Gabbana mink-trimmed coats in the past twelve months.

'Yeah, right,' said Sharon, recovering some of her composure. 'No, when I say I have a *thing* about fur, I mean that I love it. The more endangered the better. Of course, you can't get hold of much of the hard-core stuff any more. You have to make do with antiques. They're not quite the same, but every time I put one on I still get that "fuck you, Daddy" rush. I've got a leopard jacket that belonged to Marlene Dietrich, a zebra cloak that I was told came straight from Isak Dinesen's closet and—'

'—c-c-c-cut,' yelled Will hoarsely, visions of militant

animal libbers in Balaclavas shelling the BBC swarming in front of his bloodshot eyes.

Charlie Pitchcock had sent Phoebe an enormous bunch of wilting lilies when he'd seen the footage. He'd even agreed to her suggestion that they call in Magda Marakeepski as Phoebe's personal wardrobe mistress at some astronomical figure which had sent Charlie into such a panic that he'd called Charlotte at home to get her to dig out his old asthma inhaler.

It was worth it. Everything considered, he thought, watching the crew applaud Phoebe adoringly, Operation Fast-Forward Charlie Pitchcock's Career was going swimmingly.

Things were sizzling along very nicely for Dan Hammond's organic leek-and-pork sausages too. And for his mango and pear chutneys, his rennet-free Cheshire, Red Leicester and Double Gloucester. Spurred on by Sadie, who had turned over all the menus at Tithe House to organic produce, Dan was renting land all around, expanding his original little vegetable plot by the day. The only catastrophe so far was his lemon meringue ice cream, and Sadie had salvaged that by repackaging it and selling it on to Kate as organic hair conditioner which the W11 posse were lapping up.

In September, three glowing reviews of the food at Tithe House appeared simultaneously in *Beau Monde* magazine, the *Probe* and *Condé Nast Traveller*. Following on from Todd Woodward's almost mystical allusion to the place in a front-cover interview for *Vanity Fair*, Tithe House's reputation as one of the world's great retreats seemed sealed.

'Of course, if you had a pool and access to an

aromatherapist you could get a star rating,' a glossy fashion editor from *Town and Country*, who had arrived with an entourage of nine browbeaten minions to photograph ballgowns on a pop star whose name Sadie kept forgetting, told her. 'You're very gifted, Sadie,' continued the fashion editor, catching Sadie's sceptical expression. 'You mustn't squander it.'

'Of course, a pool is ridiculous, but it got me thinking,' she told Dan when he came over later that night to play her his new lute. 'I'm at a crossroads with all this.' She gestured towards David's dressing room, which she had now converted into her private sitting room. 'I have to decide whether to do things properly and turn Tithe House into a viable small hotel, which will mean expanding the kitchen and possibly colonizing the stables for my private quarters. Or I struggle on in this rather ramshackle way, wasting my talents, running a business that's barely profitable, working my fingers to the bone.'

Dan looked at her immaculate slender fingers with their perfect half-crescent-mooned nails and smiled.

'It sounds to me as though you've already made up your mind,' he said softly. 'Any fool can see that you're a natural, but if you really decide to do this for real,' – he cupped her chin in both his hands and looked searchingly into her eyes, steeling himself to say something sacrilegious – 'you're going to have to start borrowing from the banks.'

'But you agree in principle,' she said, stepping back from Dan's all too distracting grasp. 'You can see the potential. For your business too.'

He flinched at her terminology. He preferred to think of himself as running a co-operative. 'Sadie, I came here to get away from all that insatiable capitalist crap. If we get bigger we end up selling our souls to the fascist-pig banks.'

'Not,' said Sadie, smiling her most enigmatic, Hartnellian half-smile and thinking of the alimony she could get if she finally agreed to divorce David, 'necessarily.'

Nick had learned to regard Phoebe's phenomenal surges of euphoric energy with a certain foreboding. In his experience they invariably heralded a great downturn in her emotions, or a series of dinner parties and makeovers. Either way it was fairly exhausting.

So far the dinners had had the upper hand. In the past two months they had entertained most of the upper levels of the BBC, five Oscar-winning thespians whom Phoebe had coaxed on to the show — and their extensive entourages — Jacques Chirac, who'd just been elected President of France and had agreed to appear, Dominick Dunne, who'd been covering the O.J. Simpson case extensively for *Vanity Fair*, and the editors of the *International Gazette* and the *Probe*, as well as Warren Pickering, the editor-in-chief of the *Python* ('just to keep the tabs sweet,' explained Phoebe to a mystified Nick). She had also played host to the editor of the *Spectator*, whom she had seated next to the editor of the Oppressed Workers' Party newspaper, to spice things up a bit. 'At least I think he's the editor,' she giggled to Nick. 'They're not really supposed to have a hierarchy, but he's definitely got the biggest desk.'

She was in her element. The *Sunday Times* magazine had anointed her and Nick the new prince and princess of Camelot, and the women's magazines couldn't get enough of her. Nick was genuinely happy for her, especially since

Phoebe had been such a critical and commercial success. But sooner or later, he knew, the crash would come. And what worried him most was that with all the advance ticket sales for *infidelity* on Broadway, it didn't look as though he was going to be around to catch her when it happened.

'We've bought a house,' she said triumphantly.

Nick had flown back from New York where the entire production of *infidelity* had been thrown into jeopardy by Equity, which was threatening to sue Ambrose personally for importing fifty per cent of the London cast, and was feeling a little raw. He had been living Guy Swanson, his brooding character in *infidelity*, for almost eight months, and it was starting to affect him mentally. He tried to resist asking how much it had cost. He was used to Phoebe's spending being out of control.

'You're cross. Even before I've begun you're cross.' She walked over to where he was undressing in the bathroom and began massaging his buttocks. Gazing at the mirror, she could see her negligee fall open, revealing her taut, small breasts which had been criss-crossed, bondage style, with wide silk black ribbons.

'No, I'm not.' He turned around and pressed her against him. He was so exhausted his bones ached, but Phoebe was clearly in the mood for some entertainment which he didn't think he could possibly provide. His only option was to divert her.

'Come and tell me all about it,' he said, leading her out of the bathroom and over to the sofa. 'And if you promise to make it thoroughly entertaining, I promise not to so much as flare a single nostril.'

'Ah.'

'Where is it?'

'Holland Park. Kate found it. It's absolutely magnificent. It's early Victorian and used to belong to some famous explorer who stuck conches everywhere and – with the rent we're getting from the house in LA—'

'How much is it?' he asked eventually, and regretted the question immediately.

She tipped her pointy little face to one side and looked at him quizzically. 'Do you want the truth or an appalling lie?'

He looked at the bondage ribbons that were starting to bite into her smooth white skin and thought of the delays on the *infidelity* and Lars von Snoren projects, which were preventing him from embarking on two obscenely lucrative films Gloria had lined up for him. 'Do you know what, darling? At this precise moment, I think the more appalling the lie the better.'

Chapter Thirteen

During the first six months of Kate's marriage, Cressida continually locked herself into her bedroom and threatened to develop ME until her drama teacher astutely cast her as the lead in *Poor Cow*. This transformed her lethargy at school but proved exhausting for the rest of them. Cressie threw herself into rehearsals with a dedication that made Dustin Hoffman look slipshod, while giving even less time to her studies. But at least it brought about a temporary peace settlement between her and Kate, which was consolidated when the two of them sat down and sobbed through Princess Diana's *Panorama* interview.

Now that Cressie needed to raid Kate's wardrobes for antique clothes that could be shrunk and boiled in the washing machine for an authentic poverty-stricken look, she *had* to be marginally polite to Kate. The trouble was that Cressie's margins were so tight they made Morton's look profligate. What with all the extracurricular activities and the long journey to and from St Catherine's every day – it was the nearest state school Ambrose could find that lived up to his academic expectations for Cressie while salving his conscience — she was as crotchety as a Bach fugue.

Kate tried to help her with her homework. But since Kate had never been that academic herself, it was a disastrous experiment that started off badly with geography — the only continental basins Cressie was interested in belonged to the hairdressers that did her lowlights when she was on holiday, and the only countries Kate knew anything about were the ones she was importing from — and went rapidly downhill when Kate tried to help out with her English comprehension.

'Why the hell do they have to bring chickpeas into it?' wailed Cressie one night over the Foreword to *Wuthering Heights*. She and Kate were busy at work on the kitchen table. 'I didn't even know they had hummus in those days. And what the fuck has it got to do with writing letters? Did they smear it on them as some sort of secret code?' She tossed her hair so violently that Kate, who was up to her eyes painting ayurvedic symbols on to a pile of pumice stones that had just arrived from Sri Lanka, where the people supposed to be painting them were on a go-slow, worried she'd damage her brain. Not that anyone would notice. Kate was beginning to think the only reason she'd got into St Catherine's was because Ambrose had dedicated all the royalties from *gotcha!* to the PTA fund. Squinting from the fumes of her lead-free organic paint, she padded over to Cressie's side and leaned over her shoulder.

'Look,' wailed Cressie, pointing triumphantly to the offending paragraph. 'Post. Hummus. What kind of fuckwit writes about lentils and literature?'

'It's not actually anything to do with food or with the post,' began Kate tactfully, hardly believing her eyes. Her mouth twitched dangerously. 'It's posthumous. It means after someone's died.' Her voice wobbled.

'You mean like when Sharon Weiner died on *Friday with Phoebe* when she told that crappy joke and no one laughed? I should think it's the only place she's ever been and not got the clap.'

Kate stared at her stepdaughter in wonderment. How anyone could be so academically dense and at the same time so street-savvy was beyond her. As were Cressie's moods, which continued to be more unpredictable than the Dow Jones. Allegra helpfully suggested they get her checked out at the Hale Clinic. Several costly allergy tests later, it was declared that Cressie's stress levels were unfeasibly high for a girl her age and that she had a parasite lurking in her gut, picked up from one of Allegra's film sets.

Kate was beginning to feel that she had a parasite too, picked up in Vanbrugh Terrace, but she sensibly kept this to herself. It wasn't easy, especially since the tests had meant that Cressie had missed out on going to see Oasis at Knebworth. Still, at least she could heap it all on her wicked stepmother, which sounded much better than blaming it on a parasite.

Ambrose had been exceptionally patient throughout the traumatic line-learning and method acting that followed. But then, as Phoebe tartly pointed out, it was easy for him to be tolerant when he spent eighty per cent of his time in New York. Even so, Kate couldn't help feeling that he secretly blamed her for the disastrous start to family life.

There was certainly no lack of lust in their relationship. He was very physical for an intellectual. In fact, he was very physical for a non-intellectual – she doubted whether Podge and Jack Dunforth combined would be a match for him. But his notebook, into which he jotted down all his new ideas for characters and which she initially found so charming, was never far away. Princess Diana might have had three in her marriage but Kate had at least three hundred and thirty-three in hers, and she couldn't help feeling that her darling husband might turn out to be an incurable workaholic.

She supposed she might have contributed to Cressie's stress levels, albeit unintentionally. The second thing Cressida had ever said to her was that her bedroom sucked. It hadn't been decorated since she was ten and was, in Cressida's view, entirely inappropriate – not least because no matter how many posters of Take That and Nick Wilde she stuck up you could still see the Winnie the Pooh wallpaper underneath.

Kate had to agree and, even though the first thing Cressie had ever said to her was that her father had continued to write love letters to her mother until just a few months before his second marriage took place ('Just thought you should know, Kate. Rebound relationships can work, just so long as both parties know what they're getting into'), she forgave her and decided to decorate her room as a surprise while she was on one of her jaunts to Capri.

At the precise moment when Allegra would have pounced on Brad Haven, had her daughter not shown up, Kate let a crack troop of builders loose on the entire top floor of Vanbrugh Terrace. It hadn't been easy: a rush job (who knew when Cressida would reappear?) which had been paid for out of Kate's own pocket, and which had only been finished in time thanks to Kate calling in some favours from the builders, who had worked on What Katy Did Next.

Taking her cue from Cressie's wardrobe, which had gone

all gypsy-style recently, she had the walls painted bright fuchsia and sky blue. Then she imported a hand-painted box-bed she had tracked down from an old gypsy caravan and ran up floor-sweeping chintz curtains for the windows. Tor tracked down a traditional lace counterpane on one of her forays into Hay. Then Kate had discovered some Romany prints in Bermondsey market for which she made some painted frames. Lastly she strung some coloured Mexican lights around the fireplace and lined the drawers with wrapping paper made from reconstituted tea bags that Magda had come across in Tasmania when she'd been shooting a chemical fertilizer ad.

It was a disaster, of course, as Kate knew it would be the moment Cressida arrived back from the airport, head to toe in the Versace bondage leather that Allegra had worn the year before at the Venice Film Festival. She hated the entire floor and said it gave her migraines. The only positive outcome was that Kate had discovered her favourite 1960s cocktail dress, which had once belonged to Marisa Berenson, screwed up behind the door to Cressie's room, where she had been using it as a draught excluder.

'You might have consulted her first,' fulminated Ambrose on the phone, after he had endured an hour of Cressida's ranting, followed by a tearful call from Kate. His mood wasn't enhanced by the ulcer Sharon Weiner had developed during the rehearsals for the Broadway run of *infidelity*, which was threatening the entire schedule of the movie adaptation.

Kate had struggled valiantly to maintain her composure, which only meant its collapse was all the more spectacular by the time she got on the phone to Sadie.

'Well, really, darling,' said Sadie somewhat distractedly

— she was in the middle of a blind tasting of Red Leicester recipes. 'I don't know which of you is the more foolish. Ambrose for indulging those wretched children of his, or you for not making more of an effort to be with him.'

Poor Ambrose. If anyone was suffering from stress, it was him. *infidelity* was easily the most powerful of his trilogy, but it was also the most politicized and controversial. It wasn't easy transferring such a topical play to New York, where half the nuances were likely to fall on stony ground. And while the critics there were profoundly in awe of him, they were also secretly furious at the idea of yet another Brit taking over Broadway.

On top of which, this was the first play he'd ever directed. He was suffering from acute insomnia in his suite at the Stanhope. And he was racked with indecision about whether or not, now that he was the son-in-law of David Crawford, Right Honourable member for the New Democratic Party, he was going to have to give up his lifelong affiliation with the Labour Party, of which, he reminded himself mistily, he'd been a member ever since he'd left Harrow. He missed Kate dreadfully, and at the same time fretted that she was already regretting marrying a man who was fifteen years older than she was. Why else would she ring her mother constantly?

Life wasn't any more serene for Kate. The final straw was Ambrose missing his plane back from New York, thereby missing their first wedding anniversary and the first night of *Poor Cow* and sending Cressie's hormones into free-fall.

'I hate you,' she had screamed as Kate went backstage (in reality a set of converted pungent loos) to congratulate her after the performance. Cressie's face was streaked with tears and her beautiful blond hair, which had been under a stifling wig for the past two hours, clung to her head like bleached coconut matting. She was so distraught she didn't even notice the enormous bunch of flowers Kate had brought her.

'It's all your fault. You're a bloody workaholic and you've driven Daddy away.' And with that she had locked herself in one of the cubicles until Kate had promised to go home.

It was all bloody Roberto's fault, thought Kate miserably. He was such a slave-driver she ought to call him Mussolini. Ever since he'd married Berniece he had become more financially ambitious than ever, and now he wanted her to open a shop on Bond Street. In fact the only thing more upwardly mobile than Berniece's social ambitions was her hair, which had never come to terms with the end of the eighties.

It was Berniece who had found them the Bond Street site one day when she was leaving the hairdresser's. It was rather a good one, Kate grudgingly acknowledged, bang opposite Chanel, though of course it needed gutting. But now the whole venture was hopelessly behind schedule – a fact of which Kate was hourly reminded by Roberto, who called her with regular sepulchral updates.

'That's another fifteen thousand pounds on top of the revised estimate, then,' he would say, after cataloguing the latest disaster. He said this every time, until she wanted to scream at him for keeping her from her husband's side, conveniently forgetting that she had been just as keen to expand.

Not that screaming would have done any good. Roberto still couldn't understand why she couldn't have kept the aluminium frames that were there and slap a bit of marbling paintwork on them. It worried him that Kate seemed intent on importing the shabby chic style lock, stock and distressed milkmaid stool to Bond Street when it seemed to him that the area badly cried out for a bit of gold leaf.

In his way, Roberto was feeling as put upon as Kate and Ambrose. Berniece had decided to send Serenity to boarding school and had been dragging Roberto off to far-flung rural idylls so that they could both be inspected by various ferocious headmistresses. So far they had done Cheltenham Ladies' College, Bryanston in Dorset, St Mary's Ascot, St Mary's Calne in Wiltshire, Malvern College in Worcestershire. ... the list went on and on. Berniece had even dragged him up to Ampleforth in Yorkshire, only for them both to be humiliated when the headmaster pointed out that the school only took boys. No wonder he was squealing at the thought of spending an extra £20,000 on a skylight for the new shop, thought Kate indignantly, when he was about to get done for £25,000 worth of fees a year. And no wonder he kept lecturing Kate about the virtues of multitasking.

'All in all,' she told Sadie wryly, 'Roberto and I are having so much acupuncture to relieve the stress it's a miracle there are any pricks left in the northern hemisphere.'

There were, however, and most of them came in the shape of Kate's builders, who seemed to have such an aversion to closure that she was thinking of packing them all off to Sadie's for a spot of psychotherapy.

It was no good confiding in Roberto. Every time she tuned into what he was saying he seemed to be debating the same point he had been days earlier when she had tuned out.

'... and then she take me to some prison called The Abbey, right up in Scotland. They seem very keen on sport,' he added suspiciously. He had watched with mounting horror as a group of fifth-formers with thighs more rugged than the Rockies had scrambled across some Astroturf with lacrosse sticks. The last thing he wanted was for Serenity to develop into a lesbian shot-putter.

'Is bloody expensive,' he continued bitterly. 'The train fare alone is gonna kill us.' She began to long for the good old days when all he ever did was bang on about his precious profit motive.

All in all, it was easier to switch off and get on with her multitasking. On top of everything, she had woken up one morning with a burning desire to design baby clothes, and had now added cashmere vests and tiny delicious beaded mittens to her repertoire.

Still, something positive came out of Roberto's moaning: the idea of Cressie being incarcerated in a prison for the next seven years, where she would be subjected to freezing showers and daily swims among glaciers, was extremely appealing. And she couldn't help harbouring a vague but surging hope that she just might have stumbled across a solution to her own familial problems.

It was true that Ambrose was vehemently opposed to private education. In fact *slappers!*, his brilliantly excoriating diatribe against the British class system, written at a precociously early age when he was in his year off between Harrow and Magdalen College in Oxford, had been set in a discredited boarding school in Devon. The lead character, a dissipated, disillusioned headmaster, was a thoroughly despicable creature who had haunted Kate for weeks after she had read the play.

That didn't stop her ringing up for a few prospectuses, just for research purposes. Once she started, she couldn't stop until she had phoned practically every boarding school in the country. She found herself curling up in bed less and less with the complete works of Engels or Karl Marx and more and more with the latest exam results from Bedales.

One by one the brochures began plopping through the letterbox: plump, glossy manuals that shimmered on her doormat with all the self-satisfaction and sparkling production values of high-class fashion magazines. Kate was deeply impressed by their facilities – the pictures of happy, confident girls tapping away at acres of computers or laughing gaily as they swarmed across the hockey fields or flew through picturesque fields astride photogenic palominos, manes and blond-streaked adolescent hair streaming behind them like a L'Oréal ad. The fees were definitely worth it. She began leaving the brochures casually lying around in the hope that Cressida might take matters into her own hands, but to begin with Cressie was too busy emoting with *Poor Cow*.

'Of course, it's hilarious really,' began Cressida one Saturday, as she filed her nails insouciantly on the soles of one of Kate's special Guadeloupean shell flip-flops and scattered her script all over the white floorboards. She was seated upon the counter next to the cash register, swinging her legs, and dressed in a pair of over-the-knee black socks, stilettos, a Jailbait T-shirt and a minuscule gym slip which she had rescued from the Oxfam pile.

'What's hilarious?' Kate looked hopefully in her direction from where she was pinning some dried cornflowers on to a muslin curtain she had draped over a battered leather armchair which she had found in Bath on one of her forays to PC World. She had begun to see a way to Marcus's heart – it involved a blatant one-way flow of favours on her part. But Cressida was an altogether tougher proposition. Still, perhaps she was about to share with Kate one of the insights she had gleaned about her character in *Poor Cow*, which she normally saved up to tell Ambrose on the phone.

'All these old crones spending a hundred quid on eye pillows made from fluff gathered from a pig's arse. When it's quite clear that what they all really need is a good shag.'

Any faint hope Kate had harboured about her customers not hearing Cressida's pearls of wisdom evaporated when the cluster gathered round a new collection of jewellery made from what looked like fossilized twigs at the far end of the shop swivelled in Cressida's direction with sheepish expressions on their faces.

She couldn't really blame Ambrose for indulging Cressida and Marcus – though she was sorely tempted. It was the lone parent's burden. Or that's what Charlotte Pitchcock said. She did wish he'd come home, though. On the rare moments when she wasn't with customers, builders or Roberto, she found that she missed him more than she could ever have imagined.

When the call had come from Jenny Stewart sending her to Israel, Martha, like the diligent, professional war reporter she had become, blew her top. As far as she was concerned, she and Tim were doing really crucial work out in Chechnya and the trip to Israel sounded like the kind of lightweight story anyone could do.

'If I'd realized you wanted me to join Sunbathers Anonymous, I would have taken things a bit easier,' she said, sounding outraged, although it might just have been the crackly satellite phone, thought Jenny optimistically. She was wrong. Martha would have slammed it down but now that she had finally got one of her own she had become very protective of it.

'Oh, don't be like that,' clucked Jenny, running her eye down her list of stories. She couldn't decide whether to lead on Jemima Goldsmith and Imran Khan's wedding or the fact that the Spice Girls were on their way to selling more records than any other female band in history. 'It's precisely because I appreciate how hard you've been working that I wanted to give you a break. Not that Israel's a playpen,' she hastily corrected herself. 'But it shouldn't be quite so chaotic. The peace talks have reached a very delicate point, and you're the only person I know who can get all the nuances across to the listeners without them nodding off into a coma. I'm sending Tim to Zaire. Fabulous story on the outbreak of a new flesh-eating virus. Anyway,' she added as an afterthought, 'it's about time you covered a story on your own.'

Martha was elated – and terrified. Jenny must rate her if she was sending her without Tim – but in the past three years she'd never been *anywhere* without Tim. He'd become her father figure, teacher and confidant all rolled into one. Their closeness was compounded by Martha's reluctance to take any of her leave – she was currently owed fourteen weeks' holiday – in case, once she got home, she lost her nerve and found she couldn't face covering any more trouble spots. That was her official reason. Unofficially she was frightened that she wouldn't be able to stop herself from camping on Nick Wilde's doorstep until he was forced to call the police.

There was much sobbing on both parts when the time came for her to say goodbye to Tim, even though Jenny had promised she would only be needed in Israel for a few weeks. Tim had become as dependent on Martha as she was on him.

Not least because ever since rationalization at the BBC had demanded that all reporters be able to file for television as well as for radio, the way Martha looked certainly hadn't harmed their success rate in getting stories on to the nine o'clock news. Not that he'd ever dared tell her that. She would have hit the roof.

'Now don't go all hard-core in my absence,' said Martha, clutching his linen jacket tearfully. 'You know they won't screen anything too upsetting, so it's just self-defeating in the end.'

Tim looked down at her shiny head and freckled nose thoughtfully, marvelling at how much she had changed since he had first met her that fateful day when she had stepped off the bus with her Prada rucksack, so thin and pale and nervous, like some victim of heroin chic. Talk about naïve. She'd made Mother Teresa look like a raddled old cynic. And now look at her. Dear Martha. He'd miss her in other ways. Her dedication, her hard work, her integrity – she was the only female reporter he'd ever known who refused to bat her eyelashes or flirt in any way in order to get a story. Not even when Tim had asked her to bat for England. Not that she needed to. She looked better in a rumpled, filthy flak jacket than most women did in an evening dress.

Anyway, she was right not to flirt, he thought proudly. There were lots of soldiers who'd be happy to take up the offer of a drink or a kiss with a woman correspondent – not least because there were so few women on the front line that most of them were desperate. But that didn't necessarily mean they respected the women who flirted with them, or that they were likely to trust that kind of correspondent with a story. In fact they were more likely to be dismissed as lightweight. Martha had instinctively grasped this and as a consequence was considered anything but a pushover.

'Take care,' he said in a muffled voice, hugging her to his turquoise silk shirt until she almost passed out from the Kouros fumes. 'I've a sad hunch those Middle East talks are all going to blow up in our faces.' She hugged him and ran towards the small twin-engine plane that was waiting to take her on the first leg of a complicated journey, unaware of just how much her life was about to change.

Charlie Pitchcock rewound the videotape for the tenth time and watched intently as Martha's shiny bitter-chocolate-coloured hair flapped wilfully across her face while she delivered a brief but moving report from the devastating scene outside Hebron where a huge bomb had just exploded. It was pretty impressive. And so were her legs. Her measured, unemotional tones brought a sense of order to what was clearly a confusing and frightening vortex of anarchy. And so did her legs. As people rushed around her screaming, she remained an island of size-ten (he estimated, and he was good at that sort of thing) calm. If she could look that good in that horrible African kaftan thingie, he could barely contain his excitement as to just how sexy she would look once Magda had got hold of her. She made you proud to be British.

More to the point, she was exactly what he needed now that he was being tipped to be a future director-general of the BBC.

It was true that he had had a scintillating run of ratings winners in the past few years, the crowning glory of which was *Friday with Phoebe*, which could apparently do no wrong as far as the viewers were concerned. The critics loved her too, and had unanimously eulogized her show until it drew nine million viewers every week – an unprecedented figure for BBC2. Charlie had been so chuffed when the first set of statistics had come in he'd rushed out and bought himself some rather impressive-looking Edmund de Wahl pottery – or rather Charlotte had, and had told him to go and collect it. Anyway, it gave his office a suitably artistic touch. 1995 was turning out to be his best year yet.

Phoebe was being compared with Parkinson in his heyday, but without the boring obsessions with Yorkshire and cricket. 'Parky knocked for six,' screamed the *Python*. 'Phoebe comes up stumps,' trilled the *Sun*. The Hollywood A-list was lining up to take part in her show, videos of which had become cult dinner-party viewing in the canyons and foothills of Los Angeles, where Phoebe's charity network continued to meet regularly and toast her in her absence. The downside was that Phoebe's expenses were spiralling by the week. Her demands were out of control. Charlotte said she must have had a troubled childhold to be so impossible now. Somehow Charlie didn't think that disseminating this information to the crew of *Friday with Phoebe* would improve the atmosphere on-set, which was now about as harmonious as a Sex Pistols medley.

In many ways, Charlie had the uncomfortable suspicion that his secret weapon, his great white hope, his cast-iron ratings winner, was dottier than a Damien Hirst and that one day everything would come crashing around them. The DG had already sent him a couple of alarming memos and he had had to take Warren Pickering, the editor of the *Python*, out for an excruciatingly expensive lunch at Le Manoir in order to quell some unsavoury rumours.

'The bottom line,' said Warren, who was known as

Warren Peace for his ability to whip up a Tolstoyan drama out of a crisis, 'is that we've got quite a bit of info on the lovely Phoebe and we need to work out how best to use it to both our advantages.' He tapped his nose knowingly before slugging back the second half of the Château Lafitte 1947. Charlie winced inwardly. He had a vague suspicion that Warren expected him to collude on Phoebe's foibles, just as he'd heard that some soap producers dished on their stars in order to keep their show in the headlines. Charlie liked column inches as much as the next controller, but he was even more terrified of Phoebe than he was of Warren.

'Er, not sure I know what you mean, Warren, old chap,' he said. Warren's magenta-and-purple spotty bow tie winked at him malevolently until he could feel one of his asthma attacks coming on.

Warren leaned back in his chair and placed his podgy fingers on the pristine white layers of linen. 'Are you trying to tell me that Phoebe is more spinned against than spinning? Listen, let's cut the crap. We all know what she's up to. We've got tapes, visuals, you name it—' Suddenly he fished into a briefcase and pulled out a sheaf of long-lens shots of Phoebe hurling an ashtray at Will; Phoebe rolling up a fifty-pound note as she knelt down beside an intricately carved Chippendale table inlaid with fine lines of white powder. Sweating profusely, Charlie looked at Warren's baby face.

'Like I said,' began Warren, his voice as smooth as the pasty skin on his blameless-looking face, 'we're all really behind Pheebs at the *Python*.'

With a dagger, thought Charlie.

'The last thing we want is for the whole thing to go belly up. After all, she's hardly some B-list soap star who can be replaced like that.' He snapped his slimy fingers and a crumb of herb-and-ricotta bread flew into Charlie's eye. 'And we love the show. We really do. What's good for your ratings is good for our ratings. So what I propose is that in return for keeping shtumm about Phoebe's little, er, eccentricities, you give us a stream of little exclusives – either you can make 'em up or we will. You promise not to talk to any of the other papers, Phoebe adorns some of our parties and backs some of our campaigns. At the moment, for instance, we've got a lovely little project going in south-west India—'

'Where all those people died in a flood?' said Charlie, mopping his brow with Warren's napkin by mistake.

'Yeah, yeah, that's right,' said Warren impatiently. 'Well, we're rescuing a baby elephant. Flying it back to Whipsnade. Poor thing's had a helluva time. The readers have been heartbroken. We did a phone-in to name it and we got 456,000 calls. That's more than when we dropped out of the ERM and we asked them to think of ten ways to string up Norman Lamont. Anyway, by popular demand she's now called Rachel – after the Greek one in *Friends*. P'r'aps Phoebe could see her way to being photographed with Rachel on her arrival . . .'

Charlie banned everyone who worked within a radius of five miles of *Friday with Phoebe* from talking to any of the press apart from the *Python*. To encourage Phoebe to collaborate with the *Python*, Charlie heard himself agreeing to her demand that they commission Norman Foster to designer an *en suite* bathroom for her dressing room in White City. She justified it on the grounds that they'd get lots of publicity, and since she'd already sold the story to *Hello!* who was he to deny her? In any case Holland, France, Germany, Spain, Greece, Japan and Australia had all signed up for the second series.

At this rate, the show might even run into the black. Even more importantly, as far as Charlie was concerned, Charlotte thought it was great.

What with the success of *Phoebe*, all that was lacking from his CV was gravitas. As the controller of BBC2 he had any number of successful light entertainment and art documentaries to his name. His skill, as well he knew it, was to make the kind of watchable television that viewers felt was intelligent and probing, without it being much of either. Of course there was *Newsnight* on weekday evenings, which as Charlie always said, usually just before he slashed its budgets, was the absolute jewel in his crown. But in reality he couldn't care less about Jeremy Paxman, who had been very rude to him on-air the time he'd been hauled on to the programme when his Japanese porn season had caused an uproar. The fact was *Newsnight* wasn't his baby and in any case it was on far too late for Charlotte ever to catch it.

What he really needed was a topical show that could go out on a Saturday night with heavyweight political guests, film footage of the week's events, a mini-debate and perhaps some street or audience vox pops — without everyone falling asleep. That meant finding a charismatic anchorman. Preferably one that was good-looking, size ten and a woman.

In her lucid moments, Phoebe wondered why she ever resented Nick. But lucidity was an increasingly rare guest in her poor exhausted mind. And when it departed, her brain was filled with misremembered, half-dreamed shadows from her and Nick's past. The herbal sleeping pills reluctantly prescribed to her by her homeopath no longer had any effect, and she had been reduced to bulk-buying industrial-strength tablets from a Wigmore Street specialist who put her on a course of Prozac. And just for insurance, she had worked her way down Harley Street until she had a collection of diazepam, temazepam, prazepam, oxazepam, lorazepam, nitrazepam and triazolam. And when they made her feel groggy, she picked herself up with a bunch of stimulants. Nick's ability to sleep like a baby drove her mad, and she assumed – wrongly – that he didn't realize what was going on.

During the day she seemed fine. She had energy to spare. The long dark hours of insomnia only made her marginally more highly strung and fidgety than usual. There was a restlessness that anyone who didn't know her well mistook for stamina. Only Nick, who remembered Phoebe's old playfulness, felt disturbed. She assured him she was fine. She took up writing her diaries, which she hadn't done since they'd gone out to LA almost four years earlier, when Nick had begun work on *The Meaning of Loss*. They – and the past – began to consume her. She said that all the travelling had thrown her circadian clock out of whack and now she only needed four hours' sleep a night – and wasn't it brilliant?

Nick didn't think it was remotely brilliant. Her eyes were bright, her infectious enthusiasm undiminished, and she seemed to achieve Herculean amounts every day, filming, researching, socializing, working on the house on Holland Avenue and posing for what seemed to Nick an endless stream of glossy magazine shoots. It was only when she tried to focus on anything that required an attention span of more than ten minutes that he could see her struggle. Her repartee was a little blunter than it had been, her capacity for rational analysis a fraction reduced. But so far only he had noticed.

He tried to talk to her about it, attempting to steer a ridiculously circuitous conversation towards the subject of her getting some help. 'God, Pheebs,' he'd said casually, 'there's no big deal about it. There's a place outside London where everyone goes for everything, from heroin abuse to a mild lack of beauty sleep. It's like Champney's . . .'

But she had flown into an hysterical rage, smashing one of her Meissen figurines, and then subsided in such an abject, breathless heap over it that he had been on the brink of calling an ambulance, when she suddenly stood up and walked calmly out of the room and into the taxi that was waiting to take her to the studio. He hadn't broached the subject again.

Instead, at the start of 1996 he suggested they escape to Palm Springs for a long weekend. He thought the bracing climate and sedate surroundings would do them both good. Phoebe was much keener on Las Vegas and in the circumstances – he had been stuck in Los Angeles fitting in yet more scenes for *The Meaning of Loss*, which was making very slow progress indeed now that most of its cast were contractually tied up with other projects – it had seemed reasonable enough. Especially as Phoebe had flown out to do a series of interviews with Nicole Kidman, Zack Wilson, Winona Ryder, Sylvia Ireland and Warren Beatty and was on the brink of exhaustion.

'Oh my God, there's the Pyramid,' she squealed excitedly as their plane circled the stony dunes of Las Vegas and the black shining planes of the Luxor Hotel glinted beneath them. Thousands of lights twinkled unevenly like tipsy Bluebell girls in the cool of the desert night. Her chocolate-coloured fingernails gripped Nick's hand so emphatically that when he looked down he saw blood. She was too hyped up to notice.

'That witch Sylvia kept us waiting five hours for three days running,' Phoebe said, tip-tapping down the steps of the aeroplane in unbelievably high Christian Louboutin ankle boots. 'It's 'cos she's got no bloody hair. Pre-Raphaelite, my fanny. She's got so many extensions I'm surprised they haven't made her apply for planning permission. Even her pubes, apparently. They kept detaching themselves and sliding down her legs. It's the diet pills, apparently. Makes all the follicles frazzle and drop out . . .'

Phoebe was in turbo-tongue mode and talked all the way from the airport and even as they climbed exhausted into bed, which was flanked by four onyx sphinxes and a golden asp. Nick had long since discovered the best policy was just to let her get on with it.

'So anyway, I asked her if the bald patches were in preparation for some part and she absolutely freaked. Insisted they change all the lighting and then tried to get me to change my hair colour so as not to compete with hers. Talk about clash of the sodding Titians. Zack Wilson's no better. Apparently they practically have to wheelbarrow in the coke for him before he'll agree to be miked up. Honestly, what makes them think they can behave like that . . . ?' she continued, stubbing her cigarette out on a sphinx.

She raised her head from Nick's chest expectantly, waiting for some insight. But he had already fallen asleep. Phoebe gazed at the gilt snake coiled round the bed-head disconsolately. Talk about a pain in the asp. Nick was no fun these days.

She knew that he had doubts about the Vegas trip and was eager to prove him wrong. The next day she was determined they'd have fun. And they did – it was almost like the old times. The brazen, vulgar good humour of the town had them both chuckling the whole time. They watched the mock-fight between the two pirate ships on a man-made Cut-throat island, tried to feed the sharks swimming in one of the hotel foyers, and enjoyed the simple pleasures the way they once had – walking together in the hard, cleansing sunlight, grinning at each other as they played the slot machines.

Nick, always ready to compromise for an easy life, she thought sourly, had complied with everything she wanted, including, towards the end of the day, a massive spending spree in Neiman Marcus. She hadn't even bothered to try on the clothes before getting them wrapped.

But again, as they crawled into bed after a long night in the casino, the demons engulfed her. It was all right for him, she thought bitterly, frantically ruffling under the sheets to see if she couldn't locate his asp. In the time it had taken her to get undressed for bed and douse herself with anti-ageing unguents, he'd already dropped off. He never had problems sleeping. Even when she was aching with tiredness her mind wouldn't stop racing. When she did doze off it was only to wake up a few minutes later shaking and sweating, her eyes swimming in tears. Starlight had told her to keep a pen and paper by her bed so that she could write down all her dreams. She was already on her second volume. And it was definitely a horror story, which invariably culminated with her doing something terrible to Nick.

If only the draining schedule of *Phoebe* were all that was driving her demented, she thought, dragging her nails through the hair on Nick's chest one last time before she slipped out of bed and went into the bathroom to reapply ome make-up. Trust Nick not to get it. Surely it didn't ake a genius to work out that the real problem was that she vas sitting in the wrong chair. It was all very well for Charlie Pitchcock and all those creeps on the newspapers to drool on about her brilliant interviewing techniques, her knack of drawing people out, her wit, her charm, her way with the udience and her ability to lure the cream of Hollywood over to White City. Did they really imagine all that was ny consolation for the fact that her acting career was in the gutter? Did they think she could even bear to watch any of her own programmes? The disappointment and self-disgust were so acrid she could feel it oozing out of her pores.

She hurriedly pulled on the little beaded slip dress she had bought in Neiman Marcus and gave Nick one last contemptuous look. You'd think her bloody husband would have guessed.

There were little honey-traps encouraging you to gamble everywhere you walked in Las Vegas. She was amazed the hoteliers hadn't installed them in the bathrooms so that people needn't waste time when they were on the loo. She would have. Then they really could gamble all through the wee hours. She teetered along the ferociously lit corridors, her crimson satin mules twinkling like the buttons on a slot machine. She liked this town; it had as little sense of day and night as she had. And about the same lack of propriety, she thought, making her way down to the casino.

First salmonella, now mad cows,' said Rose coolly as she and Eliza went through their daily notes on the day's headlines. 'It looks like Chris Newton-Evis is going to have to wave u revoir to that little yacht he's had his eye on.' She pushed a copy of that morning's *Guardian* across the table to Eliza who scanned the banner headline that screamed the scientists new warnings about BSE.

'D'you think it's just media hysteria? And more importantly, do you think we should be branching into other areas – diverging from food and going towards companies that deal in something stable and uncontroversial?'

'Like arms to Indonesia, for instance?' asked Eliza archly. 'As a matter of fact I think we should be getting more and more involved. Food scares are the next big thing. I predict that by the end of the decade there will be meltdown in this area, and companies armed with the necessary knowledge as well as our media expertise will clean up.'

Rose looked across at Eliza, with her impeccable sweep of hair and her long, racehorse legs twisted elegantly round the spindly frame of her chair, and wondered how anyone who looked so pure could be so contaminated with cynicism.

She knew Eliza well enough by now to recognize when she was in a dangerous mood. Eliza was bored. Her affiliation with the NDP, which had been so exciting when it started, was beginning to frustrate her as it became increasingly clear that they would never get into power. Her think-tanks were fine as far as they went but they were unlikely to change anything much. With each new opinion poll showing Tony Blair's lead in the polls increasing, she grew more and more restless.

In theory she ought to able to offer her services to any political party that sought them. But her relationship with David meant the press would have a field day if she went to work for the enemy. Politics wasn't the only area where David was giving her Blaired vision. She missed Martha, Kate and Sadie horribly, but there appeared to be no chance of a reconcilation with any of them. Worse still, since Sadie had begun divorce proceedings, she was haunted by the awful fear that David might ask *her* to marry him.

At one stage the thought of spending her life with an urbane, sophisticated, intelligent, attractive, wealthy man would have thrilled her. On paper – and once the press had got hold of their story they were never far from the papers – they were quite a package. But she had her own money; she didn't need a prop to make her feel sophisticated or intelligent and there was no disguising the soullessness at the core of their relationship. For a year or so she had told herself that this didn't matter. She had her career – and there was no doubt David had been good for it. She had never been one to dream of conventional happy endings. The only family values she admired belonged to the Borgias. But this void she felt when they closed the door on his Dolphin Square flat at the end of the day was beginning to sap her sense of purpose. Everything they did seemed designed to augment their careers. She no longer knew where the social life she led for her work ended, and her own life began. Perhaps it didn't.

Oh my God, I can't believe it . . . Lachlan?' Phoebe blinked uncertainly in the scorching brightness of the foyer and swayed tipsily on her mules. Lachlan's eyes flashed like comets and his hair tumbled over his collarbones like a great enveloping cloud. He was wearing his usual undertaker's suit, though this one was obviously the expensive version. He looked like the fifth horseman of the apocalypse.

'Hello, Phoebe,' he said lugubriously, surveying her creamy décolletage and glassy-eyed stare.

'It *is* you. I thought I was seeing the Vegas equivalent of pink elephants – pinko militants.'

'If indeed I am me, then I suppose me is you. Whoever that is.'

She eyed him caustically. 'Good, well, that's cleared that up, then.' She trotted off a few feet down the carpet, with its stampede of spades, hearts and diamonds, and then turned back. 'Christ, it's like walking through an acid version of *Alice in Wonderland*. What time is it?'

'Time is a meaningless concept,' he said dourly, wiping his brow with the huge white cuffs dangling out of his jacket. He was hopelessly overdressed, given that the dress code in most of the hotels hovered around gym locker-room level.

'Oh, never mind that.' Phoebe grabbed his wrist to examine his Rolex. 'Five a.m. The night is young. Come on,' she said, leading him to the lift. 'I'm celebrating and in the absence of any life-enhancing companions with which to share my *joie de vivre*, you'll have to do.'

The pyramid-shaped bar was even more hideous than the rest of the hotel, complete with lagoon and resident swans around which a few mournful-looking, extraordinarily fat people were squeezed on to extraordinarily tiny sphinx-shaped stools, twiddling cocktail sticks in a half-hearted attempt to drown their sorrows. So much for the A-list clientèle of which the hotel's pamphlet had boasted, thought Phoebe sourly. There was precious little in the way of film stars tripping about the place, though there was no shortage of box-office gross.

'Oh Christ, I hate swans,' announced Lachlan, breaking out into a cold sweat again.

'Hmm, and you such an ugly duckling ... well, you can't leave me,' said Phoebe, suddenly sounding shrill. 'You absolutely can't.' Lachlan had turned whiter than his shirt and then a murky shade of blue. She thought he was going to vomit. Torn between not wanting to leave him in case he disappeared and worrying about the health of her John Galliano, she trotted over to the reception desk and told them a cockroach had appeared in her and Nick's suite but that they were not to disturb Nick on any account. Fifteen minutes later she and Lachlan were reclining in the Presidential Suite with its Olympic-sized Jacuzzi and panoramic views of Cut-throat Island.

Lachlan perked up when he saw the magnum of champagne waiting for them and the Nefertiti heads perched in their emerald recesses. 'Presidential, my foot,' said Phoebe, cracking open a magnum of Dom Perignon. 'Penitential would be closer to the truth. I bet not even Bill Clinton has stayed in this shag-palace. In fact, what are you doing here? And don't start on that mumbo-jumbo about doing being in the perception of the beholder ...'

'Since you ask,' replied Lachlan, colour and equanimity rising as fast as the champagne was sinking, 'I'm doing about two million. Which is what they're paying for my one-man show over at the Humongous. So far my biggest audience has been twenty-eight — and I refer of course to the dress sizes of the two women who turned up. But the management are happy. They think it makes them look classy. So this—' He threw an expansive arm towards the room. '—is on me.'

'How sweet, but actually I think it's on the house.' She reached over and stroked the dark curls lapping his shoulders. His pouchy, stubbled face was quite attractive really. And his hazel eyes, great mournful, muddy-looking puddles, suddenly reminded her of one of her first-ever holidays with Nick up in the Scottish highlands.

She fished in a little antique crocheted bag and withdrew a wad of dollar bills fastened with an elastic band. 'Anyway, I won this this afternoon while Nick was in the pool. Twenty-five thousand dollars.' She threw it up in the air and it fell about them like greasy rain. 'Now we can be just like *Indecent Proposal*. So I trust you'll put your renowned imagination to good use and come up with something truly indecent, Lachlan.'

She brushed her lips gently against his before sashaying into the bathroom to check her reflection. Not bad for 6 a.m. She squirted some Fracas on her wrists and between her thighs. Lachlan, who had followed her in, pulled her unsteadily towards him and they both landed in the orange Jacuzzi. Phoebe flipped the Cleopatra-head tap on with her heel and Lachlan poured the remains of the magnum into the whirling water. In the circumstances, it should have been ass's milk, but Phoebe decided that champagne would probably smell better and refrained from complaining. Lachlan began to kiss the white expanse of her throat, reaching his hand into her dress, cupping her breasts and squeezing the top of her thigh with the other. Her skin felt as soft as talcum powder, and as he worked his hands upward and downward beneath her wet dress he discovered she wasn't wearing any underwear. Clumsily, he worked his fingers into her and began sucking on her stiffening nipples. 'Oh, Phoebe, I want to fuck you,' he grunted.

Not very lyrical, but that, she supposed, was what you got for dating a prize-winning poet these days.

She accidentally left the remainder of the twenty-five thousand dollars in the Penitential Suite. Heaven knew how much was there after they had ordered another four magnums of the hotel's most expensive champagne, tipped them in the Jacuzzi, tipped the bell-boys a thousand dollars each, and Lachlan had used some of the bills to make a paper mâché cast of Phoebe's buttocks. She had crept out of the room without giving Lachlan, still comatose in the Jacuzzi, a farewell glance. And slipped into her room as Nick was pouring his second cup of coffee at the breakfast table that had been elaborately set for two on the balcony. He looked up at her, trying not to take in her faintly stale aura and instead arranging his face into a template of concern. 'Couldn't sleep again, poor baby?'

'No,' she said, daintily straddling his lap and undoing his fly. 'But I'm full of vim and vigour.' He kissed her eyebrows, lingering over the jagged little scar, and she sighed.

She did love slipping from one hot, damp — or in Lachlan's case sopping wet — set of loins to another. She always found it so invigorating. The biggest hit yet. And, in a sweetly poignant way, it reminded her of the old days.

Almost three years after she'd sent Martha off on a month long assignment, Jenny Stewart put her foot down and insisted that Martha come back to London. 'They want to give you and Tim an award,' she explained one evening as Martha sat on her balcony at the King David editing a report for *From Our Own Correspondent*. 'For outstanding services to wars or something. Although in Tim's case it could just as easily be whores. Not that I don't admire him hugely, you understand. And that's why you've got to come back. He won't and they'll probably change their minds if they know neither of you will show up. So I'm afraid, Martha, I insist.'

Reluctantly, because she was having such a fascinating time exploring Jerusalem, and with a certain amount of trepidation, because she hadn't been home in almost three years, Martha wound her way slowly back to London. *En route*, she stopped off at a draconian spa in Deauville which she had read about ages ago in one of the *Vogue*s Kate had sent her, so that she could be thoroughly scrubbed up and defoliated before she faced everyone at home. Which is where Charlie Pitchcock finally tracked her down.

'I can't hear you,' yelled Martha above the whooshing of the hydrotherapy treatment that was being administered to her by a woman with a pseudo-scientific seriousness and the people skills of a Nazi officer. The spa had been trying to get her to switch off her mobile for days in the hope that she would relax, but old habits refused to die.

'It's Charleeee Piiitchcock,' he tried again patiently. She must be caught up in a riot some place he didn't know about. 'Sorry if I've got you at an inconvenient moment.'

'Not at all. Just a sec,' she shouted as the Nazi began heading for her breasts with what looked like a sandblasting machine. She leaped off the table and grabbed a towel.

Outside the treatment room she resumed the call. She had been away so long that at the start of the conversation his name only vaguely rang a bell. By the end she had agreed to front a new current affairs programme that promised to be Charlie Pitchcock's most audacious experiment yet.

Chapter Fourteen

———◦◦◦◦◦———

'The problem, when you really think about it,' said Kate, her hands overflowing with some Abergavenny seaweed that Tor had Federal Expressed her that morning, 'is there just aren't any decent dusters around. I mean, why do they always have to be yellow? Why not pale pink and embroidered? Or beaded? No, no, wait – what about patchwork? That would hit just the right rustic note ...' She trailed off and gazed past Ambrose thoughtfully. 'There's so much potential for beauty – and it's just wasted.' She looped another frond around some soaps made from buffalo spittle.

'I can see you might have a point,' said Ambrose, simultaneously thinking that she looked like a water nymph emerging from Narcissus's pond, patting Nibbles morosely and trying to sound mesmerized. He had dropped into the shop to try to break the news, stewing on the back of his tongue all week, that he was going to have to go to New York yet again, and found her threading crystals through the chandelier. Thanks to Nick and Marty Shicker, who had somehow quelled the final outbreak of insurgency from US Equity, *infidelity* was finally due to open on Broadway

– eighteen months later than planned, amid unprecedented amounts of hype, which Sharon Weiner's Oscar nomination had only increased. Marty had also unilaterally decided to alternate *infidelity* with the other two in the trilogy, which of course meant lots more rehearsals and copious amounts of rewriting. Ambrose had started on *gotcha!* last week and had become so embroiled that he had almost entirely rewritten it, so that it was no longer the middle of the set but a prequel.

Set in the aftermath of the Falklands War, *gotcha!* was a complex, thought-provoking depiction of a godless society that allowed Ambrose plenty of scope for exploring all his favourite motifs: amorality, greed and agnosticism. Plus it had the odd window of opportunity for Marty Shicker's favourite motif – nudity. In its original incarnation, it was, as *The Times* put it, '*sublimely well crafted. A soaring achievement of visceral intensity.*' Unfortunately it was also extremely depressing, and working intensely on it was having a deleterious effect on Ambrose's moods. His entire oeuvre now seemed to him meretricious and empty, which was worrying; he couldn't get the third act to work any more and the whole play was close to collapse. He fingered a slimy sliver of seaweed despondently.

It somehow seemed an apt metaphor for his life. He wished he could rattle off something frothy like Tom Stoppard. It hardly seemed fair that some had comedy and Tony awards thrust upon them, while he was condemned to toil in the Siberian wastelands of depressed and twisted psyches. Even Martin Amis got to take pot shots at life from the safe confines of a literary eyrie without ever having to deal with bolshy unions and megalomaniac directors. Ambrose sighed. What with all the Equity problems, the

endless flights to New York, and painstaking negotiations with actresses suffering from PMT – post-mammary
enhancement tension – he was beginning to feel less like
an artist and more like a factory shop-floor steward.

'I think it's a huge gap in the market, actually. Tor says
it would be really easy to get hold of enough patchwork to
do quite big bulk orders. Would you believe she's found a
local factory? Well, it's more of a barn really, where they've
got this huge over-stitching machine that's just rusting away
at the moment. It used to make serapes and then the bottom
dropped out of the market. The man who owns it reckons
the machine could easily be adapted. He's desperate to get
in more orders, apparently. A case of seraping the barrel,
I suppose. But it would be easy to start wholesaling them.
Wemyss and Sons have said they'd be very interested in
stocking a What Katy Did Next line of products. Between
you and me, I think they'd sell Nibbles' pee if we put it in
a nice bottle and plonked our logo on it. That would give
Roberto's flow charts something to think about.'

'Ingenious,' said Ambrose absent-mindedly. He couldn't
for the life of him imagine what serapes did or who Wemyss
and Sons were. What *he* really wanted was for his wife
to accompany him while he wrestled with the egos of
Broadway. But having dedicated a number of his plays
to lambasting the bourgeois values of his father, foremost
of which was his father's insistence that Ambrose's mother
give up her teaching career upon marriage and spend the
rest of her life in pursuit of his comfort and happiness,
he could hardly insist on it. Still, he couldn't help wishing
Kate would learn to delegate a bit more.

She had been through four manageresses in twelve
months. It was quite obvious that she ought to take

on Sky, Tor's daughter, who not only organized all her siblings while Tor got on with bossing the outworkers, but even managed to handle Tor. Kate, on the other hand, was clearly intimidated by Tor, whom she thought spectacularly creative, beautiful and resourceful, which she was. But then so, thought Ambrose proudly, was Kate. Tor had an imposing beauty that clearly bored her – she had less vanity than any other woman he'd ever met and didn't exactly make the best of herself. And because she valued it so little, others inevitably came round to that point of view too. Whereas Kate ... He looked across at her stretching towards the chandelier, tendrils of hair and seaweed curling round her shoulders while Nibbles jumped up at the pale blue chair she had placed on the counter and was now balanced on. Kate was simply inimitable. He sighed again.

If only he weren't constantly being visited by the niggling feeling that somehow their marriage was ... insubstantial – yes, that was the only word for it. It was all very well being together in their separateness, as Paulina, the lead character in *rape*, had expressed it in one memorably tear-jerking speech, but Ambrose was beginning to despair that Kate even registered their apartness any more.

'Darling—' Kate's voice, muffled through a mouthful of seaweed, intruded on his misery like a sleepwalker. 'Listen, this is taking a bit longer than I'd anticipated. You'd never imagine seaweed could be so moody, would you? It definitely has emotions. I can feel the vibrations.'

Ambrose fished instinctively inside the pockets of the floor-length tweed coat Kate had bought him for his Sainsbury's notebook and began to scribble something down. Kate caught the words 'vegetation' and 'anthropomorphism' and eyed him warily. It was exhausting being a muse sometimes, especially when the artist was in danger of getting under everyone's feet.

'Why don't you and Nibbles nip across to Julie's, order a nice bottle of Merlot and I'll join you in twenty minutes or so?'

Ambrose thrust his hands back deep into his pockets and wandered disconsolately across the road, Nibbles whimpering at his ankles. They must make a pathetic sight, he thought wearily: two old dogs with nowhere to go. Even his children could no longer bear to be around him. Cressie at least had made that much clear when she had started casually leafing through those dreadful boarding-school manifestos. Two years old, and his marriage was as dried up as the wizened walnut shells Kate had turned into phenomenally chic mirror frames — and he had thought only life in his plays was this depressing

Just as Kate was looping the last seaweed frond around the chandelier, the phone rang. Reaching gingerly for the hands-free button with her toe, she answered it, thinking it must be Roberto with news on Bond Street. It was Marcus, fishing for a free present from the shop. She spoiled Marcus horribly, she knew. When he'd announced that he wanted to be a film director — and in preparation had learned the dialogue to all of Quentin Tarantino's films — she had bought him a state-of-the-art video camera which he now used constantly to film all of them. Cressie played up to the camera horribly, wearing ever shorter skirts and emoting with an intensity that made Joan Crawford look laid-back.

Somehow Marcus got the best out of Cressie — out of all of them. He had a good eye and knew how to light them. His lazy, lopsided smile and indolent acceptance of her meant that he got away with blue murder – midnight blue, her favourite colour, thought Kate, marvelling at how their relationship had been transformed since the early days. He'd even helped her out with all the spreadsheets Roberto kept sending her, organizing a computer programme for her and even accompanying her to PC World when she finally agreed that she needed her very own Mac.

In fact, putting aside the prune poisoning incident, and his vast collection of horror videos and the unhealthy obsession with insects, he was kind and tolerant. In Ambrose's frequent absences, she had found herself not only forgiving Marcus for his serial girlfriends, the trail of detritus he left all over the house, and the anarchic little piles of rubbish that erupted spontaneously on every spot he passed, but rather relishing them.

Still there was no escaping the fact that he coasted along on a jetstream of charm and good looks – and little else. And occasionally she attempted to provide some parental guidance.

'If you spent as much time learning about the microbes on your curriculum as you do reading up about the sex lives of earthworms you'd already have a PhD in biology,' she said curtly one evening after she had taken up a bowl of overcooked pasta. 'Talk about creepy.'

Marcus grinned and began tucking into the pasta. It looked disgusting – like something one of his insects might secrete – but he was always very appreciative of her cooking. Whereas Cressie had taken to calling A la Carte Restaurant Service very loudly on the hall telephone for takeouts. Another reason for Marcus's position as Most-Favoured Stepson.

He was watching *Chainsaw Massacre 3* with the life-cycle

of the fruit-fly mapped out on the floor. Kate could have sworn he was meant to be studying the life-cycle of aphids; Marcus's big – his only – act of rebellion was never to study what was actually on the curriculum. The nub of the matter was that Ambrose's son needed him. And so did she.

And now Ambrose was back, waiting for her across the road at Julie's – and here she was deliberately loitering in the shop. For some reason the thought of an informal drink with her husband made her nervous. He was so distracted lately, so clearly bored by her. The notebook and pen that had initially charmed her now haunted her. She had tried replacing the notebook with a Smythson one, on the grounds that it would at least be more aesthetically pleasing. But Ambrose had freaked. The Sainsbury's yellow ones were his lucky talisman. He had stockpiled about two hundred of them. But Kate felt that the notebooks were sucking the life out of everyone around him.

She ambled to Julie's. There was no sign of Ambrose. She scoured upstairs and eventually asked at the bar, where she learned that he had left half an hour ago. Looking at the clock, Kate realized it was nine-thirty. Ambrose must have been waiting on his own for her for an hour and a half. Swamped in remorse – and not liking the familiar suffocating feeling – she decided indignant outrage was the best defence. She stormed home, to find him slumped in front of Marcus's video of *Friday the Thirteenth Part IV* with the remains of one of Cressie's Thai takeaways in front of him, and slammed her way up to bed. Alone.

Sometimes Magda wondered whether Phoebe hadn't given her a job as her personal stylist just so that she could torture her. It wasn't as if the glory was that great. And the money certainly wasn't. She could earn more from one Virginia Slims ad than she could from an entire series of *Friday with Phoebe*.

Really, thought Magda disapprovingly, the tenacity with which some celebrities could abuse their internal organs and still keep their biggest one intact never failed to impress her. Here was Phoebe's face, an expanse of perfection: her flawless skin unadulterated by a single epidermal glitch. Her mesmerizing emerald eyes were as sleepily inscrutable as ever.

And yet, judging by what everyone said, she was packing away the booze and pills as if there were no tomorrow. She was permanently on a diet, and when she wasn't in the TV studios she was in the gym. She spent so much time weight-lifting with Gary, her personal trainer, that there were more bulges on her arms than in a maternity ward.

Magda didn't approve of gossip — at least not when it concerned herself — and in her way she was so fond of Phoebe that she considered her an extension of herself. But she had to admit that her behaviour had become increasingly erratic. And the dissolute state of Phoebe's new bedroom in Holland Park was shocking. It wasn't just the handcuffs, the scores of books, magazines, newspapers and other bits of paper that lurked in the folds of the blankets and eiderdown like secret landmines, but the discarded plates, cups, lipsticks, even underwear that frothed over the peaks of duvet like clouds of sea foam. It was Harvey Nichals meeting Mount Vesuvius. The whole room looked like a bad acid trip. And whoever heard of having duvets, blankets *and* eiderdowns, thought Magda.

'I'm the opposite of a snake shedding its skin,' said

Phoebe, intercepting her gaze. 'I keep adding layers. I'm permanently cold – and yet I have to sleep naked. It's a compulsion.'

She thinks she's Marilyn Monroe, thought Magda reprovingly, although she clearly didn't have Monroe's weight problems.

She had always been upbeat, but not as abnormally, relentlessly cheerful as this. Still, Magda put it down to her having spotted a picture of Sharon Weiner looking heinous in *Hello!* 'If ever anyone was born to be airbrushed it's her,' said Phoebe loftily, stubbing her cigarette out in one of her antique cerise pink coffee cups. Magda winced. Phoebe used to be so fastidious.

'Now I know I've got it somewhere,' chirped Phoebe, still in her peignoir, a lacy Georgian one Magda had found for her in Vienna when they were making *Mozart the Man* – and none too spotless, she noted. She watched as Phoebe dived under one of the layers – she knew that Phoebe had started keeping a diary again and the bed was strewn with crumpled pages from it. Phoebe eventually emerged with a scrap torn from the pages of Italian *Vogue*. It was a photograph of Winona Ryder in a couture Chanel black-and-silver cobwebby shift. There was no price in the captions, always a very bad sign in Magda's experience, but she doubted if any potential Chanel customers would get change out of £20,000.

'Yes, well, I can't see Charlie-boy forking out for that,' she said – and instantly regretted it. Phoebe's mood changed and she went from sunshine to thunderstorm in a flash.

'And since when have you been so concerned with budgets?' Phoebe spat accusingly. Her peignoir fell open over her luminous skin. She looked small, muscular and preternaturally tense, like a salmon caught on a hook, thought Magda, wondering by the by which brand of exfoliant Phoebe used.

It was a fair comment. Magda had never knowingly underspent in her life. But Charlie, under huge pressure from the DG about his spiralling budgets, and even huger pressure from Charlotte not to screw things up now that she was expecting yet another baby, had read Magda the Riot Act about Phoebe's wardrobe expenses – not quite daring to read it to Phoebe herself. Magda sat down calmly on a low Victorian nursing chair, covered in lime velvet and purple fringing, that was placed opposite the bed, and began pulling out some sketches from her bag.

'Or is that what happens when your career goes into free-fall?' snarled Phoebe, her sleepy eyes suddenly snapping open. 'You start becoming a bureaucratic little penny-pincher. Why shouldn't he fork out? I make more money for him than anyone else on that fucking channel.'

Magda ignored her. It was too early in the day to do battle. 'Why would you want to wear something Winona's already worn?' she asked reasonably. 'Now look, I thought this, in a kind of emerald metallic thread I found in Istanbul, would be just the job when you interview John Travolta—'

Phoebe jumped off the bed and snatched the sketch from Magda. 'I hate green,' she said sulkily.

'No, you don't. You wear it all the time. You begged me to get you a green wimple on *My Lady of Shalott*, even though I told you green dye was hard to come by in 1278 . . . Anyway,' continued Magda, catching a violent-looking grimace, 'it was just a thought . . .' She rummaged in her bag. 'What about this? *C'est chic, n'est-ce pas?* It's based on a vintage coat

I found in New York. The original's a bit knackered, so I thought I could make it in orange-and-red patchwork silk over a red-and-gold dress from Vivienne West—'

'Oh, for Christ's sake, I'm sick of Charlie's pathetic penny-pinching and your cheap little knock-offs—'

'Well, excuse *me* for thinking of the licence fee-payers,' said Magda, beginning to sound mutinous. She had spent most of her time on an M & S shoot the day before whizzing up designs for Phoebe. Phoebe looked at her incredulously. The only licence either of them really cared about was one that would allow them to kill Charlie.

'I'm sick of the whole damn thing!' screamed Phoebe, hurling a coffee cup of ash at Magda. She was storming around the room now; her peignoir had fallen to the ground but she seemed oblivious to her nakedness. She was throwing papers on the floor, kicking plates out of the way and pulling clothes out of her wardrobe, hysterical little cries catching in her throat.

'I'm just wasted in this fucking country. Chat fucking show hostess.' She began ripping up a yellowing copy of the *Python* which had a picture of her sitting on an elephant under the headline *Who's a Big Girl? Chat-show darling Phoebe Keane joins the* Python's *Save Our Rachel campaign*.

'I'll come back *une autre fois*,' said Magda, trying to pick a dignified path past a plate of two-day-old frankfurters and a pile of Agent Provocateur knickers. 'When you're feeling better.'

'Better?' screeched Phoebe (it was extraordinary, Magda reflected later, the way she kept her energy levels up. Obviously she was doing a whole cocktail of amphetamines – not that the press would be finding out from *her*). 'Better? What's to make me feel better?' She knelt by the bed and began to sob. Magda moved toward's her.

'Don't touch me, you traitor,' screamed Phoebe. 'Don't think I don't know where all that crap about me is emanating from, you witch. You poor, jealous old witch. Is that why you spend all your spare time dreaming up ever more hideous outfits for me?'

Magda looked at Phoebe crouching on the floor in a small, marshy puddle of crumbs and spilt Diet Coke, and to her surprise felt distaste instead of pity. '*Au revoir*, Phoebe.'

She walked to the door, only to be beaten there by a flying bowl that, fortunately for both of them, hit the lintern rather than her head. 'I'll tell you when you will be fucking going,' screamed Phoebe.

'I doubt that,' said Magda in as authoritative a tone as she could. 'I doubt that very much indeed.'

Martha watched Kate struggle with a tin opener while she struggled with her own internal dilemma: should she risk offending Kate by offering to rescue her and save them all from what she could see even now was going to be an inedible meal, or let her get on with it?

It had been Kate's idea to have Martha over to meet them all for dinner. Martha would have been just as happy to go out — she was as nervous about meeting Cressie and Marcus and Ambrose on their home turf as Kate evidently was about playing hostess. But Kate had insisted. 'Don't worry, I've been practising. I can even cook one or two dishes rather well now,' she had enthused at the end of their first reunion, which had gone better than either of them had dared hope.

Martha had never quite forgiven herself for not realizing earlier that blood was thicker than any amount of war reporting and insisting that she get time off to go to Kate's wedding. Consequently she had been secretly dreading seeing her sister again. Almost as much as she was longing for it. But something about Kate had changed. Her success with What Katy Did Next had given her a confidence and an inner calm that, Martha now realized, had always been missing before. She was even more beautiful than Martha remembered, magnificently so. But there was also something impressive about her now, even if there was a sadness in her eyes and a stillness in the way she sometimes spoke.

For her part, Kate had been astonished at the transformation in Martha. She had cleaned up beautifully. Even more miraculously, she had finally got fed up with living rough and had put down the deposit on an airy eighth-floor flat in a postwar block overlooking Regent's Park which she had asked Kate to decorate in cool, minimalist style. The change was even more visceral than that. Martha radiated confidence. It was as if she had finally discovered that she quite liked herself.

Martha could hardly recognize herself either. She no longer panicked in front of a camera; words and information didn't forsake her the moment she found herself in an interview situation. She wasn't at Jeremy Paxman's level yet, and sometimes she kicked herself for letting her guests off too lightly, but Charlie told her this was no bad thing. 'They open up more in the end, because they trust you,' he told her over lunch at the Ivy. She had a feeling he was just pacifying her but enjoyed the compliment all the same. And to her astonishment, she loved walking into the audience for the floor discussions.

The pilot of *And Now* had been a triumph. Martha was a revelation. Smart, confident and sexy. With *And Now* as his bid for serious but populist current affairs, and *Friday with Phoebe* as his glitzy flagship, Charlie Pitchcock was feeling very pleased with himself indeed. Any doubts he had had about whether or not to let Martha loose in front of a live audience had evaporated when he saw her chair a debate on the government's policy on prisons.

As with *Friday with Phoebe*, the figures for *And Now* were terrific and, as Charlie liked to tell the DG, he didn't just mean those of his two presenters. Martha's interview with Ann Widdecombe had been electric, and the politician's views about manacling pregnant prisoners to their labour beds had made all the following day's papers. And when Laurence of Suburbia, now relaunched as a virulent newspaper columnist and born-again Christian, came on the same show to plug his autobiography, she coaxed him into saying that working women should be abolished, which effectively blitzed any chances his book had had of making it on to the bestseller lists. He'd been drunk, of course, and when Ann Widdecombe had pointed this out, he had turned on her. 'And you are ugly, but in the morning I shall be sober,' he had slurred, parroting Winston Churchill.

'But still stupid, alas,' she had replied, as the audience burst into spontaneous applause.

'Don't you ever miss your old job as party chairman?' Martha had asked him sweetly.

'God, what planet have you been on?' he drawled insolently, peering down his nostrils at her. 'That position's been totally discredited.'

'Isn't that why so many people think you'd be so good

at it?' asked Martha innocently. The audience had erupted. *More front than Ann Widdecombe*, Julie Burchill wrote in the *Guardian*. After that the scoops came thick and fast. She interviewed Hillary Clinton in Washington and was allowed to film Nick Leeson in jail.

The press loved her, although they wished she'd play the celebrity game more by appearing in skimpy dresses at awards ceremonies and inviting *Hello!* back to her lovely home.

Martha loved the secure anonymity of her block's portered hallways, the slightly antiquated luxury of its layout, and she adored its views of the trees in Regent's Park. Sometimes she would wrap herself up in a blanket and sit with a little tumbler of whisky on her balcony watching dusk fall or the birds flutter round Snowdon's aviary. And just occasionally she would allow herself the melancholy luxury of thinking of Nick and their time in Bosnia. She knew they would never end up together – and she sometimes wondered whether it wasn't this certainty that made him such an enjoyable fantasy. She was alone, but for the first time in her life she felt comfortable about it. Even the news, splashed across the tabloids, that Donna Ducatti had signed a million-pound contract with Radio One to present the breakfast show didn't cause her a single twinge, at which point she decided she finally had got her life under control.

But best of all, she was reunited with Kate. Only once they had made it up did each of them realize how much they had missed the other. Not that Martha had felt able to discuss Nick – even with Kate. It seemed so transient, almost like a dream. How could you love someone you had known so fleetingly, so long ago? Not that it mattered. He was blissfully married. And that was that. She would just have to get on with her life. After all, increasingly, it was a very nice life. And if Kate wanted her to sit down with her new family over something that made Pot Noodles look like Marco-Pierre's finest, so be it. Still, what with their frantic schedules – and Martha's workload was huge once filming of her show began in earnest – it was months before she finally made it round to Vanbrugh Terrace for their inaugural dinner. And when she did, she was shocked to find she was extremely nervous at the prospect of meeting Ambrose and his children.

Martha gazed round the expansive cream kitchen with its beautiful little chandelier, distressed pale blue chairs and faded rose-printed blinds appreciatively. Even if Kate was a little intellectually awed by Ambrose, as she had intimated, she certainly didn't seem to have any problems imposing her sense of style on his home. The doors opened on to a brick terrace, and she breathed in the scent of the large, drooping pink roses outside.

'Are you sure I can't help?' she began tentatively, as Kate began the hopeless task of stirring some congealed *tagliatelle carbonara* that would be better used for underpinning the Winchester bypass. Still, Martha thought, eyeing the pristine Black Forest gateau Kate had picked up from Maison Blanc, at least they could gorge themselves on chocolate.

'No, everything's under control,' lied Kate in an attempt at breeziness. She caught Martha looking at the cake. 'Except that the Chocolate Nemesis cake I tried to make from the River Café turned out disastrously, so I had to nip out and buy one. Honestly, I should get my money back – those recipes are s'posed to be foolproof. Here,' she said, tossing some of Dan's new turnip-and-baked-apple chips into a soup tureen, 'help yourself to some crisps and relax. Marcus will be here any minute. He's such a help.'

On cue there was a clattering in the hallway, a smattering of expletives — and Cressie appeared before them wearing a gym slip so skimpy it was more a case of gym-slipped. It was amazing she hadn't been arrested. She threw her satchel on to the table and took off her regulation maroon cardigan to reveal a minuscule pale blue T-shirt with the words *I woz not 'ere: Glastonbury '96* stretched tightly across two missile-sized breasts that were clearly heaven-bound. Or rather more accurately, thought Martha, trouble-bound.

'Sorry I'm late,' she said insouciantly, scraping her finger across the top layer of chocolate cake and affecting not to see Martha. 'Lucy thought she might be up the duff and she asked me to go to the doctor's with her. Turned out she only had wind.'

Kate decided not to rise to the jail-bait. Let Ambrose deal with it. 'Cressie, meet my long-lost sister Martha.'

Cressie spun round and raked her eyes over Martha's slick black Donna Karan trouser suit, her burgundy lips and the shiny black hair which sprang over her shoulders like a panther.

'Oh, hi,' she said uncertainly. 'Are you the brainy one?'

Martha met her gaze evenly. 'Are you?'

Cressie rolled her eyes, which were ringed in an M25-sized orbit of black kohl, and tossed back her Sun-In streaked hair. 'Hardly. I'm on a level with Kate. We're so thick we thought the Nasa space project was a loft conversion in Clerkenwell.'

Martha looked at Cressida sharply and then across at

Kate, who was busy stabbing the cheese sauce with a blunt instrument. She hoped Kate hadn't tried to woo Cressie by pretending to be dumb. In any case, it was quite clear that the little minx wasn't quite as intellectually challenged as she made out.

Cressie perched herself on the edge of the table, allowing Martha a panoramic view of her sun-kissed thighs. Martha decided that the sun was probably the only thing that had kissed them. Cressie, for all her posturing, wasn't as hard boiled as she pretended. It was all a big act designed to stress out her parents.

'Gosh, Kate, cooking? I thought you'd given that up. Amazing you've got time. It is November, after all. Shouldn't you be busy putting up Easter decorations in the shops? Kate's so talented,' she cooed, turning suddenly to Martha. 'It's super having a really homey stepmum'. She fluttered her eyelashes, which were so heavily caked in mascara Martha was surprised her eyelids hadn't developed biceps. She was very beautiful, in a blank, angelic sort of way. And Martha didn't trust her an inch.

'Does that mean you're not a rock fan?' said Martha, nodding at Cressie's T-shirt.

'No, it does not,' came an outraged squawk. 'I would have sold my left tit to go. But the parents – you know . . .' She rolled her eyes conspiratorially.

'Cressie's never really got over the break-up of Take That,' offered Kate helpfully from the inside of the oven, where she was desperately trying to chisel some cinderized ham and cheese off the grill. Eventually she emerged triumphant with the entire grill, which she placed on a metal tray and sprinkled with some dissolving fluid.

'Oh, excuse me while I puke into my popcorn,' hissed

an indignant Cressie. 'It's Lucy who liked them. I'm like, Lu-u-u-ce, the only thing more putrid than Take That would be an attack of crabs. And she's like, yeah, but Robbie's so cute. And I'm like, oh, pulease. And she's like . . .'

Whatever Luce was like was lost to the rest of them for ever because by now she had sauntered over to the fridge and submerged herself in its cavernous depths. When, Martha wondered, had the middle classes become so obsessed with huge fridges? Probably at the same time they'd stopped cooking and started buying obscene amounts of recipe books instead. Cressida poured herself a giant cranberry juice to which, when Kate and Martha weren't looking, she added a slug of vodka, marched back to the kitchen table and began leafing through *Hello!*

'It says here that Phoebe Keane keeps a tendril of her dad's pubic hair in a locket round her neck. How gross. And look—' She pointed to a fashion shoot featuring Miriam Harper with very blond hair and a very low side parting. 'Miriam Harper's gone all Hitler Youth. Oh, and here's a picture of Sharon Weiner being almost trampled to death when she opened the Harrods sale. Just look at that Dixie band scarper. Isn't that the top of Mohammed Al Fayed's pate – there, by Sharon's Manolo? Talk about being undersoled.'

Half an hour and ninety-seven deconstructed pages of *Hello!* later, there was more rumbling outside the kitchen door. 'Ah, and you must be Marcus,' said a relieved Martha, as a gangly six-footer with the lopsided charm of a puppy and even more lopsided combats bounded in and hoovered up the cheese, ham and dissolvant scrapings. 'Er, wouldn't you prefer these?' asked Martha, pushing the vat of crisps towards him. Marcus smiled genially and tipped the scrapings into the crisps before demolishing the lot. 'Bitchin',' he announced when he'd polished them all off, having turned only slightly green.

Martha instantly took to Ambrose, who, having at least got one draft of *gotcha!* in the bag, was at his most attractive. Witty, gentle and sexily crumpled – she hoped Kate knew how lucky she was – he was profusely apologetic for being so late. 'But at least I've finally finished the play – or at least made a start of finishing. And do you know,' he said, oozing bonhomie and kissing Kate, 'I even think that it might be redeemable?'

Unfortunately, by the time they sat down that was more than could be said of Kate's supper. The table setting – an autumnal vignette straight out of Caravaggio, taking in half of Sainsbury's fruit and veg department *en route* – looked ravishing. But the *carbonara* was so overcooked that the sauce had entirely vaporized. 'They should rename it Shakespeare's favourite dish – because it's Hamless,' chortled Cressie, who had by now imbibed half a bottle of vodka. Kate blushed.

'I don't mind,' said Marcus loyally. 'I'm thinking of going veggie anyway.' Staunchly he tried to help himself to more but the serving spoon snapped in half.

'Delicious crudités,' offered Ambrose helpfully, munching on one of Kate's vegetable arrangements.

'Oooh er, not 'alf,' giggled Cressie helplessly. Any minute now, thought Martha, she was going to topple into the Black Forest gateau. That really would be a chocolate nemesis. 'Talking of crudités, Dad, it said in the *Python* yesterday that Sharon Weiner ought to forget about Broadway and get a part in *Open All Hours* on account of her legs never closing.'

There was a deathly silence.

'I hear you're a bit of an Internet whizz,' said Martha, turning to Marcus. 'Kate says you've been really helpful getting her sorted out with computers.'

'Yes, well, we all know why Marcus likes to surf the Net,' said Cressie, swaying dangerously. Her kohl was halfway down her face by now. But she still looked beautiful. 'It's not so much you've got mail as you've got hard-core porn. He thinks no one knows. Is that what that film with Virginia McKenna was about?' She smiled sweetly. 'I'm afraid I never saw it – too young. *Porn Free*, wasn't it?'

Ambrose looked reprovingly down his long patrician nose. He wasn't sure what was worse – Cressie's jolly-hockey stick and gymkhana phase, which had sat very awkwardly with his politics, or this dreadful teenage imbecility. Unable to decide, he did what he always did and ignored her.

'Tell me, how are you enjoying television, Martha? You're doing a brilliant job.'

'Thank you,' said Martha, sounding surprised. She still couldn't get used to people she admired complimenting her, and it took all her willpower not to tell them that actually she was a hopeless fraud and that anyone would be better at it than she was. 'I'm loving it, to be honest. It's probably the most challenging thing I've done in some ways.' She wondered why Ambrose found it so difficult to deal with his own daughter and whether his benign neglect was why Cressie pretended to be so unintelligent. Perhaps being stupid was her ultimate revenge.

'Really?' He nibbled thoughtfully on a piece of raw kale. 'Even more than your time in Sierra?'

Cressie's eyes, which had been in danger of closing,

suddenly snapped open. 'Oh my God, don't tell me you've actually driven a Ford and lived to tell the tale.'

Ambrose winced. Martha tried another tack. 'Have you thought about what A-levels you want to do, Cressie?' she asked gently.

Cressie arched her exquisitely plucked eyebrows in minimal enquiry. 'A-levels?' she repeated blankly. 'I'm afraid these days I'm concentrating more on my spirit levels.' She reached over to help herself from the bottle of gin that was in front of Ambrose. The inevitable happened and she finally slid off her chair at his feet, taking the chocolate cake, two cabbages and half a cucumber with her.

Nick held the fort brilliantly while Ambrose was in London working on the rewrites of *gotcha!* That is to say he charmed the American media, who, chafing about the endless postponement of the play's glittering first night on Broadway, had been spoiling for some scandal about Ambrose or anyone else remotely concerned with the trilogy. He worked the chat-show circuit relentlessly and was so witty on the David Letterman show (he had mastered a brilliant impersonation of Bill Clinton) that he was asked back twice. He said all the right, soothing things about Equity in an interview he did with the *Washington Post*, which went some way towards plastering over the cracks. And when Lars von Snoren called him back to San Francisco to redub yet more of his scenes in *The Meaning of Loss* and announced that he was thinking of reshooting it as a musical, not one murmur of complaint passed his lips.

Apart from Phoebe, whose behaviour, as was even apparent from her phone calls, was growing increasingly erratic, things were going swimmingly.

Some days – those on which she called him twenty or thirty times – he managed to console himself that he was the one bearing the brunt of her neurosis. Then he wouldn't hear from her for three or four days – she would leave all the phones in the house on answer machine and switch off her mobile. And he would go out of his mind with worry. He even contemplated breaking his contract and flying straight back to London to sort Phoebe out, but when he tentatively raised the issue, Marty threatened to sue his bollocks off and Sharon threatened to kill him. In any case, he didn't even know if Phoebe was in London: her shooting schedule was taking her all over the world.

And then, just as he was ready to lose both his testicles and his life, Phoebe would call him out of the blue, sounding so rational and well balanced he felt guilty for being paranoid about his wife. He would go out on the town and celebrate, with whoever happened to be around – and almost got used to seeing the previous evening's festivities chronicled in the *New York Post* the next day. It didn't matter what he did – from having a quiet night on his own at the movies to dinner in a fashionable restaurant with Marty and the inevitable coterie of young Hollywood actors and New York supermodels – journalists seemed to find him. No incident involving Nick – whether it was lifting a forkful of pizza to his mouth or emerging from Prada with a present for Phoebe – seemed too trivial not to warrant a photograph in the newspapers. It was getting so that if he didn't make the day's gossip columns he momentarily wondered whether he'd been out the night before.

✳   ✳   ✳

'And what's really weird,' said Kate, 'is that just when you'd expect Ambrose to be snapping out of things — I mean, they've just about come to a deal with Equity — he's gone all sort of lethargic and peculiar. He just spends all day locked in his study refiling old notebooks.' Morosely, she gazed around Martha's sitting room, which, glowing in the candlelight that Martha preferred these days as it enhanced the twinkling lights in Regent's Park, looked wonderfully chic yet cosy. Despite her anxieties, Kate couldn't help marvelling at the transformation in her sister's domestic situation. Never mind Martha Stewart, Martha Crawford was becoming Miss Homemaker 1997.

'What's he working on?' asked Martha.

'*gotcha!, infidelity* — oh, who knows, he's been rewriting all three so much they're all in a muddle, from what I can make out.'

'Bloody hell, Kate, aren't they due on stage next month?'

'He tore up the London versions. Totally rewrote them. And then tore the new versions up too. Now he's totally blocked. Half the original cast have had to fulfil obligations elsewhere . . .' Kate looked at Martha desperately. 'Martha, there is no trilogy.' Her eyes filled. 'The most terrible thing is watching his confidence drain away. And the closer the deadline, the more he crumbles.'

Martha made sympathetic noises. Then Kate was off again.

'And the other most terrible thing is that I'm so completely uninvolved in the whole thing. It's as if he thinks that emotionally or intellectually I just won't be able to cope if he so much as suggests that everything in the great Ambrose White scheme of things isn't perfect.'

'Well, it's totally obvious what needs to be done,' said Martha, digesting the situation rapidly – if nothing else, covering war zones and interviewing slimy politicians had revved up her brain.

'I mean, it's not as if I've never been to the theatre or don't have any views,' blurted Kate.

'Look, can I just get a word in? You should offer to do costumes—'

'Oh yeah, just like that. Ambrose only ever works with Golden Globe winners—'

'So? You're brilliant and he knows it. And Ambrose needs to think of something to postpone the opening – and fast.'

'He tried to stage a heart attack but he's a crap actor.'

'But he's a great interview,' said Martha. 'I've seen him on Larry King.'

'Won't do them,' said Kate blankly. 'Not at the moment.'

'Not even for his sister-in-law, who would promise to give him the gentlest run of his life?'

'But even you would have to broach the subject of the plays sooner or later. And knowing you, Martha, you'd have to get a dig in about the unions and then Ambrose would be off saying something totally incendiary – and bloody Equity will call a strike again.'

They sat in silence for a few moments, a million sketches for Falklands uniforms whirling around Kate's mind and ratings graphs formulating in Martha's. She graciously decided to overlook Kate's jibe and instead beamed broadly at her own ingenuity. 'Preeeecisely.'

*   *   *

Catching sight of Ambrose through the window of Julie's, Kate checked herself nervously. He looked somehow lonely, sitting there hunched over his glass, his voluminous hair draped over his lofty forehead. He seemed so alone. What with his recalcitrant children and ex-wife, his actors, producers and audiences, she was used to seeing him surrounded by admirers. Even when there weren't people pressing round him, he always seemed happily contained in his own thoughts. But this evening, on his own, he looked both solitary and vulnerable. Her heart lurched, not because he looked attractive, though he did, in an imposing sort of way, but because he seemed so forlorn. She wanted to creep up on him unawares and put her arms around him, but the door of Julie's had a bell that clattered every time it opened and Ambrose immediately looked up at her, his pale grey eyes taking in her worried expression.

'So——' they began in unison. 'How has your day been?' And they broke off in awkward laughter.

'Busy,' said Kate. 'You?'

'Sour,' he said wearily.

There was a pause. Kate gulped back her Merlot. It was slightly too cold and made her feel sick. She tried again. 'Did you know that pregnant wasps lay their eggs inside other creatures' bodies because if they don't their baby larvae will start eating their mother's uterus from within?' She froze. How had that got out of her mouth?

Ambrose looked at her in a daze and, reaching for the bottle of Merlot, took a swig from it, an act that was so out of character that Kate found herself giggling nervously. Cautiously she reached for his hand. He clasped it so tightly her heart twisted guiltily. She ordered them some food — Ambrose always preferred her to choose —

and little by little led him towards Martha's interview proposition.

'My career's over,' he said blankly. 'And my daughter's a walking nightmare out of *Beverly Hills 90210*.'

How did he know about that series? wondered Kate. Then she remembered Marcus's pile of unmarked videos. So that's what he was watching when he pretended to be stocking up on blood and pillage.

'Oh, Cressie's not that bad,' lied Kate. 'She's just a teenager.'

'So's Marcus, but you don't get him teetering around in stilettos and shrink-wrap and saying "I'm like so over them" all the time.'

'Well, he doesn't say anything much, to be fair,' said Kate, smiling. She could smell victory in the air. Whatever happened now, she felt that Cressie at least would be out of her hair. 'It's not fair to compare them. Cressie's a raging torrent of hormones, whereas the one and only time I ever see Marcus moved is when Aston Villa loses.'

'Perhaps boarding school really would be the best place for her,' Ambrose whimpered. 'After all, no point sacrificing the best interests of your children on the altar of your youthful principles.'

'Quite. And even Tony Blair went to public school.'

Ambrose looked at her pensively and went very quiet.

Kate, who, thanks to Roberto, was used to dealing with over-the-top emotions, bundled him into a taxi and let him sob over her and Nibbles, who always enjoyed licking up a nice salty downpour. 'And of course your career isn't over. Do you know who Martha told me she'd most like to interview?'

Ambrose shook his head mournfully.

'And it's not just because she's your sister-in-law. The producers think it would be a real coup as well. In fact,' added Kate slyly, 'they're putting her under a lot of pressure to get you on the show. You'd really be helping her out.'

'Oh God, is her job on the line, d'you think?'

'Could be,' said Kate, stroking his hair tenderly and allowing herself the gentlest of smiles.

Nick wasn't the one suffering from paranoia. Phoebe was slipping into a state of heightened neurosis brought on by anxieties about her career, her looks and her marriage, all of which she felt were fading into oblivion despite numerous signs to the contrary. Always a light sleeper, she was now suffering from nightmares. She would wake four or five times a night in the big four-poster, with a rush of adrenaline, screaming and shivering, sweat pouring down her. She would call Nick and then put the phone down before he could pick it up, convinced that he must be with someone else.

She spent a fortune on gifts to compensate for her endless losses of cool; but she couldn't help herself. The control freak was out of control. It didn't help that she was convinced that everyone on the set of *Phoebe* was gossiping behind her back. Her suspicions weren't entirely groundless. Even Will, her hapless director, had felt honour-bound — on behalf of his beleaguered crew — to beard Charlie in his office one morning about Phoebe's increasingly alarming tantrums. The ratings, however, were a marvel.

'Okay, okay,' said Charlie genially, slightly taken aback by the strength of Will's outburst. 'So she can be a bit imperious at times. But frankly she's the queen of the corporation right now. And that means she can do no wrong.'

'Even if you end up losing one of the best technical crews I've ever worked with?' thundered Will, his mild disposition for once outraged. 'Because Her Travesty is driving us all mad. The other day we had to delay everything for six hours while Phoebe had a freak-out about her hair. She was being photographed for *Vogue* and she wanted that "just cut" look. Apparently it's very big on the catwalk. Only she didn't want to lose any length. So do you know what we had to do? Fly in her frigging hairdresser from Paris so that he could give her extensions so that he could cut it to the length it already was. Have you any idea how much that little exercise cost? M-m-more than I earn in a month, that's for sure.'

He stormed out of Charlie's office, banging the door so hard that for one terrible moment Charlie thought his Edmund de Wahl pottery was going to come to an untimely end before Charlotte had had time to get it insured.

Chastened but not cowed was how he later described his mood to Charlotte, who was in the middle of an antenatal class and breathing in a most distracting manner. He was not about to let the jewel in his crown slip through his fingers. Not until that jewel began to show signs of tarnish. It would happen, of course – Charlie was too much of a realist not to know that – but until it did, as far as he was concerned, Phoebe could put the entire output of Colombia up her nose. And most of Harley Street's tranquillizers.

Chapter Fifteen

'And finally, the death this week of François Mitterand, the former president of the glorious republic, has concentrated all our minds on what's so great about the French—' Donna paused for dramatic effect. '—absolutely nothing.' Cue laughter from her zoo. Cue zany jingo, and a deft segue into the Fugees.

Martha flicked off the radio and stretched luxuriously beneath the dreamy mosquito netting Kate had draped over her bed to soften the stark purity of her room. Forcing herself to listen to radio's highest paid DJ had been a very effective form of therapy. Okay, so the show topped the ratings across its time slot, but that was probably because of the wads of cash Donna threatened to give away every week. It was basically a glorified lotto show. The much-trumpeted current affairs angle amounted to a few cheap, xenophobic jokes. Any pretence the show had had of being a sophisticated mix of current affairs and hard-hitting interviews (now where had she heard that formula before? she thought smugly) had long since evaporated in a puff of plugs, studio gimmicks and inimitable Donna touches. The upshot was that Donna had become stupefyingly famous, in and out of *Hello!* and the tabloids so often, that the joke circulating round Fleet Street was that she'd had keys cut for all of them. Because she was utterly shameless she had no compunction about kissing and telling with nauseating regularity – always for a tidy sum. It was said that if and when Donna ever gave birth, she wouldn't stop at selling the pictures, she'd sell the firstborn as well. She was, as Kate remarked to Martha one morning as they flicked through the front pages, laughing all the way to the bonk.

The best bit was that Martha really didn't care. She padded to the kitchen with a stack of *Economist*s and a clipping Charlie had torn out from *GQ* which christened her the thinking man's crumpet. She thanked her lucky stars. Charlie might have his weaknesses but at least he would never let her open supermarkets with her boobs bursting out of a lacy jacket. Donna's dress sense hadn't improved with experience. Fenton Wigstaff, who had appointed himself custodian of the Best and Worst Dressed lists that were syndicated to all the newspapers, had continuously targeted Donna in the past year, turning her wardrobe into a national joke. His judgment on the silver hipsters she wore to the Sony Awards was 'sad, shocking and scary'. When she had donned a brown-and-olive flapper dress to the Royal Variety Performance he had called her 'a magnolia blob wrapped in reincarnated crap'. Martha almost felt sorry for her – when she'd stopped chuckling.

She was generally feeling good about herself. She was pleased that she had been able to mediate between Ambrose and Kate. In fact it had proved surprisingly easy. Ambrose had come on the show, said some things about US Equity which had been wildly distorted by the press and badly received by the Americans – and the trilogy had been postponed for another two months. Plenty of time for rewrites and for Kate to climb on board as costume designer – much to Ambrose and Kate's mutual delight.

Despite the barriers they had allowed to spring up between them, it was plain they both adored one another. If only her own love life could be sorted so easily. But Martha was beginning to believe she would be a confirmed bachelor. It was funny, she thought, opening the doors to her balcony and bathing in the early sunshine, her career was scintillating and her relationship with Kate was better than ever. Yet her social life was about as exciting as a disquisition on European fiscal reform. As for her love life – Marcus's insects definitely had more fun.

But she wasn't unhappy. She often thought of Tim O'Mara and their life on the road, but with a fond nostalgia rather than the sharp stabs of pain she had expected. She had put that part of her work behind her. Being nominated for a BAFTA for a series of reports they had done from Sierra Leone had helped, and even though in the end they hadn't won, it was nice to know that what they were doing wasn't unrecognized.

'You see,' she had told Tim over a crackly line to Rwanda, 'people do listen. We can make a difference.'

'Yeah, so long as it doesn't clash with Euro 1996,' he drawled. 'You got out just in time, babe. The food's terrible here, by the way. Even you wouldn't be able to do a thing with it.'

She had chuckled, picturing his laconic smile and flamboyant shirts, which must be a little frayed round the collars by now, it was so long since he'd been home. She had gone shopping the next day and bought him a new suit in

Paul Smith and a couple of Versace shirts and posted them to him. She had so much to thank Tim for; not just helping her professionally, but for being an emotional rock. The three years she had been away would always seem special, even magical – not least, she knew, because twenty-nine days of them had been spent with Nick Wilde.

Phoebe entirely endorsed Kate's plans to send Cressie to boarding school, as Kate knew she would. 'Darling,' Phoebe drawled, as they had eaten lunch at Nobu – or rather Kate had and Phoebe had pushed a bean sprout round her plate – 'you can't have a social life, a career, a husband, children *and* a really first-class wardrobe. Something has to go. And in my experience, it ought to be the children.'

Beyond the wraparound windows, Hyde Park twinkled gloriously in the spring sunshine, cars had scooted down Park Lane like miniature Tonka toys, and the world – specifically London, and any minute New York – seemed at her feet. Phoebe spoke so convincingly that it was only later that Kate realized that her experience of children was less than minimal.

Even Ambrose's implacable opposition to the public school system had evaporated after the fateful dinner with Martha. It wasn't that he objected to the idea of Cressie rebelling – he hoped that any child of his would have the good sense to do that – so much as the way she was doing it. The minute the Met Bar had opened, Cressie and Lu-u-uce had taken up squatters' rights there, becoming more permanent fixtures than the tables, the bar staff or Tara Palmer-Tomkinson. Cressie's voice, which she had struggled to inflect with cockney pathos for her role in

Poor Cow, was now a miserable marriage of Mockney and Valley-speak. She hated everything, yet her entire conversation was pockmarked with 'likes'. Every statement went up at the end like a question until poor Ambrose was thoroughly confused. The day *Tatler* had rung up to ask her to pose for a cover shoot with a group of junior league It girls had been the final straw.

So one gorgeously bright – in every sense – morning, two days before they were due in New York, Kate and Ambrose set off with Cressie for St Eleanor's. It wasn't an entirely relaxing drive. Kate was tense about leaving Sky in charge, even though in the two weeks she had already been working for Kate she had transformed the accounting system and re-dressed one of the windows almost as well as Kate herself might have done. And Cressie, who secretly couldn't wait to start boarding, sobbed all the way down, so that by the time they reached Exeter she looked as though she were the victim of the most appalling child abuse.

St Eleanor's was an imposing Queen Anne pile set in fifty astonishingly lovely acres, all busily rolling down towards the South Devon coast, and filled with four hundred girls all busily rolling their own ciggies. Ambrose's BMW swept through the gates, which bore the motto *Altiora Petamus*. The long scrunch up the gravel drive was accompanied by the heady scent of aliums. Kate's heart lifted. Cressie would surely enjoy herself once she got over the initial shock of being outside the M25. The formal elegance of the house itself, which had been a wreck before it had been rescued by a public school trust in the 1960s, had been softened with lichen and fronds of Virginia creeper.

They were expected; a decanter of sherry and some peanuts had been set on a silver tray. The headmistress, a

Miss Lambert, who was something of a stately ruin herself, was waiting for them behind a vast walnut desk. Almost before they sat down, she began pouring, her hands shaking slightly more with each glass so that by the time she began tipping Ribena into Cressie's, half of it ended up on her tweed skirt. Not that it mattered, thought Cressie, eyeing her drink with disgust – the skirt was so old it was hard to tell what its original colours might have been. She perched on the arms of a gleaming leather chesterfield so that the true brevity of her own miniskirt could be unappreciated by all, and wished she'd worn something with sufficient fabric to conceal the hip flask Lu-u-uce had given her as a leaving present.

From Cressie's vantage point, things looked grim. Miss Lambert was so old and out of touch she probably thought Prada was a Russian newspaper and Tom Ford was the long-lost brother of a geriatric American president. She sipped some Ribena out of desperation. It was obvious the closest she was going to get to a Sea Breeze at St Eleanor's would be long brisk walks along the headland.

'What a beautiful room,' began Kate, more to fill the conversational void than because she actually liked the fussy wooden panelling and the dark oil paintings featuring various examples of domestic wildlife and weak-chinned school benefactors, which, she supposed, amounted to more or less the same thing.

'Yes,' said Miss Lambert, her eyes darting round the room like something out of a Busby Berkeley routine. 'We're terribly lucky. Some of our old girls have been most generous ...'

What a cheek, thought Cressie. On the scrounge already.

'Really,' continued Miss Lambert, oblivious to the puking gestures Cressie made when her back was turned, 'I have to say all our girls have been a credit to us – as I'm sure Cressida will be.'

She was certainly living on credit, acknowledged Cressie. And the fees at St Eleanor's were so huge Kate would probably be hounding her for repayment until she was sixty.

There was a pause. Miss Lambert coughed nervously. Her smile stretched so tightly across her face it quivered and her crimson lipstick leaked into the tiny crevasses around her mouth, making it look like some vast, bloody estuary.

'I expect you'd like to see round St Eleanor's?' Miss Lambert stood up expectantly; her cardigan, the colour of mouldy bread, was more shapeless than Cressie's worst attempt at an essay plan.

It was indeed a lovely place – and boarding school had certainly changed since Ambrose's day. For one thing Cressie was to have her own room, overlooking the lake and ornamental gardens. The whole place was well tended and clean, which was more than could be said for poor Miss Lambert's conversation, which was larded with accidental doubles entendres. Still, Ambrose and Kate might have overlooked them had Cressie not practically choked with laughter. She was gagging for it all right, thought Kate, feeling her hand tingle, longing to slap Cressie. She was terrified Cressie would be expelled before they managed to get the cases out of the car.

'And that's where our girls do their woodwork,' trilled Miss Lambert as she swept them past an annexe of the art department. 'Oh yes, we're very liberated here,' she continued, catching Ambrose's expression. 'Our girls love entertaining themselves with their hands. They're always banging away. We like them to be busy, so we have an after-prep activities committee. It's optional but I'd say the vast majority of them are in the club. And then there's our policy of allowing the girls to bring their pets. We've found it most effective in alleviating stress, especially at exam time. You wouldn't believe how relaxing fondling a pussy can be.'

Cressie looked almost cheerful by the time they sped away, which was just as well as another trauma awaited Kate. She was going to have to say goodbye to Nibbles, who was going to stay with his Aunt Martha. As she sobbed all over his wiry coat and fed him some last-minute chocolate doggy drops, Kate was only marginally comforted by the thought that Miss Lambert would doubtless have described her as giving her bit of ruff a right old stuffing.

Nick was surprised that Ambrose, who famously despised chat shows, had appeared on Martha's programme, and even more astonished that such an astute tactician should apparently have made such incendiary remarks about US Equity that the opening has been postponed yet again. Still, the extra two months had been a blessing in disguise. True, the 'minor' amendments meant that the plays bore no resemblance to their previous incarnations, but if Nick wasn't mistaken they had improved, becoming less hectoring and ultimately more moving. And whoever's idea it had been to draft Kate into designing the costumes was a genius. They were slick, modern and, best of all, understated. Even Sharon loved them.

Kate was in her element. Doing the costumes for all three plays was incredibly pressurized. Actually it was designing the costumes for Sharon that was stressful. It was written into all her contracts that she was allowed to keep whatever she wore in every production, so not entirely coincidentally she had developed an allergy to everything except cashmere.

Being involved in Ambrose's work had boosted Kate's confidence enormously. For one thing Ambrose and she were talking again – properly talking. Not just about what had happened to them that day or the mating rites of gerbils, but discussing ideas. Ambrose had taken to showing her early drafts of his new film script and once or twice Kate had scribbled little notes in the margins, even writing, on one occasion, 'Not clear, could do better ...'

And being in New York was just so exciting. Once she had rearranged their suite with a patchwork velvet bedspread and a small coloured Venetian chandelier that Tor had shipped out, and draped some 1950s silk scarves she had bought in the flea market on the corner of 26th Street over the lampshades, it almost looked like home.

On her rare free moments, she took off into the icy cold and walked for miles down the Bowerie, past former crack houses, plunging off at tangents, wherever her eyes or sense of smell took her. She spent hours in Chinatown, finding herself on the very edges of the Lower East Side, among jostling Koreans, listening to the babble of languages, sniffing the bittersweet aromas of the mysterious vegetables laid out on their stalls and almost tasting the exotic, delicious scented soups that always seemed to be cooking in the back. And all the time she was making notes – for her next collection, for Dan and for Tor and Sky. It was all very inspiring. But the best news of all – the really exciting, wondrous event that was turning her life and emotions upside down – was that she had just discovered she was pregnant.

She could never put her finger on the precise moment when she had stopped regarding babies as boring nuisances and home-wreckers. A year or two ago she would have wanted to kill any child who tampered with the linen spray displays in What Katy Did Next. But now that had all changed. She kept telling herself that babies grew up, learned to hate their parents, turned into drug addicts, murderers or Cressie. But to no avail: she still felt her heart somersaulting every time she saw a baby cry, smile, or even throw up. It had taken a while to get pregnant – she had almost thought it might never happen. But now she was. And she sometimes felt afraid that life couldn't get much better.

In late February, Naomi Campbell finally committed to a date for an interview with Phoebe – in New York. 'She's bound to cancel. Naomi *always* cancels,' said Magda airily. She still hadn't forgiven Phoebe for wrecking her sketches, which were about the only thing she'd never managed to claim on insurance. Phoebe didn't care. It meant a fortnight at least in New York and not just as an adjunct to Nick Wilde.

The trip was fraught even before she got there.

'Oh, come on, Phoebe,' said Charlie, pouring her a glass of lukewarm champagne when she stormed into his afternoon, having turned up four hours late for work. 'No one at the Beeb travels first class. Not even the DG. The licence-payers would have a fit.'

'Fuck the licence-payers,' snapped Phoebe, ignoring the glass he held out to her. 'What precisely do you take me for?'

Charlie was about to frame what he considered to be a brilliantly diplomatic response when his secretary, who was under strict instructions to interrupt him on the flimsiest pretext, rang to tell him that his wife had just gone into labour.

'Er, you're not going to believe this, Phoebe, but the baby's finally about to make its entrance.'

She appeared not to have heard. 'Have you any idea, Charlie,' she began coldly, 'what a cheap impression this is going to make on Naomi Campbell?'

'Phoebe, sweetheart,' he said, grabbing his mobile phone and sweeping out of the door, 'let's all sleep on this. I'm sure you'll find that tomorrow club class looks really rather jolly.'

Phoebe was in floods of tears for the rest of the day and the messages from crew members complaining on her behalf to Charlie were so numerous that the midwife threatened to ban him for life from the Lindo Wing if he didn't switch off his mobile. In the long hours until Cosmo appeared, Charlie mentally redid his budgets scores of times. There was no way he could lose a first-class fare among the expenses for the show, not with the way BBC accountants crawled over everything these days. He contemplated making up the difference himself. It might almost be worth it.

'Why don't you pop her on Virgin Upper Class?' gasped Charlotte, between epidurals. 'It's supposed to be frightfully nice – tons better than club, and a hell of a lot cheaper than BA's first class.' Charlie kissed the moist crown of her head gratefully. His wife was a genius.

Initially, Phoebe was not remotely impressed by this compromise, even though Charlie stressed what a big deal it was, given his department's special relationship with BA, etc. After a massage or two in the VIP lounge she began to feel marginally appeased, however, and when she found herself seated next to Miriam Harper on the plane, her cup — or at least her champagne glass — almost ranneth over. At the very least she'd get some interesting gossip, and at the best she'd get the promise of an interview which would merit her going on a huge splurge at Bergdorf Goodman's and shovelling it on her expenses.

Not that Miriam instantly recognized her as an equal. For a good twenty minutes, while they settled into their respective seats, Miriam refused to take off her sunglasses. But little by little Phoebe made it apparent that she was a highly successful television star in Britain, and that seemed to thaw her. As a final whammy, Phoebe revealed her connection with Nick, and that was it. Miriam couldn't have been friendlier, gushing about Nick's integrity as an actor and how much she longed to work with him. Dropping Nick's name wasn't something Phoebe planned to make a habit of, but she justified it to herself on professional grounds: an interview with Miriam was virtually in the Vuitton bag.

Miriam Harper was the hottest Hollywood starlet around, with a neck almost as long as her list of delicious ex-boyfriends, which made her a brilliant clothes-horse. She wasn't a bad actress either, as Phoebe graciously conceded. Still, it helped when you were Marty Shicker's niece — although, according to every interview Miriam did, nobody in the business had been aware of this fact when she started out. Yeah, right, thought Phoebe. With her dainty freckles and honey-coloured hair, Miriam was every inch America's dream Wasp. And now she was their indie queen as well. She had also worn the most daring outfit to the Golden Globes last year, a skimpy Gucci number that Fenton Wigstaff had declared 'decadent, delicious and divine' and which looked to Phoebe as though it had been made from a single piece of dental floss.

'Tell me,' said Phoebe silkily, folding her dainty little legs up on the seat and drawing her pistachio pashmina over both of them, 'have you ever been to any fashion shows?'

'Once,' began Miriam in her plinkety-plonk Wasp-speak. 'Giorgio flew me out to Milan.' She pronounced Milan to rhyme with yarn: 'But to be honest, it got a little embarrassing. I received so many invitations after that and I was terrified of hurting anybody's feelings, so I felt I couldn't go to any of them in the end.'

They were interrupted by one of the stewardesses, crouching gingerly by Phoebe's aisle seat with what looked like a giant leather egg resting on her lap.

'Miss Harper, I do hope you don't mind me asking – and of course if you say no I'll understand. But we've got the England rugby squad sitting in premium economy. They're attending some charity event and they were wondering whether they might get you to sign their ball so that they can auction it for charity. They reckon they could get quite a lot for it.'

At this point, an enormous man with slicked-back hair, whom Phoebe had correctly identified as a bodyguard the moment she walked on board, despite the book of crossword puzzles he had clamped to his knees, swivelled round menacingly.

'It's all right, Ajax,' purred Miriam, smiling graciously and pulling out a Mont Blanc fountain pen from her Gucci agenda, which, Phoebe couldn't help noticing, was personally embossed with a message to her from Tom

Ford, 'I'm always happy to fondle a nice juicy ball.' She scribbled her signature and, after a thoughtful pause, added a limerick.

> There was a rugger bugger from Wadham
> Who asked for a ticket to Sodom
> When they said we prefer not to issue them, sir
> He said, Don't call me sir, call me madam.

The stewardess read it, her lips moving gently until she got to the last line. She blushed pomegranate and burst into peals of laughter.

'That is brilliant,' she gushed. 'They'll be thrilled, Miss Harper. Um, Miss Keane—' She fished in her apron pocket for a scrap of paper and, finding none, ripped off a corner from the spare in-flight magazine in the overhead locker. 'I don't s'pose I could trouble you to put a paw-print on this – for my cleaning lady.'

'The thing is,' Miriam continued, while, behind the curtain, the rugby squad burst into a spontaneous rendition of 'For She's a Jolly Good Fellow', 'I'm learning that, style-wise, you have to be your own person. I mean, take the Golden Globes. I must have been sent half a million dollars of free clothes. It's probably even worse for you in London, being so close to Paris and Milan. You must get bombarded. But can you imagine anything more degrading at the end of the day than being a walking billboard for a designer? I mean, it's such a terrible abuse of one's talents, don't you think?'

'Oh, terrible,' murmured Phoebe.

'Your dress is lovely, by the way,' trilled Miriam.

'Thank you,' purred Phoebe, feeling slightly better.

Something about Miriam made her want to punch her in the collagen.

'But then your British high street is so marvellous, isn't it?' cooed Miriam, reaching for her eye mask, popping a sleeping pill and turning out the lights.

From the start, Phoebe's New York odyssey got off to a treacherous start. The night she arrived, *Vanity Fair* confirmed that it wanted to do a cover shoot and interview with the entire cast of the three-play marathon, which they had finally agreed to call simply *trilogy*. This included Kate, in her role as costume designer and Ambrose's wife. No mention, however, had been made of Phoebe. And no mention of this fact had been made *to* Phoebe, as everyone was terrified of her reaction. Nick, hoping she wouldn't get to hear of it and that she would be safely back in London by the time it happened, tried his usual approach of lying emotionally low and avoiding confrontation, a tactic that was about as effective as little Belgium trying to get out of a world war even as the jackboots were marching in.

Phoebe did hear about the shoot, from page six of the *New York Post*, and promptly went into a froth of activity, visiting the gym twice a day, having her personal trainer visit the Westbury last thing at night – which, since she'd become so manic about getting her beauty sleep, was about nine o'clock. Then she spent the next nine hours in a fug of chemically induced torpor that was doing nothing for the zing of her skin or the sparkle in her eyes. When she wasn't having facials, colonic irrigation, hot stone massages and eyebrow makeovers – she had already been to Anastasia, 'plucker to the Stars', five times in a fortnight – she was prowling around Manhattan on the lookout for that perfect peekabo outfit or driving Magda mad with a snowstorm of faxes instructing her to Fedex half of John Galliano's collection over from Paris.

'You're going to have to say something,' said Kate gently over a hot dog with Nick in the park. Phoebe, having deigned to slot in a bit of work for the BBC between hydra therapies, was filming Naomi Campbell being filmed for some advert.

Nick looked at the ketchup congealing on his roll despairingly. It was all right for her. Kate would actually have preferred not to be in the shoot, although Roberto was so excited at the anticipated publicity fall-out that Kate had already had to restrain him from getting some commemorative mugs made. Phoebe, on the other hand, minded very much indeed.

'I can't. It would be so humiliating.'

'There's got to be a way around this,' Kate said to Gloria later over a decaffeinated frappuccino. Something about Gloria's talons reminded her of Nibbles' sweet little fangs. She missed him horribly.

'There is,' said Gloria matter-of-factly, her bony little fingers strangling her paper cup until the froth ran over the sides and scalded her claws.

Kate looked at her hopefully.

'Shoot the bitch.'

Kate looked shocked.

'For a later issue, I mean,' said Gloria, intercepting Kate's expression. She didn't want to upset the wife of a man who, now she had finally got around to reading some of his work, she had decided was a literary genius. 'We call *Vanity Fair* and tell them Nick won't play unless they agree to do a profile of Phoebe in a forthcoming issue – you know, one of the less important months. She *is* some kind of TV phenomenon in England, right? It would be a smallish piece, not in the main bit of the magazine, and just for the UK editions, but better than nothing . . .'

'Would they do that for Nick?' asked Kate in awe.

'Are you kidding?' Gloria snorted. 'God, you English kill me. He's just about the biggest indie box-office draw at the moment, although with the release of *Green Cover* I do hope his indie status is about to go mainstream. He also happens to have one of the most powerful agents in the business representing him. Plus, if *trilogy* does half as well as everyone thinks, it's gonna be huge. Not that he has a clue, of course . . .'

'Could you fix it, then?' asked Kate tentatively. 'So Nick doesn't have to know the specific details?'

Gloria peered at her over her tinted bifocals. 'Naturally, it's all part of the service,' she said, her voice unexpectedly icy.

Not for the first time, Kate wondered why they were all always so eager to make life as painless as possible for Nick, and heard herself volunteering to break the news to Phoebe that she would not be needed at the *Vanity Fair* studio.

Some long-suppressed impulse caused Eliza to skip off work extra early in order that Guy, her hairdresser, could twist her long platinum locks into Medusa-like coils that shone like embroidered buttons all over her scalp. 'I've got to hand it to you,' Guy had said, surveying his own artistry appreciatively, 'you don't surprise me often. But when you do, it's sensational. There's me thinking you'd come in for the usual French pleat, and here's you exiting like some Versace model.'

On the way back from Guy's she had dropped into Gucci and bought a backless flesh-coloured dress. She had then got into the shower, dried herself roughly and slavered some Dr Hauschka oil all over her body so that the dress clung indecently to her gleaming curves. Looking in the mirror, she noticed with satisfaction that even the outline of her pubic hair was visible. The effect, particularly after she powdered her still-damp face and mouth into pale perfection and ringed her eyes in deepest indigo, turning them into two hypnotic black holes, was sensational.

David was waiting, as he always was these days, outside for her in his silver Mercedes. Probably found the stairs too tiring, thought Eliza. It was cold – he liked to keep the interior of his cars fresh – and she could feel her nipples popping out like champagne corks. Cold interiors for a cold man. He was so fastidious that he even used filtered water in his screen washer. At first this had amused Eliza but now it irritated her.

The only time he hotted up these days was when his secretary gave him the month's clippings from Dempster showing him and Eliza at one of the many glittering public events they attended. He was so busy trying to get the NDP into bed with New Labour that he went to anything and everything he thought might raise his profile, dragging Eliza with him. In the past year she'd done more hobnobbing than if she'd worked a lifetime in a McVitie's biscuit factory and shaken more hands than a Saudi Arabian executioner. It wasn't so much a social life as a champagne socialist one, she thought mordantly. She clutched her embroidered evening coat around her for warmth. In the cool, pine-scented dark David reached over and pecked her dryly on the mouth.

'You've changed your hair,' he remarked, ever the observant dandy.

'Do you like it?' She patted the wet coils and smiled mischievously.

'I'll give you the verdict when we get into the light,' he said coolly.

The circular gravelled driveway to Bernie – or Sir Bernie, as they were now to call him since he had been knighted in John Major's final New Year's Honours – Higginbottom's house was packed with more chauffeur-driven cars than the forecourt of Jack Barclay's showroom. 'Pompous asses,' muttered David, deftly backing the Mercedes into a sliver of space beneath a large oak tree. He still hadn't forgiven Bernie for putting Kate out of work. But, since the demise of Laurence Patterson, Bernie, to the chagrin of some of the snobbier New Democrat MPs, had become the party's biggest financial benefactor.

Closing *Domus* had been a psychological turning point for Bernie's cement businesses, which had taken a bit of a pummelling with the Gulf War and the building recession. In the past two years, his fortune has increased tenfold. He'd opened a chain of discount mobile phone warehouses which he was poised to float any minute. The indoor holiday parks had taken off spectacularly. Meanwhile, the publishing company which Tatty headed up was doing remarkably well, having followed the success of Xtra with a string of deeply unglamorous niche magazine with names like *Rolo* (aimed at chocaholics) and *Solo*, which was aimed at lonely urban singles and boasted the most extensive lonely hearts section in the northern hemisphere.

The press, of course, adored him almost as much as the inner sanctum of the New Dems' kitchen cabinet looked down their noses at him. His outspoken, maverick views regularly made the front pages and, after a characteristically blunt appearance on *Question Time* during which he'd asked the audience and Peter Sissons to excuse his French, they'd embraced him even more. The *Python* had sent round one of its buxom reporters the following day to interview him in French, and Bernie had winningly played along in execrable Franglais. Never one to miss a marketing ruse, he had launched an amazingly popular *Sir Bernie Goes Bilingual* set of linguistic cassettes, which promised fluency in ten easy listening sessions and featured hilarious segments of Sir Bernie mangling everything from Serbo-Croation to Mandarin.

It really was nauseating, thought David grimly, slipping a proprietorial arm around Eliza as he escorted her up Lady Nancy's newly balustraded steps to the double front doors. The entire party was expected to pay court every time he threw a party to entertain his many overseas business associates.

As they listened to Chris de Burgh's 'Lady in Red' tinkling away on the doorbell, they could hear that the party was already well under way. A butler ushered them into the pomegranate-coloured hallway that had seen more dodgy brushwork than a stolen getaway car, and Eliza was immediately enveloped in a storm of taffeta as Lady Nancy greeted her warmly. David circled the hall gingerly, flinching as he peered into large rooms overfilled with Roche Bobois fitted furniture and serious-looking Arabs.

The gathering largely comprised Bernie's Middle Eastern colleagues, whom he was doubtless trying to coerce into handing over vast sites of natural beauty so that he could erect more of the huge indoor 'exotic' resorts with which he had blighted considerable swathes of Britain and northern Europe. David sighed, and gazed around dejectedly at the latest haul of pastel watercolours which Lady Nancy had sent away for by the job-lot from *Simply Splendid*'s reader offers. Above the fireplace was a magnificent aerial view of Sir Bernie's finest erection to date, Spaghetti Junction.

At least, thought David, relieving a passing waiter of two glasses of Krug, he always served a decent vintage. A little too quickly he drained his glass, only to choke on its unexpected sweetness. 'What in God's name is that?' he spluttered.

'Aqua Libra,' replied the waiter, nodding in the direction of a gaggle of sheikhs who were sipping on some lurid fruit cocktails and twiddling paper parasols.

'Is there nothing alcoholic?' asked David, trying to keep the desperation out of his voice. Obviously Lady Nancy had got the wrong end of *Simply Splendid*'s distressed gilt instructions again and gone for Shabby Sheikh.

'Cook may have some leftover trifle in the fridge,' replied the waiter archly. 'And I believe Lady Nancy keeps some Rescue Remedy in her bathroom——'

Appalled at the prospect of a completely dry evening, David wondered whether he had time before dinner to slip out to the local Reading off-licence for a swift finger or two of Glenfiddich, and whether his Gold Spot would sufficiently do the trick afterwards. He didn't even register Eliza sweeping off, her lips curling in amusement. By the time he looked round she was lost in the swirl.

Beneath the twinkling chandeliers that *Simply Splendid* declared no well-dressed house should be without, the dark, mysterious eyes of the Arab women, yashmakked up to the temples, glowed mysteriously. David didn't recognize a single one of them. They clearly weren't the *Hello!* type. On the far side of the room he saw Jim Allwater schmoozing a huddle of editors from the *International Gazette*, the *Guardian* and the *Probe*. It all looked unbelievably dreary.

He was just about to make a dash for his car, where he thought he might have a hip flask of brandy bobbing around, when he was accosted by Lady Nancy, her normally rapacious cleavage savagely bound in a swathe of pomegranate silk taffeta that would clothe most of South-East Asia.

'Hello, David.' She beamed, her crinoline bobbing around her like a giant water bed. Feeling unaccountably guilty, as if he had been caught in the act of something naughty, he seized her plump bejewelled hand and kissed it. Two large ruby blotches erupted on her cheeks and, to his horror, she began fluttering her eyelashes before tapping him tartly on his wrist with her lace fan.

'Now, you naughty man,' she trilled, throwing herself between him and the porticoed front door, 'don't think I don't know exactly where you were heading. You wouldn't be the first,' she confided in a lower voice, wheeling him back towards the crowd. 'Jim Allwater was halfway down the drive before Sir Bernie caught up with him.' She fanned herself violently. 'I can't tell you what a trial tonight's been. So many minefields. Bernie was convinced the London women were bound to turn up with bare bosoms and backs flashing like Belisha beacons. He was furious that I hadn't stipulated a dress code, but of course I knew no one would turn out if they thought we were entertaining the Middle East, what with there being no alcohol and all. Though strictly between us' – she lowered her voice again marginally – 'there's a crate of gin in the nanny's bedroom.'

She looked so hot and red that David thought she might spontaneously combust. 'So I said, Bernie, now don't insult our guests' intelligence by spelling it out. We had quite a row about it, I can tell you. Thank heaven's no one's let me down.' She surveyed the long sleeves and demure necklines approvingly. 'Now, David, I'd like you to meet someone very fascinating.'

His heart sank as Nancy carted him off in the direction of two sheikhs. 'Ahem,' said Nancy loudly. 'Allow me to introduce Sheikh Manahani and Sheikh Abdullah.'

For the first time that evening, David's smile actually made it as far as his eyes. Sheikh Abdullah was one of the most powerful men in Dubai, with business interests all around the world that constantly required the ministration of top-class lawyers – and rumour had it he was looking to change law firms. David's hand readjusted the knot in his tie in an automatic gesture and he relaxed slightly. At least there were people here who made his presence worthwhile.

He spent a good half-hour charming both men, completely forgetting about Eliza. But the marvellous thing was that he never had to worry about her. She could hold her own in any situation, whatever the crowd. If anything, she was a little too self-sufficient. But, by God, she was decorative. And the way she had so superbly judged the evening's dress code – damping down her normal slinky style in favour of that rather fetching, demure velvet thing she had on – was a tribute to her sensitivity.

He was on the verge of clinching a verbal agreement to represent Sheikh Abdullah whenever he had business in Britain when Sheikh Manahani interrupted them. 'Is it me,' he said, anxious to try out his new *Sir Bernie Goes Bilingual* course in colloquial English, 'or is it hotter than a pig's fart in here?'

'I should say,' said Sheik Abdullah urbanely, 'it's boiling as a pope's prick. Don't know how the women are coping in all their fabric.'

'I think one of them has just found a solution,' said Sheikh Manahani, his eyes on stalks.

There was an audible gasp and a pool of empty space around Eliza as she allowed her velvet cloak to slip to the floor. For the first time that night – and the last in their relationship – David saw her in almost all her considerable physical glory: a reckless angel in a backless, almost frontless flesh-coloured dress that had been expertly cut so as to render its wearer as close to indecently exposed as Western – though not necessarily Arab – law allows.

Phoebe had finally wrapped her interviews with Naomi Campbell and was now herself being wrapped by a white-coated regression therapist in rose-scented pages torn from her diary and dipped in sheep's amniotic fluid which would allegedly finally give her the closure she craved on her miserable childhood. Focusing on the positive, which wasn't easy as the aubergine ink ran all over her buffed body and dribbled over her breasts, Phoebe tried to expel all feelings of negativity, but they seemed to have taken up asylum-seeker status and wouldn't budge. The one bright spot on her otherwise occluded front was being able to have lunch and go shopping now and again with Kate. She really was a sweet girl. And she had the most terrific taste.

Phoebe actually had a lot to congratulate herself on. The Naomi rushes was a riot – they had gone shopping together and Phoebe had roped her into a couple of shiatsu sessions.

Then they had taken in a ballet and Naomi had ended up performing the dying swan on the stage of the Met. All in all, Phoebe had not simply achieved what most chat-show hosts failed to do – to get a whole hour of material from Naomi – but she had drawn things out of her that had never before come to light.

But as ever, Phoebe was caught between two polarized sets of emotions. On the one hand she realized that if she made enough of a stir in New York it might be the key to a whole new, extremely prestigious career as a celebrity interviewer in America. She began to monitor Barbara Walters closely, and considered consulting a voodoo specialist about getting a doll made of her. On the other hand she was still a serious actress and must not get too successful doing anything else in America, where she still harboured serious ambitions to snag a major film role. And she was devastated that *And Now* seemed to be going so well and that all the newspapers now called Martha the thinking man's crumpet. She was the queen interviewer at the Beeb. There wasn't room for another.

Charlie, hot out of a screening room in White City where he had watched the unedited Naomi footage and, after all these months, still clueless as to the cause of his star's angst, called her to congratulate her. He caught her mid-irrigation.

'It's fan-bloody-marvellous,' he gushed, relief burbling out of him. This would show the rumour-mongers that Charlie Pitchcock knew how to back winners. 'You got things out of her no one else has. Showed the human side and all that. You're a total genius, Phoebe. Keep this up and I foresee BAFTAs galore. Big kisses.'

Disgusted, Phoebe pretended her mobile had gone

down and switched it off. How typical of Charlie Pitchcock-up, as she had begun thinking of him, to assume that hanging around for Naomi Campbell for days on end until she deigned to grant them a few hours of her time was the crowning achievement of a life. As far as Phoebe was concerned it symbolized just how far down the tubes her career had got wedged. It was colonically fatigued. And it would take more than some energetic enemas to flush it out.

Phoebe's mood swings were starting to frighten even her. She was worried she might do something really stupid, such as starting a liaison with someone really unsuitable. All her adult life she'd made a point of collecting the names and addresses of ghastly men – the more potentially damaging to herself the better – in a little crimson leather book she perused on rainy days. The incident with Lachlan had reminded her how rash she could still be, but at least he was pretty harmless and, by her standards, the episode hadn't been too humiliating. But she felt she ought to get on top of the situation before it got out of hand. By way of distraction, she asked Kate to go shopping with her. It was while they were trawling around Chinatown one day that Kate's pains first started. Not wishing to disappoint Phoebe, she had ploughed on, until at last the stabbing sensations were so strong, and she had turned such a ghastly shade of grey, that even Phoebe had noticed and suggested, not entirely enthusiastically, that they take a taxi back to the hotel. By the end of the day Kate had lost her baby. And Phoebe, to her chagrin, was going to have to spend the last two days of her trip going shopping on her own.

✳   ✳   ✳

'So, tell us why you went to India,' said Phoebe, smiling sweetly at Miriam Harper, secure in the knowledge that, for once, Miriam's olive Helmut Lang was not a felicitous look. It had been Charlie's unwelcome idea that they do a bit of the interview in front of a live audience in the Plaza Hotel, and Phoebe had to admit it was a brilliant one. At this rate HBO would be gagging to buy the series. Miriam rarely gave interviews to anyone, but after Nick and Phoebe had invited her out to dinner, and Nick had hinted that there might be a role for her in Ambrose's next play, she had been putty in their hands. The BBC press office had managed to whip up a flutter of interest in the media and most of the newspapers had sent along reporters to watch.

Miriam was considered to be Hollywood royalty. For some reason, the normally voracious press gave her an easy ride, even though it was common knowledge within the industry that she slept with anything with a pulse.

'Does that include lentils or does she just stick to mung beans?' asked Phoebe when Nick delivered this information.

'Frankly I don't think she makes any distinction,' said Nick, 'but for God's sake don't even hint at it in the interview.' He'd only told Phoebe because she'd been working herself up into a vortex of inferiority complexes. She takes her role as America's sweetheart very seriously.'

To begin with it all went brilliantly. Miriam was charm itself to Phoebe, whom she trusted as one of her own kind by now, and opened up in a winningly naïve way. In fact the whole thing was going swimmingly. Too swimmingly.

'Well, I wanted to find myself,' said Miriam coyly in

response to Phoebe's question about her last role as a nun.
She blushed a delicious rose pink and stared down at her
hands, clearly uncomfortable.

'Oh, sweetie,' soothed Phoebe, reaching over to pat
Miriam's hand and, in the process, allowing the camera an
unfettered view of the beautiful fantail silk pleating at the
back of her lace dress, 'all you had to do was look under
the nearest man—'

There was an audible gasp from the audience, followed
by hisses. Phoebe, momentarily thrown by the reaction,
forgot which camera she was addressing and began swivelling
her head disconcertingly.

Miriam's ample lower lip trembled and her eyes began
to look dangerously damp.

'So how is Mitch?' Phoebe asked, flustered. For the
first time in her professional life as a chat-show host, she
had fluffed the meticulous research she insisted on. Mitch
Willoughby and Miriam had broken up very publicly a
fortnight earlier, as all of America knew, having been fed an
endless diet of photos showing a more or less make-up-less
and fragile Miriam emerging alone from various restaurants
and shops over the past few days.

A fat tear – the single last carbohydrate in Miriam's
body, as Phoebe reflected later – rolled down her cheek
and the audience began a slow handclap. Miriam decided
to milk the moment for all it was worth. Struggling bravely
to hold back the tears, she eventually gave way to them and
had to be escorted sobbing from the stage.

The headlines couldn't have made it more explicit.
'Little Miss Nobody insults America's Princess,' thundered
the *New York Post*. 'Overdressed, over-made-up and over
here,' screeched the *Daily News* over an unflattering picture

of Miriam and Phoebe, which looked as though it had been doctored to show a bad case of cellulite proliferating up the entire length of the backs of Phoebe's thighs.

'Academy Award-winner Miriam Harper was yesterday the victim of a curious outburst of spite and vitriol from a chat-show host,' wrote the *New York Times*, which was the only paper not to have sent a journalist to cover the story. 'Phoebe Keane, of the BBC, made sly allusions to Miss Harper's private life and joked about her various affairs in front of a live audience. Miss Harper, famously private about her love life, broke down in tears and had to be escorted from the set. Miss Keane, a little-known one-time actress, is believed to have met with some success for her show in England. However, she is unlikely to be asked back to conduct more interviews in America. See page 13 and "When Professional Jealousy Comes between Actresses", page 5 of Metro.'

Utterly mortified, Phoebe retreated back to England, leaving Gloria waving a red flag and Kate, who was reeling from her miscarriage, feeling that somehow she had been deserted.

Chapter Sixteen

To the outside world, Kate's life was perfect. Glossy magazine perfect. She was travelling all over the place, especially to India, where she was having some of her more elaborate pieces embroidered and beaded. Her career was more stimulating than she had dared dream. So much so that Roberto was already negotiating to open a third shop and Berniece was negotiating to send Serenity to finishing school in Switzerland. But six months after the first miscarriage, Kate still couldn't put it behind her. Instead of leaning on Ambrose, she threw herself into her work.

And there was plenty of it around. Wemyss, the glamorous department store in Manhattan, was so ecstatic about the way her blankets, bags and throws were selling that they wanted her to open a concession within their Fifth Avenue store. They had also offered her an obscene amount of money to design an exclusive range of crockery, bed-sheets and, ironically, some babywear for them. *Trilogy* was up for seven Tony awards, including one for best costumes.

To her chagrin, Kate noticed that Ambrose seemed far

less affected by their inability to have a baby than she was
He had started on *Endymion*, a screenplay of the life of Keats
and for once his work seemed to be going smoothly. Marty
Shicker shrewdly snapped up the rights before Ambrose had
time to launch into three hundred or so rewrites. Nick was
slated to star and hoped against hope that he might be able
to convince Marty to cast Phoebe as Fanny Brawne – after
all, she'd played her brilliantly in one of her Euro-puddings
But Marty wouldn't budge. He wanted a name that mean
something in America. Miriam Harper had recently won
an Oscar for her uncanny portrayal of a repressed young
Victorian woman in *Villette*. And even though everyone
agreed that it was her stagey British accent that had really
walked away with the award, Marty Shicker insisted on her
And since everyone also agreed that the film stood the best
chance of being a hit if Liggers Pictures made it, Ambrose
conceded. No one had dared tell Phoebe that Miriam was
in it. But already the buzz about the film was gathering
momentum before the first frame had been shot.

People magazine had voted Kate and Ambrose one of
their fiftiest hottest couples, not that Kate took any notice
of such things, of course, but it had amused them both.

On a personal note, she had begun seeing more of
her father again, after he – and to give him credit it was
definitely David who had instigated it – had invited Kate
and Martha round to dinner at his flat in Dolphin Square
True, he had split up with Eliza and was clearly in need
of some female company, but he had courted them so
assiduously and so thoughtfully that they had both decided
to give him a second chance.

'After all, we're not condoning what he did,' said Kate
uncertainly.

'And the quality of mercy is not strained,' added Martha, who hadn't seen her father more than three times since she'd been summoned from Israel almost two years earlier.

'No. Only filtered where Dad's concerned,' said Kate.

Something about him had changed. He wasn't exactly humble, but somehow he seemed less sure of himself. It was a change that would have been imperceptible to all but his family. But they did notice it — and considered it a change for the better. He even cooked them dinner — coq au vin, though Martha had to rescue the crème brûlée. The evening had been such a success that they had vowed to repeat it just as soon as they all found time. And to crown a spectacularly successful year, Cressida had announced that she wanted to spend the summer holidays on Operation Raleigh. This had caused Ambrose a minor pang since he still couldn't help feeling that any self-respecting teenager of his ought to be out brandishing placards in their spare time. But since it was better than the alternatives — Peter Townend had been hotly courting her in the hope of persuading her to be one of his debs of the year — he acquiesced.

All in all they ought to have been in a relaxed state of mind. How ironic, then, thought Kate sadly, that one of America's sexiest duos was finding it almost impossible to conceive.

She had had four miscarriages in eighteen months. The doctors told her she should stop trying for a while, and give her body a rest. But they didn't understand how badly she wanted a child. She had been for tests but so far nothing had shown up. Unable for once to control the situation, she was beginning to panic, convinced, apart from anything else, that she was desperately letting Ambrose down.

✳   ✳   ✳

Given that the BAFTAs had never deigned to acknowledge any of her film work and had taken two and a half years to pay tribute to her show, Phoebe spent the first few weeks after the television nominations had come in pretending that they were so tawdry as to be unworthy even of comment, let alone her presence. But once Charlie had been tipped off that *Friday with Phoebe* was a shoo-in for at least two of the three categories it was up for, she went into a frenzy of anticipation and mounted a ruthless campaign in the press. She had a lead position in any case, because since her drubbing in the American papers, and her championing of elephants, the British tabloids had taken her to their hearts in a vicelike clamp of hypocritical sentimentality. In return they were royally entertained at the Holland Park house. No tabloid hack was too junior to be invited for tea and a heart-warming gossip. While Nick was away shooting yet more scenes for Pain in the Lars, Warren Peace was treated to so many after-work drinks that Phoebe even contemplated adding his name to her red book. But she decided he wasn't really dangerous enough.

'I trust you'll be wearing something suitably spectacular, Pheebs,' he said, nibbling on his cocktail stick thoughtfully.

'Don't you worry about that,' she replied, leaning over and adjusting his bow tie. 'When have I ever disappointed?'

But Warren did worry. Sensing the chance to stage-manage the entire event for the benefit of his paper, he wanted to mastermind every detail. His damp pasty cheeks glistened like radioactive potatoes in anticipation.

He wanted something uplifting for his front page, and he didn't just mean morally. The trouble was that Phoebe had got so scrawny it would take a dress with more plush upholstery than a Rolls-Royce to give her any hope of a cleavage. Without her screen make-up and the benefit of skilful studio lighting, he could see that she was ill. Something was eating her. Which was ironic, he thought, since she clearly wasn't eating anything. Still, he wasn't ready to run the hysterical anorexia headlines yet. Phoebe was the *Python*'s golden girl and she shifted copies like nobody's business. Someone else would come along eventually and replace her, but until they turned up Phoebe was their best bet, and Warren wasn't going to let her go without an epic struggle — or without a few taunts.

'I know you won't let our readers down, Phoebe,' he grunted contentedly, as she sloshed some more Buck's fizz into his glass. 'I'm relying on your natural competitive spirit. After all, the glamour stakes are very high this year and you wouldn't want to see Martha Crawford getting the better of you.'

Phoebe took a taxi from the station to the home where her mother had resided ever since her Alzheimer's had made her a danger to herself, and made it wait outside while she went through the motions of filling her mother in on the latest twists in her life while the former stared through her the whole time, apparently more captivated by her dwindling packet of cigarettes than her daughter. Phoebe kissed her powdery cheek and gave her twenty packets of Rothman's before she left.

'At least she's not in any pain, Mrs Wilde,' offered

the nurse encouragingly as she walked Phoebe to the exit. Depressed, Phoebe took the taxi to the estate – same rain-stained concrete, same urine-soaked lifts – where she'd grown up and asked the driver to wait. Grudgingly, and after she'd tipped him up front, he agreed. Even though she'd dressed down in a pair of jeans and trainers, she looked incongruous as she walked quickly down the graffitied corridors to her brother's flat. She looked like a model who'd been temporarily placed against a scenic backdrop of deprivation.

She dreaded these trips back to Wolverhampton – she knew it must be hard for Nick to deal with her silences afterwards. Sometimes they lasted for days. But then his family wasn't a dysfunctional mess like hers. She always got drunk on the train back and she always vowed she wouldn't return. But her family were like a car crash, and she kept returning to the scene of the accident. It took her ten minutes to find the flat she'd spent fifteen years in. The Chaucer Estate was a maze of blocked corridors, barricaded entrances and no-go stairwells. Every so often she lost her way and found the route cut off by a steel wall that had been erected since her last visit. The place was half derelict. Like Hartley. Hartley and Tanya. The aspirational thrust of those names never ceased to astonish her. She found it hard to believe her parents had ever harboured any hopes for any of them.

Through the flimsy chipped doors, voices floated across the derelict landscape; snatched rows, flickering televisions – fragments of lives that were being repeated across the estate in the other identical blocks.

Hartley opened the door bare- and sunken-chested, his thin, muscular arms as white as mozzarella.

'Made it, then,' he said dourly. 'I watched you weave your way up here. Took you longer than a pissed whore.'

She smiled brightly, even though the visit to her mother had left her feeling shaky, and tried to hug him. Silently, he led her into the living room, where the television was on mutely. She tried to ignore the overflowing ashtrays, the empty beer cans and the sour smell of the place, and wondered if she'd ever get over the guilt of leaving him sufficiently to stop coming back. But there was so much she wanted to talk to him about. Their childhood – the bits he could remember and she couldn't and the parts she had blotted out – came back increasingly to torment her these days. She wanted to ask him about their father – about the times he'd beaten Hartley up and then tried to slobber all over her. And somehow she had to broach the time she had sought comfort in Hartley's bed, after their father had collapsed one night in the living room and he had kissed her tenderly, over and over, and see whether what she had tried so hard to blot out had really happened.

It was one of Hartley's bad days and he wasn't in the mood for anything other than grunting. It wasn't for want of trying or investment – on her part – that life had never quite taken off for him. But nothing ever went right for Hartley. His taxi business had gone bust. Then he'd taken a stake, with some of Phoebe's Euro-pudding money, in a road haulage company, but that hadn't worked either. He'd tried scheme after scheme until his energy and enthusiasm for everything except Sky Sport had died, and now he couldn't seem to hold a job down. After a few stilted minutes, she suggested they drive out to a country pub for lunch. His sunken eyes gazed back at her with so much scorn not even the haze of cigarette smoke between them could disguise it. She left after forty minutes, took the taxi to the station and, when she got back to London, went straight to Laurence Patterson's flat, charmed her way past the porter and sat outside his neoclassical mahogany door until he came home.

Phoebe was secretly terrified that she would be snubbed at the awards and come away empty-handed. Even worse, she dreaded that Martha might win and she wouldn't. It didn't help that the newspapers pitting them against one another compared their ages (not that anyone was completely sure of Phoebe's), their dress sense, their addresses and of course their bodies, and generally created mischief. 'Two too much,' squealed the Python over a largely invented story about their alleged rivalry and how they had banned each other's teams from fraternizing with one another. Not that it was completely wide of the mark. Phoebe would have loved to have made Martha's life a misery, but she never got the chance because Martha was so busy swotting up on her guests that she kept a very low profile around White City.

Not that that stopped Phoebe from spraying the lifts with her favourite Fracas every time she got in – just in case Martha had been in before her – or from fastidiously wiping all the chairs before she sat down. They were even pitched against each other for one of the categories – that of best original format. Phoebe definitely seemed to be winning the PR war: the press, growing weary of Martha's aloofness, were becoming palpably testy towards her.

Even so, raddled with nerves, Phoebe was in a foul mood when the night of the awards finally came round.

'You look fantastic,' said Nick, straight off the plane from
LA. After an epic struggle of his own, he had persuaded
Lars to give him two days' compassionate leave. Before he
could kiss her properly she had moved away from him. In
fashion terms, he thought bitterly, it was true; she did look
fabulous. The emerald and amber bias-cut Julien Macdonald
dress glowed like traffic lights against the lambent silkiness
of her skin, and featured a split deeper than the one that had
recently finished off the Tories. She had set off her slender
neck with an enormous square-cut topaz that dangled from
a thin ruby-coloured length of velvet. With her shiny copper
hair cupping her head like a silk scarf, and the two curls
of black liner above her eyes, she looked more exotic than
ever. But Nick could no longer ignore the fact that she was
ill. She had lost so much weight her body, once curvy and
sensuous, was like that of a prepubescent child.

'Shouldn't you take a wrap?' he asked. She needed to
cover her arms, which had become so scrawny and over-
worked-out that they looked like overcooked vermicelli.
It's pretty cold at these things. It's pouring outside and
it looks as though it might thunder.'

'I'll be fine,' she said glassily. He decided to take one
for her anyway.

They drove to the ceremony in silence. Nick was on
tenterhooks. He had been thrilled when Phoebe had been
nominated. He still felt a surge of pride whenever he saw
her on television. It was as if the old Phoebe – the witty,
sometimes acerbic but always entertaining Phoebe – had
somehow been reconstituted and forever frozen as airwaves.
Certainly there was precious little sign of her in real life any
more. But on air she was still brilliant, charming, effervescent
and inimitable.

'Why did you bring the shawl, Nick?' Her voice was hard and impersonal.

'I thought you might be cold. I really don't want you getting ill.'

'Crap,' she snarled. 'Is there no end to your control freakery?'

He didn't rise to her bait. It was imperative to retain equilibrium. But by the time they had reached Marble Arch, Phoebe had worked herself into an hysterical rage. Still screaming a tirade of abuse, she tugged at the door and leaped out at the traffic lights just as the car moved off. Weaving unsteadily through the speeding cars, she looked like a madwoman, dressed in her jewels and long emerald dress, which was already damp and clinging to her like fronds of seaweed. Frantic that she was going to get killed, Nick asked the driver to circle round the Arch until they caught up with her again. He then leaped out and grabbed her, pushing her back into the car.

'Look, if you don't want to travel with me, fine. But at least make a decent entrance on your own.' He watched the car disappear into the blaze of tail-lights as they twinkled down Park Lane, and set about the dispiriting task of hailing a taxi at six o'clock on a damp evening.

Donna Ducatti had spent most of the intervening hours between rehearsals for the awards and the actual ceremony locked in the loo. She was nervous on all fronts. She'd done plenty of daytime TV. But presenting the BAFTAs was her first big attempt at serious prime-time gravitas. And just when she ought to have been concentrating on polishing her witty aperçus, she found herself horribly distracted by body hair.

Ever since the *Python* had published an unflattering shot of her armpits at a charity tennis match under the headline, 'Thatch of the Day', she had developed a phobia about it. Bunty Leigh's comments about vulgar presenters' dresses hadn't helped, particularly since now that she looked at it in the cold fluorescent light of her dressing room, her gown was tackier – and considerably messier – than a sangria-soaked fortnight in Megaluf. The shop assistant had told her the feathers elongated her neck and made her look like a swan. Ugly duckling was probably closer to the truth. She could just see Fenton Wigstaff's headlines now. She didn't know why she didn't write them herself and save him the trouble.

It was all right for Bunty. He just had to squidge his way into the same tuxedo he'd worn when he'd accompanied Princess Margaret to the first night of *Shocked and Amused* back in 1969. 'And it still fits like a glove,' he had boasted to Donna before disappearing into his dressing room to be sewn into his corset.

The viewing figures for *Art House*, the unbelievably pretentious late-night show on to which Bunty invited his luvvie friends, were so low they defied all radar, but Bunty was an old hand at em-ceeing awards ceremonies, whereas this was Donna's first shot and she was determined not to mess things up. She ran through her speeches and ad libs for the nine hundredth time, and applied some more blusher, also for the nine hundredth time. By the time the first guests started drifting in she was surfing on a wave of panic and gin, and her cheeks were so blotchy and red they looked as though they'd been tie-dyed in ketchup.

Meanwhile, at the front of house, the reporters, clustered like anoracked carrion behind the ropes, immediately noticed that Phoebe and Nick arrived separately. It had taken Nick ages to find a taxi and he was soaked through by the time he arrived. 'Not with the missus?' chirruped a reporter from the *Digger*. Unsure whether Phoebe had made it there and not wanting to say the wrong thing, he rushed past them in silence, with his head down.

'Stuck-up git,' muttered one of the reporters. 'Just 'cos he's big in Hollywood.'

'Dunno how Phoebe Keane puts up with him,' agreed a blond reporter wearing what looked like a black hankie. 'And what a mess.'

In the mêlée before they all sat down to dinner, Nick fell on Ambrose with such an obvious air of desperation that Ambrose wondered briefly whether he should take him home. But he couldn't abandon Martha on her big night. Kate, who was feeling weak from her miscarriages and wasn't in the mood for celebrating, had gone to see Sadie, promising to watch it all on television. Secretly, she couldn't face being caught between Martha and Phoebe, who had both begged her to come and lend some moral support.

Phoebe was missing, presumed posing for the paparazzi. And Martha was nowhere to be seen. Since they had arrived she had been assailed from all sides by colleagues and friends. When she finally reappeared, looking radiant in a simple black satin column, she was accompanied by a triumphal Charlie Pitchcock. Ambrose stood up to introduce her to Nick, and was surprised to see that they already seemed to know one another.

'We met in Bosnia,' said Martha, who was by far the

more composed of the two of them, even though her heart was thwacking so loudly she feared her ribs would crack. After all this time she was finally face to face with Nick, and her emotions were so tumultuous she hardly dared look at him. What if he weren't the same? What if he had never felt as intensely about what had passed between them as she had? As she still did?

Ambrose watched them greet each other awkwardly. Was it his imagination or was there a palpable *frisson* when they kissed one another politely on the cheeks? Martha, who looked more and more lovely each time he saw her, seemed almost rattled. But then so did Nick. For the rest of the evening he studied them from behind his programme, noting the way they leaned in to one another when they were talking, and the way that, whenever they thought anyone was watching, their gazes studiously avoided one another.

Her stomach exploding with nerves, Donna finally sailed on to the podium with Bunty. She looked like an explosion in a tin-foil factory and knew it. But ever the consummate professional, she tin-soldiered on, even though the fumes of Bunty's Miss Dior eau de toilette were threatening to asphyxiate her, and her heavily rehearsed ad libs had so far met with stony silence from the audience.

Phoebe, meanwhile, had decided to make herself at home backstage so that she didn't have to suffer the indignity of a million camera angles of her face in defeat – or throwing up when Martha beat her to best format. Gulping down vodka martinis, she kept telling the make-up artists and behind-the-scenes staff that she had acute eczema on her hands, which was why she couldn't sit out front and applaud any of the winners. Charlie, meanwhile, was table-hopping shamelessly under the pretext of congratulating the winners, but in reality to take down their telephone numbers.

Lachlan O'Hennessy, whose series on modern poetry had been a surprise smash hit, was next up on the podium to receive an award for services to art. He said that he didn't wish to thank anyone but wanted to share a little joke instead. The audience gazed at him grimly, expecting some existential tirade on death. 'So Rachel meets Ruben in this old people's home,' he began lugubriously, his eyes glinting wickedly. 'And she gives him such exquisite hand jobs that he declares undying love for her and she looks forward to ending her days with him. And sure enough they live happily ever after until Leah arrives. Ruben dumps Rachel and she is distraught. "Do I or do I not give the best hand jobs in town?" she asks plaintively. Ruben shrugs wistfully. "I used to think that was the case. But then I met Leah and — oy vey . . ." "So what does Leah have that I don't?" asks Rachel tearfully. "Parkinson's," says Ruben gleefully.'

After this supremely tasteless joke, the audience collapsed and filming had to be suspended for ten minutes. Fortunately the ceremony wasn't going out live and Lachlan's contribution to the evening's overall vulgarity at least broke the ice. Then it was Lachlan's turn to present an award.

'And the winner of the 1997 BAFTA for Best New Light Entertainment format is — is—' began Lachlan, fumbling in his undertaker's pockets for the relevant information. 'Oh, bugger, I've lost it . . .' There was a nail-biting delay during which he rummaged noisily in his pockets, which were roomier than a Blackpool boarding house, and Phoebe managed to toss back another two vodka martinis. 'Ah, yes, found it, thank God,' groaned Lachlan. 'The winner is *Friday with Phoebe*.'

There was an unseemly scramble as Phoebe skittered on to the podium and raced to collect the award before Charlie Pitchcock and Will got there. By the time *Friday* had won two awards, one for best presenter, one for most original format, Phoebe had miraculously found the use of her hands again. Charlie, meanwhile, was talking into two mobiles at once, giving blow-by-blow accounts to the DG and to Charlotte, who was stuck at home with the children after their Croatian nanny had run off with Charlotte's cleaning lady.

Phoebe gave a charming speech in which she thanked her director, Charlie, Magda, her guests and, pausing tremulously, Nick. The hacks scribbled away busily. Then it was Martha's turn. After missing out on the joint award she and Jim had been up for two years ago, she had never really expected to win anything. So she was astonished to receive the Churchill Award for Current Affairs. Trembling, she walked on to the stage, allowed Bunty to press his paunch up against her, and then found herself face to stony face with Donna, who had read out the award and was at that moment wondering whether the evening could get any worse.

It could. Smitten by Martha's classic elegance, which reminded him of Jackie Kennedy in her heyday, Bunty stepped back on to Donna's trailing hems just as she was trying to hurry along the proceedings by shuffling Martha off the podium. There was a heart-stopping ripping sound as Donna's fishtail detached itself from the rest of her dress, leaving a four-foot gap at the back. 'Whoops,' said Bunty archly. 'Bet Richard Branson wishes he could get his trains to leave that quickly. Shame you didn't take the fake tan all the way up, Donna,' he remarked, surveying her legs languidly. At which point it was very hard to inject anything into the remains of the evening, let alone gravitas.

Phoebe swept off in the waiting limo without giving a backward glance at Nick. Martha, who had spent most of the evening with her heart pounding – a state of affairs which, she was peeved to note, didn't abate once she had received her award – watched him pityingly.

'Let me give you a lift in my car,' she said, as lightly as she could. 'Charlie's spared no expenses tonight. It's chauffeurs all round and you're on my way home,' she lied, silencing his embarrassed protests. 'In fact I'd be glad of the company. I'm a bit too wired to go straight to bed.'

They drove back in silence, each huddled in their separate corners. Between them the corrugated leather seats stretched like undulating prairies. Martha made a few attempts at small talk and Nick did his best to respond, but she could see his heart wasn't in it. He was obviously really cut up about Phoebe, and she was an idiot to keep on feeling the way she did. On the Bayswater Road they passed an enormous billboard for *Green Cover* with Nick, twenty times larger than life, looking down on the wet streets in that confident, laconic, sexy way of his which made women around the world feel they had some kind of personal involvement with him.

They drew up outside the Holland Park house. Nick buried his head in his hands, his fair hair flopping over his face. Instinctively, Martha placed her hand on his shoulder blade. 'Would it help to talk?'

'Only if you can tell me what else I can do to make this work,' he said bitterly. 'No, I thought not.' He opened the door. On the pavement, he appeared to waver slightly, but he was just fishing in his pocket for something. He leaned in to give the driver a tip. 'I hope this hasn't spoiled your evening too much,' he said, looking at her with such sad, sweet eyes it took all her self-control not to yank him back in. 'I think your award is brilliant. And much deserved. You look lovely, by the way. But then you always have.' He reached across and kissed her gently on her forehead. She closed her eyes softly and willed herself to hang on to that moment for ever.

The car whooshed off along the gleaming wet road and Martha turned back to look at Nick's forlorn figure. She had half a mind to make the driver circle back for him. Something about his eyes — a kind of bleak acceptance — made her worry for him. He had always seemed to be blessed with vast reserves of serene resilience before. She couldn't bear to think that they might be destroyed. But what if she did go back? What then?

A lot had happened since their time in Bosnia together. Even if she and Nick had connected on some deep level — and she was sure that was the case, though they had never explicitly discussed it — it was all a long time ago. And they had been different people. Or at least he had. In that world he had been her friend, her equal and the man she most wanted to be with. Here he was a big film star — even bigger than he had been when they had first met. Film stars didn't inhabit reality, not even nice ones like Nick. But at least he'd been getting on with his unreality while she had just been putting her life on hold. The realization struck her like a punch to her solar plexus. She sat huddled in the corner of the car, memories crashing in her mind like meteorites: her lack of grief when her so-called relationship with Jack had finally ground to a halt; her inability to commit or even begin to care about anyone else since; the way she sometimes felt as though she were being sucked through a tunnel without ever touching the sides. She was still in love with Nick. The realization made her feel sick and heady; euphoric and incredibly sad. When she got back to the flat, she wrapped herself in a duvet and sat on the balcony listening to Chopin on her Discman and waited for the sun to rise.

Slipping off his shoes, Nick tiptoed across the chequered hallway to the drawing room so as not to disturb anyone, took off his jacket and poured himself a large whisky. The lights were blazing downstairs but the silence told him Phoebe must be in bed. He sat nursing his drink and his hurt for a while, before creeping warily upstairs, wondering whether he should sleep in one of the spare rooms or whether that would simply antagonize Phoebe more. He didn't have to wrestle with the dilemma for too long because as he reached the landing she appeared at the door to their bedroom, in a transparent black negligee. The velvet choker still at her neck looked, from a distance, like a livid scar. She had removed most of her make-up apart from around her eyes, which glittered unsettlingly in her white face. She had been drinking; a bottle of champagne dangled from her arm. Leaning in the doorway, she reminded him of a 1930s siren; a troublesome vamp who should have been confined to the two-dimensional world of the screen. She was just too exhausting for real life.

'Hello, Nick,' she began. 'Care for a glass?' He stood there mutely. 'No, of course not,' she jumped in before he had worked out a response. 'You couldn't be happy for my success for even one night, could you? Don't think I don't know exactly what's going on underneath that magnanimous exterior of yours.' She was beginning to shout. He remained still and silent, waiting for the artillery to retreat.

'You are such a coward, Nick Wilde. I can understand you lying to your public, but to yourself? It's just pathetic.'

'I don't know what you're talking about, Phoebe,' he said wearily. 'I'm too tired to follow any line of argument. I'm going to bed.' He turned away and she darted in front of him, blocking the doorway.

'You know, I think you're right. You genuinely don't know what I'm talking about. Ever. That's just the problem. And you know what else I think?' Her voice was dangerously high-pitched. 'It's over.'

Wrung out by the endless assaults, he turned away and shrugged in a reflexive action that tipped Phoebe into violent fury. She ran up to him, dragging on him like a wild animal; screaming, waving the champagne bottle. Her strength took him completely by surprise. He turned to try to ease her off his shoulders, and in that moment she shattered the bottle of champagne against the wall and lunged it towards his face. She was screaming that she hated him and sobbing. In the confusion of limbs and clothes, he didn't feel the pain at first. She slid against the wall in a crumpled heap and looked so demented and abject his first thought was to somehow get her to take a sedative. It was only when he had settled her in bed and the blood from the wound on his temple began to stream into his eyes that he remembered his own cuts. He staggered back down the stairs, feeling sick, and made for the door to get some fresh air.

✳   ✳   ✳

She must have dozed for a few minutes because she dreamed that she was back in Sarajevo listening to a siren. When she came round, she realized it was the buzzer to her flat. Stiff from the cold, she got up and walked slowly to the door, looking blearily at her watch. It was four in the morning.

He was still bleeding, but the gushing had turned into a gentle seeping. She wanted to get him to a hospital but he was worried about the story leaking out. Tentatively she picked out the glass and bathed the wound, which looked worse than it was, made up a bed for him and put the kettle on. Unemotionally he told her what had happened. She could see that talking about his marriage was torture for him and he tried to be fastidiously objective and brief.

'It's me,' she said, at one point, reaching across and placing her hand on his arm and relishing the shivers that ran up and down her spine, despite herself. 'I'm your old friend, Nick, not a reporter from the *Digger*.'

'I'm sorry,' he said, attempting a smile. They sat in silence for a while, nursing their tea, Martha sucked into one corner of the sofa, Nick in the other. At that moment the gulf between them seemed bigger than ever.

Eliza stuck her nose into the final chapter of *The Path to Spiritual Enlightenment* and tried to ignore the elbow of the passenger next to her, which was digging into her right bosom. She hadn't been this far back in a plane for ten years, but now that she had decided to take a sabbatical and find herself, travelling business class was a luxury she couldn't afford. Still, it would have made concentrating on *The Path* easier. Distracted by the headlines in her neighbours' newspapers, she asked the stewardess for a copy of the *Digger*.

'*Thigh and Mighty!*' was the screamer on the front page, which carried two photographs showing Nick and Phoebe arriving separately at the ceremony.

'*Five reasons Nick Wilde should leave his wild ways and uncouth manners behind him,*' ran the copy. '*First, he arrived without his gorgeous, award-winning wife Phoebe Keane. Second, he looked as though he'd spent all of five minutes getting ready for his wife's big night. A crumpled crisp packet would have looked smarter. Third, he hardly spoke to anyone all night. Fourth, he consumed at least three bottles of champagne. Fifth, he tried to upstage Phoebe by arriving in a garnet-coloured shawl that looked ridiculous on him. Phoebe, of course, was a model of graciousness, even thanking her wayward spouse from the podium. What's the matter Nick? Can't bear the missus to get some of the spotlight too?*'

The queue for the loos was endless. The next few months were clearly going to be littered with spiritual challenges, thought Eliza. Deciding that initiative was part of her personal growth plan, she slipped past the stewardesses into first class. She began mentally chanting: Oh God, oh God, please don't let me bump into any of my clients. And collided with Ruby Miles, who was on her way to Bombay to write a piece on Bollywood for the *Face*. 'Good grief,' giggled a now decidedly tipsy Ruby, taking in Eliza's grey jogging suit and the title of her book in astonishment. 'Do you come here often?'

Having flirted outrageously with the ground staff, told them she was an impoverished geography student and promised to show them her contours, Ruby had been upgraded and was now swigging her way through first class.

'Sadly I'm in economy,' said Eliza flatly. Best to get that out of her system sooner rather than later.

'Mm,' said Ruby, licking some beads of caviare that had become lodged in the corner of her mouth. 'Well, come and sit with me here.' She patted a large semicircular upholstered seat near the bar. 'I'm sure the stewardess won't mind. It'll save me from driving them mad. I've seen all the watchable movies and that's normally the point at which I get seriously angsty. Let's talk. Tell me, is this new, er, approach of yours part of a zeitgeist New Labour-y kind of thing?'

'I hope not,' said Eliza, sinking into the creamy leather sofa gratefully. 'It's more of a personal journey. I'm taking some time out.'

'Well, good for you,' said Ruby, hugging her knees against her voluptuous breasts. She smiled approvingly, revealing an endearingly gummy smile that Eliza had never registered before and running a hand through her tousled hair. 'I always wanted to go slumming round the world, but I never had the money. So here I am,' she said, 'working my passage. More champagne?'

They both looked at one another and began to giggle.

'Tell you what,' said Ruby, ordering some more smoked salmon for them both, 'I'll take you on a clubbing mission if you fix up a trip for us both to Enlightenment.'

'Done,' said Eliza, grinning. Hadn't Yogi Togi told her that the path would have twists and turns and move in mysterious directions?

Kate took a sip of Dan's ginseng-and-almond infusion and furrowed her brow in deep concentration. It was ages since she had been down to Tithe House, but Sadie had been quite insistent on the phone that she come.

The minute Kate arrived she could see why things had sounded so urgent. Sadie wanted Kate's advice on the mail order business Dan had set up which was losing money hand over fist – so much in fact that Sadie had put all her plans to enlarge Tithe House so that she could turn it into a proper small country hotel on hold. One look at the books told Kate why the mail order had gone awry. Dan was a fantastic cook and obviously a perfectionist – she was profoundly impressed by all his products – but he had far too much stock to be profitable. And he ought to be making more ready-prepared organic meals with high margins and not concentrating so much on vegetables and fruit. He desperately needed more gift ideas – little nests of high-density organic chocolate; delicious olive oils; and, of course, his fantastic lemon candles – to tempt people into spending before they even got to the pages with the vegetable boxes. And the packaging, which should be pale green with dark brown lettering, was a grey mish-mash.

The difficult bit was telling all this to Dan. He was bound to resist and tell her that she was symptomatic of the whole messed-up food system. She had heard him before on the radio about the dangers of turning the entire output of small Third World countries over to fashionable crops that were entirely dependent for their popularity on the whim of a bunch of housewives in places like Notting Hill or The Wirral. He cared passionately about changing the world over to organic food and he wouldn't take kindly to advice about bumping up gift products and cutting down on the veggies. The problem was Dan's principles were bankrupting her mother, thought Kate with a mixture of fondness and exasperation. Why hadn't Sadie told her things were so desperate?

The following morning Kate slipped out of the house shortly after dawn and strode across the fields to Hunter's Copse. As the twigs snapped beneath her wellingtons and she breathed in the damp earthy smell all around her, she felt her cares begin to melt away. She climbed to the top of the hill and breathed in deeply, almost overcome by the beauty of the view. She had forgotten how therapeutic she had always found these country walks when she was still living at home, and how much she missed the countryside. Memories of her childhood, long-neglected fragments of school-friends, of her father teaching them to ride, of Sadie always being there in the background, working so hard, in ways Kate was only just beginning to appreciate, to create a warm, harmonious home, made her feel inexplicably nostalgic. She wondered if she and Ambrose would ever have a family of their own, and sat on the grass, brooding, watching the clouds ripple across a periwinkle sky, turning it into a giant piece of tie-dye.

She had no idea how long she had been there when Dan came running up to find her.

'What is it?' she said, seeing the look of urgency on his face.

'It's your father,' panted Dan. 'He's had a heart attack.'

Chapter Seventeen

———◦◦◦◦◦———

'Bloody typical,' thought Kate as she, Martha and Sadie anxiously watched David coming round from the anaesthetic. Linked to the cardiogram monitor via a trellis of thin wires, he almost made a touching sight. Even so, she thought it a bit rich that, after all he had put them through, all he had to do was have one little heart attack for the women in his life to come running. No sign of Eliza, of course, who was apparently in India getting in touch with her inner self. Inner colon, more likely, thought Kate, whose recent experiences of India had left her stomach in a rather fragile state.

Dan had driven her and Sadie up in his clapped-out Morris Traveller. A stagecoach might have been faster, but she appreciated the gesture. She kept trying to meet Martha's eye, but Martha seemed woefully distracted.

The room must be costing him a fortune, thought Kate indignantly, seethingly aware that he had somehow forgotten to pay Sadie's BUPA subscription for the past year. Not that Sadie seemed to hold it against him. She had overseen the flower arrangements, extracting all the carnations and chrysanthemums before they became part of the decor, and superintending the delivery of a selection of his favourite first editions. She was, Kate noticed, presiding over events as if they were still married – which, as she pointed out, technically they still were. She seemed to be in her element.

He stirred and the machine next to him went wild; momentarily mesmerized by its graceful peaks, Kate thought how good a facsimile of her father's cardiogram would look reproduced on her new line of crockery. She wondered whether it would be considered tasteless to get them to print out a copy. She tapped her fingers restlessly on the window ledge. What was it with her and hospitals this year? She felt she had seen enough of them to last her a lifetime. And yet if she thought she might actually get a baby at the end of it, she would willingly have volunteered to spend the next nine months in one.

'Why don't you and Martha get yourselves some tea?' Sadie asked tactfully. She desperately wanted to be in the room on her own with David so that she could rearrange his hair, which in its current hospital-swept style looked as though it might be thinning. If she could just comb it she'd establish once and for all whether she really was no longer attracted to him, or whether it was just the shock of suddenly seeing him look ten years older. 'I'll wait here,' she said, sounding brave. 'I don't think much is going to happen in the next half hour or so.'

Relieved, they scuttled off to a little bakery round the corner where other hospital visitors were trying to exorcize the sickly-sweet smell of medicine and antiseptic in the steamy fug of steam from the cappuccino-maker and cigarette smoke.

'Is everything okay?' said Kate, when they had ordered

some doughnuts. Martha seemed strangely on edge, and merely grunted.

'Oh God,' remembered Kate, 'I'm so sorry I missed the awards. You were fantastic, by all accounts. I wish I'd seen you win. Mum called – trouble at t' tills – and I thought I'd better get down there straight away. Story of my life, I'm afraid. I'm constantly double-booking. Forgive me?' She paused and noticed for the first time that Martha's eyes were ringed with dark, bruise-coloured circles; her cheeks were unnaturally flushed and her eyes glittered restlessly.

'Are you going down with flu?' Kate asked, concerned.

'I'm fine,' lied Martha, her eyes taking in Kate's ghostly pallor. Having talked non-stop about her miscarriages in the beginning and cried buckets on Martha's shoulders, she had become withdrawn and unwilling to broach the subject recently, which worried Martha enormously. She was certain Kate was working her way towards asking her for the biggest favour of her life. One which in normal circumstances Martha would gladly have gone along with. Only in this case she was pretty sure she would have to let Kate down. So all in all she was rather grateful to skirt the issue as much as Kate seemed to be.

'On second thoughts, I think I might be,' said Martha uncertainly. 'No, I'm not. Um, Nick Wilde stayed with me last night.'

Kate looked at her stunned. 'Stayed stayed? Oh my God. Ambrose said he thought there was something strange going on between you at those awards. But . . . bloody hell, Martha, when did all this happen?'

Kate stirred her coffee and absent-mindedly dropped six lumps of sugar into it.

'Well, you know we met in Bosnia?'

'Yes, you said, but you also said nothing happened.'

'It didn't. And in the most profound way it did. Only I didn't know he'd felt the same things I was feeling—'

'But you know now that he did?'

'I think so,' said Martha uncertainly.

'Think?' Kate almost screamed in frustration. She stabbed her doughnut and an arc of strawberry jam spattered her orange cardigan.

'Well, obviously he was overwrought. He'd had a terrible row with Phoebe.'

'Oh, they're always rowing,' retorted Kate. She was suddenly uncomfortably aware that in her excitement at hearing that her sister had finally got it together with a man – and one of the world's more attractive ones at that – she had overlooked the fact that he also happened to be married to one of her best friends. 'Martha, are you sure that Nick wasn't just playing a little game with Phoebe and using you as a pawn?'

'Oh, Kate,' said Martha, relieved finally to have someone to unburden her emotions on. 'I am. I know it seems unlikely, especially with my record with men. But that's what's so amazing with Nick. I just know he's genuine. I can feel it. It's almost visceral. It's terrible and wonderful at the same time. I mean, I know it sounds corny, but I really feel as though I've found my soul mate ...'

Kate looked at her stonily. 'Martha, repeat after me, Nick Wilde is married.'

'He told me he felt the same connection when we were in Bosnia.'

'Connections, connections. Martha, we're talking about breaking up a marriage, not installing a BT line. And anyway, that was nearly four years ago,' said Kate angrily.

'Half a lifetime ago. I hadn't met Ambrose then. Nibbles hadn't even been born.'

'But that's just it,' cried Martha, her eyes flashing excitedly. 'It's still there. That bond—'

Kate looked at her sister's radiant expression and for the first time she felt really fearful for Martha. All through their lives she had believed she had been struggling to keep up intellectually with her, never really realizing, until now, that emotionally she had always been light-years ahead. How could Martha, who had always been so cynical about celebrity, fall for Nick Wilde of all people – and for his spiel? How Phoebe put up with him was a mystery, but her justification was that they had a history that went way back. Martha had no excuse. And the one thing of which Kate was sure was that she wouldn't let Martha be screwed around by Nick the way she had been by the appalling Jack Dunforth.

'Listen to me, Martha,' said Kate firmly, placing her hands over Martha's. 'Whatever the outcome of all this is, you must promise me that you will go all out for your own happiness and not put your wonderful, questioning, perspicacious intelligence on hold the way you normally do when men are around.'

Martha smiled beatifically. 'Honestly, Kate, anyone would think I was an habitual fuck-up.'

Kate looked at her bleakly. 'Oh, Kate,' said Martha, helping herself to a piece of Kate's massacred doughnut, 'it's so good to have you back as a confidante again.'

Calling a cab from Martha's flat early in the morning to take him to the airport, Nick was struggling to decide whether to drop in to see Phoebe before flying back to LA when his mobile rang. It was Magda. Phoebe had been taken to hospital. 'She's not receiving visitors, Nick. Not any. The doctors say she needs complete rest,' said Magda apologetically. Phoebe had told her under pain of death not to allow Nick near her. 'But I'm just taking in a few of her favourite nighties and I wondered whether you had any message for her?'

He had gone straight to the hospital, of course. How could he not? It wasn't as if his conscience wasn't clean. He and Martha had stayed up talking most of the night, before he had finally tumbled into a doze – alone on the spare bed in her little study.

The hospital was a low-built, all-white box in St John's Wood, reeking of moneyed neuroses and shielded from curious eyes behind a high brick wall and a screen of plane trees. The press, thank God, hadn't got wind of anything yet. Even so, the doctor who eventually saw him was clearly discomforted by his presence and perfunctorily polite.

'Ah, Mr Wilde, your wife is doing well, all things considered. The fractures to her ribs should heal completely eventually and the bruising and contusions on her face won't leave any lasting damage. Thank heavens.'

'I don't understand. What happened?' asked Nick in a panic. Had Phoebe been so drunk when he left that she had fallen down the stairs? Or had she – God forbid – rushed out into the street after him and been involved in a car accident?

The doctor looked at him searchingly. 'She's under heavy sedation. The injuries aren't life-threatening but that doesn't mean they don't hurt like hell.' He lingered on the final word. 'She's expressed a wish to be left alone for the moment. You'll understand, I'm sure.'

He escorted Nick back to reception and Nick walked numbly to his car. He obviously believes I hit Phoebe, thought Nick, feeling sick. The idea that anyone could ever imagine him hurting his wife was unbearable. He went to the airport and boarded the plane as if he were on automatic pilot. When he arrived in LA he went straight to his hotel room and sat with the lights off, watching the dusk turn to night, seeking comfort in the monotonous hotel hum, waiting for a sign of what he might possibly do next.

He must have been sitting there for hours because when the phone rang he could only reach for it stiffly. It was Martha.

'How did you know where I was?'

'Oh, a mixture of intuition, infallible detective work and bribery. Seriously, Nick, that's the wonderful thing about mobile phones — they tend to follow their owners around. Anyway, I've had a terrible day, watching my father act out *Emergency Ward Ten* and twisting us all round his little finger again. And I was wondering whether there was any chance of being twisted round yours.'

He said nothing.

'Are you okay?'

'I've been better.'

'What is it?'

'Phoebe. She's in hospital too.'

'What's wrong?' Martha's heart was pounding somewhere between her kidneys. She despised her concern, because she knew it was only rooted in a fear that this would change everything between her and Nick.

'I think she must have hurt herself somehow after I left. She's bruised and battered with a couple of broken ribs. The doctor seemed to think I was the one responsible.'

'That's rubbish. You can't watch over her twenty-four hours a day.'

'No, I mean he thinks I did it. Oh, and Phoebe's obviously told them she doesn't want any visitors. Especially if they're married to her.'

Martha was swamped by a tumultuous muddle of emotions. Nick had been agitated when he had first arrived at her flat. But then he had just walked out on his wife. But what if ...? She banished the thought to the back of her mind. He was the gentlest person she had ever met and, deep down, he probably still loved Phoebe. She was astonished to find that, at that moment, this thought caused her no anguish at all. She must really love him more than she had ever loved anyone.

Giving up her flat – or at least renting it out to a Japanese banker at a vastly inflated rate – had, at the time, simply seemed the sensible thing to Eliza. She had been increasingly aware that all was not right with her relationship with David, and any number of photographs in Nigel Dempster's pages showing them looking glamorous and at the same time heavyweight and utterly, cosily together could not convince her otherwise. Finishing with him just before his heart attack hadn't been brilliant timing – she'd had to make a few concerned-looking visits to see him in the hospital (taking care not to clash with Sadie, Martha or Kate's visits) when really she would have preferred a clean break. But as soon as she was satisfied that he was making a typically speedy and efficient recovery, she felt she could move on to the Next Phase of Her Life.

She was beginning to realize how much she had sacrificed to be with him. She missed Kate and Martha more as time wore on. Self-flagellation was not something Eliza had ever gone in for much (although she'd been happy enough to whip the daylights out of Podge). But even she was beginning to think that running off with the husband of a woman she had once regarded as a second mother hadn't been her finest hour.

And once she had decided to repudiate all her worldly goods, or at least auction them off to the highest bidder, following it through had been surprisingly easy. Yogi Togi had been gentler and more understanding than she could have hoped. It was he, after all, who had suggested that she pack copious amounts of her favourite Jo Malone lime-and-basil shower gel to get her through the darker moments of India's notorious plumbing.

Thanks to Yogi Togi, she had explored much uncharted territory of the soul. Still, the path to enlightenment had indeed proved long, twisting and racked with infection. She should never have hooked up with Ruby, but the chance to explore some Bollywood studios had been irresistible. And, though she hadn't yet fully admitted this to herself, anything that put off the fearful moment when she would finally have to shack up with Yogi Togi in his ashram had to be good thing.

Wisely, she and Ruby abandoned their first plan, which was to stay in an impoverished-looking hostel heaving with burly Australian backpackers, and had checked into the five-star Imperial Taj instead, before making a short trek to Rajasthan to see the sights. Stupidly, Eliza had stopped using her water filter system by the second day because it looked so uncool and made all the drinks taste like the dreg-ends of a very public swimming pool. She'd got ill at the first whiff of unfamiliar amoeba.

Ruby had proved a surprisingly devoted nurse, even going so far as to remove her Walkman earphones at night in case Eliza suddenly needed her. She was genuinely concerned about Eliza, who, for a good twenty-eight hours, was almost delirious, bathing her with the precious Jo Malone, and reading to her from a copy of the Kama Sutra she had picked up at the airport.

For Ruby had fallen passionately, deeply in lust. Sometimes she would just sit quietly for hours contemplating Eliza, who even in the depths of fever, with her hair tangled and unwashed, was icily beautiful. Halfway through the third day, when the fever showed signs of abating and Eliza's incomprehensible babble began to metamorphose into something more coherent, Ruby was so relieved she cracked open a small bottle of champagne from the minibar and drank it all by herself. While she was curled up on an armchair dozing, Eliza, pulling herself up into a seated position, reached for her hand mirror and, seeing the state of her hair, made an unsteady attempt to go to the bathroom by herself. She collapsed shakily by the door. Startled out of her sleep, Ruby leaped up in a panic. 'What are you doing?' she said sternly, helping Eliza back to bed. 'You're still under bed arrest.'

'My God, what's happened?' croaked Eliza feebly, catching sight of her reflection. 'And how the hell did my hair get like this?' She did look as though an almighty hair raid had taken place on her scalp, but even so, her reaction was completely over the top. Anyone would think Eliza had never seen herself with a hair out of place, mused

Ruby. She would probably require counselling – but not even this realization put Ruby off her.

In the Technicolored rainbow of India, Eliza's clotted-cream pallor seemed impossibly exotic. Ruby sensed very strongly that Eliza was gay, but she also realized that this truth had never dawned on Eliza. It was going to take a lot of gentle coaxing and probing. Ruby was particularly looking forward to the probing and began racking her brains to find excuses for extending her assignment so that she could stay on in India. It shouldn't be difficult. In four days in Rajasthan, they had run into so many well-known fashion designers looking for inspiration and cheap factories – not to mention all the Groucho regulars professing to be looking to escape the media rat-race – that Ruby had rechristened the place Pradastan.

As the weeks wore on and Lars lived up to his soubriquet by sneakily making his long-suffering cast reshoot almost every scene in *The Meaning of Loss*, Martha's faith in Nick was tested to the full. Kate's words in the bakery, now she'd had time to reflect on them, were making an impact. It didn't help that Lars had dragged his cast off to the Mojave Desert, which was uncontactable by telephone.

She carried on as normally as possible, going to the studio, seeing Kate and Sadie and visiting David, who was rapidly getting back to his confident old self, which was a shame, as everyone preferred his new, slightly cowed self. At nights she made excuses not to go out, preferring, she said, to research her notes for the show. Then she would have a long bath, cook herself some comfort food, and, wrapped in her favourite blanket, retreat to the balcony, watching the light turn soupy and listening to Chopin's *Berceuse* in D flat major or, when she really wanted to wallow, to Satie's *Gymnopédies*. This went on for about three weeks. She was almost happy in her melancholy.

Satie was on the CD player when the doorbell pierced her reverie. It was George the porter, behind the largest bunch of roses, peonies and berries that she had ever seen. Impatiently, he thrust them in her arms and then spent what seemed like for ever – she was desperate to know who they were from – extricating his legs from the trailing tendrils of ivy. The note, when she finally located it, was buried deep within a tangle of leaves and thorns. Her heart somersaulted. It was his writing! Hands trembling – this was ridiculous, she thought – she tore open the envelope. After at least ten drafts, he had scrawled one line.

We all need signs sometimes. I'm below your window. All my love, Nick.

She rushed to the balcony and saw him over on the other side of the road, by the railings, looking up at her windows. His coat collar was turned up against the chilly night wind and his hands were thrust deep into his pockets. She tried to call to him, but the roar of the traffic was too loud. She thought about flashing him a Morse code signal, but she didn't know any and she had disconnected the outside light months ago. She stood there in the dark waving to him, feet apart but separated by an inability to communicate It began to rain. She tried her best whistle, learned in Bosnia, an ear-splitting screech that was achieved by placing two sets of fingers inside her mouth. He still didn't hear. Not stopping to get dressed or put on shoes, she rushed downstairs and into the street, dodging the traffic and luminous puddles. He was turning now, about to walk off. She rushed up behind him, her socks a soggy towelling mess. She tugged at his coat. He turned back, his startled scowl giving way to a broad grin as he swept her into his arms.

The honeymoon between Cressida and St Eleanor's was definitely over. The other girls were such prigs they made Jane Austen look debauched. Cressie had gone there, county-hunting for drugs, sex and rock and roll, and had found only Ribena, biology lessons and extra music tuition for those who wanted it. Safe sax was about the closest she was going to get to fornication, she thought disgustedly. If she could only get Ambrose to buy her a pony it would be all right, but he was too busy having nervous breakdowns over his precious plays, and Kate was always in some bloody aeroplane. She briefly considered slashing her wrists, not properly but just to wind Kate up, but decided against it. It sounded a bit painful, and anyway Matron would probably just give her an enema which was what she recommended whenever any of the girls got a bit run down. Something was going to have to give because the dire situation at Alcatraz, as she had renamed St Eleanor's, was doing her head in.

In the end, it was Tracy Coles, one of the school cook's daughters, who rescued her. She gave Cressie an E one night when Cressie had bunked off hockey practice and was lurking behind the bike sheds by the school kitchens. Tracy, a vision in frosted pink lipstick and purple satin hot pants, was a worldly import from the local comp with a heavenly body and a nose for trouble. It took about two minutes for her to sniff out the cause of Cressie's discontent, and another ten before she'd persuaded her to run away with her to join her boyfriend Skunk's commune.

Kate was in the middle of a fascinating meeting with Bo Wemyss III when her mobile went. She didn't recognize the number flashing so she turned it off without answering. There were more important things to deal with at the moment than a call from some airhead wanting to reserve a pashmina flannel. This summit with Bo Wemyss, for instance, to which she had been flown out in Bo's own not so little seven-seater Ryton, with its toffee leather interior and full-time pilot and chef.

Bo Wemyss, whom until now she had never actually met in the flesh, having made a fortune from his two-billion dollar chain of department stores, was almost certainly in America's top ten list of richest men, and definitely in its top five smallest. Not that this was widely known, thanks to decades of clever advertising that always showed him seated on top of an eighteen-hand stallion.

In any case, Bo was a complete recluse and never travelled anywhere, which made the Ryton even more of an extravagance. Mischievously, some of the press persisted in calling him Little Bo Peep, even though he had long ago given up trying to go against the family grain by becoming a sheep farmer.

When he had walked stiffly down the dark wooden staircase, his spurs clanking behind him, his Levi's creaking rhythmically, Kate realized why Bo Wemyss shunned the public eye. It wasn't just that he was tiny. His face was so wind- and sun-chapped that it looked as though it had been modelled from slurry, and he wore a toupee that, if he'd been an actor, would have been booed off the stage for overacting. He was, in all senses of the word, hairy-looking.

He was also the biggest thing to hit retailing since money.

Their meeting took place in a huge room in Bo's log cabin – more of a log skyscraper actually – with a column made of entire tree trunks and festooned with more dead heads than Kate had seen even on her trips with David to the House of Commons. Bo strode awkwardly across the room and settled himself in a leather armchair as deep as Lake Tahoe that made him look even tinier. They must have to airlift him on to his stallions, Kate thought, or more likely airbrush him on. His press release said he loved dangerous sports and was five foot nine. Presumably that was after he'd abseiled up his wallet.

Bo didn't beat about the bush. Having spent the first thirty years of his life being lambasted for being the black sheep for not going into the family business, he had subsequently thrown himself into it with a vengeance. The Wemyss Corporation had long owned a consortium of hotels around the world, bland international palaces with the same reassuringly luxurious accoutrements in each one, whether in Chicago or Cairo.

'I'll be straight with you, Miss Crawford.' His affected cowboy drawl didn't quite mask the preppie vowels of his Ivy League education. 'They bore me to tears. Oh, sure, they make money, but I believe the time is right for a revolution in the hotel business. What folk are crying out for are idiosyncratic places the discerning world traveller can stay in. They don't want uniformity. They want personality and individuality. And to be blunt, your stores and merchandise have both these qualities in abundance.'

Kate wondered when he had ever been into one of her shops. It wasn't as if they wouldn't have noticed him. In fact they'd have heard his spurs clanking from the other end of Bond Street.

'I've seen the photographs,' he continued by way of unsolicited answer, 'I've examined the figures. My people tell me that everything you've done for the stores has flown out. From what I've read about you, you seem constantly to be searching for the next challenge – am I right? Well, what could be more challenging than to design a hotel, from top to bottom?'

What indeed? Kate was so excited she omitted to take into account what this would do to her attempts to get pregnant. And she completely forgot about the person who'd been trying to call her until, hours of tough negotiation with Bo later, she finally replayed her messages. It was Ambrose, sounding hysterical – something about Cressie running away from St Eleanor's.

As soon as the next two-second chunk of *The Meaning of Loss* was in the can, Nick checked into Claridge's and set about an old-fashioned courtship of Martha. It wasn't so much that he needed time to consider his feelings for her but that he wanted to give her time to adjust to being with him. These days the extent of his fame took even him by surprise sometimes. Since *Green Cover* had taken nearly $200 million at the box office, it had gone stratospheric. It wasn't just his celebrity which was at issue. He worried frantically that there might be an element of doubt in Martha's mind about whether he really had hurt Phoebe. When he realized that she trusted him completely, he realized also that he'd just been looking for excuses not to be happy because he was guilty about Phoebe. But her lying to the hospital had been the best thing Phoebe could have done. He felt sorry for her, he still wanted to help her – he supposed he always would. But he knew finally that Phoebe no longer loved him. And that had set him free.

For a while, life carried on almost normally for Martha, with the blissful exception that she was happy. She went to work as usual, he read scripts, and in the early evening he went round to her flat and watched while she cooked.

They would stay up all night talking. This time it was Martha's turn to disinter her past. She found herself telling him everything, from the time she had cried because Kate had got a part in the upper-school production of *Twelfth Night* and she hadn't to the shameful way in which she had allowed herself to be manipulated by Jack. Anything to distract him.

'The really awful thing is that Kate didn't even want to play Viola. In the end she pulled out. And they still didn't give it to me.' She laughed. 'Story of my life.'

'What do you mean?' He put his head on her lap and wondered when it would be seemly to get her into bed.

'Oh, you know – perfect parents, perfect sister, perfect home. I was the klutz. The one who needed a brace. The one who was crap at games. Kate was always bright. There was a time when she was more academic than I was.'

'What happened?' asked Nick in surprise.

'Mum steered her towards Art. And Style. And Making a Perfect Home. Which of course she did. Perfectly. And Dad took me in hand. You know the sort of thing – brisk walks accompanied by brisker pep talks. About my potential and reaching for the stars. That sort of thing.'

'Actually, I don't know. I was completely thick at school. I was dyslexic, although no one knew much about it then. It didn't help that my brothers, Luke and Zack, were such brainboxes. And 'cos Dad's job meant we were always on the move I went to about sixteen schools – by the time I was twelve. It's a great recipe for becoming the class nerd. I was a total outsider.'

'You?' asked Martha in astonishment.

'And probably a creep,' he added.

'I'm so sorry.' She placed her hand on his knee and leaned against him as she'd always imagined she'd have leaned against her brother.

'He was right, wasn't he? Philip Larkin, I mean.'

'About parents fucking you up?'

'Yeah. But sisters do a pretty good job too.'

He would always go back to his hotel at the end of the evening, until the night she asked him to stay. 'I can't bear to think of you going back there alone now. Hotel rooms are too sad when you're on your own.'

He looked at his watch. 'Three years, eleven months, four days, eight hours and twenty frigging minutes. Jesus, woman, I thought you'd never ask.'

It was ironic, Ruby mused sadly, that the person whom she would most like to seduce appeared to be oblivious to the fact. And it was odd, she thought, sinking into the silky folds of the sari she had draped across the chaise-longue, that Eliza could be so worldly in many ways and yet so clueless when it came to her own sexuality. Surely she hadn't imagined the physical as well as the mental chemistry between them. The way Eliza had blushed so sweetly the night before when they had gone skinny-dipping in the hotel pool; the way she had stopped pulling her knees away when Ruby 'accidentally' brushed her own against them when they were at lunch; the way she had leaned her head on Ruby's shoulder in mock-torpor the night they had gone to see *Prisoner of Love* at the local open-air cinema, and kept it there a little too long. It was Eliza who had read that poem from *The Prophet* the meltingly hot day they had gone to see the Taj Mahal, her creamy skin turning dewy under a fine veil of perspiration. When they had lain down under a tree for a few moments it was all Ruby could do to stop herself from taking Eliza in her arms. Instead she had watched her drift into sleep, her thin linen tunic becoming a transparent gauze over the warmth of her body.

Ruby's own sexual inclinations – long suspected during her career as a groupie and finally confirmed by the humiliating incident with Lachlan – had never caused her a moment's unease. She decided that she would let things run their natural course. But so many meaningful glances had passed between them and come to nothing that Ruby wondered whether she shouldn't suggest they go their separate ways – anything would be better than this constant state of vulnerable arousal.

She was about to go for a swim on her own when Eliza wandered in from the bathroom in a towel, her damp hair coiled down her back. 'Would you brush my hair,' she asked in a small voice. 'My father used to do it when I was little. I found it very comforting.'

Ruby took the Mason & Pearson – Eliza's pride and joy – and sat down on the edge of the bed, while Eliza knelt in front of her. Silently she began to brush the angelic white tresses, gentle sweeping strokes at first and then, when the tangles were out, beginning to run her fingers through. Slowly, Eliza let her towel slither to the floor. Mesmerized, Ruby took in her slender back, the curved outline of her breasts, which turned up adorably at the nipples, and watched as the drips of water from Eliza's hair traced their way down between her breasts and over her belly and between her creamy thighs.

Finally Eliza spoke. 'Please do *something*,' she said primly. 'Or I shall die of embarrassment.'

'All's well that ends well,' said Kate brightly, as they sped back to London from Devon.

'It would appear so,' said Ambrose dryly.

Thank God for Scorcher. The minute Ambrose had rung him to see if he could help in any way, he had leaped into his car and driven the forty or so miles to the Love-Inn, the very unlovely commune run by Skunk, Tracy's aptly named boyfriend. After an hour or two he had even persuaded Cressie that she should at least agree to *meet up* with her parents.

Needless to say, Cressida hadn't been remotely grateful to see Ambrose and Kate when they had finally arrived after two gruelling flights and a midnight drive from Heathrow. The hippie commune turned out to be housed in a former Watney's pub of uncertain vintage. And the hippies, far from plotting the downfall of capitalism, were all desperately working out how they could lig their way into Glastonbury.

She did seem to tolerate Scorcher, at least, and as soon as they'd established that she was okay and not being held against her will, they had tactfully withdrawn, leaving Scorcher to see if he could draw anything more out of her.

'As rebellions go,' said Ambrose, 'it's livable with, I suppose.'

'Look, tell me if I'm interfering, I won't be at all offended,' began Scorcher, after the three of them had left Cressie at the Love-Inn for the night and gone for supper to a nearby pub. 'But as someone who's spent their entire adulthood reliving their teenage years, I sort of know where Cressida's coming from—'

'Please, go ahead,' said Ambrose bitterly. 'It's obvious I've ballsed up.' He reached into his pocket for his cigarettes and then remembered he'd given up.

'Have one of these. They're only rollies. The doctor seems to think they'll slow down my consumption. He doesn't seem to have worked out that someone who's played bass guitar for twenty years has got to have pretty nimble fingers.' He cackled mischievously, and Ambrose gratefully accepted the squashed-up little offering.

'Blimey, if this is the sum total of your ballsing up, I don't think you'll have much problem getting past St Peter. Or is it St Paul? I can never remember which one's sitting at the gates.'

'What did Cressida have to say for herself?' asked Ambrose.

'Oh, the usual stuff. She feels a bit misunderstood, a little bit sidelined. But the great thing is that she's smart enough to realize that she's basically just going through the usual teenage motions. The main problem is that school. I mean, I'm all for a bit of élitism when it works. I was invited to Eton to talk to them about music once, and I've debated at the Oxford Union. This house believes that drugs are mind-reducing. We won, as a matter of fact. But if you don't mind my saying, Ambrose, Cressida's place seems totally archaic. That Miss Lambert sounds as though she ought to have a demolition order slapped on her.'

'I couldn't agree more,' said Ambrose, sounding relieved. 'So where now?'

'Well, it may sound a bit radical, but I think you should let her pay her own way for a bit. There's nothing like a spot of hard labour to make a kid think twice about not getting qualifications. So why not let Cressie come and work for me for the summer? She's mad about horses and Douggie Kenwood can always do with another groom. He's a bloody hard taskmaster, too. She won't be getting off lightly. I bet you anything that after a couple of months she comes away with a helluva lot more insight into real life than she would after seven years at St Ladidah's.'

The idea had a certain appeal. For one thing it sat much more happily with Ambrose's egalitarian principles than St Eleanor's. But perhaps it was a convenient abdication of his responsibilities.

'If you're worried about keeping an eye on her,' said Scorcher, 'what with the other stable lads and everything — don't. I'll make her my personal responsibility. She can stay in the house with me. Don't look so horrified, Ambrose, I won't be setting her any bad examples with wild parties. I may look like an old degenerate, but it's all a big con. The sad truth is that these days I'm cleaner than a nun's conscience.'

All things considered, thought Kate, as they approached London, Ambrose was in as good a mood as she'd seen for a long time. Who knows, if she could only arrange for them to have a quiet night in so that she could whip him up some spaghetti hoops, she might even feel brave enough to tell him that she was going to be even busier over the next few months doing a hotel.

That first night she had invited him to stay, they had spent the first few minutes fumbling with their drinks and giggling awkwardly. Then he had pulled her towards him, and pressed his mouth against hers with an urgency she feared she might never satisfy. For a while they had stood there, kissing passionately, before she had astonished herself by pulling off his clothes and leading him to her bedroom and pushing him gently on to the bed, beneath her cool mosquito net. He had pulled her on top of him, tearing at her clothes until she was naked too, and run his hands up and down her body, kissing her throat, her breasts, her toes and finally kissing her all over. The ceiling fan whirred above them but, even so, the sweat poured off them – as it was to do many more times that summer.

Martha was delirious with happiness. She loved him with a vehemence and selflessness that she had only ever expected to feel for her children, if she ever had them. He moved in then and there. Not that he had any possessions with him. He bought new clothes when he needed them. And always came back with things for her – a rare recording of Chopin's Nocturnes; a 1920s history of the Balkans and a pair of antique diamond earrings that was delivered late one afternoon just as they were waking after one of their tangled encounters.

And when he had enough shirts and jeans, he stopped going out altogether. He wouldn't be going anywhere for a few weeks, until he was needed on location for a thriller that was about to start shooting in Toronto. She took a fortnight off work and they didn't leave the flat. They were the eye of the storm. Occasionally she would descend for food, and it was then that she saw the first headlines. Phoebe's version of events, in which she and Nick had had a colossal, violent row that had culminated in him throwing her down the stairs, had somehow 'leaked' to the press. After that she sent George the concierge out or they ordered food in. The more frenetic things got in the outside world – and she could tell from the frequency and high pitch of the messages Sadie and Kate left on her machine that they were frenetic – the more serene the atmosphere became in the flat. She unplugged the phone and the radio and the television and when she wanted contact with the outside world – for she was less used to solitariness than he was, it turned out – she would sit on the balcony while he played the piano to her. She was so happy it hurt. But only because she knew that her happiness must be at the cost of someone else's pain. But that was all right too. Because she knew it couldn't last.

Chapter Eighteen

For a few magical, deluded weeks it seemed that Martha and Nick had succeeded in shutting out the whole world. The media, off chasing stories in the South of France, seemed to have forgotten about them. *And Now*, Martha's TV series, was coming to the end of its summer run. For once Nick had a brief respite between filming engagements, as Lars looked dangerously close to being happy – or at least not suicidal – about the new batch of rushes for *The Meaning of Loss*, and the film he was due to shoot in Toronto had been postponed after his leading lady announced she was five months pregnant.

When they felt like taking a hike on Hampstead Heath they would wait until dusk and swaddle themselves in sunhats and sunglasses and climb across the rank-smelling fire escapes that ran in a ramshackle fashion through the spine of the building like crooked vertebrae. George seemed to derive as much delight as they did from outwitting the few desultory reporters who were still posted outside the block. 'It's like *West Side Story*,' he wheezed at Martha one day. 'Haven't had so much fun in years.'

'Anyone would think you were John and Yoko. You can't stay in bed indefinitely, of course,' grumbled Ambrose good-naturedly as he sipped some more of the vintage claret George had got for them. He had taken to calling in on them nearly every day, now that Kate was more and more tied up with work. 'You're practically hermits. You'll go mad in the end. Love will sour. Mark my words.'

Martha, who had been absent-mindedly dismembering a rose, threw the petals at him. 'Spoilsport.'

'What do you expect from a professional doom merchant? He's made a very lucrative career out of making people feel suicidal,' said Nick playfully. 'Anyway, we're conducting vital research into the Internet. Martha's going to write a piece about it for the *Spectator*.'

'I only say it out of concern,' said Ambrose defensively.

'You and Kate ought to try staying in bed all day,' said Nick, tilting back in his chair, one loafer dangling elegantly from his bare foot.

'It would be nice to see Kate at all,' said Ambrose wistfully. 'You're right, I probably am jealous. Anyway that walking toothpick of an agent tells me that with the delays on your Toronto film, we might be able to start shooting Endymian – which is why I'm rather keen on you getting dressed.'

It was true. Initially Gloria had been so horrified at the thought of Nick starring in yet another art-house offering about an obscure poet, probably a gay one at that, that she'd accidentally tipped the contents of her decaf extra-lite moccatino all over her cream Jil Sander. But the bullying tactics of Marty combined with the diffident charm of Ambrose, of whom she was becoming increasingly enamoured, despite his crooked British teeth, had convinced her that it would simply emphasize his diversity. She knew Nick loved the script — he practically knew it off by heart already. Plus, for once, he had some spare time. He might as well put it to good use.

'Is it my imagination or has Ambrose dipped his soul in some Clairol? He's lightened up so much I hardly recognize him,' said Martha later, as they shared a bowl of green curry in bed and Nick licked flecks of fragrant rice from her tummy button.

'He was never that heavy, if the truth be told,' said Nick, working his tongue downwards. 'God you're a fantastic cook. I can't decide whether I prefer the taste of you or the curry.'

She kicked him playfully.

'It's just you and your sister,' he continued later. 'You both put Ambrose on such a high pedestal you need binoculars and a megaphone to communicate.'

In the bath, he surprised her by saying that Ambrose might have a point. 'We can't hide away for ever.'

'Why?' said Martha, soaping him so thoroughly it was clear it was going to be a long bath. 'What's the point of engaging with the world when it's so much friendlier and more interesting here?'

'Because we have to face up to things sooner or later.' He gazed down at her. 'I really want this to work for us, Martha, and that means it has to work on all levels, not just as some mad, hedonistic lost weekend.'

Two weeks later they packed up and headed for Rome, where shooting was commencing on Keats's death scene. It was at that precise moment that the tabloids, scenting blood, or at least the whiff of a potential punch-up between Martha and Phoebe, began circling. The *Probe* sent a reporter and photographer to shadow Nick and Martha in Rome, with strict instructions to get pictures of Martha in compromising or unflattering situations. Warren Peace stepped up his visits to Phoebe, who, between snivelling about her loyalty to Nick and saying she couldn't possibly consider pressing assault charges, fed him a delicious flow of titillating tales about his ruthlessness, his mediocrity and Martha's grasping connivances at the BBC, as well as her inability to master the basic principles of personal hygiene. And the broadsheets, officially disdainful of the entire affair, spent pages and pages analysing the tabloids' obsession with it all.

Kate gazed wistfully at the pudgy hands leaving chocolatey fingerprints over some pale rose satin-embroidered mules.

'Theodora and Alyssia, put that down immediately,' barked Charlotte Pitchcock. She bent down to scoop up Cosmo, who was crawling at full speed towards an artful pile of Wenge wood incense bowls, squashing the little creature that was crushed in a Bill Amberg sheepskin papoose against her breasts in the process. Poor little mite, thought Kate. It was a wonder he didn't suffocate. Talk about the baby slings and arrows of outrageous fortune. God knew how any of the Pitchcocks' ever-proliferating brood survived. Not that it mattered, she thought sourly. They bred like rabbits.

Cosmo turned round and gave his mother an angelic gummy grin. Kate felt her stomach list queasily. After her last miscarriage she just didn't seem able to get pregnant. For months and months, the longing she had felt every time she saw a child — any child — had become a powerful force.

She puzzled over whether the yearning had anything to do with the shock of her father's heart attack — intimations of mortality and all that. At any rate, seeing him there in hospital, all helpless and frail-looking, had, to her surprise, deeply affected her. The upshot was that she sometimes wondered how much longer she would be able to bear her aching need for a baby. She threw herself into more and more displacement activities and deliberately avoided friends who were in the process of starting families. But there was no escape; only a kind of fragile evasion that threatened ultimately to destroy her. The more she sought to inure herself against the pain, the more catastrophically she felt it on the rare occasions she found herself unavoidably confronted with a small child.

'Ohmigodohmigod — I know I should say you shouldn't have, Scorcher. But I'm just so glad you did.' Cressida clapped her hands over her mouth and jumped up and down again in excitement, her breasts jiggling enthusiastically inside her tight little Aertex shirt, as if they too couldn't wait to get a peep at the seventeen hands of pure Arab that galloped past them in Scorcher's paddock. 'She is such a beauty I could ... well, I could cry,' she said, suddenly feeling lachrymose. Never in all her life had she seen such a vision of beauty as Lady Godiva.

'Blimey, don't do that,' said Scorcher, flinching. It was hard to say who was friskier at that moment, Lady Godiva or Scorcher's libido. 'Save your energies for riding her. She's not exactly going to be a pushover, you know. Douggie says she's quite a goer.'

'Then we're perfectly matched,' giggled Cressida, sidling

up to Scorcher and giving him a sly kiss on the cheek. A gentle pink blush seeped across his pallid, abused skin, as if Cressida had just tipped a glass of red wine over a piece of old white leather. She giggled again and Scorcher motioned for Douggie to bring Lady Godiva over so that Cressida could mount her.

'Aren't you coming?' Cressida asked him from somewhere behind Lady Godiva's lustrous, tobacco-coloured mane. 'It's such a glorious day.'

'Er, later,' he mumbled, wishing Cressie would mount him. 'I've got a bit of business to sort out ... one or two problems laying the final track.' Cressida looked crestfallen.

He ambled off towards the converted barn where his recording studio was, tearing his gaze from Cressida's haughty silhouette as she cantered across the field towards Poacher's Copse. He had to stay away from her. He tried to distract himself with thoughts about the weather and what Thomas Hardy might have had to say on the matter. Cressida was right, it was a gorgeous day; the sky the exact same electric blue as his new Lancia, the sun blazing like some epic hallucination and tiny neat clouds scudding across the sky like *Playgirl* bunny tails.

With her long treacle-coloured hair flying out behind her and her tight jodhpurs that were the same colour as her unblemished, golden skin, she looked like a tantalizing streak of nakedness. The jodhpurs clung to the contours of her very shapely legs as snugly as the very expensive body lotion she liked to slather all over herself – she looked the mane chance, all right. Forlornly, he entered the studio. There were no problems with track eleven, which was entitled 'Girl on a Horse' and which he hoped

Cressida would never realize was about her; nor with track ten, 'Jailbait', which he fervently hoped Ambrose wouldn't realize was about her. In fact there weren't any problems with any of the tracks, all of which were, either directly or obliquely, about Cressida. The whole thing had gone off amazingly smoothly. Douggie seemed to think it was one of his best pieces of work in years. And Douggie had never been wrong yet.

The problem, he thought sadly, trotting over to the fridge and pouring himself a large tumbler of elderflower juice, wasn't the new album at all but the feelings that had inspired it. Cressida was roughly thirty years – actually twenty-eight years and three months – too young for him. Even if he hadn't been terrified of Ambrose's reaction if he ever discovered that Scorcher harboured feelings that weren't strictly avuncular towards his sixteen-year-old daughter, he was sufficiently bourgeois these days for the age difference to be a significant problem. In any case, although Cressida had been spending an inordinate amount of time dawdling in his studios, he wasn't such an old fool yet as to imagine that it was anything other than advice about the horses that lured her over.

He couldn't blame her. She had taken to the saddle like a butcher to slaughter. Apparently she had ridden when she was small with Allegra, who had gone through a phase of fancying herself as a horsewoman during the filming of a steamy Italian remake of *National Velvet*. But when Allegra and Ambrose had split up, the riding lessons had become spasmodic – along, from the sounds of things, with a good many other treats. It was no wonder Cressida was given to moments of imperiousness, thought Scorcher fondly. The poor kid was desperately insecure. Ambrose had probably done his best, poor sod. It couldn't be easy bringing up a couple of teenagers on your own — three if you counted their mother — but they did seem to have had a miserable time, what with him working and being away so much, and then being wrapped up with Kate.

Cressie had been frightened when Douggie first suggested teaching her to steeplechase. But when Scorcher explained how therapeutic he'd found being with horses after he gave up drugs; when he promised that he would personally oversee her instruction; when he gave her his word that he would make time every day to go riding with her, she finally agreed. And within weeks she was galloping through his fields and jumping hedges as if to the manor house born. It was then that he first noticed what a voluptuous, accomplished woman she was growing into.

He could honestly say that his initial intentions had been entirely honourable. He had even attempted to fill the gaps in Cressida's woeful education, painstakingly working out a curriculum for maths and science studies to be taught by Professor Martin Ffinch-Chaffin, the same retired Oxford don who had schooled him. He had personally drawn up a reading list for her, composed of great works that had seen him through his darkest hours in prison, including *The Brothers Karamazov* and *To the Lighthouse*. She soon abandoned that Valley-speak that drove Ambrose berserk and even wrote a couple of what she laughably called essays — on *Tess of the D'Urbervilles* and *The Mayor of Casterbridge*, two of Scorcher's favourites.

'Blimey, Cressie,' he couldn't help expostulating when she presented the first of her two great streams of consciousness, both of which were unblemished by any kind of punctuation, 'how much does it cost to teach someone so little?'

'A hell of a lot, I'm afraid,' she said good-naturedly. 'Daddy's distraught. But the fact is I'm just not academic and the sooner we all admit it the happier we'll all be.'

It was true. Cressie's idea of a good read was Dick Francis and *Hello!*, and the only mathematical problems she was interested in solving were to do with whose round it was in the local pub where she went every Friday with the other grooms.

Scorcher was touched by the struggles she must have engaged in as the daughter of one of the country's leading thinkers. When he finally saw her dissolve into unselfconscious giggles – great bubbling cascades of them – after Lord Riley, his snootiest hunter, had emptied his bladder over a rare rose bush that Phillips, his head gardener, had just transplanted, he realized that he had fallen in love.

He knew he was no work of art. At a pinch he might qualify as a gargoyle. He also knew that Ambrose would surely be making alternative plans for Cressida – finishing school in Latvia, soup kitchens in Islington, or whatever it was millionaire lefties like him organized for their daughters these days. For an hour or so he twiddled desultorily with some faders and mixers on his console, gave up and wandered over to a sofa where a pile of Cressida's discarded *Hello!*s lay. Looking at them was sweet sorrow.

Glumly he stared at Nobby Decker, lead guitarist with the Smash and once the nemesis of many a hotel room, whose grinning skull stared demotically back as it bobbed contentedly in his guitar-shaped pool in California. Draped languidly across a lilo shaped like a plectrum was his new blond wife, Candy, who must be all of nineteen. On her lap was a chubby baby who looked young enough to be Nobby's great-grandchild.

May the saints preserve him from such ludicrous indignity. 'What do you think you look like, Nobby?' muttered Scorcher to himself. 'You must be ninety-three if you're a day, you silly bugger.'

'He looks pretty happy to me,' said Cressida softly, striding towards him, her jodhpurs dusty from the ride and her polo shirt – God forgive him for noticing – sticking damply to her swelling breasts. Surely it couldn't be good for her to go riding without a bra, he found himself fretting. She stopped in front of him and climbed on to his lap facing him, as she had climbed onto Lady Godiva an hour earlier, and chucked *Hello!* on to the floor.

'What was it you told me two months ago about living life according to your own rules and no one else's?' she said sternly, cupping his chin in her hands and gently kissing him on the lips.

'Well—' he began gingerly, when she let him surface for air. 'I think I was just making a point, Cressie, about Dostoyevsky. I mean, we all have to observe certain rules, otherwise what you get is anarchy.'

'Is that what you were doing when you were banged up for smuggling drugs into Japan?' she said, the corners of her adorable pouting mouth curling up wickedly.

'I was young—'

'Thirty-three—'

Scorcher cursed his cuttings.

'And I didn't have the benefit of your common sense . . .'

'Oh, you silly man,' said Cressida, laughing, bouncing up and down on his lap and causing such undue agitation in his nether regions he thought his jeans would burst. 'Don't you know that's what's so great about you? Apart from your charm, your kindness and your incredible generosity, I mean. The really seductive thing about you is that you are one of those blessed people in life who doesn't have to follow any rules at all.'

'That's where you're wrong, Cressie,' he said sadly, reluctantly moving her hands from his fly. 'Anarchy is for the young.'

Undeterred, Cressida removed her shirt. 'Well, that's me sorted, then. Now, Scorcher, I'm probably a lot heavier than you, so don't try and buck me off. And give me three good reasons why you're not prepared to even try and give us a go?'

'Age, age and age,' he said weakly. He was still struggling with the euphoric discovery that this wondrous, lithe creature found him attractive and ... What was it she'd said about his charm and generosity?

'Age cannot wither him nor custom stale his infinite variety. See, my expensive education did teach me something. And if you're worried that I may not have sufficient experience,' she continued, wilfully misconstruing him, 'I can tell you I've got bags of enthusiasm.'

'That is not what I meant and you know it.' He sighed as she unbuttoned his shirt, nuzzled her face, still damp from the ride, against his bony chest, and reached her hand into his jeans. He groaned and closed his eyes, shooing away Ambrose's sorrowful recriminations. Douggie Kenwood always said the final hurdle was his downfall.

✷   ✷   ✷

Kate plucked at an imaginary hair on her embroidered pashmina sarong, then examined the ceiling – hideous – while Jonathan Crombie, her consultant gynaecologist at St Mary's, peered between her legs. She coughed and then scowled. After countless visits she would have hoped to have overcome her embarrassment by now. But no.

And nor, by the looks of him, had Jonathan Crombie, who couldn't be more than twenty-three. She watched while the strawberry-blond tufts of his spiky haircut bobbed up and down between her knees, and waited for his conclusion.

'Well, the good thing is that it all still looks perfectly healthy there, Mrs White.' He beamed. 'Which is no small achievement when you consider the physical trauma of the past eighteen months.'

Kate had had enough of this flim-flam.

'If it's so healthy, then why isn't it working?' she snapped.

'Hard to say – the causes of the four miscarriages all appear to have been different—'

'Yes, well, now I don't even appear able to conceive.' Kate glowered at him in accusation.

'Mmm ... Well, that's not uncommon in these situations. You've been through a lot of stress, and you're working terribly hard—'

Kate rolled her eyes. She'd been subjected to this litany of blame endlessly. And how dare Jonathan prepubescent Crombie lecture her about working too hard when Ambrose was so busy he couldn't even make it to the consultations? It was just typical of the male supremacist culture that ruled these bloody hospitals.

'Yes, well, I'm not about to give up work and retreat to the kitchen, however much the reactionaries in this country night like that,' said Kate. 'So we'll just have to find another solution—'

'Well, of course, there are various options,' began Jonathan Crombie. 'IVF, for instance, although as you know the success rates aren't brilliant and it would certainly help your chances if you were to cut down on your travelling, just a litt—'

'What about surrogacy?'

'Yes, that's always a possibility, though it's a huge undertaking. I think there are a number of avenues we should explore before we go down that one. But that said, I could arrange for you to have a meeting with one of my colleagues who specializes in that area—'

'Er, great,' said Kate, looking at her watch and realizing she was meant to be at a meeting with the architect of the hotel, which she and Bo had agreed to call Cocoon, in fifteen minutes. 'In the meantime, have you got any literature on it? That way I could bone up on it on my own, which would save us all a lot of time in the long run.'

Five minutes later she was on her way to meet Jake Tavernier, a stack of leaflets on IVF and surrogacy plus the odd one on stress management that Jonathan Crombie had managed to sneak in with the rest of them, bulging out of her straw basket.

Gingerly, Kate stepped across two deadly-looking joists and tried vainly to blend in with the greyish blur of activity all round her. Her dark curls sprang out stubbornly from her bright yellow hard hat like a family of baby moles who had been trapped underground. When she reached the centre of the space, she looked up, awe-stricken, at the gaping hole where the atrium would eventually be lowered into place. All around Bo Peep's latest hotel in Soho, workmen were beavering away in various mysterious states of activity, most of which seemed to involve laboriously unscrewing the tops from their flasks of tea, borrowing each other's copies of the *Python*, and taking it in turn to nip out to Prêt-à-Manger.

'Coming along nicely, isn't it?' crooned Jake Tavernier, London's most fashionable architect, appearing, as usual, from nowhere, with his Palm Pilot glinting malevolently in the blinking shafts of sunlight and the sleeves of his Yohji Yamamoto shirt flapping like unpaid invoices.

Kate didn't think it was coming on at all nicely. Unless you counted being three months behind schedule, fifty per cent over budget, and having a building site that looked more like a post-modern pile of bricks that should be exhibited in the Tate than a place anyone might ever stay, as progress. Cocoon indeed.

'What happened to the Grade One-listed cornicing?' she asked in a small, constricted voice, panic bubbling up like water in geriatric plumbing.

'Oh, that,' said Jake loftily. 'Had to rip it out. Felt wrong.'

'But the council'll go mad,' expostulated Kate. So would Bo. Only that morning she'd received a three-thousand-word e-mail from him eulogizing the joys of olde British buildings and how their ancient features should be integrated into a holistic modern synthesis – or gibberish to that effect.

'Keep your hard hat on,' soothed Jake, flicking an invisible piece of moulding from his Comme des Garçons black artisan trousers. 'They'll soon shut up when the building wins every award going. And just look at this magnificent work of art,' he crowed, rubbing his lily-white hand up and down a miniature sample of a jagged glass tread, which was all they had to show so far of the hotel lobby's central staircase.

She was distracted by a loud altercation about genetically modified foods on the radio between Percy Irvine, the very ambitious First Secretary at the Ministry of Food and Agriculture, and a nutritional and wellbeing expert who sounded uncannily like Dan. Dan was definitely coming off best.

'Well, that was our beloved government,' barked Donna Ducatti. 'Too tight to spend on the NHS, but happy to pour millions into Frankenstein foods. And while we're on the subject of the NHS, how come it's so crap now and yet worked perfectly well when it was set up on a fiftieth of the money? Okay, so medical research wasn't quite as accomplished as it is today. There were no sex-change operations on the NHS, no free artificial insemination for lesbians and multi-flavoured sex aids weren't liberally distributed among buggers hell-bent on a quiet night in a public toilet with half a dozen strangers . . .'

Good old Donna, thought Kate, scowling. Liberal as ever. And twice as bloody popular, if the rapt attention of the builders was anything to go by. It was going to be one of those days, she thought glumly, only marginally appeased to see Jake Tavernier in such pain she thought he was going to demand an epidural, as he attempted to prize a piece of broken glass out of his right index finger.

Cressida pressed her tumescent breasts against Scorcher's gnarled chest and giggled as she picked bits of straw out of his matted hair while Lady Godiva and Dostoyevsky, Scorcher's favourite stallion, stamped the ground so loudly it shook. 'Talk about feeling the earth move,' she sighed blissfully, tweaking his nipples. Scorcher groaned. They had to stop meeting like this. Come to think of it, they had to stop mating like this.

It had been Cressida's idea, of course, to sneak out that first night and make love in one of the stables. And it wasn't just the stables. It was anywhere public. Last week, shortly after posing demurely for the *Harpers & Queen* society snapper at Lord Trickett's hunt ball, she had led him up to the minstrels' gallery, where she had proceeded to lift up her pale pink DKNY ball skirt to reveal an immaculate silhouette of a horse that had been topiaried out of her pubic hair, before pressing him against a sixteenth-century tapestry which, much to Lady Trickett's pride, had been featured in several English Heritage guides as well as on the front cover of *Simply Splendid*.

And simply splendid it had been. But that wasn't the point. This was the problem with addictive personalities, he thought, quivering at the memory of Cressida's very pleasurable addictions. Her appetite for life, he mused, watching her tongue work its way expressively down his body again, was even larger than his.

But it had to stop. Otherwise how would he, Scorcher, ever look Ambrose in the eye again? How could he have, if not exactly violated his daughter, guardianship of whom had been entrusted to him, then certainly not repelled her advances? He closed his eyes and tried to summon up Ambrose's sombre features. But all he could muster was a giant hologram of Cressie's tongue.

The other problem was that she was huge fun. She had vast stores of energy, adored all the sporting activities Scorcher had assiduously cultivated over the years, and could drink staggering amounts of alcohol without staggering at all. On the contrary, it simply gave her the Dutch courage to live up to her horse's namesake and ride starkers at night. And she had a huge repository of filthy jokes.

She was also brave, loyal and devoted to his horses and grooms, and she had made herself completely indispensable in his life. Organizing the servants, taking his shambolic research notes for his historical treatise in hand, reorganizing his fan club, and setting up a Scorcher website. At first he thought she did it because she was bored, but as the summer wore on, and Cressida's natural ebullience melted into something which he could only describe as tenderness, he realized that she was deliberately finding ways to make it hard for him to send her home – and that knowledge touched him more than he could say. He would have to give her up, of course, but not yet, he thought, gently caressing the golden hairs on her sunburned back. Not yet.

As it turned out, Cressida was the least of Ambrose's concerns that summer, as he discovered when he flew out to LA for a summit with Marty Shicker to discuss the death scene in *Endymion*.

'Don't get me wrong,' said Marty, slurping his way through a mountain of risotto in Spago's. 'I love the pathos of it. But it is a bit of a downer – Keats dying so young, I mean.'

'History often is,' said Ambrose, clenching his fist so tightly round his glass of Château Lafitte it was in danger of snapping.

'Well, I was getting to that,' said Marty hastily, mopping his voluminous forehead with a corner of the tablecloth which he mistook for his napkin. 'Do you think we have to be quite so literal? I mean, I totally support the integrity of your work. But wouldn't it be more creatively satisfying if we kind of avoided the whole death thing? If we could finish it before Keats does, for instance, and maybe inject a little more sex? Think what a feel-good little movie we'd have on our hands. I can see the posters now: Endymion – Mad, Bad and Dangerous to Know . . .' He trailed off.

'That was Byron,' said Ambrose stonily.

'Yeah, whatever,' said Marty. 'The thing is, the public's in a bit of a vulnerable place right now, what with Princess Di leaving us. I don't know if they can take two deaths in one year. And I feel so strongly about this movie, Ambrose, that I want it to have the widest possible audience.' His voice shifted down an octave and it dawned on Ambrose that he was attempting to method-act his way through Sincerity. 'I see Keats as being the first rock-and-roll superstar,' he continued. 'A kind of forerunner for Sting . . .'

Ambrose winced.

'Plus,' continued Marty, fanning himself with the menu 'I've a strong presentiment that if we can treat the erudite issues which are at the centre of this movie – especially the one about beauty and truth – in a popular way that reaches out to the widest possible number of people, the Academy will not be able to resist garnishing Endymion with every award going. Not of course that that matters but—'

'Of course not,' said Ambrose hastily, wondering if Nick was absolutely wedded to the death scene.

He tried to broach the subject two days later when he dropped in to see Nick on the set of Endymion, shooting on which had now shifted to Kent. But Nick had other things on his mind. For weeks after the Princess of Wales had died, the newspapers had carried nothing else. But now they were manically casting around for stories to fill the void.

'It's just so unfair,' thundered Nick, tilting back his neck so that the light bounced sharply off his profile as if it had been painstakingly organized by an experienced director of photography. It was only nine o'clock in the morning but already the stretch of meadow outside his trailer was flickering in a heat haze. Ambrose looked at Nick closely as the shafts of sunlight threw the delicate angles of his face into dark relief. He was such a beautiful boy, even with his hair dyed jet black to play Keats. And yet strangely virile, without a trace of the crass action-hero machismo of so many Hollywood leading men. No wonder he scored so highly with male audiences as well as female ones.

'You'd think it would have been enough for them to annihilate my character, but they're doing it to Martha too,' he said bitterly.

Ambrose shrugged. 'It means nothing. Newspapers have become like wallpaper – no one really notices what they say any more.'

'That's crap and you know it,' retorted Nick angrily. 'It's the wallpaper effect that's so dangerous. Every day they paper a bit more of your soul up there and no one notices until eventually the whole place looks different. The things they say about Martha are just despicable,' he continued. 'Christ knows Phoebe's cunning, but I didn't know she was this bloody clever. She's got the tabloids eating right out of her hand as Saint Fucking Hard-Done-By, and meanwhile Martha's portrayed as some brainless, callous slut who slept her way to the so-called frigging top. Do you know the

Python even insinuated that she made Donna Ducatti's life a misery at BSR by constantly undermining her? As if anyone could undermine Donna, for Christ's sake.

'You know what really gets me?' he continued shakily. 'It's the sheer bloody hypocrisy. They can write all the shit about me that they want, and at the end of the day it all comes down to this: Wilde by name, Wilde by nature. What a guy, what a career, and just watch it soar. But when a woman gets involved in something like this it's all over for her. She's either portrayed as a saint or a whore of Babylon. And yet none of them has a clue what she's really like, because what she's really like doesn't have anything to do with what sells.'

While Nick ranted – and Ambrose wimped out of asking him if he'd mind reshooting the end of *Endymion* – Martha was stretching lazily across her bed, ostensibly reading through some research notes for the new series of *And Now*. She was still reeling from the sensation of seeing some of the first rushes of *Endymion* in a small screening room in Wardour Street the night before. It was the first time she had been to any of his films. They sat, hand in hand, watching his beautiful face up on the screen, and she fell in love with his physical beauty all over again. And when she turned to look at him, his face so much smaller and more vulnerable in the flickering light of the cinema, she saw that he had been watching her the whole time. 'To see your reaction to the distortion of celluloid,' he told her later.

'And did I pass?' she asked softly, as they stepped out on to the wet Soho pavement.

'It wasn't a test,' he said, kissing her.

By the end of November, filming of *Endymion* had finished and, battered by the long dark evenings and the even darker stories in the press, they decided one night to take a holiday in South Africa. *And Now* was due to start its new series any minute, but Martha felt like being reckless. On the spur of the moment they caught a flight to Cape Town so that Nick could show Martha around. Martha felt deliriously happy. Her life was almost out of control, but as long as she had Nick she felt profoundly secure.

It was while they were sipping tea in the British Airways first-class lounge at Heathrow that Kate finally caught up with her on the mobile.

'Kate,' said Martha guiltily – she hadn't been keeping in contact with her sister nearly as much as she ought to have lately. 'Where are you?'

'The M4,' said Kate tearfully. She was on her way back to Cocoon from a meeting with Bo in his log palace, and was late for a session with Jake Tavernier, who wanted to explain to her exactly why he'd had to rip out the listed ceilings on the first floor. 'I've been desperately trying to get hold of you, Martha.' Her voice was almost accusing. Martha recognized the tone. Kate was working up to asking her a favour. 'There's something I've got to ask you.'

Martha's blood froze. She'd been dreading this for months. She'd even been to a specialist – only to have her worst fears confirmed. The chiffon dress Nick had bought her in Rome that had been flapping pleasingly against her skin in the air-conditioning felt almost painful now. She walked across to a stretch of empty chairs where no one would hear, listening while Kate explained that her last hope of having a child was if Martha were to become a surrogate and carry a baby for her. Martha heard her voice, shakily, sounding as though it were coming from somewhere else, explaining about the abortion, how it had permanently damaged the wall of her womb and why she would never be able to have a baby for anyone. She couldn't remember exactly what Kate said. Something very quiet, like, 'I see. Well, I hope you're very happy with Nick. You certainly must be in love to overlook everything he's done.'

And then the line had gone dead. She had walked back into the lounge and on to the plane in a trance.

She had sat for hours barely talking, going through the motions of watching the films on the flight, instinctively avoiding the newspapers, especially the British ones, when the stewardess came round with them. Pretending she had a headache, she took a sleeping pill and drifted fitfully in and out of the present, never completely able to block out the roar of the engines or the insistent rhythm of her guilt. Hours later she was unsure whether she had slept at all as the plane soared over a spectacularly steep spine of mountains.

'That's Devil's Peak,' said Nick excitedly, pointing out of the window. Drowsily, she reached for his hand and he smiled.

'It's going to be all right, Martha,' he said. 'I'd forgotten how beautiful it was.'

The airport was far smaller than she'd expected, but even so she could see that at the end of the corridor to the arrivals lounge there was a small reception committee of photographers and reporters waiting for them. After the discreet anonymity of the flight, the throng came as a shock. 'How did they know?' asked Martha blearily, fishing in her bag for some sunglasses.

'It's a small town. Not a lot happens. They'll go away in a minute. They probably just want to welcome one of their own home,' whispered Nick, trying to conceal his growing sense of alarm. The last time he had been home it was as a relative unknown. He had thought that here, if nowhere else in the world, there was still a refuge of peace waiting for him.

'How do you feel about becoming a father, Nick?' a young reporter with turquoise eyes and a blond Afro frizz asked, thrusting a microphone across Martha and into Nick's face. Martha's stomach lurched. In her disorientation, she wondered whether somehow her conversation with Kate had been overheard and the reporter had got the wrong end of the stick.

Another journalist, with thinning grey hair, produced a copy of the *Python*. 'Shouldn't you be at home with your wife, *sir*?' he asked insolently, as Nick took in the banner headline.

'Phoebe to have Nick's twins,' was the screamer, beneath a picture of Phoebe, smiling tearfully as she posed coyly in a low-cut pink Galliano dress, on the Cupid's love-seat in the garden of the Holland Park house, one hand placed proprietorially over her swelling stomach.

'I believe you. Of course I do, Nick,' Martha began, shivering, as they sat on the balcony of the Mount Nelson Hotel looking out towards the ocean. But her voice sounded small. 'I love you and so I believe what you tell me,' she went on mechanically. 'But ... it's hard when Phoebe is so insistent. Shouldn't you issue some kind of denial?'

'What's the point?' he said bitterly. 'It would just degenerate into some slanging match.'

'You can't ignore it,' she pleaded, unable to bear the thought of this hanging over them and destroying their idyll. She wanted Nick to draw a line under his life with Phoebe. 'Wouldn't it be best for everyone if the real father got involved?'

He gave a bitter little laugh. 'I doubt if even Phoebe knows who the real father is.'

Martha looked at him, startled. She had heard gossip at the BBC to the effect that Phoebe had had a fling with Lachlan.

'Lachlan? Is that what people thought?' he said scornfully. 'Christ, poor Lachlan had about as much chance of holding on to Phoebe as a weasel trying to stop a bolting horse. Lachlan, Las Vegas, January 1996. I think that's right. He may have had two or three sessions with Phoebe – but the dates don't work. She called them sessions, by the way, it's not my terminology. Martha, it could be any one of dozens of men. Literally. Hundreds even.'

'What are you saying?' said Martha, suddenly sounding frightened.

'Phoebe liked sex with multiple partners. Or rather she liked the transaction of power that occurred every time she took someone to bed. It was an addiction. Years ago, before we met, she used to turn tricks, for fun as much as anything. I don't think she ever forgave me for depriving her of the excuse to carry on that particular little game.'

'And you knew all that time?'

'God, no. For years I genuinely thought we were love's young dream. I was a hopeless idealist. Either that or so wrapped up in myself I didn't notice what was going on under my nose. And by the time I did find out — there comes a day when you can't keep orgies and prostitution a secret even from idiots like me — there was nothing to be done. No anger to be felt. No gnawing jealousies to harbour. She was such a fuck-up, you see. And I actually thought I could help her.' He raked his fingers through his hair, which was fluttering in the evening breeze.

Martha pulled her shawl around her and felt her world collapsing. All these months she and Nick had been together she had thought they had become as close as two people could get, but she realized now there was so much he hadn't told her. What else was lurking in his past? Feeling tears stinging the backs of her eyes, she stood up abruptly and headed towards the room. He grabbed her wrist roughly and pulled her back.

'Martha, I didn't tell you because I wanted to wipe the slate clean. Not because I don't trust you. It's more a case of not trusting my own judgments. So much of what happened was crazy. I needed some distance to think. To sift it through my mind and work out what really happened. Please, don't make us both suffer for a past that neither of us could control.'

He pulled her towards him and began to kiss her face wildly until she began to kiss him back. Of course she trusted him. But the twisted tentacles of his relationship with Phoebe were starting to threaten their life together, and with a cold, sinking clarity she began to see what a fool she had been to ever think things could be otherwise.

Chapter Nineteen

'I guess that ensures the Beeb *can't* sack her now,' said Ruby, scanning the morning's headlines admiringly. All of them, apart from those on the front page of the *Financial Times*, seemed to be outdoing one another in saccharine sentimentality as they alerted the world to the momentous details of Phoebe's pregnancy. It was amazing. Anyone would think Nato wasn't about to bomb Iraq again, or that Bill Clinton hadn't been found having a curious relationship with cigars. Or that a peace agreement hadn't just been reached in Northern Ireland. Because the big issue of the day was whether or not Phoebe would be able to continue dressing stylishly throughout her confinement.

Tugging the linen sheet off Eliza's bed and wrapping it around her naked body, Ruby padded over to the desk, where Eliza was applying a light coating of powder to her porcelain skin, and kissed the nape of her neck tenderly. Reaching into Eliza's caramel leather jacket, she squeezed her left breast lovingly. 'I always suspected I was married to a genius,' she cooed.

'*I* didn't father the child, you know,' said Eliza, dousing herself in Chanel No. 19.

'I don't suppose Nick did either,' said Ruby, brushing away some croissant crumbs that had become trapped in her cleavage.

'What do you mean?' asked Eliza, swivelling round in her chair sharply.

'Well, the dates don't exactly add up, do they?' said Ruby, counting on her fingers. 'Five months pregnant, yet Nick and she parted seven months ago – May 1997. Along with half the country, the bloody date's stamped on my brain. Even I, with my lack of maternal instincts, can see a flaw there.'

'Oh, for heaven's sake, Ruby,' said Eliza, flushing angrily, 'what do you take me for? I've been through all that with Phoebe and it's a classic case of the man not being able to make up his mind. Just because he'd left her it didn't mean he didn't carry on sleeping with her for as long as he could. One could almost feel sorry for Martha.'

'Oh, surely not,' said Ruby, a little too tartly.

Eliza glared at her. 'And what's that supposed to mean?'

'Nothing, my little angel of death. You're just doing your job. And doing it brilliantly. If only Monica Lewinksy had consulted you when she decided to spill the beans, she might be running for President now instead of being famous for running after one. As it is, Phoebe's totally wiped the floor with Nick and Martha as far as gaining the public's sympathy is concerned. Judging by what the papers write, Martha's an evil-smelling, foul-mouthed, no-talent, cellulite-ridden bitch from hell who slept her way to the top.

In fact, according to the tabs, the only things she hasn't had a passing acquaintance with are the basic tenets of hygiene – tipping them off about her old flat was a nice one, by the way. I loved that double-page pic of it in the *Python* under the headline "Twelve Diseases You Could Catch Here".'

'I am, as you pointed out, simply doing my job,' said Eliza coldly.

'And your ruthless efficiency wouldn't have anything to do with the fact that – God knows how many years ago – you got pissed off because Martha and Kate forgot to tell you about some family summit they were having with Sadie and you've never got over it?'

'Not that it's any of your business,' Eliza began in a voice that could have frozen the Equator. 'I didn't even know Martha was involved in the equation when I first accepted Phoebe as a client.'

That was also partially true. She had been in India while most of the drama had been played out in the press. But it was also true that she had read up on all Phoebe's cuttings before she had finally signed the agreement to represent her – and that she knew exactly how much Martha was implicated in the whole affair before she did so. And no one had forced her to go to the papers with those ancient snapshots of Martha's flat she and Kate had taken over a cosy supper all those years ago. It seemed a lifetime away, she thought wistfully.

'The discovery certainly didn't make the account any less appealing, did it?' Ruby looked at Eliza confrontationally. The sheet had slithered to the floor. Framed against the morning light from the window, her voluptuous body, normally such a source of comforting delight to Eliza, now seemed hostile. 'I thought you went to India to discover yourself. I hope you're happy with what you found.'

'I'm beginning to think it was better than the other junk I came back with,' said Eliza nastily.

'I'll pretend you didn't really say that, Eliza. Or that it's PMT – Post-Martha-Thrashing syndrome.'

Eliza snapped shut her Psion and, gathering up her Vuitton briefcase, waltzed out of the bedroom. 'It must be wonderful having such high-minded principles,' she called from the front door. 'Alas, some of us have to work for a living.'

What really troubled Sadie about the vicious press coverage of Martha was its utter inaccuracy. No wonder Nick and Martha had escaped to South Africa as soon as he had finished filming *Endymion*. Poor Martha was so debilitated by it all she had even decided not to do the next series of *And Now*, much to Charlie Pitchcock's chagrin.

Not that the coverage bore any relationship to the daughter Sadie knew. Like Nick and Martha, she had long ago cancelled all the papers. But there was no escaping the news-stand headlines. The besmirched tatters of her daughter's reputation turned her into an articulate literary lioness. She regularly sat up late into the night over David's old computer, composing angry letters to every editor on Fleet Street. When Angus Deayton made a jibe about Martha on *Have I Got News for You* she wrote him a letter saying that he would no longer be a welcome visitor at Tithe House, a gesture that was slightly diminished, as Kate pointed out, by the fact that Tithe House was no longer welcoming any visitors. Dan's mail order had taken off like a rocket – or ruccola, as Sadie preferred to call it. And thanks to Eliza he was in such demand in the media as the country's most attractive foodie (the *Python* called him Dish of the Day) that Sadie no longer had time to run a small country retreat.

She bullied David mercilessly until he eventually tabled a motion that proposed curtailing the freedom of the press, even though he knew that everyone realized he clearly had a vested interest and that this would eventually make him a laughing-stock. Her only consolation was the knowledge that, to judge from Martha's letters, her daughter's sanity apparently remained intact.

'They do seem to be putting it all behind them,' she said one night, looking up from a letter Martha had sent. The paper smelled faintly of pine; she could almost feel the sunshine rise off the pages.

'Yes, well, it's all very well for people who can just up and leave all their problems.'

Sadie looked across at Kate in surprise. Kate met her gaze defiantly. She wanted to tell Sadie how her precious daughter had betrayed them all – though she wasn't certain whether she considered the abortion itself, or Martha's failure to confide in her closest family, the greater treachery. Instead she found herself earnestly asking Sadie whether she thought it was possible ever to be a truly good mother without being able to cook.

'It's just that whenever I think of us altogether at Tithe House, we're gathered round the kitchen table and you're cooking something delicious,' she said, tears channelling down her face. Sadie looked at her uncertainly, not sure whether to laugh or sympathize. 'Even Martha managed to make that mangy little flat homely whenever she rustled up a meal,' Kate continued wistfully. 'Whereas all I ever seem able to do is make wonderful ... stage sets. All the right props are there in all the right places. It just never feels like home. I'm hopeless. It's probably just as well I can't have children.'

Sadie slid on to the sofa next to Kate and hugged her, stroking her hair for what seemed like hours until Kate's sobs subsided. Eventually Kate drifted into a doze on her lap, aware only of the fact that her mother's hands, after all these years, still smelled of hand cream and rosemary.

Without the ballast of Martha in her life, and denied, as she saw it, her last chance of motherhood, Kate threw herself into her work with a brittle energy that constantly threatened to teeter into collapsed exhaustion. When she wasn't in meetings with Jake Tavernier or Roberto or wading through Little Bo Peep's endless e-mails, she was stuck on a plane somewhere. There had been a mini-riot when her homeware department opened in Tokyo and the Katy beaded hot-water bottle cases had sold out overnight. Then there were building sites to be visited in New York or Moscow, where she had been approached to set up a department store. Ambrose, who was happily preoccupied with a new mystery project with Nick that they kept e-mailing one another about, spent most of his time hugging his computer. Even Cressie had stopped bugging her. They hadn't heard a peep for weeks; even her regular pleas to Ambrose to up her allowance seemed to have dried up – presumably because Scorcher was paying her way over the odds to be one of his grooms. That was probably why she was so keen to stay on there. At least she had finally found something she was good at. In fact she was so good at it that Ambrose seemed to be coming to terms with the idea of Cressie becoming a full-time groom. Even more miraculously, all things considered, Kate found herself almost missing Cressie — an indication of just how lonely her life had become.

Most heartbreaking of all, she barely had time to see Nibbles, who had been on stud duty all summer, in a doomed attempt to calm him down, and had apparently fathered his first litter when Kate was thirty-five thousand feet over Helsinki. It was this last nugget of news, relayed breathlessly on to her mobile answer machine by Marcus, that finally caused her to dissolve into tears halfway down the metal staircase of a 747 that had just deposited her in Moscow. She couldn't even mother her dog properly.

She desperately wanted to call Martha. Her fingers punched out the numbers a hundred times. But at the last moment she would find anger at what Martha had done swamping her like poisonous gas. How could she? And worse still, how could she have kept it from them all for so long?

Nick looked up from his iMac, where the notes he'd been working on for Ambrose about Detmar Hibsen, an obscure, 1930s South African archaeologist he had first discovered when he'd been surfing the Net for groceries back in London, were starting to come alive and hold him prisoner. Shielding his eyes from the glare of the late morning sun, he scanned the shimmering turquoise pool that seemed to fall over the cliff into the Atlantic and contentedly sipped a banana daiquiri. He couldn't believe how good life felt. He knew that the British media were still mauling him – and that things would get worse when *Endymion* came out. But out here it was hard to care. Even Ambrose had given up sending anguished pleas for them to come home and face up to things and had started instead sending him the very first drafts of the Detmar Hibsen screenplay.

Nick hadn't realized how much he missed his brothers and his parents, Chrissie and Mike. Phoebe's lack of family had, he supposed, made him wary of overwhelming her with his own. Zack and Luke had, as predicted, become a fiscal lawyer and neurosurgeon respectively. But they had also set up a small-time acid jazz band to which they devoted many more evenings and weekends than the public were prepared to devote to seeing them. All in all, Luke and Zack had turned out to be thoroughly likable, even vaguely eccentric individuals; slower, more conventional and, looks-wise, cruder versions of Nick, as if they had been made from the leftovers of Nick's chiselled features. They were immensely kind, with equally good-natured wives.

It was Luke who had found Nick and Martha the enormous thatched cottage perched precariously above Hout Bay when they had decided to stay in South Africa. With its pale blue louvred shutters, tumbling thatch and lush gardens, Rose Cottage had been in the same Russian émigré family for seventy years, until its last owner, a frail but renowned ornithologist called Ernst Lubitov, had died six months ago. With its impossibly pretty cottagey exterior and gorgeous gardens which spilled spectacularly over the cliff, it had a welcoming but secretive air that Martha and Nick immediately identified with. But the real selling point was the hopelessly overgrown veranda which snaked round the entire cottage, and on the east side gave mesmerizing views straight down to the rocks and sea several hundred feet below. They rented it while Mr Lubitov's cousin, an oil executive in Houston, decided what to do with it. The estate agent had been thrilled to offload the place, which he found old-fashioned and dark.

'Of course, if Rose Cottage does come up for sale, you'd want to rip the interior out and practically start from scratch. I mean, this kitchen is practically antediluvian,' he gushed, roaring up in his Golf GTi and sweeping them through the house and grounds at a hundred miles an hour.

'As for this veranda,' he said distastefully, pulling a tendril of ivy to one side, 'we can probably organize a JCB for you.'

They loved the ivy. It gave them a feeling of intense privacy. And the minute the estate agent had roared off to get the papers for them to sign, leaving them to explore the grounds, they had christened the veranda in their own inimitable way. The estate agent had returned earlier than expected and Martha had had to muffle her moans of pleasure as his shiny black shoes came tip-tapping on to the cool tiles.

'As I was saying,' he crowed obliviously as they finished getting dressed, 'it needs a bit of work, but you won't regret renting it. And as I'm sure you've discovered, it does have this magnificent pool. State-of-the-art. Mr Lubitov, bless him, was a dedicated swimmer. And he must have been ninety-one if he was a day. Don't get me wrong,' he added hurriedly, as they signed the papers there and then, 'it's got all mod cons.'

'Including one that drives a convertible Golf,' said Martha under her breath. Nick had quietly taken him to one side and offered him a huge bribe if he would tell the press that they'd rented somewhere else. He and the Golf had roared off into the sunset and, a few hours later, a cluster of desultory hacks had set up camp outside a palatial spread on the other side of the bay which belonged to an Arab family who visited it once every two years.

For once the estate-agent-speak wasn't overblown. The Olympic-sized pool was indeed magnificent. But then Nick and Martha thought most things about Rose Cottage were wonderful, including Anthony, the wonderful factotum who had served Mr Lubitov faithfully for thirty years and promised to do the same – God willing – for them.

They didn't want to change a thing. The smell of beeswax emanating from the dark wooden floors, the lingering sweetly bitter smell of Mr Lubitov's pipe, the way his chair was angled by the French windows so that he could watch the sun arc across the sky from one side of the bay to another, were all things they left as they had been. And every evening, at six o'clock, they dedicated their first toast to him. As for the thick curtain of ivy shielding the eyes of Rose Cottage from the burning sun, Nick slung up a hammock behind it and spent long languid afternoons avoiding writing about his archaeologist and endless hours conducting his own archaeology on Martha's body.

Martha's cooking rapidly won over Nick's mother and provided an instant bond as she and Chrissie shyly swapped recipes. The rest of the family were soon eating out of the palm of her hand too – and old Mr Lubitov's ancient Le Creusets. Martha admired the Wildes' easy respect for one another, the way they could spend so much time in one another's company without feeling suffocated, and compared it wistfully with the behaviour of the splintered remnants of her own family. Now and again the memory of her father looking pale and vulnerable in his hospital bed would cause her a pang of remorse. The problem with her own parents' dedication to leading the perfect life, she decided, was that when things finally had unravelled, the shock had hit them all like an exploding mine.

'You're not bored, are you?' Nick asked one day, looking up from his notes. She loved the way his South African accent had resurfaced, the odd little staccato consonant popping through his languid tones like machinegun fire. She gazed out beyond the palm trees towards the curtain of hibiscus that almost completely covered the balustrade, where, every evening, they sipped cocktails, overlooking the spectacular scenery of Hout Bay, and smiled slowly.

'How could I ever be bored? Here? With you? It's the most beautiful, serene place I've ever been.'

They sat hand in hand, mesmerized as usual by the view. The sun slipped across the sky like a flat orange disc, hovering flirtatiously above the white-crested waves. To the west the mountains blurred into the horizon like a long line of sentries up to their knees in water. Martha was well aware that South Africa had a cauldron of problems to deal with, many of them violent ones. But here, in Rose Cottage, she had never felt so protected. Nick kissed the freckles on her tanned shoulders, wiping the last lingering droplets of water from her neck with a towel. She wrinkled her nose and pushed the tendrils of hair out of her eyes.

'How did you ever manage to tear yourself away from here?' she asked him.

He place a hand theatrically against his temple and adopted a cod Laurence Olivier accent. 'I had to act,' he intoned.

'Shame it never came to anything,' said Martha. Nick

picked her up as if she were a baby and deposited her back in the pool.

'Do you think it's possible to change the person you are within a family without destroying that family,' she asked him later, as they lay, head to head, along the balustrade, watching the sun skim through the sky towards the water.

'What do you mean?'

'Well, I'm not the person I was ten years ago. I'm not insecure or jealous of Kate any more. I'm not overwhelmed. I don't have this great shuddering feeling that at any moment life is about to sweep on past without me.'

'And that's good, isn't it?'

'But where do I fit into the Kate and Martha and David and Sadie matrix?'

'But surely they've changed too? That's what happens in life. People move on. It doesn't necessarily mean you lose them.'

'But that's just it,' she said wistfully. 'I think I might have. Look, I didn't tell you this before because I couldn't bring myself to think about it at first, let alone talk about it, but when I told Kate about the abortion she went mad. We haven't spoken since.'

'I know,' he said gently.

'You do?'

He leaned over and kissed her neck. 'Surely you've learned by now that I always research my parts thoroughly.'

'Mmm,' she mumbled, rolling on to her stomach so that he could put some suncream on her back. 'And they are such big parts. But why didn't you say anything?'

'Because I could see it was something that had to work its way through your many complex thought processes first.'

'You are amazing,' she said, sitting up and stroking his face. 'Most people would have felt desperately insecure that their partner was harbouring a Deep Dark Secret.'

'I just happen to think it isn't always necessarily good to talk. At least not till you're sure what you want to talk about. And are you?'

'I think so. I think what I'd really like is to see Kate,' she said in a small voice.

'Let's invite her out here,' he suggested.

'Just like that?'

'Why not?'

'Because for the past two months she hasn't answered a single one of my letters or returned any of my calls I think she's been making a voodoo doll of me.'

'Don't worry, she's probably sold it as a key-ring accessory by now. Anyway, ask her whether she'd like to be a matron of honour.'

'Excuse me?'

'Marry me. Please.'

'I'd love to.' She bent over and kissed him lightly on the lips. 'But unless I'm mistaken, you're still married to Phoebe.'

Nick sat up suddenly. 'Oh my God, I'd genuinely forgotten ... Well, that's soon rectified.'

Martha raised one eyebrow sceptically. 'I'll be here. Though I can't guarantee Kate will.'

'Ask her.'

'I will.'

'Good. One more thing.'

'Yes?'

'Meet me on the hammock in fifteen minutes.'

✳   ✳   ✳

It couldn't go on like this, Martha thought, as she sipped her glass of wine in the moonlight, and watched through the ivy curtain as Nick swam up and down the floodlit pool, making ghostly little effervescent ripples. It was too perfect. They would get bored. Or he would. But they had talked about that. Nick was more of a realist than she would ever have imagined.

'If we do tire of lotus-eating – and it is an if,' he had said early on after one of their extended hammock sessions, their bodies still gleaming with sweat, 'we'll go back to California, somewhere near San Francisco. We can both work there – and at the same time we'll be just as distanced from the grotty bits of real life as we are here.' She had looked sceptical that time too. 'It's true, my darling – you'd be amazed how money can cocoon you, provided you know where to go.'

Martha did write to Kate. She tried to call her too. But Kate had become almost impossible to track down.

'She's travelling all the time,' explained Sky apologetically, when, for the umpteenth time, Martha got her instead of Kate. 'It'll get better soon,' she said encouragingly. 'The opening's soon – the pressure of all that has been driving her mad, as I'm sure you know. Things are bound to calm down after that.'

Martha was too embarrassed to ask what opening that might be.

'Gosh, this is amazing,' cooed Tatty, bounding up to Kate and Ambrose, who were standing beneath an atrium in Cocoon that appeared to be constructed from a single sheet of glass. Kate had just finished explaining at great length via a satellite link-up to Little Bo Peep why Jake had decided they had no option but to rip out the original walnut panelling that ran across the back wall and install a neon pink expanse of cascading water, and why nothing in the hotel quite matched up to her e-mail descriptions.

Tatty was pretty amazing too, thought Kate, introducing her to Ambrose. She hadn't seen her since her marriage to Mark Lacy. In fact it was touch and go as to which was the bigger transformation – the hotel or Tatty, who was clad head to toe in black Gucci leather. Her fluffy pompadour had been superseded by a sleek John Frieda layered cut. The go-faster blond highlights had been replaced with a subtle vegetable dye. She looked expensive and sleek – and a good stone and a half lighter. And she had two gorgeous healthy babies.

'And I do think it was brilliant of her to call it Cocoon and not The Cocoon,' continued Tatty, nibbling on a carrot shaped like a flower which was garnishing her cocktail. 'It's so much more modern-sounding without the positive article, isn't it?'

'Definite article,' Ambrose corrected her absent-mindedly. 'Yes, it is, isn't it?' He beamed, sipped on his Sea Breeze and looked over at Kate proudly. Slightly flushed from her virtual encounter with Bo, she looked radiant in a periwinkle silk cheongsam she had picked up in Chinatown in New York, and which she had popped over some gold silk sari-style trousers from Georgina von Etzdorf and a pair of embroidered Emma Hope mules. This was how he liked to see her best – animated, slightly winded and completely absorbed in her work. If only she could stop brooding about not having children and realize that it didn't alter his love for her one iota.

'How nice to meet you at last, Tatty.' He smiled down at her slightly moist, flushed cheeks. 'I've heard so much about you.'

'Oh, gosh, have you?' said Tatty, turning scarlet with pleasure. 'Oh well, I don't get out much these days. Two babies in nineteen months, you know. Mark can't get over how organized I am in my professional life and how hopelessly disorganized I am when it comes to getting pregnant. I just keep forgetting to take the pill. Still, it's probably all subliminal ...' She trailed off awkwardly, fanning herself with her Fendi baguette. 'Gosh, is that Sharon Weiner over there talking to George Michael? I'm amazed he's got the balls to show up anywhere these days.'

'Sharon certainly seems to be enjoying his company,' said Ambrose. 'And over there,' he went on, wheeling Tatty round, 'that's Henry Kissinger chatting to Liz Hurley. And that's Peter Mandelson about to throw his drink over Donna Ducatti. It'll probably make front-page news. Kate tells me hotel lobbies have become the literary salons of our time and I think she's probably right.'

'Oh, I'm sure she's right. In fact Mark and I are in the process of launching a chain of internet café franchises inside hotel lobbies. That's where Mark is. In New York. Signing on the dotted line as I speak probably. I brought Mummy along instead. And she brought along Daddy and my little brother Freddie. Not so little now. It's his first proper London outing. I'd better go and find them.'

Ambrose looked at her admiringly. 'You're quite a business dynamo, aren't you, Tatty?'

'Oh, it's not just me,' said Tattie shyly. 'Mark's a natural. He just needed some confidence.'

Sadie floated over, a vision in purple Missoni, and kissed Ambrose on the cheek as a waiter sped past with a plate of marinated seafood. 'I am *sooo* proud of Kate. And Dan. He was the food consultant,' she said, turning to Tatty. 'Good heavens,' she exclaimed, craning her neck as a storm of flashbulbs went off. 'Is that Cressida? My goodness, she's grown.'

Cressida had indeed put on about six inches, thanks to the pair of emerald patent bondage-y stilettos that Scorcher had bought her that morning, along with a plunging sliver of iridescent chain mail that purported to be a dress.

'Blimey,' Scorcher had gulped admiringly, when she stepped out of the changing room and began twizzling in front of him. 'Careful or everything'll pop out.'

'Hardly,' purred Cressida, nuzzling up as close to him as her volcanic breasts, which were standing to attention thanks to the cold metal, would allow. 'This dress is harder to get out of than Colditz, which, incidentally, is an apt description of my boobs. They're going to need some serious warming up later on. We ought to rechristen ourselves Pinky and Perky,' she said, eyeing up his fuchsia leather jacket and tweaking his groin gently.

'Well, you do look amazing, I grant you,' he said appreciatively. 'So we'll get it. But tonight I think you should wear something a bit more sedate. What about that little Audrey Hepburn dress over there?'

'Oh, please, Scorchie,' she wheedled, twirling the dark curls on his chest in a way that he found almost irresistible. Eight months of winning all the local gymkhanas had done such wonders for Cressida's confidence – not to mention her physique – that she had completely forgotten how much in awe of her father she was.

'If we're going to go, we might as well make an entrance. Everyone else will be dolled up to the nines. Come on, it is our first night out together in public – you don't want people to think you're embarrassed.'

Sure enough, the paparazzi, lurking in every nook of Cocoon, went berserk when they arrived. Since the release of the *Jailbait* album, Scorcher was firmly back on the A-list – all the more so since he so rarely stepped out of Meadowlands, except to the local pub. To catch him on his first outing with what looked like real live jailbait ... suffice to say that his record company couldn't have stage-managed things better themselves.

Lady Nancy Higginbottom, who had been fingering the silk organza blinds in the lobby and declaring them a rayon-polyester mix to all and sundry, 'just like my ones in the downstairs lav at home', was practically trampled to the ground in the rush to photograph Cressida's cleavage.

'My God, what a heavenly pair,' said Bunty Leigh to no one in particular. 'She looks just like a mermaid.'

'I really don't know where they drag some of these people in from,' grumbled Lady Nancy, as Liam Gallagher's cigarette bore a hole into her peach satin wrap. In his hurry to escape her – he thought he had spotted Catherine Zeta Jones arriving – Sir Bernie chucked the remnants of his Bloody Mary over her and bundled her towards the ladies' cloakroom, where a very drunk Lachlan O'Hennessy was ill advisedly giving a reading of his new version of "Moby's Dick".'

'Disgusting,' said Lady Nancy, slapping him across the face and sending him careening into Ruby and Eliza as they emerged from one of the cubicles. She then sailed into the throbbing waves of the party, navigating herself unflinchingly towards the centre, where she brusquely extricated Freddie, who was wearing an *I've Been Prioried* T-shirt, from Elle MacPherson's cleavage.

Cressida surfed through the crowd on Scorcher's arm like a beautiful shimmering nymph, ignoring Marcus's frantic gestures for her to come and be filmed by him. Radiating togetherness at the flashbulbs, they made their way over to the bar, which looked as though it had been constructed from a curved aquarium, with barracuda swimming frantically back and forth through purple inky water. Ambrose, now on his fourth Sea Breeze and basking in the adulation of the theatre critics from the *Guardian* and the *International Gazette*, blinked at the aqueous apparition in front of him and failed completely to recognize his daughter.

'Hello, Dad,' said Cressida insouciantly, the fish-tail train of her dress slithering over the shoes of the critics, who parted like the Red Sea to allow her past.

Ambrose was speechless. 'Blossomed a bit, hasn't she, Ambrose?' said Scorcher sheepishly from behind Cressida, the feathers and beads in his black thatch jiggling around like demented parrots.

'I think she looks like something from the end of the pier,' said Lady Nancy to Bunty Leigh, whom she mistook for a waiter. 'Or is she one of those dreadful Spice Gels?'

'I'd happily allow her to be the end of this peer,' muttered Sir Bernie.

'Darling,' said Bunty, seizing on Ruby, who had just emerged from the loos and looked hot and sticky but ravishing, in a dishevelled Ruby sort of way. Her red PVC miniskirt was so short it barely covered her suspenders, and he noticed she was wearing fishnets and what he believed were popularly referred to as fuck-me shoes. He beamed at her delightedly. Fastidious in every other area of life to the point of obsessiveness, he adored lack of subtlety when it came to a woman's dress sense. 'Haven't seen you for ages. What happened to that Bollywood article you were going to come and plug on my show?'

'Oh, that,' said Ruby vaguely, grabbing a magenta cocktail from a passing waiter and downing it in one. 'The thing is, I've more or less given up journalism. It's a mug's game. And talk about ageist and sexist. I'm playing the stock market instead. D'you want to see my new gizmo?'

'What an offer,' said Bunty, picking at a wasabi-covered prawn.

Ruby fished into her Vivienne Westwood black bustier and pulled out a little plastic pager. 'See, it tells me at any time of the day or night what's happening on the Nasdaq. I keep it on my pillow. I'm obsessed.'

'Your lover must be thrilled,' said Bunty dryly.

'Funny you should mention it, Bunty,' said Ruby, grabbing another cocktail, 'but actually she is. I think she finds the bleeps erotic. Either that or she's relieved that I'm finally making some money. Anyway, who cares? It's pepped up our sex life no end. Mmm, fantastic food,' she trilled, helping herself to a piece of scampi. 'This place is going to make a fortune. Who's the bloke helping her with the food?'

'Dan Hammond,' said Bunty. 'He's on my show next week. Apparently he's all the rage. Does any party worthy of the name these days. Also a friend of Kate and Ambrose, though I dare say it would be too much to

ask that a man that good-looking be available to the
likes of me?'

'Fraid so,' said Ruby, licking the remains of some
lobster bisque that had dribbled out from a won ton
parcel on to her forearm. 'He's more or less married to
Kate Crawford's mum.'

'*Tant pis*,' said Bunty, suddenly feeling frisky at the
sight of Ruby's pink tongue. 'Good God, woman, you're
practically enough to turn me straight.'

'Darling Bunty, you say the sweetest things. The problem is, as I've already intimated, it wouldn't do you
any good even if you were. Oh my God, what's that
disgusting smell?'

'I think it's what you quaintly refer to as your skirt,
though to me it looks more like a cummerbund. Wore one
quite similar once when I danced with Princess Margaret at
the Twenty-One Club. I think it's melting.'

Sure enough, the red PVC was slowly combusting down
Ruby's fishnets, leaving little droplets of simulated blood on
her legs. The skirt had done the impossible and morphed to
half its size.

'You do look dramatic,' said Bunty urbanely.

'I thought it was a bit warm,' Ruby grumbled. 'You
might have told me I was practically standing in the fire.'

'Darling, I thought they were *trompe l'oeils*. That's the
trouble with architecture these days. One can never tell
what anything is. I spent half an hour admiring some
modern art on the pavement outside before I realized it
was a dog turd.'

'And I'll tell you another thing,' said Lady Nancy later
to Ruby when she had cornered her in the ladies' room
while Ruby was hosing down her fishnets, 'that Gwyneth

Paltrow is not a natural blonde. Quite frankly, I fail to see what's so special about her — my Tatty's much prettier.'

'. . . and then the bloody sea failed to part,' chortled Bunty Leigh to Sir Harold Pinter, in full flow over one of his elaborate luvvie anecdotes. 'Special effects all up the spout, you see. In fact the only thing that did part on that set as I recall were the leading lady's legs—'

'Well, really,' harrumphed Sadie to David as Ruby teetered past, her crimson lipstick beginning to run away from her mouth. 'You'd think she could have made more of an effort to get dressed for Kate's special day.'

David winced as Ruby disappeared into the crowd. 'Oh, sorry, darling,' said Sadie sympathetically. 'I forgot she was a bit of a sore point with you.' She squeezed his arm affectionately and smiled. It was amazing how warmly disposed to him she was since his extremely generous divorce settlement. And when all was said and done, she thought, surveying him slyly adjusting his orange-and-emerald Hermès tie as he went to fetch them both another drink, he was still a very attractive man. And best of all, she could honestly say she wasn't in love with him one little bit. 'Oh, David, aren't you proud of our girls?' she asked when he returned with two glasses of Kir Royale.

'Yes, I am,' he said, sounding surprised.

'You say that as if it never occurred to you before.'

'D'you know, I don't think it has. They were so busy being truculent and emotional and not turning out exactly as we'd planned—'

'*You'd* planned,' corrected Sadie, conveniently forgetting the *grands projects* she'd mapped out for her daughters.

'—just being their own people, I suppose,' he continued thoughtfully, 'that by the time they'd got on the paths they wanted to be on, I'd got out of the habit of approving or disapproving or feeling proud or any of those things a parent ought inherently to feel.'

'Have you been feeling very unhappy, David?' she asked gently.

'Not very,' he said honestly. 'But at least I have been *feeling*. I think for too many years in our marriage I didn't feel things keenly enough. You were such a wonderful wife and mother and you made the whole family thing function so seamlessly that somewhere along the way I stopped remembering to contribute. I suppose I just got more and more wrapped up in the firm and in politics and in self-advancement and vanity. At least the last few years have made me take a cool long look at the way I want to live the rest of my life.'

Over in Holland Park, Phoebe's bedroom looked as though a squall had struck. The floor was a seething ocean of lace camisoles, satin slip dresses and sequinned sheaths, with the occasional shark's fin of a stiletto heel penetrating through the waves. Rolling on a surge of chemically induced emotions, Phoebe was at the mercy of one of her periodic bouts of indecision. It was vital that she strike the right note tonight at this launch thing of Kate's. But what was that? The press had gone rather quiet recently – without any fresh pictures of Martha and Nick to crow over they'd run out of steam, although they still obligingly camped outside Phoebe's house every morning waiting for her to sweep into the lilac limo she had bullied out of Charlie Pitchcock-Up. But she had noticed that her hit rate was slumping. Some mornings she wasn't in any of the newspapers at all. Eliza said it was a good thing. She said Phoebe should play the dignified card now and sit back and wait for the divorce settlement. But she didn't want a settlement. She wanted Nick. And it was hard to play a dignified cast-off. She didn't have the wardrobe, for one thing. Magda had come back from Ghost one day with armfuls of stretchy, floaty dresses, but they had turned out to be see-through – a discovery Phoebe did not make until she saw herself on the front page of the *Daily Express*. She had sulked for three days, refusing to go out, until Magda returned with a Jemima Khan dress instead.

'It took an entire Pakistani village six months to make,' she announced with a satisfied flourish.

'Anyone would think you wove it yourself,' snapped Phoebe, snatching it from Magda before she'd got it out of the bag.

'Well, I stalked it down all by myself, which amounts to the same thing. They're like gold dust.'

Alas, it was at least two sizes too small and refused to stretch over the twins. 'You do this to humiliate me,' said Phoebe, tossing it on the floor.

Pregnancy dressing was wearing her out. Six months pregnant, her tiny frame made her bump look even bigger than it was. She'd been through nearly all the designers now. Gucci didn't have anything in stock above a size ten. Donna Karan didn't seem to go below a size eighteen. In the end she settled on Alberta Ferretti's floaty layers and handfuls of appetite suppressants. She wanted to look ethereal and poignant, and you couldn't do that with flabby arms. At nine-thirty, two and a half hours after Kate's party had started, she stepped out of the house, doused in Fracas and several hundred slivers of burnished dusky grey-coloured dévoré and chiffon, and into Charlie's limo, which had been patiently waiting outside.

'You look fantastic,' gushed Charlie, who had been bullied by Phoebe into escorting her and sending Charlotte on ahead. Barely acknowledging him, she sat in silence for the fifteen-minute drive to the hotel, concentrating on looking ethereal and not disturbing the MAC plum lipstick which coloured her mouth in its porcelain setting like a meteor streaking across a snow-filled sky. It was imperative she get it right. All of London and half of Hollywood were going to be there – she'd heard that Leonardo diCaprio had taken out a twelve-month option on the penthouse suite. She had to make the right impression. To ensure she garnered all the headlines for herself, she had taken the momentous (in press-worthy terms) step of dyeing her silky red hair a dramatic raven.

'Bloody hell.' Marcus almost choked on a spring roll, sending its contents spewing over Cressida's chain mail. The paparazzi had gone completely insane, climbing over each other and half the guests to get to Phoebe. 'And to think she must be thirty-eight,' said Marcus, sounding awed.

'Well, of all the nerve,' chimed Sadie and David in unison.

When she was sure that they had got a sufficient number of flattering ethereal poses, Phoebe made her way towards Kate, her dress rippling around her like mist. Through a fug of deadened sensations, she was only half aware of the commotion she was causing, as a deep-sea diver might be only vaguely conscious of a mine exploding miles across the seabed.

'Kate, my darling,' she whispered tremulously, as the crowd surrounding them fell silent. 'I don't want to steal your night but I couldn't let this momentous occasion pass without marking it. You are a truly gifted woman and I wish you all the happiness and success in the world.' She raised a glass and took a tiny sip before placing it on a passing tray. She turned on her heels. Within twelve minutes of arriving, she was gone.

'What a vision,' trilled Bunty admiringly. 'She looks like Louise Brooks. As for her timing – perfect. Gertie Lawrence couldn't have done it better herself.'

'Putrid, more like,' said Ruby in disgust. 'It makes me sick the way that manipulative little cow screws everyone. And for the record, I liked her better with red hair. Now she looks like Snow White.'

'I've a good mind to slap her,' said Sadie. 'My hand is itching.'

'Not wise,' said David, 'but understandable in the circumstances.'

'She is mind-bogglingly brazen,' agreed Ambrose, scribbling something on his Sainsbury's pad. 'She's almost a case study.'

'Well, I think it was very brave of her,' said Kate suddenly.

'Kate,' they all chorused in unison.

'Well, it's true. I'm sorry. I know everyone here thinks Martha is a saint, but I happen to believe there are always two sides to every story. And I'm sorry if that breaks up everyone's cosy little image of our great reunited family. At least she came.'

And with that, she stalked off into the swirl, trailed by Bunty and half a dozen Japanese film crews.

*　　*　　*

Even if the presence of so many film stars, writers and artists hadn't been enough, Phoebe's contentious appearance at Cocoon's opening party ensured it made the front pages of every newspaper.

'Pity there aren't any pictures of Kate, apart from in the *Indie*. Still, it does sound like an amazing success,' said Martha wistfully from the hammock. Normally she and Nick didn't take the British papers, but Luke had buzzed over that morning with a pile of them. 'I couldn't decide whether you'd be more upset at seeing the Phoebe coverage or missing out on Kate's big moment,' he said awkwardly. 'So I checked through it all and actually the stuff about Phoebe seems to have calmed down – not that I've been following it, but this seems pretty muted. Just stuff about her looking a bit on the thin side. You can't win. They said she'd put on too much at the beginning.' Luke blushed. 'Pity you couldn't be there.'

'Pity we weren't invited,' said Nick.

'Yes, we were,' said Martha defensively. 'Ambrose asked us.'

'Not the same.'

'Well, she probably didn't think we'd come.'

'Why?'

''Cos we never go anywhere,' giggled Martha. Later in the afternoon she grew quiet. 'I do miss her, you know,' she said softly. 'Do you mind?'

'How could I? It would be strange if you didn't. I've got my whole family around me. It's about time you redressed the balance. Go on – invite her out. Maybe she'll even drag Ambrose along. It's about time we allowed some of the outside world in.'

She looked at his sunburned face. The dark hair, which

she had almost grown used to, had finally begun to fade in the bleaching South African sun and flopped in his sea-green eyes. She always used to think he looked so much younger than she felt, but now they seemed to have caught up with one another. History had given them a shared past and future. She loved him and, at that unMartha-ish moment, she knew suddenly that she always would.

Phoebe opened the door to be confronted with a bunch of roses and lilies the dimensions of a medium-sized rainforest. From behind the thickets Kate's voice emerged, muffled. 'I just wanted to thank you for being so supportive the other night. It really meant a lot to me,' she said, brushing aside a frond of ivy that had got tangled in her hair. 'I mean, I know things are a bit strained, to say the least, between you and Martha, but I don't want you to think that has anything to do with—'

'Come in,' said Phoebe, wrapping her jade-coloured silk kimono around her milky breasts, which had been peeping out from its folds. 'How lovely to see you.' She yawned and ran her dark fingernails through her unusually dishevelled bob. It was midday but clearly she had just woken. Kate felt slightly embarrassed. Barefoot, Phoebe led her across the flagstoned hallway and into the ballroom-sized drawing room, still shuttered from the night before.

'Drink?' she asked, pouring herself a tumbler of orange juice. She glanced at the carriage clock on the mantelpiece. 'Oh my God – look at the time. I didn't get to sleep until God knows when – terrible backache.' She shifted uneasily in the deep purple velvet armchair she and Kate had bought together on one of their shopping trips in New

York. Plus I had all this research to do. I'm interviewing Monica Lewinsky next week and you wouldn't believe all the reading I've got to do. You will stay for lunch?'

Over a minute salad, Phoebe chatted animatedly, as if they had only seen each other the day before. Her old perceptiveness and charm were as effective as ever. By the time she had eked out what was left of a bag of coffee into two cups, Kate had told her just about everything. Phoebe, she realized, as she made her way home feeling strangely deceitful, had given very little of herself away.

She decided not to tell Ambrose that she had seen Phoebe. But they began meeting regularly. They would have lunch in Orsino's; once or twice Phoebe even cajoled Kate into taking a yoga class with her. They went for manicures and pedicures. Phoebe would regale her with gossip about the guests on her shows, and laugh at all Kate's stories about Little Bo Peep. It was a strange spring, full of secret assignations and funny, frivolous outings of the kind Kate had never really indulged in before. She designed and orchestrated the decoration of a nursery for the twins. And Phoebe presented her with an exquisite emerald bracelet — very rare, Georgian — which she'd had inscribed, *To my darling Kate. Friends for ever.*

'Don't you ever want children?' Phoebe asked her idly one day when they were lying on Phoebe's four-poster. 'You have such an eye for children's things. You can't tell me you don't have maternal urges.'

Normally enquiries along these lines made Kate run a mile, but she found herself opening up to Phoebe and telling her just how much she longed for a baby, how she'd even asked Martha to assist her, and how her own sister, because of a careless abortion, had been utterly unable to help.

Sometimes the exchanged confidentialities were almost too intimate. When Phoebe casually mentioned one evening over supper on Phoebe's bed that she used to make ends meet when she and Nick had both been struggling in the early days by visiting rich men in their hotel rooms, Kate had been shocked into silence. But then Phoebe had giggled, kissed her lightly on the nose and teased her gently about her prudishness, until Kate began to wonder whether she wasn't as hopelessly old-fashioned as Phoebe said she was. Months later, when she looked back on those warm, late spring weeks, she realized it was almost as if she had been having a clandestine affair. Their friendship had become so intense that it seemed perfectly natural that, just as they laughed a lot, she should find herself weeping that night as they lay on Phoebe's four-poster, just as she and Martha used to snuggle under the eiderdown on her mother's big bed at home in Tithe House. That was the night when Phoebe made her promise to Kate. And it was the night when Kate realized she would do anything for Phoebe.

Chapter Twenty

————◦◦◦◦————

Despite having bought most of Waterstone's stock on the subject over the years, Kate had never got beyond the pregnancy chapters, and consequently knew next to nothing about childbirth. But she was fairly sure that La Perla underwear wasn't recommended for the actual labour in any existing book.

'Well, it's going to be a hot tip in my book,' said Phoebe, dabbing at her moist face with a huge Parma violet powder puff Kate had bought her in Space NK. The summer sunshine was streaming through the hospital windows and the heating was turned up full blast as usual. 'Not to mention a hot tit,' she added sourly, lighting a cigarette. Her continued smoking had shocked Kate but Phoebe said that Dr Michaels, her obstetrician, thought it was better for her stress levels that she carry on.

'It says here I'm going to need copious amounts of cabbage leaves to help the swelling in my boobs after they're born. Talk about vegging out.' She tossed Miriam Stoppard's birthing book on to the growing pile by the bed in disgust. She was suffering from terrible indigestion, which, she claimed, prevented her from eating.

'That would be the baby pressing against the alimentary canal,' said Kate uncertainly, trying to sound knowledgeable because she knew it calmed Phoebe.

'Alimentary, my dear Watson,' said Phoebe, grimacing. Her research into labour had begun and ended with a few hammy Hollywood films in which the heroines twisted and writhed in agony as they lashed against brass bedposts. This strange lull, now that she had been given an epidural, was proving a bit of an anticlimax.

'Well, well, well . . . Nelson Mandela's getting married again. Keep up the good work, Nel — and keeping it up is what will be required, believe me . . .'

'Oh, for God's sake turn her off,' snapped Phoebe. Kate obligingly extinguished Donna and smiled patiently. The mountains of hi-tech equipment around her — and Kate's twenty-four-hour presence — were supposed to be making Phoebe feel much calmer. But it didn't seem to be working. Phoebe was in hyper mode. Kate had turned down the lights and lit one of Dan's honey-and-ginseng candles and the room was bathed in a shimmering light and a deliciously soothing scent.

'I'm serious,' Phoebe said, as Kate adjusted the straps on her eau-de-Nil nightie so that she could massage in some of Sadie's rosemary hand cream, which apparently did wonders for stretch marks. 'Vickers & Snood have asked me to write a practical, humorous manual on the subject. You know the sort of thing — lots of jolly bons mots and the occasional picture of me with my tits hanging out. They're offering oodles of dosh and, since I can probably write it in about ten minutes, I'm rather tempted. But actually the La Perla's for *Hello!* They're coming in at six to do the whole story — *moi avec* smiling infants.'

'But Phoebe, how do you know the twins will be here by then?'

Phoebe looked at the little antique diamond evening watch Nick had given her and which she never took off. It was eleven in the morning. 'They'd better be. I've booked Magda and a make-up artist to come in at five. I hope she remembers to bring concealer. Do you think the babies will need a spot of Touche Eclat? I've heard they can look revoltingly blotchy to begin with.'

Kate looked at her wryly. Becoming Phoebe's confidante had been a gut-wrenchingly mixed experience during the past few sensitive months. It ought to have been depressing — heaven knew, Phoebe had problems. But being in the glare of Phoebe's friendship was, as Kate had discovered, like being in the full heat of the sun — exhilarating and intoxicating. She never wanted the sun to go in and consequently she took her role as Phoebe's New Best Friend very seriously. Since that night on the four-poster, when Phoebe had promised that she would make her godmother to the twins, and their legal guardian if anything were to happen to her, Kate had thrown herself into a vicarious state of pregnancy which would have alarmed Ambrose if he'd only been around to see it, instead of taking himself off to Alaska to do some more research on Detmar Hibsen.

Sometimes Kate suspected she was far more involved in the whole process than Phoebe, who frequently behaved as though she'd forgotten she was about to give birth to two tiny humans. 'Phoebe, did you actually *read* any of those books I gave you? The twins might not be here for days.'

'You are not serious?' exclaimed Phoebe in horror.

'It's all in the books,' said Kate. Ever since Phoebe had asked her to be her birthing partner, Kate had taken her role very seriously. She had more or less put work on hold – much to Sky's joy and Little Bo Peep's utter consternation – and had spent days packing and repacking vast hampers and suitcases with anything and everything she thought might be required for the long sojourn in hospital. She ran around like a slave trying to please Phoebe, who occasionally remembered to thank her.

'Oh, those,' pouted Phoebe. 'They make me nauseous. All those pendulous bosoms and industrial-sized stretch marks. Haven't any of those publishers heard of retouching?'

'Anyone would think you were frivolous.'

'Any chance of some more champagne?' asked Phoebe weakly from the depths of her pillows.

Kate fished out another bottle from the hamper. They were getting through the stuff rather faster than she had anticipated. At this rate they'd have to toast the babies' arrival with Estée Lauder's Night Repair.

'It is nice having you here,' said Phoebe, applying some Clarins Beauty Flash Balm to the circles under her eyes.

'How could I not be here for the arrival of my god-children?' said Kate fondly, stroking Phoebe's arm. Phoebe leaned back against a skyscape of Harrods goosedown-and-feather pillows that she had sent Kate out to get and visibly relaxed.

'It's not that bad really, I must say, this labour business,' she said, swigging back the champagne.

'Well, the nurse did say you weren't very dilated,' said Kate cautiously.

'Well, I wasn't very delighted with her. Honestly, the bloody fuss she made about not wanting the anaesthetist to give me an epidural yet, when it was obvious I was in agony.'

'Strictly speaking you're not supposed to have one till you're at least five centimetres dilated ...'

'Frankly, the way these hospitals try and interfere is sick,' continued Phoebe, obliviously. 'Anyway, now I've had her removed, we should be able to get through this entire thing without further interference. Then you can nip out and get one of those dishy doctors to snip the cords at the end.'

Kate eyed her warily. The effects of the epidural would wear off soon and, thanks to Phoebe's summary dismissal of Nurse Grossman and all other hospital staff, they'd be in big trouble. 'Don't worry,' said Phoebe, 'I have an enormously high pain threshold. On the set of *Toulouse* I had to have every centimetre of my body waxed, pubes included, and I didn't even wince. The director said I was a freak of nature and that if there were an Oscar for best all-over depilation, I'd win it. Ohmigod!' She clutched at Kate's patchwork pashmina.

'What is it? What's the matter?' asked Kate anxiously.

'A fucking pain in the groin, that's what.' Phoebe gripped Kate's throat for what seemed like minutes before releasing her, panting.

'How long did you say this could go on?' she gasped eventually.

'Quite a time—'

Phoebe began to sob hysterically, in between heaving herself off the bed, staggering to the door and yelling into the corridor for someone to come and administer some more drugs as soon as possible. Exhausted, she crawled back to the bed, tears streaking her make-up. Her neat crimson lips twisted in pain as another contraction seized her. She looked at Kate piteously. 'I'm frightened,' she whispered.

Kate held her hand tightly and kissed her damp forehead. 'You're going to be just fine,' she soothed. 'All of you.'

'I'm going to call the girl after you,' said Phoebe, when the contraction had subsided. 'Or Caitlin, at least. To avoid confusion.'

Kate turned pink with pleasure.

'It was Nick's favourite name.' Phoebe writhed again as another contraction engulfed her in a vicelike wave.

'She's not going to make this easy for us,' Nick said to Martha gently as he padded up to her in the kitchen, where she had disappeared to rustle up a five-course banquet for supper. His parents were coming over for supper and she'd got up at the crack of dawn with Anthony to go to the market and find some fresh lobster, thyme and garlic.

By five o'clock in the evening, however, she'd got as far as crushing the garlic and basil in her pestle and mortar so violently that Nick had told her to stop. Trying to relax, she allowed herself to be distracted by the recent issue of *Hello!* which had found its way into Rose Cottage, complete with half a dozen lavish spreads of Phoebe, the twins and — most woundingly of all — Kate, in the Portland Hospital. Guiltily, she tried to slip it under a tea towel.

He saw her doing it, and grasped her wrist. 'I didn't think even Phoebe would succumb to this. She's obviously died and gone to *Hello!*'

'They're lovely-looking babies,' Martha said.

He tilted her chin up towards his until her dark eyes had

no choice but to meet the piercing gaze of his azure ones. The black dye he'd needed to play Keats was finally starting to grow out and he looked less hauntingly consumptive, almost like the old Nick. 'I'll take your word for it. They're not mine, Martha. I hope you believe me.'

'Of course I do. You don't even need to say it.' She tried to look away but he was holding her face too tightly. It was true – she did trust him. Implicitly. Yet there were too many loose ends. Of course the twins weren't Nick's – but why did Phoebe insist so publicly that they were, unless she had some grounds for believing it? Why wouldn't Nick talk about it – even with his lawyers? And those words of Kate's, '*you must love him to overlook everything he's done*', no doubt uttered in anger and frustration, had repeatedly come back to haunt her. Since the news of the twins' birth had reached Rose Cottage this was the first time the subject had been raised. Neither of them had dared acknowledge that they even knew the babies had arrived.

Outwardly, Nick and Martha were more settled than ever. Their life in South Africa had moved into a different phase, from indolent pleasure-seeking to a more regulated, but no less pleasurable, sense of placid industriousness. Nick was becoming more and more involved in the early stages of Ambrose's script for the Detmar Hibsen biopic and had started to do some serious research in Cape Town's main libraries.

Martha, meanwhile, had discovered the unexpected joys of keeping house. She had reorganised the utility room so that it worked just like Sadie's and there was a constant supply of lavender-scented linen and big white fluffy towels. She had opened up the shuttered-off rooms in the rest of the cottage, polished floors until the house was steeped in beeswax, dusted, tidied and painted until the place looked like something out of *Domus*.

After that first night in Cape Town they hadn't discussed the situation with Phoebe. The more they avoided the subject, the more taboo it became. Nick's family, sensing this unexploded landmine in their midst, sensitively tiptoed round the issue – not easy when you were touching six feet five. It all made things ten times worse, in Martha's view, as she was longing to get things out in the open. It was the only time she had ever known Nick not confront something head on.

'I do believe you. Of course I do, Nick,' she said now. 'I love you and so I believe what you tell me. But ... it's hard when you refuse to discuss anything.' She regretted it as soon as she'd said it. It sounded so much like a reproach, and she'd always vowed she would never reproach him with anything.

'There's nothing left to say,' he said bitterly, thrusting her away. She went to the sink and began washing her hands perfunctorily. 'It's in the hands of the lawyers, who seem to think that provided I make Phoebe a generous enough settlement, she'll back off sooner or later.'

'I see,' said Martha quietly, wiping her hands on her apron and getting out a chopping board.

'And just so you don't accuse me of keeping any other secrets from you,' he said gruffly, 'they're talking ball-park figures of around ten million.'

'I-I didn't know you were worth that much. I'd have zoomed in on you a lot sooner,' she tried to joke.

'I'm not. Nothing like. Art-house movies and the Almeida don't exactly set my bank manager on fire.' It was true. His fee for *Green Cover*, his first American blockbuster, had been relatively low, especially once Gloria had taken her cut. Nick was comfortably off, but he and Phoebe had always lived just beyond his means and he had been shocked, although not aghast, money never having been an overriding motive with him, to learn that until the profits from *Explorer* – the Detmar Hibsen project and first film where he'd get a cut of the box-office takings – rolled in, he would be quite a bit in debt.

'But you know what the press are like,' he continued wryly. 'And lawyers. They think anyone famous must be worth a bomb.' He sounded wearier than he had since they'd arrived. He must have been spending more time with the lawyers than she knew. 'Frankly I'd give her the whole lot right now just to get her off my back. It's what she wants, after all.'

'Mightn't it help if you had a blood test?' Martha suggested tentatively, fixing him the perfect Bloody Mary.

'You sound just like the lawyers.' He sat down heavily, toying with one of Martha's cheese straws.

'Well, I'm sorry,' she said, hurt. 'I just want to help. I have a vested interest in getting this sorted out too, you know. I love you.'

'I know. I'm sorry. It's just that it's all so sordid. I was hoping it wouldn't come to this. She's so deluded she probably thinks I am the father. Forcing blood tests on everyone would destroy her.'

Martha's eyes raked him up and down like search-lights.

'Frankly I'd happily give her everything if it meant making a clean slate of it all,' he continued, fiddling with the pestle. 'That's why I haven't been talking about it. I just want to put everything behind us.'

She trusted him. Of course she did. But this was like stepping into a hall of mirrors. Unmaterialistic as Martha fundamentally was, even she couldn't understand why Nick would willingly hand over everything he had to someone who was clearly trying to destroy him.

'She had a pretty shitty childhood,' he said slowly, willing himself to see how far he could open up to Martha. 'She was brought up – and I use the term loosely – by her older brother and her father in a tower block in Wolverhampton. Her dad was an alcoholic and a compulsive gambler who stayed out more than he came home and liked to beat up his kids for entertainment. Phoebe walked out about ten years after her mother. How she got the money to get into drama school isn't too hard to guess. But I admired her more than I can say for doing it. I never probed too deeply. I know it all seems very dark and mysterious. She used to go and see her mum sometimes, I know that – in the early days, I mean. To try and stage some kind of reconciliation. But then the visits petered out, although she stayed close to the brother. She never talked about it. There's a lot I don't know myself – and that's quite odd in itself, I admit. But Phoebe's somebody who needs her little pockets of fantasy. That's probably why she wanted to be an actress. She and I had a pact from the start that there would be areas of our lives which would be fenced off.' He gave a dry little laugh. 'I just never realized quite how much of hers would be.' He stood up and began laying the table mechanically. The subject was clearly closed.

'It's all right,' Martha said gently, handing him the Bloody Mary. 'Now, if you don't mind, I've got a meal to cook.' Gingerly she lowered the lobster into the boiling water and waited for it to stop squealing. Nick wandered on to the veranda with his Bloody Mary and gazed across at the lowering sun. Things would be fine. He'd find the money to pay Phoebe — as much as she wanted. Marty Shicker said *Endymion* was going to be huge, and the previews in America suggested he might be right. He'd marry Martha. They'd get a normal life back one day. Whatever normal was when you lived in a fame bubble.

He clung to the thought — constantly repeated by his family — that, despite the tensions of the last few weeks and the constant visits to the lawyers, he was happier than any of them could ever remember him being. He'd fallen in love all over again — twice, with Martha and with Cape Town. It felt like home. Martha seemed to like it too. Everything would turn out fine.

But of course it wasn't all right at all.

Phoebe got her figure back and returned to the studios in White City in record time. Four weeks, to be precise. It seemed a little fast to Kate, and she couldn't help thinking it was a shame that Phoebe hadn't allowed herself more time to get to know the babies. She felt certain that if Phoebe only spent more time with them she would gain more confidence and wouldn't feel the need for round-the-clock maternity nurses. In addition to Caroline, the Norland nanny they had interviewed together, and who had started while Phoebe was still in hospital, she had employed Sarah, an Australian ex-teacher who was in London for two years, to provide twenty-four-hour cover at weekends.

Kate wasn't entirely won over by Sarah. She found her by turns shifty and sullen. She had personally checked Caroline's references, which were excellent. But when she offered to verify Sarah's, Phoebe became evasive and said she'd do it, even though a few days earlier she'd made heavy weather of how busy she was at work. Kate didn't say anything, sensitive that at any moment she could be accused of interfering.

She had to admit that Sarah, with her long honey-coloured hair and petite honey-coloured body, was easy on the eye – and Phoebe was certainly susceptible to a graceful appendage or two. So was Marcus, who had popped round once to Holland Park to pick up a parcel from Kate for one of his girlfriends and had been unable to tear his eyes from Sarah's small, pert breasts. So difficult did he find it that he made numerous bogus excuses after that to come round and see Kate there. And, as always, he was armed with his camcorder. Sarah, of course, encouraged him shamelessly, especially when he told her he was off to film school at any minute. Kate was almost relieved when it was time to bundle him off to Capri.

It seemed strange to Kate that any nanny should forget to cover up food in the fridge, or that she would be quite so slap-dash when it came to measuring out the quantities of powdered milk for the babies' bottles. But she bit her tongue. She was probably being a nervous beginner. In any case, Kate understood why Phoebe felt the need to work so hard. Charlotte Pitchcock had let slip to her that ratings for *Friday with Phoebe* were falling off slightly.

'Nothing too serious,' said Charlotte, trying to prevent Alyssia from smearing half a Magnum over a sequinned teapot holder in *What Katy Did Next*. 'But you know what these things are like. Ever since the DG got whiff of the slide he's been giving Charlie hell over it.'

To add to Phoebe's burden there was an impending

paternity case against Nick that had all the makings, according to Ambrose, of being explosive.

'It'll end disastrously for everyone,' he grumbled to Kate from New York one day. 'What's got into the bloody woman, apart from half the men in LA and London? Nick's already said he'll give her practically all he's got. What more does she want, for Christ's sake?'

'For Nick to admit that he's the father,' Kate said. 'The money's almost beside the point as far as she's concerned. She just wants Nick to do the right thing and learn that he can't buy his way out of everything.'

'May the saints preserve us!' spluttered Ambrose. 'Beside the point indeed! That woman's gone for gold more often than an over-achieving Olympic pentathlete. And doesn't she realize that once the lawyers start crawling all over Nick and Phoebe's past, no one will come out of this well. If anything, Phoebe will come off the worst. There's bound to be some murky goings-on in her history – she's got that air – and you know how unforgiving the press can be when they sniff the scent of a fallen woman. It will end in tragedy. You mark my words. If you must spend so much time with her, can't you at least make her see sense?'

But Kate couldn't make Phoebe see much of anything, mainly because she wasn't seeing much of Phoebe at all. She had become so elusive. But the paternity case worried her terribly. And not just because, like Ambrose, she thought it would end in tears all round, but also because she hadn't liked the predatory look in Phoebe's eyes when she had informed Kate that she intended to take Nick to court. She had been sitting in the drawing room in Holland Park having cocktails with someone she had introduced to Kate as Warren Peace, a man with an exceptionally large, bullet-shaped head, who turned out to be the editor of the *Python*.

Warren seemed to be delighted by the prospect of an almighty bust-up. For some reason Phoebe had laid out all the documents in the case for his perusal.

'I've got to hand it to you, Pheebs,' he spluttered excitedly, 'the names you've named and shamed in this are real corkers. We're certainly getting our money's worth. Talk about seeing stars.' He chortled and mopped his dripping brow with one of Phoebe's Hermès silk scarves which he'd mistaken for a napkin. 'Nick will be so pole-axed when he gets served with this little lot he'll be concussed for weeks.' He gulped some more Buck's fizz. 'Well, well, well, who would have thought Nick Wilde had started out as a rent boy? Not that anything surprises me these days,' he added suavely. 'The whole entertainment industry's crawling with hookers and dealers, thank God. Present company excepted, of course.'

'Surely there's been some mistake,' said Kate, sitting down heavily. She couldn't keep the distaste out of her voice, since she didn't believe for one minute that Nick's past was anywhere near as sordid as Warren was implying. She looked at Phoebe. Her face was a perfect blank.

'I couldn't tell you before,' she said. 'You might have thought I was just trying to get back at Martha. But this is serious. Nick has to recognize his own children—' She broke off, moist-eyed. 'I can't believe this is happening. Whatever else Nick has done, I never thought he'd be this cruel.'

Kate sat next to her and put her arms around her. She was clearly distraught. That must be why she was acting so irrationally, so dangerously. The best way out of all this would be to lead her slowly towards reason. And to get rid of the oily Warren, who was practically panting.

'Can you think of any reason why he would be so adamant that the babies aren't his?' said Warren, smiling greasily at Kate. 'I mean, it doesn't seem to be the money — he's offered quite a bit to settle out of court.'

Kate shook her head. Even if she could, she didn't feel like initiating a conversation with Warren.

'It's okay, Kate,' said Phoebe, squeezing her hand. 'You can trust Warren, strange as it may seem.'

'I honestly can't think of any reason,' said Kate, shrugging her shoulders helplessly.

'Well, there was that thing about Martha not being able to have children — because of the abortion.'

Kate shot Phoebe a disbelieving look that was ignored.

'Maybe it's just that Nick doesn't want to hurt her feelings by bringing the added complication of his own children to the relationship. Especially given the remorse you told me Martha felt about her abortion.' Phoebe's voice was as smooth and silky as the scarf now blotched with Warren's sweat.

'Abortion, you say?' said Warren, rubbing his hands together so gleefully they almost created a micro-storm.

'I-I don't think we should be discussing this here,' said Kate, appalled at Phoebe's indiscretion. She must be more ill than they all thought.

'It's all right,' said Warren, suddenly the picture of concern. 'Frankly the more sympathetic a case you can make out for your sister and Nick Wilde the better.' Rather elaborately, he excused himself and went, as he put it, to the little boys' room. While he was gone, Phoebe spoke to Kate feverishly.

'I'm sorry, I'm sorry. I'm up to my neck in all this now. You see, Warren's paper has very sweetly offered to pay for my legal costs. So there's no going back. But honestly, Kate, if you knew half of Nick's faults, you'd want this to happen, however painful it might be. Martha will thank you in the end, and if you talk to Warren about the sadness she's suffered since Bosnia, she's going to emerge smelling of roses. I promise you.'

For years after, Kate would replay the events that unfolded in the smoky heat of Phoebe's lush drawing room that afternoon and ask herself whether she really could have been so naïve as to relay the personal details of Martha's adult life — Martha, who had always been so private and had given very few personal interviews — to a national tabloid, or whether she too had been sufficiently emotionally unhinged that summer to want to do her own sister irretrievable damage. Either way, when she opened the centre spread in Sunday's *Python* entitled 'My Sister's Baby Hell', saw two separate pictures of her and Martha which had been made to look as though they were the torn halves of a single photograph, and read the mawkish copy that somehow managed to be cloyingly sentimental and yet subtly damning of Martha, she knew that, whatever her motives, she had committed the worst betrayal of her life. Her only hope was to pray that neither Martha in South Africa nor Ambrose in New York would see it.

'How could you?' thundered Ambrose from the Stanhope. He was more furious than she had ever heard him.

'I was tricked,' she said lamely. 'Anyway, a lot of people have said they feel much more sympathetic to Martha than they did before.' How dare Ambrose blow up at her as if she were Cressie?

'Don't be bloody ridiculous. No one in their right mind could possibly interpret this as anything other than a character assassination. But of course, Phoebe isn't in her right mind, is she?'

'If you're going to be so horrid,' shouted Kate, feeling absurd, 'then you might as well stay out in New York for the rest of the summer.'

'Fine,' yelled Ambrose so loudly that the maid dropped a vase of flowers on the marble bathroom floor.

'Fine,' said Kate. Not feeling fine at all.

As far as possible she tried to lose herself in the gentle quotidian blur of helping with the twins. Caitlin was a dear little thing, with uncannily grown-up features and the most perfectly formed nose Kate had ever seen on a baby – Phoebe's nose. Finn, on the other hand, had lost more weight than Caitlin and had been slower to regain it. The doctors had put him in an incubator for three days and there had been poignant pictures of all three of them when they finally left hospital five days later. He kept suffering from ear infections. The pictures had been accompanied by the usual anti-Nick vitriol. Linda Lee Potter had written an excoriating piece in the *Daily Mail* castigating renegade fathers and calling for a change in the law. Donna Ducatti, controversial as ever, had delivered a diatribe on-air suggesting that perhaps Phoebe, like many modern women, hadn't done her duty by her man and thus caused him to run away.

Phoebe had been so incensed that she had sent Donna a brace of Caitlin and Finn's nappies by Parcelforce and told a journalist from the *Evening Standard* who rang her up for a nomination for the annual worst dressed list that Donna was a bigger sartorial disaster than William Hague in his baseball cap. After this, all hell had broken loose. Donna was definitely out to get her, which only stirred things up more in the rest of the press. Things were getting very messy; as Warren Peace gleefully remarked in daily conference, his circulation figures were swelling faster than a group of bulimics on a day trip to McDonald's. Meanwhile there was talk at Vickers & Snood that a collaboration between Phoebe and Andrew Morton spilling the beans on life with Nick might be an even bigger seller than her maternity tips. Kate was horrified. And so was Eliza.

'Perhaps you ought to cut down some of your extra-curricular activities,' she suggested one morning as they were going through stage five of their press campaign. 'There is a difference between notoriety and fame, you know.'

Phoebe scowled at her. She didn't know. Consequently pictures of Phoebe hitting the town with the likes of Meg Matthews and Sharon Weiner, who was in London filming, became such common currency that the press were starting to invent stories to justify their continued publication of them. The previous week the *Saturday Telegraph* magazine had run a picture of her sipping champagne from a magnum. Beneath it was a caption suggesting that she turned up at the opening of a cardigan – and that her presence could be guaranteed at the opening of a bottle. Even the *Python* had run a caption with a picture of Phoebe eating seafood at San Lorenzo announcing 'Phoebe's squids in', implying that Phoebe's attempts to get £10 million out of Nick placed her firmly in the gold-digger category.

'What do you mean?' asked Phoebe, wide-eyed. 'Newton-Evis Foods are so impressed with all the coverage they've offered to pay me two hundred and fifty big ones if I agree to be photographed feeding the twins with their baby foods. All my perfectly laid plans are coming to fruition.'

'It's the laid aspect of your history that worries me,' said Eliza waspishly. Phoebe glanced at her sharply. 'And do you need to go to quite so many premières and shop launches?' continued Eliza tartly.

'Oh, please. Just because some old reactionaries on Fleet Street think a mother's place is by the cot with her boobs hanging out. They're disgusting. Do you know, I caught two of them going through my bins the other day? I can barely go to a restaurant now without a gaggle of hacks popping out at me. And half the time there's no story at all. I feel as though I'm suffocating. I think this whole thing might be getting out of hand.' She looked accusingly at Eliza, who was about to point out that Phoebe's dismay might be more convincing if she hadn't put so much energy into tipping the press off in the first place.

'Look, Eliza,' Phoebe continued, 'I'd love to be at home more, but in case you hadn't noticed, I'm a single mother. I've got to bring in the bacon. And that requires me to keep a high but dignified profile which is where you, may I remind you, first came in.'

It was ironic, thought Kate, as she sat in the nursing rocker she had found in an antiques shop in Bath, cradling Caitlin on her lap, that while she had managed to find time at last in her timetable, poor old Phoebe had to work like a slave. And even then, she'd had to let Caroline, the first nanny they'd employed, go, because, she said, she couldn't afford to keep her on.

Kate was sure it was stress which had made Phoebe's milk dry up so quickly. The poor thing had suffered horribly from mastitis and looked so thin and drawn it was a miracle she had any strength left for the twins at all. If only there were something she and Ambrose could do to help. Money was the obvious answer, but of course Phoebe would be far too proud to accept any, even as a loan.

At least the babies were getting plumper, although she wished Phoebe wouldn't give them that stuff from Newton-Evis which Kate didn't trust in the least. She smiled down at Caitlin as she gurgled in her lap. Every so often, the baby would turn her tulip-shaped mouth towards Kate and try to suckle on her breast. Once or twice she ached so much that she was on the verge of undoing her shirt and letting her suck, but somehow they were always interrupted by Sarah.

She spent more and more time round at Holland Park, while Phoebe spent less and less. She never invited Kate on any of these drink-fuelled outings. Kate had been hurt at first, but had reconciled herself to Phoebe's way of keeping the different departments of her life separate. She told herself repeatedly that that was just the way it was and it didn't mean that Phoebe liked her any less. It couldn't mean that. Kate didn't think she could bear it otherwise. Ambrose, who found Kate's obsession with Phoebe unhealthy to the point of being distasteful, had tried remonstrating, and provoked such a violent reaction from Kate that he'd withdrawn more or less permanently into his study with Detmar Hibsen and a hundred Sainsbury's notebooks, and seized on every excuse he could find to go to wherever Hibsen had been to retrace his footsteps.

On Sundays, Phoebe's one day off, although she invariably squeezed in a media drinks party or two, Kate would turn up at brunch time, complete with jars of organic baby food and a Fortnum's hamper of caviare and blinis

– all Phoebe's favourites – and stay for the rest of the day.

One Sunday she turned up to find that Phoebe was still in bed, sleeping off the rigours of the week. She was clearly exhausted. She had continued breast-feeding the twins, despite the mastitis, because she was convinced it helped her to lose weight. When Kate arrived, the twins were out in the park with Sarah and her boyfriend, Troy, a good-looking layabout with cheekbones you could cut lines of coke on. Which is what Kate half suspected he used them for. On several visits to the house recently she had noticed Troy sitting in a rusting, faded red BMW, always with a different person, sometimes more than one. Each time she had hovered by the hall window and watched until money changed hands and the person who'd been sitting in the passenger seat walked away with something clearly in their pockets. And each time she felt irredeemably middle-aged.

Phoebe was sitting up in bed, pushing off the eye mask she always wore, even though the thick velvet curtains blotted out almost all the light. 'Oh, hello.' She smiled weakly as Kate walked in. Her face looked ghostly in the thick, dusky air. Unusually for her – she was normally so scrupulous about preserving her skin – traces of last night's make-up streaked her face.

'You look worn out,' blurted Kate. It wasn't the most tactful thing to say to a new mother.

'I know,' said Phoebe.

'Are Troy's friends disturbing you? It's not mandatory to take in all your staff's acquaintances, you know.'

'Oh, Troy's adorable. Or at least adorable-looking. He cheers me up no end with that lazy Aussie accent of his. I always was a sucker for a drawl. No, he's harmless. He's saving up to go to Bali, so I said he could stay here for a bit if he made himself useful doing some odd jobs around the house.'

There was no winning this argument, thought Kate, so she changed the subject. 'Still not sleeping?' she asked, as she instinctively tidied the room. Things had certainly slipped around the house since Caroline had gone.

Phoebe shook her head. 'Even when I take handfuls of these wretched things.' She gestured to a jar of sleeping pills nestling in the folds of the purple counterpane. 'It's as if I'm always worrying about Caitlin and Finn. I just can't seem to relax.'

'Oh, Phoebe. There's no need for that,' said Kate, sitting gingerly on the edge of the bed. She didn't want to get too close to Phoebe in her current dishevelled state. Somehow it seemed an intrusion on her privacy, even though they must have passed entire days in the past giggling together on the four-poster. 'You've got Sarah and—' She paused and added, shyly, 'You'll always have me.'

Phoebe looked at her through her narrowed eyes. Kate's devotion to her was a gratifying confirmation that her ability to cast spells on people hadn't worn off after all, even if Nick seemed to be proving immune to her magic at the moment.

'Yes, but it's not the same, is it?' she said, and sighed. 'It's not flesh and blood. I mean, apart from me there's no one to really love them. No father. No grandparents. Just me. And what if something happens to me? I can't stop thinking about that.'

'Well, nothing is going to happen to you. And if it does, there's me. As their official godmother I'm practically related. Listen, I don't know how to put this but, if it would

elp, I'd be happy to pay Caroline to come back. She seemed
ich a . . . a reliable person.'

'Oh Kate,' said Phoebe, her tinkling laughter defusing an
wkward moment. 'That's so kind of you, but really there's
o need. Sarah's wonderful. She's just a bit unorthodox.
Honestly, if I didn't know better I'd say you were just a
icker for an expensive uniform.'

Kate blushed. 'Or I could move in for a few days.
mbrose has got so many meetings with Marty Shicker
the States he's going back for at least another month.
erhaps having me here might put you more at ease.'

'Oh, that's really lovely of you—' Phoebe paused, eyeing
ate thoughtfully. 'I do feel exhausted. As a matter of fact,
r Michaels is a bit worried – but that's doctors for you.
an you believe he suggested I should go to a health farm
r a few days, to get my weight up a bit? I must say I do
ok terrible. I've dropped below seven stone. But chance
ould be a fine thing.'

'Is it the money?' asked Kate.

'No – well, yes. But I dare say I could find it somewhere.
o, the problem is Caitlin and Finn.'

'Yes, of course. You'd miss them horribly. It's unthink-
le. It would probably be completely counterproductive.
octors – honestly.'

Phoebe rolled her eyes. And then she began to cry.
On the other hand, I sometimes think if I don't get some
oper sleep soon I won't be any use to them at all. And
ve got to eat. But I just can't seem to keep anything down.
erhaps it would be the best thing all round . . . but, oh, it's
opeless.'

'Look,' Kate began, nervous as to how Phoebe might
act to the suggestion. In her current heightened state of

sensitivity, she might be so offended she would throw Ka
out. There was no knowing with her these days. And n
being able to see the twins would be more than Kate cou
bear. 'I could have them for a few days. I'd love it. I mea
I hope you don't think I'm being pushy or anything, but
it would help you out—'

Phoebe lent forward, kissed Kate gently on the mou
and hugged her. 'My God, Kate, are you serious? You do
know how much that means to me. You're the only one
could possibly entrust them with, apart from Sarah, I mea
and she's as knackered as I am. Oh, I feel so relieved . .
really was almost at my wits' end. Not to mention' – s
shifted uncomfortably beneath the crumb-strewn covers
'my tits' end. I thought not breast feeding would help. B
they're so sore they're killing me.'

Kate was so thrilled at the prospect of having the twi
to herself that she blotted out any niggling thoughts abo
the surprising alacrity with which Phoebe was able to lea
her eight-week-old babies. They agreed that the week aft
next would be best. It would give both of them time
arrange things at work.

'And since Vanbrugh Terrace is deserted I could mo
in here.'

'Oh, you really don't have to stay here,' said Phoe
hurriedly.

'But I thought it would be far less unsettling for Caitl
and Finn to have me move in here. After all, they haver
really known anywhere else, have they?'

'They'll be fine, I'm sure,' said Phoebe breezily. 'I
them good.'

'Well . . .' began Kate uncertainly. 'It could be qu
distressing for them. Not having you and being away fro

home and all their familiar bits and bobs. Honestly, I don't mind. It'll be so much nicer for Caitlin and Finn if—'

'I really don't think it's a good idea,' said Phoebe sharply.

Kate looked at her, surprised at the vehemence in her voice.

'But surely they'd be happier—'

'I said they'll be fine. God, Kate, you'd better be careful. You're in danger of turning into one of those boringly neurotic mothers.' She lit a cigarette and watched the hurt flush over Kate's face like a piranha watching the blood seep out of its victim.

Furious with herself for blushing, and for once not knowing what to say to Phoebe, Kate excused herself, saying she needed a drink. She wanted to leave the house, but the fear of never being allowed back in stopped her. She was probably overreacting. Phoebe was just being hormonal. She returned with two cups of mint tea, to find Phoebe cradling Finn.

'I thought he was crying so I got him up to change him,' she said, 'but it turned out he was just making little noises in his sleep. I don't want to disturb him again by putting him down.' She kissed the downy patch on his crown softly and looked across at Kate, her almond eyes resting lightly on the Victorian ruby bracelet Ambrose had recently given her in commemoration of the first night they had spent together. 'I'm sorry I'm so moody.' Her eyes grew moist. 'All I seem to be doing is apologizing lately,' she continued. 'It's not a lot of use, is it? Here,' she said, suddenly snatching the emerald-and-ruby drops out of her ears. 'These would look wonderful on you and they go with the bracelet. Take them, please.'

Kate blushed again, disarmed by the sight of Phoebe and Finn together. It wasn't something she saw often. There were times when Phoebe seemed to forget she had children altogether. And others when she was so tender with them it made Kate's heart lurch. 'I couldn't.'

'Please. I insist,' said Phoebe, a little more sharply. 'It would make me feel much better.'

Reluctantly Kate took them – she knew they were a gift from Nick – and sat there awkwardly while Phoebe fumbled to put them in her ears. 'I've been a bit worried about the security of the house lately,' Phoebe said. 'I didn't want to say anything in case you panicked.'

'What do you mean?'

'I've been hearing things. Prowlers, maybe. Or just some over-zealous reporters.'

'Have you told the police?' Kate asked, concerned. It was probably something to do with Troy and his dubious friends, but Phoebe was so defensive about Sarah and Troy that Kate knew better than to suggest it.

'Of course I've told the police, but you know what they're like. They can't do anything until something act-ually happens. They just told me to get a more expen-sive burglar alarm system if I was really worried. The way they spoke to me you'd think I was delusional, but I know there are people staking out this house. So you see, I'd be much happier if they were with you at your place than if I had to think of you alone here with them.'

'Yes, I see that perfectly,' said Kate.

'And you forgive me for being such an absent mother?' asked Phoebe suddenly.

Kate blushed again. 'There's nothing to forgive,' she

said. 'Oh, Phoebe, I hope you don't think I've been judging you. I know how hard everything is—'

Phoebe put a finger to her lips. 'Sssh. It doesn't matter. You don't have to think everything I do is brilliant. I love you because you don't. And I do love you, Kate.'

'I love you too,' said Kate, nervously fingering the earrings Phoebe had given her. 'And listen, why don't we give Sarah the week off when the twins come to me? She could probably do with a break.'

A few days later, Sarah duly deposited the twins at Vanbrugh Terrace.

'It's very nice of you, Kate,' she drawled, glancing around the immaculate room Kate had prepared for the twins. 'I hope Phoebe appreciates having such a good friend.'

Something in her tone of voice – a censorial gloating – caught Kate short. She refused to respond. 'It's an absolute pleasure,' she replied, drawing the curtains and looking for some matches to light the fire. 'And I expect you'd like a holiday. It's a shame that Phoebe couldn't afford to keep Caroline on—' She paused and Sarah turned expectant eyes on her. '—but at least it means I can make myself a bit useful.'

Sarah looked at her through her pin-dot, inscrutable eyes. 'Oh, Caroline didn't leave because of money,' she said.

'What do you mean?' asked Kate, turning round from the fire and wanting to slap the smirk from Sarah's expressionless face.

'She and Phoebe had words. Phoebe fired her. There was quite a to-do, actually – I'm surprised she didn't tell you. Perhaps you'd better ask her yourself.'

Kate fell silent. Sarah gathered her things sulkily. 'I'll

be going, then,' she said. 'Just one thing, Mrs White – I wouldn't have the twins in with you at night. They've just got back into the routine of being in their own room. It really would be most unsettling . . .'

The week passed in a blissful blur. Everyone apart from Nibbles, who whined almost non-stop, behaved impeccably. Kate had taken the precaution of hiring a temporary NNEB nanny – anything rather than have Sarah's sly insolence insinuating itself around her house – but Caitlin and Finn were such easy babies that, with the temporary nanny helping out, there was almost too little for Kate to do. Every night, she poured herself a glass of wine before bathing the twins herself and settling down for the evening on her bed with them in a Johnson's-baby-powder-scented cocoon of contentment.

She had the twins in with her at night – strictly against Sarah's rules, but nodding off with a twin on either side was delicious, even with Nibbles gazing at her pitifully from the foot of the bed. Ambrose called on the second night from New York, sounding exhilarated and happy – Marty thought they were all going to win Oscars for *Endymion* and the screenplay for Detmar Hibsen was cracking on nicely – and they called a rather awkward truce. Nevertheless instinctively she felt it wasn't necessary to tell him about her little guests. Somehow she knew he'd disapprove. She put it down to his loyalty to Nick and decided the less he knew about her relationship with Phoebe from now on the better.

She felt desolate when the week was up. Marcus had finally gone to pester Allegra with his video cam and cruise the Italian beaches for totty until college finally reeled him back to England, and she was dreading being on her own in Vanbrugh Terrace after the twins had gone. With a heavy heart she had driven them back to Holland Park. Phoebe had gone straight to work, so she left them with Sarah. Kissing them both tenderly, she placed the two tiny rabbits she had bought them as farewell presents next to them. Tears began to roll down her cheeks. She made a hasty exit, driving back to her own underpopulated house, which felt even emptier now the twins were gone, and for the first time in years poured herself a very large tumbler of brandy and drank it by herself.

Miserably, she agreed to a last-minute summit to discuss another hotel proposal with Little Bo Peep in Montana, more to distract herself than anything else. But she hated being so far away from the twins; it was one thing living a couple of miles away from them in London, but if anything serious happened to them while she was five thousand miles away it would take her at least twenty-four hours to get back. By the second day of her meeting she was so exasperated with Bo Peep's perorations that she decided to postpone meeting Ambrose in New York and fly straight back to London.

She was more exasperated still when Roberto insisted that she come straight from the airport to report on the summit in person with him in Bond Street, even though her flight was two hours delayed. If he hadn't been looking after Nibbles, whom Kate was almost as desperate to see as the twins, she would have boycotted the meeting. As it was, she hurried it along as fast as she could. He only wanted an excuse to show her Serenity's Swiss school reports anyway – she couldn't speak for Serenity, but L'Abbaye de la Rose was definitely finishing her off. It was gone midnight. when she finally headed back in the direction of Holland Park with Nibbles looking at her accusingly.

Unusually the house was in complete darkness and she had rung the bell twice before she realized that the door wasn't locked. She pushed against it and went into the hall, which was dark and chilly from the draught of damp night air that had been coming through the ajar door.

Disconcerted, she wandered around the ground floor, taking in the faint traces of whisky and cigarettes in the air. She wondered if Sarah and Troy had been having parties and then remembered that Troy had said he was going to Bali for a few months. She went upstairs, unable to tear herself from the eerie quiet of the house.

Being there when it was empty made Kate realize how much of it resonated with Phoebe's and Nick's ghosts. Phoebe had left the dressing room that she had laid out for him – he had never had much chance to use it – eerily intact, like a museum piece or an elaborate film set. Her scent – the heady, sweet-sour cocktail of Fracas that always made Kate slightly nauseous – was everywhere. Pictures of her lined the walls; old reviews together with caricatures and funny gossipy items were framed in the downstairs lavatory. An antique French cabinet in the drawing room was filled with silk fans, 1930s evening bags and shoes that she had worn in some of her films. The rich colours and plush fabrics were all so much a reflection of her, and like her, Kate found herself thinking, they looked their best in the soft lambent glow of candles and night-lights.

Kate felt sick with disappointment at not seeing the twins. Phoebe must have gone away with them, but where? She told herself to stop panicking and tried to suppress the thuds coming from her ribcage. She was walking reluctantly back out of the kitchen towards the front door when she heard a noise from the top floor. Perhaps it was Phoebe's prowlers. Or Troy's dodgy friends, more likely. Pleased finally to have a chance to prove to Phoebe that Sarah and Troy weren't suitable house-mates for the twins, she willed herself up the sweeping staircase, her teeth chattering, grasping a heavy bronze figurine of a horse that was in one of the alcoves as she passed.

By the time she reached the first floor, it was obvious the noises were coming from the twins' nursery on the floor above. Her heart pounding, and shivering in the cold, she climbed the second flight, placed her hand on the doorknob of their room and turned it slowly, praying it wouldn't squeak. After what seemed ages, the door opened, and she stepped gingerly into the twins' nursery, sick with fear.

The window was wide open and the room was freezing. But the stench of neglected nappies was unmistakable. It was Finn's whimpering she could hear. He had rolled out of his nappy completely and was lying in muck. A milk bottle had leaked all over the mattress and by his head was a pool of congealing milk, tears and mucus. Caitlin, in the next cot, wasn't much better, but she had fallen into some kind of exhausted doze, her chubby back pressed into the corner, against the bunny Kate had bought her.

It took Kate half an hour to clean them up and to pack a few things for them. It required all her self-control to stay calm, but she managed it, and eventually she descended the staircase laden with the twins and closely followed by Nibbles.

And then came the laughter, great fluted gales of post-party laughter. As she neared the foot of the staircase, she could make out three distinct woozy voices. Phoebe had clearly returned. Thank God. There'd obviously been a horrendous mistake. She must have left Sarah in charge. At least this would finally be grounds for getting rid of her. Cautiously, her heart still racing, she padded across the icy flagstones to the drawing room. The door was half open; she was about to walk in, but the voices, giggling and murmuring by turns, were so self-absorbed she didn't want to startle them. Instead, she stood in the doorway with a twin on each hip while her eyes grew accustomed to the flickering candlelight.

After a few moments she could make out Phoebe sitting on the floor, moaning ecstatically, her back against the George Sherlock sofa. Her legs, still in their purple silk Manolos, with the satin ribbons laced up her slender legs, were spread wide. Her head was thrown back; her dress, a shimmering beaded turquoise bias-cut slip, was up round her waist, and her small pointed breasts had escaped from the tiny straps. Sarah, dressed in what looked like an Ann Summers nanny uniform, was tipping white powder round Phoebe's nipples and licking it off, while Troy arched his bony, bronzed back and pushed his head farther between her legs. If that's what he meant by Bali, then he had a lousy sense of direction. They were clearly all so far gone they didn't even care whether Kate was there or not.

The scene was so ludicrously unbelievable, Kate had to suppress a nervous desire to giggle. On the way out, she knocked the door and it creaked heavily. She caught Phoebe's green eyes gloating at her as she was turning. The expression – mocking, full of hatred – shocked her more than anything else. Suddenly her nerves were replaced by a cold fury. She turned on her heels with the twins and ran out of the house.

Chapter Twenty-one

———◁◦◦◦▷———

Kate called Dr Michaels, who didn't seem to think she was wasting his time in the least and immediately prescribed some antibiotics for Finn. 'Poor mite, he must have been in agony. Glue ear can be very nasty at that age,' he said quietly. He was sufficiently discreet not to question the fact that the babies were once more in Kate's charge. As obstetrician to the glitterati there wasn't much he hadn't seen or heard.

She sat up with Finn all night, wishing Ambrose were there. For all his vagaries and tenuous grasp on the practicalities of life, in a flash she realized that out of everyone she knew he had the most admirably clear grasp of the moral and emotional issues of any situation. He would have known instantly what to do. Instead, Marcus had turned up, unable to keep himself away from Sarah any longer.

'I don't think it's a good idea for you to go round there just now,' said Kate blearily, when he waltzed into the kitchen at seven in the morning straight from Gatwick, and clearly determined to waltz straight out again.

'Why not?' he said, looking at her forlornly. He'd suffered one of Allegra's nervous breakdowns and an eight-hour charter delay to get back to his true love.

'Well, for one thing, it's too early.'

He looked at her, mystified.

'And for another, I've had a bit of a row with Phoebe. Nothing serious but—'

This time he looked stricken.

'But I've got to,' he said, clutching at his Ibiza '98 T-shirt in desperation.

'Marcus,' she began gently, 'Sarah's got a boyfriend.'

'I know that,' he said lugubriously. 'She's also got my camcorder.'

It was Kate's turn to look thunderstruck. 'What did you say?'

'She doesn't know it. I rigged it up in the front room. It's set to go off every night at about midnight. That's usually when she goes in there for a bit of action with Troy.'

This Tarantino fixation would have to be dealt with, thought Kate. But later. 'D'you think you can get it back?'

'No problems.' He beamed at her sweetly. 'Troy's always forgetting to lock the front door. Makes it easier for his mates to come and go undisturbed.' And he trotted off, leaving a steaming rucksack to stew on the kitchen table.

Kate could still barely digest the evidence of her own eyes, and repeatedly thought over the little tableau in the drawing room, hoping that by replaying it over and over again she would discover some detail that would make the whole scene appear less damning. Perhaps Marcus's video would shed some light. She shuddered. So much for Phoebe's prowlers.

It wasn't the decadence which dismayed her – though

if she were honest she was shocked to her core — but the irrefutable evidence of Phoebe's blatant neglect of the twins. The expression she had caught as she had turned and fled, a sort of amused disdain (for what, for whom? It could only have been for Kate), chilled her.

Eventually Finn fell into a fitful sleep. Caitlin woke up twice, wanting to be fed. By eight o'clock, Kate had fallen into a doze in an armchair by the French windows, to be woken by hammering on the front door. It was Phoebe.

She had cleaned up since the night before. The dark kohl circling her eyes had been washed away. Her face was scrubbed and pale, her cheeks were flushed — expertly made-up, Kate had no doubt. She was wearing an old black cashmere cardigan and a pale green tweed skirt. It was, thought Kate bitterly, Phoebe's idea of how a repentant mother should look. 'Can I come in?' she said in a small, reedy voice.

Kate motioned her into the hall and led the way to the kitchen, where, wordlessly, she began to brew some fresh coffee on the hob and opened the French doors on to the garden to let the unseasonably warm rays in. Phoebe perched on a kitchen stool by the island unit, hugging her knees. She looked about seventeen.

'There's nothing I can say to make this look better,' she began, twisting the hem of her cardigan. 'I'm not a saint. I have ... a weakness for men. Well, for sex actually. But I expect Martha's told you all that. Nick can't have failed to fill her in — or perhaps he thinks it's best left well alone.'

'She hasn't discussed it with me,' said Kate coldly, her back against the window, through which bright, hard sunshine was pouring. 'And I'm not interested, Phoebe. What you choose to do in your private life is your own affair. What bothers me are the twins. You do realize, don't you, that they could have caught pneumonia and that Finn has a severe ear infection?'

Phoebe looked a portrait of contrition. It wasn't any good. Kate would never forgive her for what she had done to the twins. That Phoebe could operate on so many levels, have so many secret lives, without divulging any of them to her, would have profoundly hurt at one time. But now she no longer cared.

'Oh, Kate,' exclaimed Phoebe. 'I wanted to tell you. Believe me. I came closer to telling you than anyone. But . . . well, it's not something I'm proud of, as you can imagine. It's like an illness. And don't think I'm not aware of it or that I haven't tried to deal with it in the past. Christ, there isn't a therapist I haven't been to. I'm a fuck-up. But you already know that.'

Kate, her arms folded, head to one side, willed Phoebe to talk her way out of the rubble of their friendship. The scent of autumn roses, surprisingly sharp, floated through the open doors from the garden. She wondered if she would always associate their fragrance with bitterness from now on.

'Why else would I be so addicted to getting hurt? I always have to go out and do the thing that's going to cause me most pain. Nick knew that and, in his oh-so-clever way, he used it.' Her voice trembled and she lit a cigarette. 'When we met, all those years ago – God, I was nineteen – I was so ripe for being manipulated. I could be played like a violin.'

The tears were spilling down her powdered cheeks. Kate looked at her dispassionately. For the first time, her make-up looked clumsy and masklike. It was all so clear now. Phoebe was playing her wild card. But it was still all an act. Everything in their relationship, Kate realized, with stabbing clarity, had been a charade.

'I was always the most solvent girl at drama school,' she was gabbling now. 'Everyone else went to their bank managers to try and top up their loans. I turned tricks.' She gave a dry little laugh. 'I think Nick liked it. It turned him on. And it kept him solvent too, while he had to retake a year at drama school.' She gave a brittle laugh. 'You never read about that bit in his hagiographies, do you? It was his very own *Belle de Jour* fantasy. He certainly didn't try very hard to stop me.' She paused. Kate looked at her distastefully.

'You don't get it, do you, Phoebe?' she said. 'I don't give a damn about your sordid little sex games. It's what you did to Finn and Caitlin that means I'll never be able to forgive you.'

'Kate, please, don't get judgmental on me.' Her voice was childlike now, wheedling. 'I didn't know. It was a misunderstanding. I thought Sarah had arranged cover for a day or two. Kate, you're the only one who can really help me now.'

Her voice was quivering dangerously. She was becoming hysterical. 'I do want to get better, you know. It's just that it hasn't been the easiest of times – and I love the twins. I need to get better for their sakes.'

'I doubt if I can help you. As you haven't confided in me before, I'm clearly not the person to go through this with you.'

'Oh, Kate – I didn't want to jeopardize our friendship. You have such high standards——' Her voice was rising.

Kate still said nothing.

'It doesn't make me a bad mother, you know——'

Something in Phoebe's voice — a certain sureness that, in the end, she would get her way — made Kate look at her aghast.

'I think you'd better leave now,' she said.

'Fine,' said Phoebe, sliding off the stool. 'I'll just get the twins.'

Kate shot her a horrified look.

'They are mine, you know.'

'You seem to have conveniently forgotten that for most of the past few months,' said Kate.

Phoebe's voice was measured. 'Oh, Kate, you have no idea, have you? But since you won't let me explain, then that's the way it will have to stay. I'm very grateful that you took such good care of them. But now it's my turn. Don't try and stop me, or I shall think that your concern for them is less altruistic than it might initially seem, and more the cravings of a woman who is so desperate for her own children she'd do anything.'

She tip-tapped out into the hall and Kate followed her helplessly. 'There's a tape, you know. Marcus set his camera up in your drawing room before he went away. He's got it back now. Irrefutable evidence.' She was gabbling desperately.

Phoebe turned round at the bottom of the stairs and looked at her contemptuously. 'How very pathetic of you, Kate. I don't think the police will take very kindly to that kind of voyeurism, do you? Or Ambrose, come to that.'

Wordlessly Kate watched Phoebe come down the stairs, the twins nestling on her hips, the downy hair on their drowsy heads waving fluffily in the breeze from the kitchen. They looked blearily at Kate, who stood helplessly by the front door as Phoebe swept through it and out on to the street, where she disappeared into a black taxi and was whisked away in the swirl of grimy traffic.

Phoebe's breezy confidence — borne aloft on twin peaks of defiance and deviance — evaporated, as it always did, within a day or two. Things were fine to begin with; her energy levels soared and she played happily with the babies until Sarah got back at the end of the weekend. And then she plummeted into despair and panic, convinced that at any moment the authorities would arrive to take the twins away. She was desperately worried about Marcus's tape, although she only half believed in its existence. On Wednesday, unable to stand the suspense any longer, she decided to call Kate.

A croaky monosyllabic voice answered the phone. It was Marcus, half asleep. Against the blaring music, his voice was just audible, but she had to get him to repeat the last bit.

'She's not here. She's gone. To see her sister,' he added when pressed. 'She left first thing on Monday. Or was it Sunday? Shall I tell her who called?'

But Phoebe had rung off. She could just picture Nick and Martha and Kate and Ambrose sitting smugly round the pool, picking over the bones of her imperfect past, tut-tutting from on high and plotting how to take her babies from her. It wasn't going to happen. She couldn't let it. She ran upstairs to where Sarah had just put them to bed for the night and, ignoring her protestations, scooped them both out of their cots and held them so tightly it seemed they all three might suffocate. She couldn't let anything happen to them. They were all she had.

✳　　✳　　✳

Tired from the flight and dusty from the journey to Rose Cottage, Kate arrived at their favourite time of day: cocktail hour. Nick and Martha were seated back to back on the ledge overlooking the bay. Martha, tanned and freckled, her hair loose and blowing across her face, squinted at the silhouetted figure on the veranda. In a trice she had run towards Kate and hugged her. 'God, it's good to see you.'

The reunion was an emotional one. There was so much Kate blamed herself for that she found Martha's open warmth disconcerting to begin with. They both seemed so happy in their idyll that for one crazy moment Kate was tempted not to do what she had come for. But she had to confess her betrayal of Martha to the newspapers to slot the final pieces of the jigsaw together. And she had to satisfy herself that she was right about Phoebe. It was her only hope of getting the twins. She had gone over her other options a thousand times and dismissed them. What could she have done? Called the police and told them that she had abducted two babies because their room was cold and their cots a mess? Phoebe was right – sexual licence, even the odd bit of recreational drug-taking, were hardly grounds for removing children from a mother's protection these days. This way took longer but in the end it seemed more effective.

She watched them both, so loose-limbed and relaxed in their shorts and shirts, chucking prawns on the barbecue and opening a bottle of Cape Chablis, and found herself envying Martha her sense of place. She went to bed early the first night, tossing and turning, worrying about how best to talk to them about Phoebe. She wasn't even sure what she thought they could do. Martha had changed in so many ways, some obvious — like her serene beauty — others less definable. She was more relaxed, less prickly, and she no longer made Kate feel trivial for not wanting to save the world. The upshot was that Kate hadn't felt so close to her in years. She told her about her contribution to the *Python* and, to her astonishment, Martha laughed.

'I saw it when it came out — Luke accidentally left it lying around. I was a bit shocked, but I always knew there had to be an explanation,' she said, hugging Kate. 'Anyway, I learned ages ago that the two people they write about when they write about Nick and me live in a parallel universe. They look like us. Sometimes they almost sound like us. But they're not us. As long as I have you back and I know that Mum knows the truth I don't care.'

The week began to slip by in a pleasing haze of lazy, late breakfasts, afternoon swims, the occasional ramble into the mountains or along the bay, and long, late-night talks, which rambled into the small hours. But Kate couldn't stop fretting about the twins. She owed it to them, if not to Martha, to clear things up. On the last morning, over breakfast on the veranda, she handed Martha a photograph of the twins and suddenly the dams burst and she heard herself telling them all that had happened.

'Do you think the babies are in danger?' asked Nick.

'Yes. No. Well, perhaps … I don't know. I think Phoebe is seriously unhinged. The papers have been saying her job's on the line. The ratings have slipped. I didn't take any notice and Phoebe always brushed it off. But I don't know what to believe with Phoebe any more. It's as if there are layers and layers of truth …'

'Join the club,' said Nick.

'But you were married to her,' said Kate indignantly. 'How could you live like that?'

'I don't know,' he said. 'All I can say is that we were aspiring actors when we met. Reinventing ourselves seemed like a legitimate, professional necessity. By the time I realized just how multi-layered Phoebe's inventions were, I was in too deep.'

'Just what hold has she got over you?' said Kate angrily. Martha lobbed her an anxious look that she ignored. 'Come on, Nick. I think we've a right to know.'

There was a long silence while the wind whispered through the vines which drooped languidly over the terrace.

'You've got a point,' said Nick eventually. 'I haven't been completely open with anyone.' He turned to Martha. 'I haven't even told you the whole story. I'm sorry – but then I've only just worked it out for myself. You remember, Martha, when I told you when we first met about how Phoebe had given up the offer to be a member of the RSC so that I could go and film in Australia?' He brushed the hair back agitatedly from his eyes and looked at her. She smiled encouragingly and reached for his hand.

'The film looked as though it was going to be a big deal at the time. Australia was making some really good films that were gaining international recognition.' He shrugged bitterly. 'Well, not this one. But back then I thought I was on a one-way ticket to stardom. And I was such an egomaniac it didn't bother me in the least that Phoebe was throwing away the chance of a lifetime—'

'That's not true—' blurted Martha.

'Fundamentally, it is, I'm afraid. I might have made the right noises, but all I really cared about was my precious career. The worst bit is' – he raked his fingers through his hair again and looked at the table abjectly – 'while we were in Sydney I found a letter from the director of the film, written to Phoebe – she'd slept with him back in London. So that he'd give the part to me. She'd come to see the first audition, you see, at which I was truly abysmal. She'd slipped away before the end – you can't blame her.' Her laughed bitterly. 'So she missed the part where they offered to let me do it again. God knows why. I suppose they liked the cut of my cheekbones or something. And she knew how much I wanted the part. So she fixed it for me. Just like she tried to fix everything for me.'

There was a long silence. Eventually, Kate spoke in a small voice.

'You might as well know, Nick, that Phoebe told me she slept with lots of men – for money. To pay for you to go through drama school, and then while you were both trying to get started. She said you knew and that tacitly you condoned it—'

Kate had never seen such a look of intense pain as she witnessed on Nick's and Martha's faces at that precise moment. It was as if she were the serpent that had entered the Garden of Eden and wrecked everything. Martha's hand, which had been stroking Nick's until that point, froze.

'Why are you doing this, Kate?' she asked coldly.

'No, she's right, Martha,' said Nick. He turned towards Kate. 'There's a lot about my relationship with Phoebe I'm not proud of. She had a secret life – she made it very clear from the start that this was a condition of our being together. She never once introduced me to a single member of her family, you know, even though I know she went to see her mother and from time to time she still saw her brother. And God knows what those two got up to. And you're right. I didn't ask. I thought I was doing the right thing and not interfering, though now I see it was probably benign neglect. And yes, I knew that she'd slept around — and for money. Not exactly a romance made in heaven. But I was crazy about her all the same. She was completely . . . bewitching.' He laughed bitterly. 'She still can be. Kate, you know that.' Kate felt herself blushing.

'And if she needed to have private compartments to her life, then that seemed a small price to pay. Later, when I started making money, there'd be these huge withdrawals sometimes, separate from her shopping ones — I always knew who they were for. She wanted to help her brother start a business — I never knew what kind. With Phoebe there were some subjects that you just didn't broach. I should have stopped her. But I was too damn busy being the international movie star.'

He looked at Kate, his blue eyes flashing with such earnest indignation that she was tempted to believe him. But he was an actor. How could she trust him? She just wanted to extrapolate some truth from all this. She looked at Martha helplessly.

'She said you forced her to have an abortion once because it was going to interfere with your career plans,' she continued contritely.

The muscles round his temples tightened visibly, as if she'd inflicted physical pain on him. 'It's lies, Kate. At least, if she had an abortion I didn't know about it and I certainly wouldn't have asked her to have one. I've still got the letter from Phoebe telling me it was a false alarm. I've got all her letters. They're at my mum's. I'll show them to you if you like,' he added roughly.

'Nothing that she's said – not one shred in the newspapers – stands up.'

'I see,' said Kate. There was a silence while the two sisters digested this.

'Then why don't you just put them all in the hands of the lawyers and bring an end to all this?' said Kate finally. 'You'll demolish her in court.'

'I don't want it to go to court. It'll kill her. And the facts are one thing, but who the hell's to say I wasn't just as guilty all the same?'

Kate didn't often apologize but she knew in her bones that he was telling the truth. She couldn't condone everything he'd done – but he was human. And it wasn't as if she hadn't made her own share of mistakes. She felt profoundly happy for Martha – and sick to her heart about Phoebe. She hated what she'd done, but she couldn't hate *her*. She was damaged goods. And she had casualty stamped on her forehead.

'I'm sorry I doubted you,' she said to Nick as they saw her off at the airport.

'It's okay,' he said gently. 'Why would you believe me any more than Phoebe? I told you, she's a bloody good actress.' She hugged him and he tactfully went to get a coffee while she and Martha said their goodbyes.

'I'm sorry I couldn't have your baby for you,' said Martha. 'I would have liked that.'

'Does Nick know you won't have children?'

Martha gave a little half-smile. 'Yes. We do share *most* of our secrets, you know.'

'Doesn't it make you sad?'

'I sometimes feel it ought to,' said Martha, reaching her hand across to Kate's. 'But the truth is I'm so astonished and happy to have what I have with Nick that I think it would be greedy to ask for more.'

'Why don't I feel like that?' asked Kate plaintively. 'I mean, I love Ambrose, but somehow it isn't enough. It was terrible when I kept losing the babies, but now I don't even seem able to conceive. It's so unlucky, isn't it, that neither of us can produce grandchildren for Mum?'

'Careless, some might say.'

'What do you mean?'

'Oh, Kate.' Martha smiled, affection for her sister welling up inside her. 'You might increase your chances if you and Ambrose were occasionally on the same continent for more than a week.'

Martha waved her sister off and watched her board the plane, a strangely lonely figure. She missed Kate the moment the plane took off, and yet on the drive back to Rose Cottage she felt strangely at peace. She threw herself into renovating the cottage – nothing that might make old Mr Lubitov turn in his grave, just a fresh lick of paint here, some new blinds there. She started to feel brave enough to explore by herself. She would take the Jeep out while Nick was working on his and Ambrose's Detmar Hibsen script, drive into the mountains, get out and walk for a few hours, and then drive back for a swim. And in the evenings she would sit down over a glass of wine and proof-read Nick's manuscript.

Her hikes became more strenuous, the swims more rigorous. She began to develop quite a routine. At weekends Nick would come with her. It was their way of dealing with what was happening in London, she supposed. And then, one day, when they had been walking for almost five hours along the Bainskloof mountain pass, she slipped on a ledge by some waterfalls, broke her ankle and blacked out. She awoke much, much later in a cool, white hospital room, with Nick, Chrissie and Mike by her side, and several kilos of plaster up her leg.

Her recuperation, strictly supervised by Nick, was a laborious affair. He monitored her so closely and was so stern about preventing her from doing anything the least bit taxing that she was almost relieved when he had to go to LA for a meeting with Marty Shicker and Ambrose about the Hibsen project, even though she was disappointed not to be able to go with him.

With her hikes and swimming curtailed, she spent most of her time on the veranda ledge, half dozing, half dreaming up improvements for the script with which she too had become thoroughly involved.

One afternoon after lunch, about five days after Nick had gone, Anthony their housekeeper slipped out to fetch them some provisions. She lay on the ledge listening to the waves crashing on the rocks beneath. It was hotter than usual. Little beads of sweat ran down her neck, collecting in the folds of her breasts and thighs. Once or twice she nodded off and each time she jerked awake, resolved to move away from the ledge to one of the loungers. Anthony had warned her not to fall asleep there because he was worried she might roll off and down the cliff.

She heard a door banging in the house. Anthony must be back. Feeling woozy, she waited for him to help her move off the ledge. To her left the cliff fell away vertiginously into the navy blue sea beneath. She closed her eyes and let the dizziness carry her away.

'Martha. Martha.' The voice was low but insistent. She

struggled to open her eyes but when she did all she saw was Phoebe. She closed them again. She could hear the waves crashing on the rocks below.

'Is that any way to welcome an old friend? We *are* friends, aren't we, Martha? After all, we have so much in common.'

She opened her eyes again. Phoebe, paler than ice in a 1950s, light blue, full-skirted dress, was leaning over her, two long-stemmed glasses balanced precariously in one hand, a bottle of champagne in the other.

'Is it really you?' she asked drowsily.

'It really is,' said Phoebe sweetly.

'How did you get in?'

'Through the door. I assumed you must be expecting me. I hope you don't mind, I helped myself to some cold champagne. Here, would you like some?' She poured two glasses and handed one to Martha, smiling her Cheshire cat smile. The almond eyes glinted in the sun. 'Do have some. I hate to drink alone.' She held the glass towards Martha's mouth, her hands shaking violently.

'What do you want?' asked Martha, sitting up suddenly. She felt sick.

'Actually *you're* exactly what I want,' purred Phoebe. She was wearing a huge straw hat. Her hair, still black, contrasted almost shockingly with her precious white complexion. Martha's heart began pounding so loudly she thought Phoebe must surely hear.

'May I?' Phoebe sat down next to her, smoothing her dress out about her, and drawing up her knees. She looked out across the bay.

'Impressive, isn't it? I always loved this country.' Her light green eyes scanned Martha's face. 'Didn't he tell you he brought me out here? It was years ago. Before he decided I was too adulterated to be let loose among his precious family. But I was quite a hit, I can tell you. Hasn't Chrissie ever talked to you about me? Or Mikey? ... No, I don't suppose he would. Too bloody scared. Men are all the same, aren't they? They always want what they can't have. And Mikey wanted me, only he was too spineless to admit it even to himself. God, it was pathetic watching him watching me. He was practically panting. Not that Chrissie knew. She loved me like the daughter she never had. She gave me this.' She tugged at a little silver charm bracelet around her wrist and thrust one of its charms, a small silver hat with the inscription *To my darling daughter, love, Chrissie* on it, towards Martha. 'It goes rather well with the dress, don't you think? It was a present from Nick — vintage Dior. Does he buy you nice presents, Martha?' She almost spat the words out.

'Why are you here?' said Martha coldly. Dizziness had been replaced by cold shafts of anger.

'I want that tape.'

'I don't know what you're talking about,' said Martha.

'Don't you?' said Phoebe, her malachite eyes fixed on her searchingly. 'I doubt that. And I want to broker a deal. I was going to ask you to tell Nick and your sister to back off. To leave me and the children alone. Although I probably don't have what it takes these days to be mother of the year. In fact she can have them. For the right price. Tell her that. And tell Nick that if he pays up quietly too I'll leave you all alone.'

Martha said nothing. She couldn't quite believe this was happening.

'Why have you come to me? Why can't your lawyers do this?' Her voice sounded more hostile than she thought sensible, but there was nothing she could do. Phoebe seemed not to have registered the tone.

'Oh, lawyers. I can't bear the way they tinker with the truth, can you?'

'I'm amazed you have any understanding of what truth is,' retorted Martha.

Phoebe shrugged and looked out over the sea. 'It's quite a drop, isn't it?' She opened a tiny silver case and withdrew a cigarette. 'Are you good with heights, Martha? You've been flying very close to the sun lately. Careful – a pasty-faced girl like you could end up with melanoma.'

'Oh, for God's sake, Phoebe, just because you're dressed for a *film noir* doesn't mean you have to act as though you're in one.'

'That's always been your failing, hasn't it, Martha?' The smoke from Phoebe's cigarette whirled around them in the breeze before dissipating in the clear blue air. 'No style. No sense of occasion.' Her voice suddenly grew shrill. 'How dare you presume to know just how far I would go. The fact is, Martha dear' – she was almost spitting by now – 'I hate you. And that bugs me.'

The venom in her eyes was almost tangible beneath the jagged little scar that ran through her right eyebrow For a moment, with the light half silhouetting her face, she looked almost demented. Helplessly immobile, Martha tried to stay calm. 'Look, I know that you're part of Nick's history. He's told me so much about you. How happy you were, in the beginning. How much you supported him and how hard it was for you. I'd never try to erase that. It doesn't matter what happened. I'm sure you're right and we can all sort this out.'

'Really,' said Phoebe, her voice crackling. The thought

of Nick and Martha clucking sympathetically over her miserable childhood caused something in her to snap.

He took the twisting road down to the bay as he had done all his life – extremely slowly. Occasionally he would pause, leaning out of the window of the Jeep, daring himself to admire the breathtaking views. The surf was pounding against the rocks – the wind was getting up – and the sharp rays of the sun were piercing the brilliantly coloured rock in the escarpment behind him. All these years, his secret had remained safe: he suffered from terrible vertigo, but no one, he reflected with satisfaction, had ever found him out. Not even Miss Martha, and she had driven with him numerous times to the market. It made the ten-mile journey into town even slower, but it meant he noticed everything.

He passed the parade of shops with their permanent holiday displays of lilos, sunhats and other beach paraphernalia. The atmosphere was sleepy and relaxed; even the chemist had bright yellow lilos tied up outside. That reminded him. He stopped the Jeep and got out. He wanted to get some more painkillers for Miss Martha. She never complained, but he could see the lines forming in ripples around her mouth whenever it got bad. It was silly to suffer when there was no need. He could get her some of the rosewater she was always running out of while he was at it.

'You got more visitors?' asked Mrs Kalk, the chemist, disappearing in search of Martha's painkillers.

Anthony shook his grizzled head. 'Nope. Place is as quiet as a graveyard. And so much the better for Miss Martha. She needs her rest.'

'Well, it's about to be disturbed.' Mrs Kalk's voice floated out from behind her cubicle where she was mixing up Martha's rosewater. 'Woman came in here earlier asking for directions to Rose Cottage. Specifically asked after Miss Martha and Mr Wilde. She was wearing a hat as big as your car and a dress that looked as though it was more fit for a cocktail party than a day round here.'

Anthony's mind began to race. The routine at Rose Cottage was sufficiently regulated for unexpected guests to cause considerable upheaval. Especially with Miss Martha all on her own. He should never have left her. Cape Town had its share of violence, and it had been spilling over to the surrounding bays and coves lately. While Anthony didn't believe some of the stories, he was sufficiently rattled to have considered installing some state-of-the-art security at Rose Cottage. Only he hadn't got round to getting the okay from Nick yet.

He had a strong premonition of danger. He knew enough to realize that Miss Martha and Mr Nick had had some problems back in England. What if this woman in her party clothes had come to make trouble? His heart was thumping now. He didn't wait for his change, but ran out to the Jeep and started to drive back up the mountain faster than he'd ever imagined possible. But three miles along he got stuck behind a lorry. There wasn't a hope of overtaking. It would take him another half an hour at this rate. He began hooting the horn, but the driver in front remained oblivious. He was going to have to summon up all his courage and overtake. Checking in both wing mirrors, he put his foot down and closed his eyes.

*　　*　　*

Martha said nothing. She was beginning to feel groggy. 'Oh, you can't really blame Nick,' Phoebe was saying. 'In his way he worked very hard. Nick didn't have natural talent, you see. He really had to hone it. He flunked a year. You didn't know that? He was in such a panic. He couldn't tell Chrissie or Mikey. They'd made such a huge sacrifice to send him there. He told them he was taking a year out and I paid the fees.'

Martha looked at her unsteadily. 'Phoebe, listen, I'm a bit tired. I can't really concentrate. Why don't you come back when Nick's here—'

'Oh, Martha, now you're hurting my feelings.' Phoebe's eyes flashed dangerously and she squeezed her glass so tightly it shattered in her hands. She wiped the blood on her pale blue dress and moved closer to Martha.

'You look very tense, Martha. Would you like me to give you a massage? They can be so soothing, can't they, post-operatively.' She ran a hand lightly up Martha's undamaged leg. Martha tried to move away, but she was so woozy she could barely sit up now. 'Nick always loved my massages. It's terribly precarious on this ledge, isn't it?' Phoebe went on softly. 'But beautiful. I can see why you would want to spend hours on end here, just looking at the view. Careless, though, of everyone to leave you all alone here.'

'Anthony will be back any minute,' said Martha desperately.

'Such an unfortunate, foolish accident, you falling off this ledge,' Phoebe purred. Martha tried backing away from her along the edge, but Phoebe had caught the broken ankle and had pinioned her down.

'You're hurting me,' said Martha, trying to sound calm. 'Please let me go, Phoebe. This is silly.'

'Silly? I'm beginning to think it's the best option. You know that you and Nick will never have what he and I had. You said yourself I'm indelibly stamped on his soul. The best you could ever hope for, Martha, is to ride along on his coat-tails. And it will be a very bumpy ride, believe me. Why put yourself through the unhappiness and indignity of always being second best?'

Her nails were digging in to Martha's arms so hard she wasn't sure whether the trickle of blood came from Phoebe's cut hand or her own flesh. She tried to wriggle free, but Phoebe still had her pinioned down.

'One little push, Martha. It's all so simple, don't you see? It wouldn't work out for you ultimately with Nick – you realize that, don't you? He's an addictive person too, you know. Only his addiction is me. That's why we're so well suited. Don't cry, Martha. It really is all for the best.'

Martha closed her eyes and thought of Nick and how she must cling to the thought that he had always told her the truth, just as she was clinging now to the ledge with all her strength. She pushed again against Phoebe's weight. It ought to have been easy but she felt dizzy, and Phoebe had the pent-up anger of twenty years helping her. She thought she was blacking out; thought she could hear footsteps on the veranda, but realized she must be hallucinating. Anthony must have gone all the way into town otherwise he would have been back hours ago. She twisted her head towards the sea. Perhaps Phoebe was right and this was the easy option. Easier than discovering that the only good relationship she'd ever had with a man was a sham.

*　　*　　*

The bell-boy hovered uncertainly outside the room, his bulbous eyes twitching squirrel-like from the glazed puffy folds of their sockets. Mrs Wilde, the occupant of 301, had expressly asked him the previous morning to be sure to knock and enter at 6.30 a.m. She had a flight to catch back to London and did not trust the hotel operator to remember to call at the right time. The bell-boy had been tipped generously and in advance. Yet still he hovered; a sixth sense, honed by two years in his current job, told him something was wrong. On the other hand, Mrs Wilde had hinted that a further tip would be forthcoming on completion of the job, and judging by the first one it would be worth collecting. Overcoming his qualms, he fished around on his belt for the ring bearing the master key and unlocked the door.

At first he could make out little. The whiteness of the room and its furniture, so dazzling by day, was muzzled in chiaroscuro. He walked over to the rumpled bed, hoping his steps would waken her, making further contact unnecessary. Mistaking a pile of pillows, curiously aligned like a crucifix, for a body, he drew back the covers a little. There was nothing there, apart from a few brownish-red stains. He began to sweat and found himself moving towards the bathroom as if he were sleepwalking.

It was the hair which shocked him to begin with – jagged black hanks crudely hacked into the basin and lying there like a mutilated raven. He didn't even notice the body at first. And when he did see it, splayed in a bath of foaming rust-coloured water, the scum already starting to form on the enamel, it was the mouth, agape in frozen surprise, which stayed with him. And the colour of the blood. Why didn't they ever tell you it wasn't properly red? A muffled scream rose in his gorge and he vomited into the lavatory while his legs gave way beneath him. He must have sat there for a few minutes. Perhaps he even passed out. Because when the nausea began to subside, he felt something else surging through him. She was famous. A big deal, apparently. The bell-boy never watched television or read magazines – too busy attending meetings of the dubious White Boy fraternity he belonged to – but he recognized the power of celebrity. A call to a newspaper – the international ones – might more than compensate for the lost tips. He heaved himself up from the floor, fuelled by greed and an unexpected boost to his sense of self-worth, and walked towards the phone by the bed, pausing only to pick up a handful of hair from the basin.

Epilogue

April 2000

'I never really believed her, you know.'

'But you almost did. For a split second.'

'Perhaps a very split one. When Phoebe managed to half push me off the ledge. Every day I thank God that Anthony arrived back when he did. And to think I used to tease him about that sixth sense of his.' There was a silence. She tried to make light of it. 'Exes can be so unpredictable, can't they? At least there's just the one. There *is* just the one, isn't there?'

Nick winced. Even after almost eighteen months he still couldn't talk about Phoebe with any degree of levity. Perhaps he never would be able to, thought Martha. He kissed her affectionately on the tip of her sun-freckled nose.

'Much as I love hearing of your blind trust, you must admit that finding all Phoebe's diaries and letters stashed away in the house in LA helped a teeny bit to convince you and Kate of my case?'

'Well, perhaps Kate. She was always going to be more

sceptical than me. I think she really was close to Phoebe, for a while – and at a time when she was feeling very vulnerable and alone. But when they found that letter from the RSC telling Phoebe that she hadn't got in after all—'

'—even Kate was appeased.'

'Yeah. Even Kate. And that stuff about her sleeping with the director so you could get the part in the Australian film?'

'All fantasy. At least according to the diaries.'

'You don't sound entirely convinced.' Her hair whipped round her face in the breeze and she breathed in the salty air of Malibu.

'Martha, we have to accept that Phoebe was a very disturbed woman. Who knows what was real and what wasn't in the end? It all blurred in her mind. The point is that I've learned that I'm going to have to live by what I think is right and not judge things according to what I think I can get away with.'

'Thank God for the diaries. Who would have thought Phoebe was so methodical? Kate said her bedroom was always a mess.'

'Only towards the end – she wasn't always like that, you know. She wasn't really anything like she was at the end. She was ... well, she was quite a package when we met.'

'I know,' said Martha softly.

They sat in silence on the deck of the hotel, watching the surf crash against the beach. It had been a long night. They had done the rounds of Oscar parties, some of which – at least the bits that comprised Kate and Ambrose, Scorcher and Cressida, Gloria and Marty – had followed them back to their suite. Together they had watched the sun rise over the ocean, toasted the success of *Endymion*, which had swept the boards, resulting in Oscars for Nick as best actor and for Ambrose, Marty and Scorcher, who had written the film score, and flicked through two hundred channels, basking in the international coverage.

'I suppose you're going to be totally insufferable now you've finally won your bloody Oscar,' said Martha, changing the subject.

He grinned sheepishly. 'It does feel good. Funny that. I spent years imagining I'd always turn it down. Not turn up, like Woody Allen—'

'But when the time came, you were there like a shot.'

'Just to help out dear old Detmar, you understand. Ambrose reckons the studio will want to bring the release forward now, and you know how much difference Marty said a best actor win can make to the final takings. And it is a film I really believe in.'

'Of course.' She poured him a mango-and-pineapple juice and watched the white parasols flapping in the breeze. 'It's all right. You're allowed to act like a movie star and enjoy it. Once in a while.'

He grinned. 'I didn't notice you turning down the chance to see the ceremony in the flesh – or outshine everyone else in that gorgeous shimmery dress.'

'Prada.' She sighed blissfully. 'It was nice, wasn't it?' She wriggled her toes on the warm decking, luxuriating in the fact that when the nominations had been announced, forty designers had sent her faxes offering to dress her. The dress Dior had sent had been beautiful – but somehow she didn't think she'd ever be able to wear Dior after seeing Phoebe in it that last time. 'Shame the jewels have got to go back ...' she said playfully.

'Tell me which piece you liked best and I'll buy it for you.'

She didn't say anything. The only jewellery she wanted from Nick — and she was embarrassed to admit this to herself — was a wedding ring. But it had all gone rather quiet on that front lately.

'No sign of Kate and Ambrose?' she said hurriedly.

'Probably trying to catch up with some sleep. I dare say the twins woke up at their usual ungodly hour. The fact that Ambrose just scored his first Oscar and biggest hangover all in the same night probably won't cut much ice with them. I was quite surprised they brought them. Toddler jet-lag can't be funny.'

'Oh, you know Kate. Can't be separated from them for five minutes. I thought she'd ease up when the adoption finally went through. She was on tenterhooks for months in case some relative of Phoebe's crawled out of the woodwork to claim them. But even after nobody did, and now they're legally hers and Ambrose's, she's still very protective. She must be the first person who actually meant it when she announced she was taking more time off to spend with her family.

'Kate looked wonderful, didn't she? Now that the baby's almost due she's much more calm about the whole thing. And she promises this is the last time she'll be travelling before it's born.' She poured some coffee.

'Amazing. Pregnancy really suits her.' He paused. 'Ironic, isn't it?'

'I'd say it was inevitable. Once she got the twins and relaxed a bit, it all fell into place, so to speak.'

'Well, I'm glad. I've always liked Ambrose, but now

I'm really fond of Kate. And they seem good together, don't they?'

A waiter came up with more coffee. 'It was fun, wasn't it, in a crassly but deeply enjoyable way,' Nick said, luxuriating in the bliss of victory. 'I couldn't decide which was the most delicious bit – watching Marty finally chat up a woman born in the same decade as he was, or seeing Donna Ducatti stuck outside, interviewing celebrities for Sky.'

'A banana-shaped tragedy wrapped in recycled candy wrappers,' recited Martha dreamily from Fenton Wigstaff's review in the *LA Times*. 'Not that I necessarily subscribe to that view myself.'

''Course not. And it was terribly gracious of you to pause and give her a few quotes.'

'Well, I don't like to harbour grudges. Especially now there are rumours she's being shunted on to Radio Two.'

'How very noble of you.'

'Oh, Donna's not too bad. Actually I never told you this, but when I was in hospital with shock after the whole Phoebe saga she wrote me a note. A lot of people did actually. Made me feel everyone didn't hate me after all.' She stopped, feeling awkward. She knew that Nick blamed himself for the mutilation she had suffered at the hands of the press and berated herself for even raising the subject.

'Do you think Kate will ease off the work permanently?'

'Relatively speaking, yes, I really do – at least till the twins and the new baby are at school. All that manic working was just a way of impressing Ambrose. Who didn't really want to be impressed in that way at all, of course. He just wanted someone who would love him. Unconditionally. In the way that men always do. And now that Kate doesn't have all those silly hang-ups about not being intellectually worthy of him, she does.'

'I see,' said Nick, eyeing her carefully. 'So none of that ridiculous over-achievement syndrome was anything to do with the inadequate feelings she had about her elder sister?'

Martha stared at him in astonishment. 'Oh, please. For most of our adolescence and early twenties there was absolutely nothing about me that gave Kate any cause for insecurity – unless you count my going-nowhere career, my crap flat, my crappier car, my terrible boyfriends, my appalling wardrobe ...'

'Not the fact that you were funny and brilliant – and the best lay in two hemispheres ...'

'Oh, you'd really know about that, Mr I've-only-ever-had-one-girlfriend-and-that-was-my-wife.'

'Martha—' He was smiling in admonishment. 'Don't you ever reveal that fact to the press. And don't change the subject. I know you spent most of your first thirty years on earth wishing you were Kate, but did it never really occur to you that the feeling was at least partly mutual?'

She blushed fuchsia. 'No.'

'Well, for a bright, funny woman you certainly can be incredibly obt—'

'You know, I think when Kate does go back to work properly, she'll be a lot more balanced about things. She hasn't got to prove everything any more.'

'What about you? Isn't it about time you went back to work?'

She scanned his eyes. They looked almost violet in the early southern Californian light. 'Do you know some-thing?'

'Well, I know you're up to something.'

'As a matter of fact, Charlie has been in touch. The new Director-General's interested in expanding the *And Now* format into a whole strand of current affairs programmes. And he wants me to be involved – on the production side if I don't want to present any more. It's out of the question, of course. It would mean going back to England, although according to Charlie the press aren't very interested in demolishing us these days—'

'Really?'

'Past our fell-by date.'

'With puns like that you should be hosting a Carry On night.'

'Sorry, it's Cressie's influence. Since the *Sunday Times* gave her that column she only speaks in headlines and captions.'

'I noticed. Kate said the subs were so appalled at her spelling and grammar that she gave up writing it down and just gabbles it over the phone. Still, it's pretty compulsive stuff, you have to admit. I can't wait to read what she made of last night.'

'Me neither. She is pretty good – who'd have guessed she had such a talent for witty observations?'

'Or that she'd ever actually go on a protest march.'

'It was the Countryside March – not exactly a hotbed of anarchists. Still, it must have cheered them all up to have Squire Scorcher on it.'

'How does Ambrose feel about having another writer in the family?'

'He'll live. Their styles aren't exactly similar.'

'And now that he's Sir Ambrose—'

'Yes, I must say I was slightly surprised that a left-wing

firebrand like Ambrose could so easily be persuaded to accept a gong.'

'Well, Kate said it was touch and go for about nineteen seconds. But as the *Python* put it, "*It was all Knight on the Day*".'

'You could have had a script editor's credit on *The Explorer*, you know. God knows you've done as much to shape it as anyone.'

She smiled at him. 'Hardly – editing's not the same as writing. But thank you. Think I'll pass, though – coat-tails aren't a very comfortable place to be.'

'They're not where you are. Anyway, stop changing the subject. Is that why you don't want to get married – Charlie's offer, I mean?'

'You stopped asking.'

'There're only so many times a man can take rejection. Even an actor.'

'But what about children?'

'Is that your answer?'

'What was the question?'

'What was yours?'

'Children.'

He sighed and took her hand, brushing it against his lips. 'The day Phoebe died – I never told you this – I got to the airport and the early headlines on the news-stand said something about the love of Nick Wilde's life being discovered dead. I thought it was you. And I realized I wouldn't be able to bear losing you. So children – yeah, they'd be great. But I don't want to be greedy. And we could always adopt. If they let Ambrose and Kate, they'd have to find us one.'

She was silent for a while, and then she told him. 'I

thought the same. About losing you. Lying in that white room – slightly delirious, I suppose – I kept hearing snatches of news from the TV in the next room, reporters talking about hanks of black hair. I couldn't remember whether yours had grown out or not. Isn't that terrible? I'd only seen you the week before. But I was so fuzzy. I thought I hadn't seen you for years. Or at least I couldn't tell. It was as if you and I didn't exist any more.'

'Er, we haven't exactly talked this through in quite the way we should have done, have we?'

'No. She's been here quite a lot these past few months, hasn't she? Phoebe, I mean. Hovering round us, making her presence felt.'

He nodded mutely.

'But we are now,' she said softly.

'I've wanted to for such a long time. But you seemed so remote.'

It was her turn to reach out for him. 'I've been doing a lot of thinking and acclimatizing. For so long she was always there. You were always really Phoebe's. And then she died and we all had to readjust. But I've learned this much. It's okay to have loved her, you know. It doesn't threaten us.'

There were tears running down his face.

'Would you like to say goodbye to her properly? Don't shake your head. Before you answer I'm going to tell you this. Your visiting Phoebe's grave won't worry me in the least. In fact I think you should. She was such a big part of your life for the best part of twenty years, for God's sake. I'd say she's been as formative an influence on your character as Chrissie or Mike. And since it's a character I love, how can I resent her?'

He nodded again. 'I would like to visit her grave. I doubt if anyone else from her family has.'

She held him tightly, the parasols flapping even harder now.

'I think it's time to go back to England,' he said, 'for a bit at least. Just so that you can find out some more about that job.'

'But you vowed you'd never set foot there again.' She looked at him.

'That was then. The fact is I'm sort of homesick for the place. And I'm desperate to know what's happened in *Hello!*'

'There's been a marriage.'

'Yes, there's bound to have been a marriage.'

'Ah, but is it a happy one?'

'You tell me,' Nick said, looking at her searchingly.

Martha gazed back at him with tenderness. 'You know what? I think it probably is.'

The End